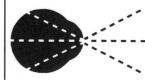
This Large Print Book carries the
Seal of Approval of N.A.V.H.

WAITING FOR SUMMER'S RETURN

KIM VOGEL SAWYER

THORNDIKE PRESS

An imprint of Thomson Gale, a part of The Thomson Corporation

Detroit • New York • San Francisco • New Haven, Conn. • Waterville, Maine • London

THOMSON
✳
GALE ™

LIBRARY OF CONGRESS CATALOGING-IN-PUBLICATION DATA

Sawyer, Kim Vogel.
   Waiting for Summer's return / by Kim Vogel Sawyer.
      p. cm. — (Thorndike Press large print Christian historical fiction)
   ISBN-13: 978-0-7862-9239-4 (lg. print : alk. paper)
   ISBN-10: 0-7862-9239-3 (lg. print : alk. paper)
   1. Widows — Fiction. 2. Mennonites — Fiction. 3. Large type books.
I. Title.
PS3619.A97W35 2007
813'.6—dc22   2006031814

Published in 2007 by arrangement with Bethany House Publishers.

Printed in the United States of America on permanent paper
10 9 8 7 6 5 4 3 2 1

For KAMRYN,
my "summer joy"
And MOM,
whose pride in her
German-Mennonite heritage
lives in me

Dear Reader,
The German dialect in this story may seem a bit odd or unfamiliar. And it should unless you are descended from the German Mennonites who initially immigrated to Russia in search of freedom from military involvement. This particular group of people spoke a unique dialect called *Plautdietsch,* or Low German. Unfortunately, it is an endangered language, with fewer than 100,000 people still able to speak it fluently.

In writing *Waiting for Summer's Return,* I relied on a handful of sources to re-create the language in the characters' dialogue. I found snippets of *Plautdietsch* in research materials at the Tabor College library in Hillsboro, Kansas. Some words were borrowed from Norma Jost Voth's *Mennonite Foods and Folkways From South Russia.* My final sources were two ladies from Inman,

Kansas, who know the language. Some of the German in the story is a combination of High German and Low German, but my best effort was made to represent the flow and feel of the Mennonites' *Plautdietsch.*

It was a joy to write this story using bits and pieces of my own rich German-Mennonite heritage, and I hope the story will transport you to another time and place.

May God bless you as
you journey with Him,
Kim Vogel Sawyer

"Gladness and joy
will overtake them,
and sorrow and sighing
will flee away."
Isaiah 35:10 NIV

1

Gaeddert, Kansas
October 1894

Oh, what an exquisite coat!

Summer Steadman stopped in front of Nickels' Dry Goods store, her attention grabbed by the sight. The wind pressed at her back, whipping strands of hair across her face. She anchored the hair behind her ear as she leaned closer to the window.

The coat, displayed on a wooden stand, had a printed card resting against its hem. Since the words were written in some foreign gibberish, she was only able to make out the price: seven dollars and fifty cents. But she didn't need to read the words to recognize the real ermine fur that graced the collar and cuffs or the elegant camel's hair fabric.

When her breath steamed the pane, hiding the coat from view, she swiped the moisture away with her hand. How sweet

Tillie would look in that little coat! Its Mother Hubbard waist and pompadour sleeves gave the coat a grown-up, sophisticated look even though it was designed for a toddler. A matching bonnet hung from the display stand by satin ribbons. Summer closed her eyes, picturing Tillie's dark curls and bright eyes peeping from beneath the ermine brim. Tillie would have loved to wear a coat such as this.

Opening her eyes, Summer pressed her palms to the glass, straining for a closer glimpse. For a moment, she considered entering the store and purchasing the little hat and coat. Her arms ached with the desire to cradle her daughter. Perhaps cradling that coat, which was the same size as Tillie, would ease her loneliness.

Reality crashed around her. No . . . cradling that empty coat would only remind her of her loss. "Oh, Tillie, my sweet baby," she whispered, resting her forehead against the cold glass as tears pricked her eyelids. Her heart tightened until she feared it might stop beating.

Forcing a breath into her lungs, Summer spun from the window and stumbled to the edge of the boardwalk. Frigid wind slapped her face, and she shivered. She needed to return to the hotel. The thought of that

12

lonely room held no appeal, but what else could she do? Her long afternoon of querying for employment had proved fruitless. There was no reason to remain outdoors any longer. Releasing a deep sigh, she turned her steps toward the large wooden building across the street.

The pungent odors wafting from the dining room made her stomach twist with queasiness. She covered her nose with her scarf and passed through the lobby as quickly as possible, ignoring the elderly desk clerk. Safely locked in her room, she sank down on the homespun blanket covering the feather tick. With stilted motions, she removed her coat and let it flop onto the bed. She sat, staring at the plain plaster wall.

What would she do now? she wondered for the hundredth time. She wrinkled her brow as she considered her limited options. She could press on to Oklahoma and claim land, as she and Rodney had planned. But she had no desire to do this on her own, and how would she take care of a homestead? Her education — well-rounded even by Boston standards — hadn't included the skills needed for planting and plowing.

She could pay someone to take her to one of the larger towns nearby where she could purchase a train ticket back to Boston. But who would welcome her? Rodney's parents had disowned him the moment he announced his intention to leave for Oklahoma. They wouldn't desire her company now that Rodney and the children were gone. Her brother and his wife would not want her, either. They had been only too glad to see her married to Rodney and out of their house. Nothing awaited her in Boston.

Staying here was the only choice. But staying presented a whole other set of problems.

Most of the money Rodney had planned to use to start their farm remained in a hidden pocket of her reticule. A sizable sum it was, but even a sizable sum would be depleted if it did not replace itself. Given time, she would have no way to pay even for this humble hotel room. If she were to stay, she would need a means of support. But there seemed to be no opportunities available here.

Her mind replayed the response given at every place of business — a firm "No help needed" coupled with a look of distrust. Did they sense the stench of death she carried? Suddenly, unbidden, a row of grave markers appeared in her memory, the first carved with the name of her husband and four smaller ones carved with the names of her children. With a groan, Summer threw herself across the bed. Her nostrils filled with the musty odor of the old tick. She bent her elbow and buried her face in its curve as tears overflowed, soaking the sleeve of her dress.

"O God in heaven," she begged aloud, "why did you not take me, too? It is surely a punishment. . . . A punishment I know I deserve, but . . . Don't leave me here alone. Let me be with my children. . . ." Sobs wracked her body until blessed sleep finally claimed her.

Peter Ollenburger entered the hotel lobby, sweeping the hat from his head the moment he stepped over the threshold. He unbuttoned his jacket with one hand, glad to be out of the biting wind. The good scents of sauerkraut, sausage, and potatoes greeted his nose, and the temptation to seat himself in the dining room and order a dinner was great. Swallowing, he reminded himself that Thomas and *Grossmutter* waited at home with beans and salt pork boiling on the back of the stove. He turned his attention away from Martha Harms's cooking and focused instead on the hotel clerk. His boots clumped against the wooden floor as he

15

crossed to the desk. "*Guten tag,* Bernard."

Bernard Harms blinked behind round-lensed spectacles. "Why, Peter, what brings you into the hotel? You have daylight hours yet to make it home."

Peter chuckled. "*Nein,* I am not checking in. You are right it would be foolish. I am here to . . ." He scratched his head. What he was planning to propose would start the townspeople's tongues to wagging, for sure.

"*Ja, ja,* here to . . . ?"

Peter felt heat climb the back of his neck. "I am here to talk to that *frau* whose family is buried east of town."

Bernard's eyebrows nearly disappeared into his hairline.

The heat in Peter's neck increased. "*Ach,* Bernard, I know what thought you have! Put it from your mind." He coiled his fingers around his hat. "My son has been home since he broke his ribs. He is behind on schoolwork, and this I do not like. I cannot help him much — a big stupid man I am. But Reverend Enns, he tells me this woman speaks as if she has had much schooling. Maybe she can help my Thomas, *ja?*"

Bernard shook his head, the light glinting on the thick lenses of his glasses. "Hmph

16

. . . I would not mind her sitting somewhere other than in my hotel room all day long."

"She is here now?" Peter was not sure if he wanted Bernard to answer *ja* or *nein*.

"She is here — she returned a bit ago. She is in room seven."

Peter twisted his hat in his hands. Despite the unseasonable chill of late October, his palms began to sweat. "*Sieben. Ja,* I will go and ask her, then."

Bernard came around the corner of the desk. "I will go, too. It is not proper for a single man and a single lady to be without a chaperone."

Peter nodded at Bernard's words. He would not even propose this if his wife's grandmother did not reside at his home. Although *Grossmutter* was crippled from arthritis, slowing down the work she could do, her mind was sharp. A good chaperone she could be.

Bernard leaned his elbow on the edge of the high desk. "Will you pick her up here each day to come teach Thomas?"

"*Nein.* With the cold weather coming, I cannot ride back and forth from home to town every day to fetch her." Besides, Peter understood from the reverend that this woman needed a place to stay that would

17

cost no money. Reverend Enns was sure she would return to the East when she had regained her strength. She would need her money for travel, the reverend had said. Trading room and board for teaching would be a good exchange; the woman would not have to spend her savings.

"Then she will . . . live with you?" Bernard almost whispered the final words.

"She will live in my house, if she says she will come."

"In your house?" These words seemed to squeak out. "Peter, have you thought this through?"

Peter scowled. *"Ja."* For sure, he had thought it through or he would not be here.

"But where will the woman sleep?"

"With Elsa's grandmother, in her room." He had not yet mentioned this idea to *Grossmutter,* and for a moment he felt guilty for involving her without her permission. But the old woman was a kind-hearted soul. Surely she would not disagree.

Bernard shook his head, his expression solemn. "Peter, it cannot be done. Even with the grandmother there, the woman cannot live under your roof. The council will never approve it. She . . . she is unmarried. And she is not of our faith."

Peter bit on his lower lip, causing his beard to splay forward. He had not considered that the council might disapprove. He scratched his head. "I am a bumbler for sure. I had thought . . . But now I do not know. . . ." He bit his lip again. Thomas needed help, and he had felt this woman was the answer to his prayers. But now? He sighed. "I guess I will not talk to her after all. I did not think all things through." He turned to leave.

Bernard caught his arm. "Peter, what about the *shariah?*"

"*Shariah?*"

Bernard nodded. "It is snug and dry."

Peter stroked his beard. "The *shariah* . . ." He used the *shariah* for storage, but he could move those boxes and barrels to the barn. The woman would have her own little place, close enough to walk to the house and work with Thomas each day but far enough away to keep the gossip hens from clucking too much. Peter grinned. "Bernard, you are a clever man."

Bernard puffed out his chest and tapped his gray temple with one finger. His eyes sparkled. "Come, Peter. We will go ask her." He led the way down the dim hallway to room seven and knocked briskly on the closed door.

Peter held his breath. What would the woman think? A woman left as she had been, in a strange town without a man to support her, was bound to feel helpless. No doubt she mourned all she had lost. Four *liebchen* and her husband, the reverend had said. Peter understood mourning. How he had mourned his Elsa when she had gone to glory. She had been his playmate in childhood, his best friend in youth, and his dearest love. Yet he, Thomas, and *Grossmutter* had managed to go on together, with God's help.

And now God had put this woman and her plight on his heart. He hoped she would see the sense of his plan. Thomas needed someone, and Peter was sure it would do the woman good to have someone to fuss over. It was a good plan now that Bernard had thought of the *shariah*.

It seemed a long time had passed since Bernard knocked. No sounds came from behind the door. Peter looked down at Bernard, concern filling his belly. "You are sure she is in there?"

Bernard nodded, his forehead creased in contemplation. "I saw her come in. She looked sad — more sad than any other day since she started staying here last week."

Peter's brows came down. "You do not think she would do something . . . foolish?"

"You think she might . . . ?"

Peter swallowed hard. "When one is deeply sorrowful, one can be foolish."

Bernard raised his fist and pounded on the door. "*Frau* Steadman! *Frau* Steadman!" His shrill voice carried down the hall.

They heard a scramble from behind the door, then a key in the lock. The doorknob twisted, and the door swung open to reveal a disheveled, wild-haired woman. Her eyes bore dark smudges; her cheeks looked hollow and pale. Her blue dress hung on a frame too thin for it. Peter's heart turned over in pity, but at the same time he wondered if the reverend could have been right that this woman was well educated. She did not give the appearance of great intelligence as she gaped at the men with wide red-rimmed eyes.

"Yes? W-what is it?"

Peter stepped forward, making a little bow. "*Frau* Steadman, *mein name ist* —" With a shake of his head, he reminded himself to speak English. "*Frau* Steadman, I am Peter Ollenburger. I have come to ask you to move to my home and —" His sentence went unfinished. Much to his surprise, the woman's face suddenly turned white, and then with a little cry she collapsed in a heap at his feet.

2

"Ach, what did I say?" Peter threw his hat aside and leaned over the crumpled frame of the woman. She had gone down so quickly, there had not been time to react. But he could not leave her lying there like a tossed-aside sack for grain. He scooped her into his arms — "As weightless as a feather tick she is!" he declared — and carried her to the bed. He rested her gently on the mattress, and she lay there just as he'd placed her, as if lifeless.

"Bernard, go and get Dr. Wiebe. I will stay with *Frau* Steadman."

Bernard disappeared, leaving the door open. Peter spotted a pitcher and bowl on the dresser. He splashed water into the bowl, took a clean handkerchief from his pocket, and soaked it in the water. The handkerchief dripped on the floor as he crossed to the bed. Keeping as much distance between the bed and himself as he could, he leaned forward and laid the rough wadded square of dripping cloth across the woman's forehead.

Neither a movement nor a sound did she make.

Peter willed, *Hast, Doktor. Bitte hast.*

He examined the woman's face. So pale and thin, with hollows in her cheeks. His arms still felt warm from the slight weight of her body — such a small burden she had been. He shook his head, pity twisting his heart. Surely it was not his words that had sent her into a faint. Had she eaten at all since the last of her family was put beneath the ground?

He remembered the first numb days following Elsa's death. His desire for food had fled him, too. Only knowing Thomas and *Grossmutter* depended on him had made him force food into a belly that resisted it. This woman had no one depending on her, no one to entice her to eat. She was in a poor state, for sure.

"Heavenly Father, touch the heart of *Frau* Steadman and help it beat again. Take away her sorrow and give her joy," Peter prayed aloud into the quiet room. "Let her grow strong, and let her find her way home." His prayer was interrupted by the sound of feet on the hall floor. He went to the door and peered out, his chest filling with relief when he spotted the doctor on Bernard's heels.

"She has not yet wakened." Peter watched from the doorway as Dr. Wiebe opened his black bag and withdrew a small vial. The doctor popped the cork on the vial and swept it back and forth below the woman's nose. At the second sweep, the woman suddenly coughed and twisted her face away, struggling to sit up. The doctor corked the vial and dropped it back into his bag then placed a hand on the woman's shoulder.

"There now, *Frau* Steadman. Lie still for a little while yet." The doctor's calm voice soothed Peter, but from the woman's stiff pose he did not believe she was soothed. The doctor glanced briefly at Bernard. "Bernard, could you bring *Frau* Steadman a glass of water, please?" Bernard rushed out once more, and Dr. Wiebe turned back to *Frau* Steadman.

"W-what happened?" The woman's voice sounded hoarse.

Peter stepped forward. "I am sorry if I frightened you." He peered over the doctor's black-suited shoulder at her white face. Her brown eyes appeared almost black against the alarming pallor of her skin. "I am a bear of a man, for sure."

The woman's brow furrowed. "Who are you?"

"Peter Ollenburger. I —"

The doctor held up his hand, stopping any more words. "*Frau* Steadman, I want you to rest. After you have had some water" — Bernard entered, as if on cue, and handed the glass of water to the doctor — "I want you to eat some bread and broth. I will bring it myself."

The woman shifted on the bed until her back rested against the headboard. She took the glass with both hands, but at the mention of broth and bread, she grimaced. "Please . . . I am not hungry."

"There is no choice being offered." The doctor's tone turned stern. "Whether you are hungry or not, you must eat. Your strength must be kept up."

"For what purpose?"

Her bitter words seemed to take Bernard and the doctor by surprise, but Peter understood. He answered, *Zeit fürs weinen und zeit fürs lachen . . .*"

The woman stared at him as if he had suddenly sprouted purple ears and a tail. He thumped his head with his hand. "*Ach,* my foolish mouth. I choose words from the Good Book — Ecclesiastes, the third chapter. There is a time to weep and a time to laugh, a time to mourn and a time to dance." He stepped closer. "You must eat to gain strength for the day when your heart will once more laugh and dance."

"I've no reason to laugh or dance."

Peter understood this, too. Just east of town were her reasons buried.

The doctor rose. "I will be back soon with soup and bread. You must eat." His tone let the woman know he wouldn't accept a refusal.

She closed her eyes and rolled to her side, facing away from them.

Dr. Wiebe motioned to Peter and Bernard to step into the hall. Peter retrieved his hat from the threshold and closed the door behind him. Once in the hallway, the doctor spoke earnestly. "I am concerned. She appears very weak. Although she has no fever, which tells me she has not contracted the typhoid fever that killed her family, she has no one here. I am going to speak to Reverend Enns. Perhaps he can find a family that will take her in and see to her needs. If she does not begin eating, she will end up buried with the rest of her family."

Bernard's eyes became huge behind his spectacles. "Typhoid fever? That is what took her family?"

The doctor nodded, then pointed his finger at Bernard. "You say nothing. I have taken every precaution. Before I brought her to the hotel, I insisted she bathe while I boiled all of her clothing. Her family is buried, along with their clothing. After I settled her here, I sent some men out to burn her belongings. There is no threat of danger from this woman — I would not have brought her here otherwise. But some would not believe it. If people are fearful, no one will take her in."

Bernard looked at Peter. "Peter, tell the doctor what you were thinking."

Peter felt heat climbing the back of his neck again. The doctor looked up at him, his expression expectant. Peter cleared his throat. "Well, you see, my boy needs help in his studies. I thought to ask the woman if she would help the boy in exchange for a room and food." The heat spread to his ears. "The room would be in my *shariah.* Bernard thought of that."

Bernard nodded, as if pleased to be included.

"I was thinking of a place with a family — with a woman who would cook the meals

28

and see that she ate." The doctor sucked in his lips for a moment. "But it might be good for her to be with someone who relies on her a little more than she relies on them."

Peter gave an eager nod. "*Ja.* Both Thomas and *Grossmutter* could benefit from this woman's presence."

Dr. Wiebe smiled. "I think it is a good idea, Peter. What did she say?"

He shrugged. "When I started to ask, down she went — *floomp!* — right on the floor." He shook his head. "I thought at first I frightened her. But maybe it was only her empty belly."

The doctor opened his mouth to reply, but before he could speak the doorknob turned and the door opened. The woman stood framed in the doorway. She held on to the wooden door as if for support. Her gaze swept past the doctor and Bernard to settle on Peter.

"Mr. Ollenburger, I would like to speak with you, please."

Summer focused on the big man who stood between the doctor and the clerk. He had called himself a "bear of a man," and the description was apt. Peter Ollenburger dwarfed the other two in both height and

29

breadth. His full beard and shaggy hair added to his bearlike appearance, but as she remembered his gentle blue eyes peering down at her from over the doctor's shoulder, she instinctively knew she need not fear him.

He swallowed, twisting his hat in his massive hands. "*Ja,* we can talk, for sure. But would you sit back down? You do not look *wachlig.*" Then he grimaced and corrected himself. "Steady. You do not look steady."

Summer squared her shoulders, pushing herself to her full height. "I assure you I am fine." Her knees felt weak. Bracing herself on the doorjamb, she continued. "When I first opened the door to you, you said something . . . something about . . . your home?" She despised the quaver that had crept into her voice. "Are you in need of a maid or a cook?"

Mr. Ollenburger's heavy brows came down. "*Frau* Steadman, you are making me feel nervous. *Bitte,* you sit on the bed there, and we can talk."

The doctor took her elbow. "*Ja,* that is a good idea." He guided her back into the room, seating her on the edge of the bed in a gentlemanly manner.

Summer had to admit she felt more secure sitting down, yet resentment welled in her chest at their concern. Where were these concerned people when her family was dying one by one and she was forced to stand helplessly by and watch them slip away? With determination, she pushed the thought aside and raised her gaze to Mr. Ollenburger.

"All right. I'm sitting. Mr. Ollenburger, would you please tell me why you came?"

The man nodded, a thick shock of wheat-colored hair falling across his forehead. He pushed back the strands with his large fingers. "*Ja*. I thought to ask if you would help me." His huge boot lifted and he stepped forward, narrowing the gap between them.

Summer had to tip her head back to look into his eyes. She noticed his ears appeared pink, which further convinced her of his harmlessness.

"My boy — he is named Thomas — he had an accident and broke ribs. He has been home healing and has missed much of school. The doctor says he must not ride a horse for many weeks yet, so no school for Thomas until January or February. Yet his lessons he needs. I cannot help him. But Reverend Enns thought . . ." He paused, turning the hat into a wad of plaid fabric.

"You . . . you are a learned woman?"

Summer nearly burst out laughing. Learned? Her education was the best Boston could offer a woman. She swallowed hard. It wouldn't do to laugh. He wouldn't understand her amusement. Giving a nod, she responded, "Yes, Mr. Ollenburger, I am a learned woman."

"Then you are able to help my Thomas with his schooling?" Hope was evident in his tone.

She nodded.

A smile broke across his face. "*Ja,* this is good. *Danke schoen, Frau* Steadman."

"Wait, Mr. Ollenburger. I didn't say I would do it, simply that I am capable of doing it."

His brow crinkled. "Does this mean you will not help my boy?"

Summer sighed and looked at the other two men, who stood stupidly to the side and listened without offering assistance. Turning back to Peter Ollenburger, she tried to explain. "Mr. Ollenburger, before I make a commitment such as you've requested, I need to know what salary you are offering."

Mr. Ollenburger turned his shaggy head to look at the others. The desk clerk raised his hand and rubbed his thumb against the tips of his fingers. Light dawned across Mr.

Ollenburger's face.

"*Ach,* of course, I need to tell you about . . . salary." He squared his shoulders. "I am not a man of wealth, *Frau* Steadman. Money I cannot offer. But I offer you a place to stay — your own *shariah* — and meals while you work with my boy." He looked so gallant as he gave his meager proposal that Summer didn't have the heart to immediately refuse.

She lowered her focus, considering this proposition. She needed money more than meals and a roof. Although, she realized, if she had meals and a roof she would not have to spend any of her remaining cash. So if she wasn't adding to her cash supply, at least she wouldn't be depleting it. Tutoring his son was certainly preferable to cooking or cleaning. Her own *shariah,* he had said. She assumed this was a word for "house" in his language. She realized all three men were waiting for her to reply.

"Is your wife unable to assist your son in his studies?"

Sadness appeared in the big man's eyes. "My wife — my Elsa — she has been gone now for six years."

Summer felt a brief stab of pain for his loss. The passing of years had apparently not removed all of the sorrow from his heart. But at least he had his boy. Grief welled up and she quickly squelched it. She forced her brain to think . . . *think*. . . . If he was a widower, there were rules of decorum that must be considered. Looking at this big, simple man, she was certain he wouldn't comprehend those rules.

"I am sorry, Mr. Ollenburger, but your position as a widower gives a new slant to this situation." She took a deep breath, organizing her thoughts. "You offered a . . . *shariah.* No one would question the propriety of my living there?"

Again, the man sought the opinion of his friends with a look of helplessness.

The desk clerk answered. "This *shariah* is on the edge of Peter's property. A good walk separates it from his place."

The doctor also contributed. "At his home also lives *Frau* Suderman, who is Thomas's great-grandmother. A chaperone she can provide." He glanced at Peter before adding, "This is a small town, so there will be some talk, but Peter has a good reputation here. The talk will not last long."

Summer nodded to acknowledge the men's words before turning back to Mr. Ollenburger. "And when your son is caught up with studies, will I be forced to leave this — this *shariah?*"

Mr. Ollenburger gave an emphatic shake of his head. "You would be welcome to stay for as long as you need to. But if you change your mind and want to come back to the hotel, I will bring you."

"Thank you. Will you allow me a few minutes to consider your offer?"

The big man ushered the other two out of the room and closed the door behind them. She heard the muffled sounds of their voices as they visited in the hallway, but she was unable to make out their words because they spoke in another language. German, she assumed. But she suspected they were discussing her, just as they must have been doing before she opened the door. It made her uneasy to be the topic of discussion, and she especially disliked not understanding what was being said.

Mr. Ollenburger needed a teacher for his son. It would be a way to fill these endlessly empty days. Her days, before leaving Boston, had been so full. Caring for the children, keeping house, preparing meals — she had insisted on doing these things herself rather than relying on servants to care for her most precious possessions. Even on the trail, as the wagon had made its plodding progress through unfamiliar cities and across varying landscapes, her time had been filled with incessant tasks. But here, in this room, there was nothing to do except remember what used to be.

She allowed her gaze to drift around the room — the bare walls, the absence of personal effects, the *lifelessness* of the room. Did she want to remain here, even if she could afford it? She had no idea what waited in the *shariah,* but whatever it was, it couldn't possibly be worse than the hollow, aching emptiness of this room. She sighed. There really was no other choice.

Summer pushed herself to her feet and crossed to the door, opening it once more. All three men turned toward her, their conversation halting. Mr. Ollenburger's fist tightened around the ridiculous little hat.

"Mr. Ollenburger, I will accompany you to your home, but first I would appreciate being taken to my wagon to collect the remainder of my belongings."

3

"I will ready your bill." The hotel clerk scurried down the hallway. The other two men exchanged quick nervous glances.

Summer's heart skipped a beat. "Is something wrong?"

The doctor cleared his throat. "It is evening. . . . The ride to Peter's is long. . . ."

Something was amiss, but suddenly she had no desire to explore it. "That's fine, then. I'll return later. I'll gather my things." Summer stepped back behind the door. It only took a few moments to prepare to leave, and she joined the men at the clerk's desk without delay. She placed the necessary bills and coins in the clerk's hand, tightened the pull string on her reticule, and turned to Mr. Ollenburger. "I'm ready."

He took her bag and gestured toward the door. Less than five minutes later she sat on a wooden buckboard bench next to her benefactor, looking down on the rumps of a pair of enormous beasts with massive chests and short horns.

Mr. Ollenburger called, "Giddap!" The animals heaved into lumbering motion.

She pointed at the pair. "Oxen?"

He nodded. "They are named Gaert and Roth." The oxen snorted, tossing their heads, and the man chuckled. "*Ja, ja,* I speak of you." He looked briefly in her direction. "Roth means red-haired, so the red and white one is Roth. Gaert, then, is the brown and white one. Gaert means strong. They are both sturdy, reliable beasts. We have a horse — Thomas's Daisy — but she is more pet than working animal."

"And what is your work, Mr. Ollenburger?"

The man's chest seemed to expand. "I am a miller. I grind the grain into flour. *Broot schleit den hunga doot.*" He chuckled. "I say, 'Bread kills hunger.' What is a meal without bread, *ja?*"

Summer peeked sideways at the man's profile. His voice rumbled like distant thunder and carried a heavy accent. Somehow its timbre was soothing. "Tell me about your son, please."

A smile broke across his wide face, crinkling his eyes. "Ah, my Thomas, my son . . .

Of course he is a bright and handsome lad. Sturdy like the oxen. Dependable, too. A wonderful boy. You will see."

The man obviously idolized the boy. She must remember this — should there come a time when reprimands were necessary, she would tread with care. "He has a horse for a pet. What else interests him?"

"Interests him? You must explain this."

Did she sense shame in his question? "Interests . . . things he likes."

Mr. Ollenburger pursed his lips as he twisted a whip in his hand. "Interests of Thomas . . . Well, he likes to read. It was the reading that got him hurt."

"Oh?" Summer raised her brows.

A chuckle sounded from the other side of the bench. "Oh, *ja*. He was up in a tree, book in one hand and apple in the other. He went to turn a page and down he came. He hit hard on a branch before falling to the ground. The branch broke his ribs."

"My goodness!" Summer placed her hand against her bodice, imagining how the fall must have hurt.

Mr. Ollenburger sent a knowing look in her direction. "He is lucky boy that the rib did not poke his lung. He has been slow moving for many weeks." He shook his head. "*Ja,* the good Lord was watching him for sure that day."

Summer set her jaw to hold back the bitter words that pressed against her tongue. Where was this "good Lord" the days her children died? Why hadn't he saved her children? She forced the thoughts away and looked at Mr. Ollenburger's profile. "How old is Thomas?"

The man's lips tipped into a warm smile. "He will be ten in January."

Summer jerked her eyes forward. Ten in January. The same age as her Vincent. Would this Thomas and Vincent have been friends if given the opportunity to meet? It didn't matter now, yet she wondered. . . . "A fine age."

"*Ja.* Still a boy, but now and then I glimpse of the man to come."

Summer had seen glimpses of the man to come in her Vincent, too. He had been so brave, standing beside his father's new grave, his chin thrust out, hands clasped behind his back. After the minister and gravediggers had gone, the youngster had taken her hand and promised, "I'll help take care of you and the children, Mama. Don't worry." *Oh, Vincent, my dear son, what a good man you would have become.*

40

Summer held tight to the seat, blinking back tears, as the uneven road caused the wagon to jolt. She asked no more questions, and Mr. Ollenburger remained silent, too, encouraging the oxen with low-toned commands and flicks of the whip over their broad backs.

Dusk had fallen by the time the wagon finally rolled to a stop in front of a simple wood-framed house. Gray smoke lifted from the chimney, and soft yellow light shone behind two-over-two pane windows. Mr. Ollenburger hopped over the side of the seat, then looked up at her.

"Remain here, *Frau* Steadman. I check on Thomas and *Grossmutter,* and then I will take you to the *shariah.*" His long-legged stride carried him across the ground quickly. He disappeared inside the house while Summer shivered on the seat. In a few minutes the door swung open again and Mr. Ollenburger stepped out, followed by a smaller replica of himself.

Summer noticed a shadowy figure, stooped over and leaning on a cane, hovering in the doorway. She assumed this was the grandmother of whom Mr. Ollenburger had spoken. She squinted into the waning light, attempting to see the woman's face, but Mr. Ollenburger and the boy stopped beside the wagon, and his voice pulled her attention away from the older woman.

"*Frau* Steadman, this is my son, Thomas. Thomas, say hello to *Frau* Steadman."

"Hello, Mrs. Steadman."

Summer's lips trembled as she peered down at Thomas. Mr. Ollenburger had said the youngster was sturdy and dependable, bright and handsome. Just one look at him proved the father had spoken the truth. Thomas was as stocky as her Vincent had been slender, as blond as her son had been dark-haired. But in his eyes she saw the same light of intelligence that had brightened Vincent's serious face. *Oh, Vincent, I miss you, son! It isn't fair that you're gone and . . .*

The door clicked, and Summer glanced at the house. The woman had gone back inside without a word. How odd that the older woman had not greeted her the way the boy had.

"I take *Frau* Steadman to the *shariah*." Mr. Ollenburger placed a wide hand on the boy's shoulder. "I must take the wagon so I can move out some barrels and boxes, or she will not have room to turn around in there."

42

Thomas's face lit up. "May I help you, Pa?"

"*Nein,* son. Doctor said no lifting yet."

The boy's eagerness wilted. "Yes, sir."

"But would you fix *Frau* Steadman some bread with jam and bring it to the *shariah?*"

"Yes, sir!" He spun toward the door.

"Verlangsamen sie!"

Mr. Ollenburger's order resulted in Thomas slowing his pace. The big man heaved himself back onto the wagon seat as his son stepped onto the stoop.

The boy waved. "I will bring that bread quickly, Pa."

"You do not run when you bring the bread."

"Yes, sir."

"Thank you, Thomas." Summer forced a smile while her heart cried. *What a nice boy. What a good friend he would have been for my Vincent.*

With firm calls to "gee," the oxen were coaxed into turning the wagon, and Summer waited until they were in motion before speaking again. "He seems to be a fine boy." Her throat felt tight.

"Oh, *ja,* a very fine boy. He should give you no trouble. But if he does, you tell me. I will deal with him."

"I'm sure we'll get along well."

"He will be hard to hold down. Poor *Grossmutter* has had a time holding him down. It is good he will have something to fill his days, that he'll be able to study again." He angled his face sideways to look at her. "The boy is tired of the sitting still. But he must. The ribs must fully heal."

Summer recognized the warning tone. She nodded. Nothing would happen to this boy. The image of the old woman in the doorway flitted through her mind. "Mr. Ollenburger, your grandmother . . ."

He released a heavy sigh. "*Ja, Grossmutter* . . . A blessing she has been to Thomas and me. And a blessing we have been to her, for sure. She has had much sickness in past years, and things have become hard for her. Her hands" — he held up one of his own hands, seeming to examine it with sorrow — "are much bent from . . . I think you call it arthritis, but she does what she can. She wishes to be useful still. The English language she cannot speak. When first we came, she refused to try. And now? I think she believes that saying of old dogs cannot learn new tricks."

He sighed again, and his tone took the quality of one speaking more to himself.

"Not much does she speak even in our language anymore — not to me. She does speak yet to Thomas. He is her light. . . ." Then he straightened, shooting her a quick glance. "Do not take offense if she does not speak to you."

Summer thought about spending the day inside that house with the old woman watching. Silently watching. She shivered again. "Are we almost to the *shariah?*"

He pointed with a thick finger. "It is right there."

Summer saw, through the murky light, a triangular-shaped dwelling about fourteen feet across on its bottom and ten feet to its tip. It appeared to be only the roof of a house, with its walls swallowed by the ground.

Mr. Ollenburger called, "Whoa," and the oxen obediently halted. The man hopped down, his heavy boots thumping against the hard ground. "I will light a lantern and then take you in." He strode to the unusual structure and ducked into what seemed to be a narrow tunnel attached to one side of the triangle. Moments later he reappeared, a lantern in his hand giving off a cheery yellow circle of light.

He set the lantern on the ground beside the wagon, the yellow circle shrinking until it barely touched his feet. She placed her hands in his and allowed him to help her down. The moment her feet touched the hard ground, he released her to reach into the back of the wagon and retrieve her carpetbag. "Come." He lifted the lantern and led her to the tunnel. "Watch your step, *Frau* Steadman. Only dirt makes the stairs. You could slip. I will cut some planks to make them safer for you tomorrow."

She realized as she stepped into the tunnel that the triangular building was like a wooden tent placed over a pit. He handed her the lantern and began shoving crates and barrels aside to make room in the center of the floor.

She raised the lantern and looked around, her heart falling in dismay as she saw what she had chosen over the hotel room. *Shariah* certainly could not mean "house" — it must mean "hovel." The entire dwelling was no more than twelve by fourteen feet — smaller than the parlor in her Boston home. Simple wood beams held up a slanted ceiling of wide planks that met at a peak in the center. Each end of the building was also constructed of planks standing up and down. Only the center part of the shelter was fully serviceable since the side walls were a scant three feet high. No windows existed in the little hut, and since the foundation was simply hard-packed dirt, it felt cool and smelled dank. Another shiver shook her frame.

Mr. Ollenburger paused in his shifting of boxes to give her a worried look. "You are cold, *Frau* Steadman. A way to bring heat here for you I must find." He scratched his chin. "When we moved into the house, we took the cookstove with us. But there is still a vent hole for a stovepipe, which I covered with a tin can pounded flat. This keeps the rain out. I will see what I can rig for you tomorrow. I must also fix a bed."

"I would appreciate a source of heat," Summer inserted, "but you needn't fix a bed. I have a bedstead in my wagon."

Mr. Ollenburger looked at her for several quiet seconds, pursing his lips, which caused his chin whiskers to splay forward. He cleared his throat. "*Ja,* well, tonight you must make a pallet on the floor — there are many blankets here." He moved to a trunk in the corner, ducking to avoid hitting his head on the slanting ceiling. When he raised the lid, Summer saw a stack of thick woven blankets. He looked at her, an apology in his eyes. "It is not much. . . ."

47

He was right. It certainly was not much. But what else did she have to look forward to? She forced a light tone. "Remember, Mr. Ollenburger, I have spent many weeks in a wagon or a tent pitched outside. It is a treat to have a roof over my head again."

Her words must have been convincing, because his face relaxed into a smile. He moved to the center of the room, straightening his back and looking upward. "*Ja,* it is a roof. It is no masterpiece of carpentry, but it will shelter you."

She let her gaze drift around the small space. "When these boxes have been removed and my own belongings have been brought in, it will feel more like a home. I'll be fine."

His brows came down into a worried scowl. He fiddled with his hat, his ears glowing bright pink. Something was clearly wrong. Just as she opened her mouth to question him, Thomas entered through the tunnel, a paper-wrapped package in his hands. He offered the package to Summer with a shy smile.

"Here is your sandwich, Mrs. Steadman. Strawberry jam on wheat bread. Pa bought the bread from the restaurant in Gaeddert. If it was bread Pa made, you wouldn't be able to eat it."

Peter gave his son a playful cuff on the back of his head, chuckling. "*Ja,* the boy is right, for sure. My baking is not so good, but you see we have not starved." He clamped a hand on Thomas's shoulder. "Remember, son, this is now *Frau* Steadman's home. You must knock before you come in next time."

The boy nodded, sending Summer a sheepish look. "I'll remember."

Peter strode to the door. "I will take out a few of these boxes to give you moving around room. The rest can wait until morning light. Thomas and I will leave you to your sandwich and bed." He picked up the nearest box and stepped through the tunnel with it, Thomas on his heels.

Summer sank down on a short barrel, placed the packet of bread with jam in her lap, and looked once more at the dismal little dwelling that was her new home.

It would be bearable if only I weren't alone. Why did they all have to die?

Peter leaned over and placed a kiss on Thomas's tousled hair. "*Guten nacht. Schlop die 'zunt,* son."

"You sleep well, too, Pa." The boy pulled the covers to his chin.

Peter left the door ajar so he could hear his son's breathing. He crossed to the wooden table in the middle of the main room and sat down. Grasping the heel of his right boot, he worked the boot free, dropped it with a muffled thud against the braided rug beneath the table, then freed his left foot and dropped that boot with its mate. He wiggled his toes and leaned back in his chair, releasing a long sigh.

The rough tabletop had been cleared of dishes but still wore a spattering of crumbs. Peter swept his hand across the surface, sending the crumbs to the floor. He looked toward the dry sink and spotted two tin plates and a mug — not enough to require a trip to the well for dishwater. It could wait until morning. There had been a time when crumbs on the table and dishes in the sink would not have been acceptable, but with *Grossmutter's* advancing arthritis stealing her ability to do simple chores, the house sometimes reflected a lack of care. Peter did not much like this, but he did not have the time to do all the household chores as well as the outdoor duties. He hoped the woman would not find their crumbs offensive.

A light snuffling sounded from Thomas's room, followed by the deeper, more rumbling noise of the old woman's snore. Peter smiled. The one time he had told *Grossmutter* she snored, her expression of indignation had convinced him he had better not mention it again. He did not mind the snoring. The sounds were comforting.

Elsa always used to say if she heard him snoring, she knew he was near. It felt good to have the boy and the old woman near. His smile faded into a frown. The woman alone in the *shariah* must be finding it hard to sleep. No snores, no snuffles, no company at all. How long had it been before he'd slept straight through a night after Elsa's passing? He could not remember now, although he was sure it had been weeks — well after the ship had delivered him and the boy to American soil.

Peter yawned, stretching. Tomorrow would be a full day. His mind sorted through the tasks awaiting him with the rising of the sun. While the woman worked with Thomas, Peter must chop some saplings to build a rope bed on which the woman could sleep, haul all of the remaining boxes and barrels to the barn and store them in the loft so the woman had room, find a way to bring heat to the shelter so the woman would not freeze when the snows came, fix the steps so she would not fall . . . and sometime during the day he must take her to where her family had camped and show her she no longer had belongings.

His chest ached with dread as he considered the last task.

She had already lost so much. He rested his elbow on the table edge and propped up his chin, searching for words that might comfort her tomorrow when she discovered what had been done to her wagon and the things inside it. For sure, belongings could be replaced. That was true, yet it seemed unkind to say so when belongings were all one had to call one's own.

"Lieber Lord im himmel," he prayed aloud, slipping into his comfortable German dialect, "I ask that you be with me tomorrow when I must show poor *Frau* Steadman that all her things are gone. Prepare her heart to accept the loss. Help her understand why the burning was needed. Thank you that my Thomas has a teacher. Let my Thomas also teach her to love again, for only with the opening of one's heart can joy be restored." He yawned, his ears popping with the stretching of his jaw.

"*Ach,* Father, I am a tired man. I must

sleep now. Let the sleep bring me strength for what awaits me tomorrow. Amen."

4

"She's awful skinny, Pa."

Peter looked at his son. "Skinny? What is this?"

"You know — too thin. Skinny."

Peter nodded. *"Ja."* He sat at the table, eating his breakfast of cornmeal mush. The early morning breeze slipped through the open front door. He liked the smell of morning in the house, but very soon they would need to keep the door closed to hold out the cold. *Grossmutter* held a shawl around her shoulders this morning. Maybe he should close the door now.

"She doesn't look very strong, either." Across the table, Thomas scooped another bite and swallowed.

Peter shrugged. "I do not know that a person must be muscled to have smartness."

Thomas gave a light laugh, one arm wrapped protectively across his middle.

"No, I reckon not. Mr. Funk is pretty skinny, too, but he's a good teacher."

"There you are." Peter lowered his brows and pointed his spoon at Thomas. "You will give *Frau* Steadman the same respect you have always given your Mr. Funk. Just because you study at home is no reason to play."

"Oh, sure, Pa. I know." The boy blinked in innocence.

Grossmutter reached out with her gnarled hand and tapped Thomas's wrist. She pointed to his bowl.

Thomas sent her a smiling nod. *"Ich esse, Grossmutter."* He ate two more bites, as he had promised, before turning to Peter. "She looks sad, too."

Peter set his spoon aside. He wondered how the woman had slept last night on the hard dirt floor of the *shariah* all alone. *"Ja,* she is sad." And sadder she would soon be when she discovered she no longer had a wagon and things to call her own. "She has lost much, son. We must be patient while we wait for her to smile, *ja?"*

Thomas looked across the table with a thoughtful expression on his youthful face. "Pa, how long did it take for you to not feel so sad about Ma dying?"

Peter stroked his beard, considering Thomas's question. This was one moment he was glad *Grossmutter* did not understand the English. "There are days, son, when the sadness still sits like a stone in my chest. Sadness comes sometimes when I look at you and think how proud she would be of you."

Thomas paused in his eating. His chin quivered. "Would she be proud of me, Pa?"

"*Ach,* but yes," he said, reaching across the table to tousle Thomas's hair. "Who could not be proud of a boy like you? Even when he falls from trees!"

Thomas grinned. "Oh, Pa."

Peter picked up his spoon. "Finish your breakfast, son. You will have studies to do and you will need a full belly for your brain to think."

"Excuse me."

Peter turned in his chair to see *Frau* Steadman in the doorway. He rose, his eyes involuntarily sweeping from her toes to her hair. She wore a different dress than the blue wool. This one was the same green as the leaves of the cedars that grew along the Cottonwood River. Like the blue one, it hung loosely. As Thomas had said, she looked skinny. But she had obviously made use of the well. Her face was shiny clean and her dark hair damp where it was swept back from her face. The circles under her eyes did not indicate a restful night for her.

He smiled a greeting and held out his hand. "Please, *Frau* Steadman, come in. Sit down. I will get a bowl for you for mush."

She entered the house, her focus touching first Thomas then *Grossmutter* before returning to him. "I honestly couldn't eat a bite."

Peter did not want to argue with her, yet he could not allow her to starve to death on his property. "If mush does not appeal, I can go to the henhouse for an egg."

"Thank you, but no."

Peter clamped his jaw, worry and irritation mingling in his chest. She must eat, but he could not force her. *Lieber Lord, what do I do?* An idea struck, and a grin tugged at his cheek. Instead of addressing the woman, he turned to his son and shook his head with great sadness. "I am sorry, Thomas, but no lessons for you today."

"Pa?"

"Disappointed I know you are, son, but I cannot allow *Frau* Steadman to teach you."

The woman moved forward one step, her skirts sweeping the floor. Her dark eyes

57

snapped. "Why not?"

"We agree — trade schooling for room and food. I cannot accept the schooling if you do not accept the payment. So . . ." He shrugged at Thomas. "No lessons today."

Thomas understood. While his eyes sparkled, he pushed his lips into a pout. "But I'm so far behind."

"You will have to study on your own, son." Peter touched Thomas's hair and brought forth a sorrow-laden sigh while Thomas played along, slumping his shoulders in disappointment. Peter peeked at *Frau* Steadman. Would it work?

She glared at him with narrowed eyes, her lips pursed in irritation. Finally she threw her hands outward. "All right. I'll eat." She crossed to the table and pushed Peter's empty bowl aside, seating herself with a straight back and raised chin. "But don't think for a moment I don't know what you're up to. And I won't always be so easily manipulated."

"Ma-nip-u-lated." Peter scowled. "I do not know what this means."

Her chin thrust out. "Oh, yes you do."

With a shrug in Thomas's direction, Peter got a clean bowl and plopped in a great lump of mush. He added a dollop of molasses and doused it with cream, then set the

58

bowl and a spoon in front of the woman. Standing beside her chair, he waited until she took up the spoon, stirred the contents into a semismooth consistency, and brought a small bite to her mouth.

Grossmutter continued eating while observing the woman with her sharp scrutiny. Peter could not tell what she was thinking.

Thomas, still sitting on the other side of the table, also watched. "Mrs. Steadman? You didn't say grace."

A blush stole across the woman's cheeks.

Peter sent a brief glowering look in Thomas's direction, then smiled down at the woman. "When I blessed the food this morning, God knew you would eat. It will digest without a second prayer." He glared once more at Thomas, who hung his head. "I will get water for the dishes. Thomas, you stay and visit with *Frau* Steadman."

Thomas raised his chin and smiled at Summer. The woman went on eating with small, dainty bites. Peter picked up a bucket, stepped out the door, and headed across the dewy grass to the well. As he turned the crank to bring up the pail, he tested the unknown word. "Ma-nip-u-lated." How he wished he knew what she meant. With a sigh, he poured the water from the pail into his waiting bucket, taking care not to splash over the rim, then threw the pail back into the depths of the well.

Back in the house he found Thomas, under *Grossmutter's* watchful eye, sharing what he had been studying in school before his accident. The woman listened, her fine brows pulled down in concentration. He peeked at her bowl and hid a smile of satisfaction. It was nearly empty. *Good. The tricking of her worked.*

He poured the water into the reservoir of the stove to heat and placed the empty bucket on the floor beside the dry sink. When he straightened, he found *Frau* Steadman waiting, bowl and spoon in hand. Her nearness caught him off guard, and he stumbled backward a step, kicking the bucket. She glanced at the bucket then looked at his face.

He felt heat building in the back of his neck. He looked toward the table, where Thomas grinned and *Grossmutter* pursed her lips.

"Mr. Ollenburger?"

He turned back to the woman.

She gestured toward the dry sink. "Would you like me to wash the dishes?"

Peter shook his head, returning to the

table to put some distance between them. "Washing the dishes is Thomas's job. It does not hurt his ribs to lift only bowls and spoons. When he is finished, he can show you his books, and you two can begin to study."

She watched as he carried Thomas's bowl to the dry sink and added it to the others waiting in the tin wash pan. "I was hoping . . ."

He heard the tremble in her voice and stopped rearranging bowls to look at her. "*Ja?* You were hoping?"

She licked her lips, hiding her hands in the folds of her skirt. He watched her eyes flit sideways to the table before coming back to him. "I know that Thomas is eager to begin his studies, but I wondered if perhaps we could delay it for one more day."

"Delay . . ." Peter looked at Thomas.

"Wait until later, Pa."

"Wait until later?" Peter said to *Frau* Steadman.

"Just one day. I would like to have the chance to settle in, to bring the things from my wagon to the *shariah*." She paused. "Would-would that be acceptable?"

Peter swallowed. He would rather wait until later to go to the no-longer-there wagon, but he knew he could not. He lowered his chin and aimed his voice at the floor. "I think to . . . delay . . . one day will not harm the boy. I will hitch the oxen."

He looked up to see gratitude in her eyes. "Thank you."

As he clumped across the ground toward the barn, he wondered if she would regret that thank-you once she saw what the doctor had done.

Summer scuffed her toe through the pile of ashes. Ashes. Only ashes remained of what was once her wagon, furniture, books . . . and memories. The minister had said, "Ashes to ashes, dust to dust . . ." as the men had shoveled soil on top of her children's graves. Her children were ashes. Her belongings were ashes. Her dreams were ashes. Hot tears formed in her eyes, and she pulled her coat tighter around her chin as she battled the desire to dissolve into wails of anguished fury.

"Sorry I am that it was done, *Frau* Steadman, but the good of many must sometimes come before the good of one." The sympathy in Mr. Ollenburger's eyes substantiated his words. He lifted his ax, using it to point toward a stand of maples along the riverbank. "I-I go now to chop the trees for your new bed. You . . . you sit and . . ." He shrugged in a helpless gesture and headed into the trees, the ax on his shoulder.

Soon she heard the hollow clack of iron against wood. Chopping trees to build her new bed, he had said. Anger, hot and consuming, rose up within her. She didn't want a new bed! She wanted her own carved oak bedstead on which her children had been born, and the quilt pieced by her grandmother, and the rocking chair in which she had soothed her babies to sleep before tucking them into the cradle that had been her own sleeping spot when she was an infant. So many precious, irreplaceable items had been inside that wagon! It was unthinkable that this pile of soot and grit was now all she had.

The wind lifted particles of gray ash and carried them away across the brittle grass. She spun from the sight, a strangled sob forcing its way out of her throat. Her gaze fell upon the row of headstones. She broke into a stumbling run and dropped to her knees in front of the graves, allowing the tears to flow.

"Oh, Vincent, all your books . . . They're gone, son." The wind whipped at her hair and dried the tears that rained down her cheeks in an endless flood. "And Rose, my precious girl, the sweet embroidery you worked on as we traveled . . . You were so proud of the posies you stitched from pink silk floss. You said you would hang the sampler in our new parlor. I'm so sorry I can't hang it for you, Rose. . . ."

She turned to another mound. "Tod, dear Tod, your carved soldiers are all burned up." She closed her eyes, envisioning the little boy lying flat on his belly in the grass with the wooden men clasped in his dimpled fists. "I'm so glad I put one with you in your grave. At least you have one left with which to play." She slapped her hands to her cheeks, gasping as guilt assailed her. "But, Tillie . . . Oh, my dear sweet baby, I didn't put your dolly with you. I kept it, thinking I would hold it when the need to hold you was too strong. And now, like you, it's gone. I should have buried it with you, my darling. I'm sorry, Tillie. I'm so sorry. . . ."

Sobs shook her. She could no longer speak. Burying her face against her knees, she cried until she thought her chest might explode. It was several minutes before she realized the sound of the ax had stopped. She peered over her shoulder. On the other side of the ash pile, Mr. Ollenburger crouched on his haunches, the ax across his knees. His wagon waited behind him, a tumble of fresh-cut saplings piled in its bed.

She turned back to the graves and cleaned her face with her sleeve. Painfully she pushed herself to her feet, but she couldn't make herself leave. Her gaze drifted down the row of markers, ending with little Tillie's. She read aloud the words engraved there: " 'An angel took my flower away, but I will not repine, since Jesus at His bosom wears the flower that once was mine.' "

"It is true."

She jumped at the deep voice that came from behind her right shoulder. "What?"

He stepped beside her. "What you said. It is true." He nodded his shaggy head, his eyes solemn. "All of your *liebchen* are now with Jesus, safe in His arms."

Anger at all she'd lost welled up like an ocean wave. "But I want them with *me!* What does *He* need with them? They're *my* children! My *children* . . ." Another sob rent her words, and she placed a hand against her lips to stifle any more that might erupt.

Mr. Ollenburger's eyes softened with understanding. "I know, *Frau* Steadman. The sadness goes very deep. It fills you until there is not room for anything else."

She nodded. The sorrow was a crushing burden. It equaled her guilt.

"There is One who can take your sadness and fill your heart with joy once more, if only you will ask Him."

Summer forced out her breath in a harsh huff. "Please, Mr. Ollenburger, do not preach a sermon to me. This God of whom you speak ignored my cries to save my children. Even if He could restore my joy, why would He? He didn't care enough to hear me before. Why would He listen now?"

The man flapped his jaw twice, as if unable to form words, then snapped it shut.

She turned away from him, wrapping her arms around herself and shivering in the cool wind.

After a long while, he spoke again, his voice of distant thunder tender in its delivery. "Why my Elsa was took from me I still do not know. She wanted even more than me to see this land where no one stops you from worshiping the true God. A land where our Thomas could grow and choose whatever he wished to be. But out at the sea, she died. She is buried in the ocean."

Summer gasped.

"So not even a grave do we have to visit." He turned, his gaze settling on the headstones. "My Elsa had been with me my whole life. All of my memories from little boy up to full-grown man have her in them. Very hard it was to say good-bye. Very hard for her *Grossmutter,* too, who had raised her since she was little girl. But . . ." He rested a large hand against the front of his sheep wool jacket, facing Summer again. "I visit her in my heart. And I talk to the God with whom she now lives. That is where I find my comfort." He shrugged, his huge shoulders bunching his jacket around his bearded chin. "But time it took to find my comfort. It will take time for you, too."

He stepped closer, his expression serious. "Do not say God is not there or is uncaring. Our God is a God who knows. He knows your pain of loss. He has felt it Himself as His Son died and He must to turn away. He knows what is found in our future, and He knows what is best for us. We must trust that He knows."

Summer turned back to the graves. "I'm glad you found your comfort, Mr. Ollenburger. But this is what *I* know — my husband believed God would take us safely to Oklahoma. God didn't. Now here I am with no husband, no children, and nothing to remind me of them. It's all . . . burnt up." Tears pricked behind her lids as she spit the words through clenched teeth. "And my joy is burnt up, too."

At that moment two curled bits of soot rose, lifted by the wind, and danced away on the breeze. Summer watched them go, the pressure in her chest increasing as they disappeared in the treetops. "My joy is now ashes, Mr. Ollenburger, and as you can plainly see, ashes cannot be put back together again."

He seemed to search for those two bits of soot, his brows pulled down.

She waited for him to refute her bitter words.

He reached inside his jacket and withdrew a rumpled piece of paper with seared edges. He looked at it for a moment, his lips pressed together so tightly his whiskers stuck out. "I found this in the bushes beside the river. I do not know, but —" He held it out to her. "It looks to be one little piece from your ashes."

When she didn't reach for it, he clasped her wrist and lifted her hand to meet the paper. "Take it with you, *Frau* Steadman. One day, it will bring you joy to have it."

He walked away, leaving her holding the shred of brittle scorched paper. Tears flooded her eyes as she recognized a page from Rodney's Bible — the page on which the births of their children had been recorded. One corner was completely burned away, and three of the four sides were singed from the flame, but each name and date was still intact, penned in Rodney's neat script.

A part of her heart ached with desire to give thanks to God for the miracle of this little scrap surviving the fire that destroyed everything else. But she hardened herself against it. If God was able to keep this piece of paper from burning up, He should have been able to save her children. She started to crumple it into a wad, but something stopped her. Instead, she folded it with great care and placed it in her pocket.

Mr. Ollenburger waited beside the oxen, his large hand resting on the shoulder of one sturdy beast. With a sigh, she pushed her feet into motion. She had made a deal with this man to teach his son, and she would honor it. Never, though, would she believe in his God.

5

Mr. Ollenburger stopped the wagon in front of the house. He turned to Summer and spoke the first words since they had left the gravesite. "I go now to clean out the *shariah* and build your bed. I will also go to town and find a stove so you will have heat. Even a small one would be plenty big enough."

Summer allowed him to grasp her hands and help her over the edge of the wagon. It seemed to take no effort for him to lift her down. She shielded her eyes from the sun with her hand as she peered up at him. "Do you need some money?"

"Nein." His chin thrust out in stubbornness, the curled whiskers bristling. "It is my *shariah*. I will provide the heating for it."

"If you're sure . . ." Wind zipped around the house and tossed a strand of hair across her cheek. She tucked it behind her ear.

"I am sure. You spend day with the boy,

get to know each other." With a push of his foot, he released the brake. "Do not expect me until suppertime."

Summer watched the wagon lumber away before she crossed to the house. Standing on the small stoop, she raised her hand and knocked. The door swung open, and Thomas stepped out beside her.

"Where is Pa going?"

"To do some chores." Summer watched the wind tousle the boy's hair. Her fingers ached to smooth the locks back into place. "He said we were to spend the day getting acquainted."

Thomas looked up at her with unblinking eyes. He seemed to be taking stock of her, and she felt a blush filling her cheeks. Finally he shrugged. "I could show you around the place. If you're going to live here, you might want to know where everything is."

"That-that's fine." Summer tried to smile, but her lips felt stiff, as if smiling would never again be possible.

"I'll get my jacket." The boy went back into the house and returned a few minutes later, a brown woolen jacket tugged over his overalls.

"Don't you need a hat?" Her maternal

worry came naturally, making her heart beat faster.

"Nah. I'll be fine."

Summer looked at the closed door. Was the old woman still sitting at the table? "Is it all right for us to leave your grandmother unattended?"

"Oh sure. She likes having time to herself." He scratched his head. "So . . . do you want to see everything now?"

She remembered Mr. Ollenburger's warning to keep the boy's activity limited. "If you're going to show me around, we will walk sedately." She bent her left arm at the elbow. "Position your arm like this."

The boy stuck out his right arm.

"No, your left arm."

With a frown, he switched arms.

Summer slipped her right hand through his elbow. "Now you may lead me around your property. Save your favorite place for last."

The boy's eyes lit with eagerness. "That would be the gristmill."

Summer nodded. "Very well. Show me everything of importance on the way. But as I said, walk sedately."

She made sure Thomas learned the meaning of "walk sedately" as they strolled around the house and headed toward the

72

northeast corner of the Ollenburgers' property. When Thomas pointed out the barn, his horse, Daisy, pawed the ground and snuffled a greeting from a small enclosure attached to the large log building. Behind the barn were the henhouse and pigpens. Summer needed no verbal introduction to the latter location; her nose recognized it well in advance.

Thomas pointed to the outhouse. "There's the necessary. Reckon that's good to know even though there's one behind the *shariah,* too."

Summer was sure her face glowed a brilliant pink at the boy's blithe comment — she had already made acquaintance with the necessary behind the *shariah* that morning, but she wouldn't have admitted it to Thomas!

"And over there," the boy said, pride in his voice, "is our gristmill. My pa's the only miller in Gaeddert."

That was the gristmill? Summer lifted her hand once more to shield her eyes, certain she had missed something. She saw only a large windmill that sat atop a high wooden platform supported by massive wood beams.

Thomas tugged at her arm. "My great-grandfather and my grandfather were millers. Pa started milling before he was my age. My grandfather's gristmill was powered by water. When Pa settled in Kansas, he thought he'd build a water-powered gristmill, too. That's why he chose land near the Cottonwood River. But he found out the river moves too slow."

The boy led her around the windmill, which towered more than thirty feet in the air, including the four-foot-high platform. The blades nearly touched the ground. Summer marveled at the immense size of the windmill.

"So he had to find a different way to power it," he went on. "Pa figured, wind's usually blowing here. Why not do like the Dutch and use wind to power the mill?"

"Very clever of him." She tipped her head back to view the entire mill. "Why did he not build it on the ground? Why up on top of that platform?"

The boy kept his right arm tucked tight against his side as he released a light laugh. "Well, the wind blows almost every day, but it doesn't always blow from the same direction." He led her to the opposite side. "Look — by hitching the oxen to the beams, Pa can turn the mill so it faces the wind. That way, no matter what direction the wind is from, the mill can keep working." His chest puffed out. "My pa's the smartest man I know."

Summer had to concede, the engineering was clearly the work of an intelligent mind. Mr. Ollenburger's large size, his humble speech, and even the simple construction of the *shariah* could lead one to believe otherwise. What had he said of the shack? It was not a masterpiece of carpentry. Well, this gristmill certainly was that. She hoped his son proved to be as quick-witted. If so, it would be as pleasant to work with him as it had been to work with Vincent.

That thought brought her to an abrupt halt. Vincent was gone. He would no longer sit at her feet, looking up with rapt attention as she read to him from Byron or Longfellow. Tears threatened, and she turned away from Thomas lest he see them and question her. She couldn't bear to speak of Vincent — not to this boy who might have been his friend.

"This-this is a wonderful gristmill, Thomas. I see why you have chosen this as your favorite spot." Her words sounded stilted, even to her ears. But the boy didn't seem to recognize her change in demeanor.

"It's my favorite spot when the harvest is done, for sure." His smile was bright. "I like listening to the grain go through the grinder. It rumbles and makes your tummy feel like it's growling from hunger. Then puffs of flour come out around the spout when it's filling the sacks. Goes right up your nose and makes you sneeze!"

He offered another controlled laugh, and Summer's lips twitched as they fought to respond with an answering smile.

"Pa ground the last of the wheat from around here only last week. He's all done now for the winter." He heaved a sigh, as if disappointed, but then with a quicksilver change, brightened again. "When I grow up, I'm going to be a miller, just like Pa."

Summer nodded. Didn't most boys want to be just like their fathers? Vincent had always said he would be a banker, like Rodney. Rose had wanted to be an artist. Little Tod had made her laugh with his declaration that he would be a cowboy — he had been most excited about the journey to Oklahoma, where he might meet real Indians. And dimpled Tillie had been too young to make plans. How sad to die before reaching an age to even make plans. Anger pressed at Summer's heart. It was so unfair that her children's dreams would never see fulfillment.

"Mrs. Steadman?"

Thomas's voice brought her back to reality. She looked at the boy, who squinted against the sun that tipped his wheat colored hair with golden highlights.

"Sun's straight overhead. Should we go get some lunch now?"

Summer looked skyward, confirming the boy's observation. "Now that you've shown me the property, we'll get lunch fixed right away."

Though she had no desire to eat, this boy must be fed. He must be fed and kept healthy so at least *his* dreams would one day become reality.

Why'd Pa bring home such a sour-faced lady? Thomas wondered as he chewed bread slathered with butter and honey. He knew Pa was worried about him falling behind on schoolwork — lessons were important to Pa. Hadn't he been telling Thomas since he was little that he should learn all he could? He understood Pa wanted someone around who would help him keep up with studies, but why this lady?

Thomas watched out of the corner of his eye as Mrs. Steadman pushed the carrots back and forth on her plate with a fork. Even though she looked real hungry, she didn't eat. He couldn't imagine someone not eating — he liked to eat. He reached for another piece of bread and the butter knife. Everybody he knew liked to eat. This lady was different from everyone else he knew.

And it wasn't just the eating. She wore her hair different, her voice sounded different when she talked, she never smiled. Of course, Thomas admitted, grumpy *Frau* Schmidt in town never smiled, either. This woman Pa had brought home didn't seem grumpy, but she sure didn't seem happy. Thomas scrunched his forehead. Was she sad? Mad? He wasn't sure.

He glanced at Grandmother. She sat at the table, and she wasn't eating much, either. She had a funny look in her eyes, like she was afraid something bad was about to happen. It made Thomas's heart skip a beat. Was she afraid of this lady? He sat up, resolve straightening his spine. Well, Grandmother didn't need to worry. He would make sure this stranger didn't bother Grandmother. He'd keep watch over her. Grandmother had nothing to worry about.

Peter slapped Roth's hindquarters as he left the ox chewing contentedly in his stall with his mate. He swung the barn door shut behind him and trudged across the yard, his feet stirring dust as his heels dragged. He released a heavy sigh — what a long day it had been. But all the tasks he'd set for himself had been completed.

Sturdy planks covered the *shariah's* steps. The shelter held a new rope bed with a freshly stuffed straw mattress. The tinners' stove from Nickels' Dry Goods sent forth its warmth, and a full woodbox promised the warmth would continue. Boxes and barrels were now stored safely in the loft. Peter rubbed his hips, grimacing with the memory of carrying so many loads up the loft ladder. Out of consideration for the woman's needs, he had left a small crate beside the bed to hold a lantern, and the large blanket chest still stood in the corner to hold her belongings.

When he allowed himself a sigh of satisfaction, his breath hung in the evening air. Stars glimmered in a sky of deep blue tinged with pink at the horizon. His feet stilled, and he tilted his head back to search for the North Star as his own father had done at day's end. He remembered standing on the deck of the ship, his arm snug around Elsa's waist, the two of them looking upward at the polestar. It had given him pleasure to think of the star as a link between his old country and his new country. Now, knowing the same star had shone for his father and his father's father, he felt connected with those who had gone before — and with those who were yet to come.

He smiled at the sky and then turned toward the house. The lamp glow in the windows beckoned. He pushed his tired feet to move again. When he opened the door, the aromatic smells of ham and cabbage and bread filled his nostrils, making his stomach turn over in readiness. But the sight of *Frau* Steadman, with a wooden spoon in her hand and Elsa's apron wrapped around her waist, gave him pause. He remained in the doorway as an odd feeling gripped him. How long it had been since any woman besides *Grossmutter* had stood at his cookstove?

He turned to find his wife's grandmother in her chair in the corner also watching the woman. *Grossmutter's* eyes, which had faded in color with age and were now a pale blue, seemed watchful, wary. Peter crossed to the old woman and placed a kiss on her wrinkled cheek by way of greeting. She nodded at him, a brief smile tipping up her lips before her attention went back to the woman.

"Hi, Pa." Thomas rose from the table and set his slate aside. "Did you get everything done?"

"*Ja,* all is finished." Peter removed his cap and coat and hung them on wooden pegs beside the door. He glanced again at the woman. Her attention seemed to be on the wooden spoon that she dragged through the simmering pot. He addressed Thomas. "*Frau* Steadman will not sleep on the floor of a cold shelter tonight, or slide on steps of dirt." The woman glanced in his direction, but she didn't speak. He cleared his throat. "Son, did you have *gut* day?"

Thomas nodded, his hair flopping. "Yes, Pa. I showed Mrs. Steadman the gristmill." He leaned forward, dropping his voice to a whisper and slipping into German. "Clever she thought it was."

Peter's eyebrows shot up. "She said this?" He, too, lowered his voice and used his familiar language.

"By the way she looked, I could tell."

Well, the boy was prideful, Peter thought. He would read things in the woman's eyes that were not truly there. He glanced again at *Frau* Steadman and saw her lift the pot,

81

using the apron to protect her hands from its hot handles. Elsa's apron in the woman's slender hands constricted his chest. He spun from the sight, concerned how *Grossmutter* would feel about the woman using Elsa's things. But the old woman was no longer in her chair.

"Son, where has *Grossmutter* gone?"

Thomas looked over his shoulder, as if surprised, then stretched on his toes to whisper again. "Hiding from Mrs. Steadman, probably. Her eyes snapped all afternoon."

This news made Peter feel unsettled. Two spatting women would be an unpleasant thing to deal with each day. But he only smiled and tousled Thomas's hair, slipping back into English. "Set the table, son. It seems *Frau* Steadman is ready for us to partake of the fine meal she has made."

Frau Steadman placed the pot in the center of the table. Thomas set out crockery bowls, plates, and spoons while *Frau* Steadman turned a crusty loaf of bread into thick slices with several strokes of Peter's best knife. Peter washed his hands, then poured milk into tin cups, imagining how good it would taste to dip chunks of bread into the milk. It was a cozy feeling, working together with his son and the woman to put the meal on the table.

When all was nearly ready, he said, "I will see if *Grossmutter* is ready to join us." He tapped on the door leading to her room and entered. The old woman sat on her bed, curled forward over her well-worn Bible. She looked up at him, and as always her eyes reminded him of Elsa's. Elsa's had not been lined with wrinkles or topped with such heavy gray brows, but the expressiveness was the same. He read hurt in them now and wondered at the cause.

"*Grossmutter?* Supper is now ready." He used her beloved German when speaking.

Slowly she shook her head.

"You will not eat? Hungry you will be when morning comes if you do not eat."

The old woman pursed her lips into a stubborn expression and looked back down at her Bible.

He sighed. "Very well. You rest then." He gave her shoulder a gentle pat and returned to the kitchen, leaving the bedroom door standing open. The chaperone should not be shut away from those she was meant to watch.

When Thomas started to sit, Peter shook his head at his son, scowling. The boy stepped behind his chair, waiting with Peter for *Frau* Steadman to sit down. She removed the apron and hung it on a wooden peg, but then, to Peter's surprise, she put on her coat.

"Mrs. Steadman, aren't you going to eat with us?" Thomas asked the question before Peter could form words.

She tied her long scarf over her hair. "No. You two enjoy your meal."

"But you hardly ate lunch, either."

The woman paused at Thomas's protest. Her cheeks still appeared pink — from the heat of the cookstove, or something else? "I don't wish to intrude."

Peter gestured toward a chair. "You would honor us with your presence, *Frau* Steadman. Please, sit down and eat with us."

Many silent seconds passed before she removed her coat and put it back on the hook. Her steps seemed stiff as she moved to the table. She seated herself, and Peter pushed in her chair. She lowered her gaze, her hands in her lap. Thomas thumped his chair backward and sat across from her, and Peter sat between the two.

Thomas reached his hand for Peter's, as was their custom, and Peter took it. Peter closed his eyes and prayed, remembering to use English. "Dear Lord, bless this food and the hands that prepared it. Let it nourish our bodies so we may do your service. Amen."

Thomas took a slice of bread and carried it directly to his mouth; Peter wished to wilt from embarrassment. "*Ach,* the boy forgets his manners." He reprimanded, "Wait until a full bowl you have and all have been served before you begin to eat."

The boy blushed, and Peter took up the ladle to dip servings of soup into their bowls. He filled *Frau* Steadman's bowl first, but she did not touch her spoon until he and the boy also had filled bowls. Finally she took a small bite of cabbage and carrots, putting her spoon back on the table while she chewed.

"Do you like it?" Thomas asked hopefully.

She swallowed, nodding. "Yes. It's quite flavorful."

Thomas beamed at Peter. "I shared Grandmother's recipe with her. She said she'd never had *kraut borscht* before."

"One has not lived until one has eaten good *kraut borscht,*" Peter proclaimed.

A small gasp escaped *Frau* Steadman's lips, and she dropped her spoon with a clatter against the tabletop.

"Are you all right?" Thomas sent the woman a puzzled look.

She picked up the spoon once more with a hand that trembled. "Yes. Yes, I'm fine. Just clumsy." But she did not laugh at herself, and she could not force herself to eat any soup.

Peter and Thomas each ate two servings between a constant flow of banter and sharing of the day's events. When his own stomach was full and the boy had put down his spoon, Peter instructed, "Clear the table now, son, but leave the pot on the stove in case your *Grossmutter* chooses to eat some later. I will walk *Frau* Steadman to the *shariah*."

Peter shrugged back into his jacket while *Frau* Steadman put on her coat and scarf. After retrieving a lantern, he held the door for her. She passed in front of him, and then they walked in silence through the twilight. While most women he knew were talkers, this one was not. He wondered if he should try to fill the quietness between them, but his clumsy tongue could not find words of worth to say. Not until she was ready to duck through the tunnel did he finally speak.

"*Frau* Steadman, I thank you for that fine supper."

Her delicate profile, lit by the lamp's glow, showed the muscles of her jaw tensing. "I enjoyed cooking at a real stove again after . . . after so many campfires."

Peter nodded. He had not considered cooking could be enjoyable, only necessary. He cleared his throat. "I started a fire in the stove out here before I left, so you will have heat. It is only a tinners' stove, for to heat a tinners' shears" — he shrugged, wishing for the wealth to provide a better source of heat — "but Nickels assures me if you keep closed the back damper and open the front one, you will feel warmth. It also has a hot plate on top. Later we will get you a coffeepot, if you would like."

"That would be nice." Her voice was a mere murmur.

"I will see that your woodbox stays well filled. A lamp sits beside the bed." He dug in his pocket, bringing out a packet of matches. "Start these on the stove to light your lamp. When you need more oil for the lamp, tell me, and I will bring a jug."

She still wouldn't look at him. "I appreciate your efforts to make the *shariah* comfortable for me."

"In time, I will find a chair for you so you need not always sit on the bed." He realized these plans indicated he expected her to stay. He felt the heat in his neck building at his presumptuousness.

But the woman did not seem to find insult in his words. "Thank you," she whispered.

They stood silently in the lantern's glow while the wind teased her scarf, tossing it to and fro beneath her small, pointed chin. Finally she lifted her eyes to his. "Good night."

Such a peculiar expression on her face. As if she were waiting for something. What did she want from him? *"Guten nacht. Schlop die gesunt."* The words slipped out effort-lessly.

She tipped her head, her brow furrowed in puzzlement. "What?"

"I said for you to have good night and to sleep well."

Her brow smoothed. "Oh. That-that sounds lovely." But she didn't smile. She turned toward the tunnel. "You sleep well, too." She slipped inside the shelter, sealing the door behind her.

6

Summer touched the head of a wooden match to the flame within the belly of her new stove. When the match flared, a memory of a campfire appeared behind her eyes, and with the image of the campfire's glow came a row of faces, shadows dancing across their dear features. Then came the image of a row of headstones bearing the names of her children. Pain stabbed her heart. She lit her lamp quickly so she could blow out the match.

The lantern illuminated her small room well enough to see her new bed of strapped saplings and rope holding up a plump mattress of blue and white ticking. She pressed both palms to the mattress. The resulting crackle let her know what was inside. Turning, she seated herself. The ropes creaked as she settled her weight. While the straw mattress was certainly not as soft as the featherbed to which she'd become accustomed in her previous life, it would be much better than a bedroll on the ground. It was kind of Mr. Ollenburger to ready it for her.

Thanks to the stove — a tinners' stove, Mr. Ollenburger had called it — the room was considerably warmer than it had been last night. Between the new warmth and the new mattress, perhaps she would be able to sleep tonight. But probably not.

She closed her eyes, replaying supper as the ache in her chest grew. She hadn't wanted to sit at the table with the man and his son. She hadn't wanted to remember past meals with Rodney at the head, herself at the foot, and the children seated along the sides of their cherry dining room table. Of course, the simple room, the chipped crockery bowls and tin cups on the rough table — none of these things were reminiscent of sitting down for a meal in her home in Boston. Yet when she'd seated herself at Mr. Ollenburger's table, she had been transported to a former time and place.

When Mr. Ollenburger prayed and asked God to bless the hands that had prepared the food, she had almost fled. Then when he said one hadn't lived until sampling *kraut borscht,* she regretted not having done so. None of her children had sampled the soup flavored with dill weed and vinegar. None of her children ever would. The longing for her family nearly overwhelmed her. Sitting here alone in the shanty, all she had were her memories.

And memories were not the best company. From her coat pocket, she withdrew the scrap of paper Mr. Ollenburger had discovered by the river. She unfolded it, pressed it flat against her lap, and read down the list: Vincent Rodney, Rose Amelia, Tod Frederick, and Matilda Nadine. With each name came a vivid mental picture. She closed her eyes, savoring the images, crushing the paper to her chest. For long seconds she allowed herself to imagine that she held her children next to her heart rather than only their names printed on parchment.

With a deep sigh, she set the paper on the little crate beside the bed. She crossed to the chest to bring out blankets, pleased Mr. Ollenburger had left the trunk for her use. Although she didn't have much to store — only her remaining two dresses, her coat, reticule, and nightgown — at least she could keep those items dry and clean in the trunk.

She turned, arms laden, to make her bed. She stood still for a moment, examining the crude yet sturdy construction. Thinking back on the day and all Thomas had shown her — the log barn, animal pens built of neatly trimmed saplings, the towering gristmill — it seemed clear Mr. Ollenburger was a man who could fix things. Her foolish heart had come close to asking him to pray for her when he'd walked her to the *shariah* this evening. Perhaps his prayers would be strong enough to fix her broken heart. Her own were to no avail.

With a sagging spirit, she put her bed in order and blew out the lamp, sealing herself in a mournful, murky gray. She slipped between the covers and pulled the rough blanket clear to her chin. After a few moments, her eyes adjusted to the dismal gloom, and she stared at the rough beams overhead, her mind picturing the flower-sprigged paper that covered the ceiling of her bedroom in Boston.

Boston . . . If only she hadn't found that newspaper article. If only she hadn't shown it to Rodney. Rarely had she gotten her way with Rodney, but this time she had been persuasive.

"Think of it, Rodney — working side-by-side under the sun, building our house and plowing our fields, depending on no one but each other. How adventurous it would be! Can you not imagine it?"

Her words came back to haunt her, bringing with them another fierce stab of pain. Why couldn't she have been satisfied to remain in Boston? Why couldn't she have simply tolerated the distant affection offered by her husband? Why had she thought she needed more of his time and attention?

When her parents died, her brother had taken her in with reluctance. His wife had said boarding school would be beneficial, and off she was sent. When she reached a marriageable age, her brother and his wife had introduced Rodney to her and indicated it would be in her best interests to become his wife. Rodney had chosen their neighborhood, their home, and most of their furnishings — things befitting the son of bank owner Horace Steadman. Rodney had said they would start their family immediately, and they had, bringing into the world four wonderful children in the space of eight years.

Summer resented that so many decisions had been made for her. Never had her life been her own. Not until she found the article and convinced Rodney to go along with her scheme of beginning life anew in the lands of Oklahoma. She remembered the joy of moving through their spacious home, selecting which items they should sell and which they should take to pack into the wagon they would purchase in Missouri. Rodney often scowled, but he allowed her to have her way for the first time in their marriage.

They had argued fiercely over the box of books. Books are heavy, Rodney had insisted; books are necessary, she had countered. She had been told the frontier lacked reading material, and she would not allow her children to grow up uneducated. Finally Vincent's pleas convinced Rodney to allow the crate. How her heart had leaped with satisfaction as the train to Missouri had pulled out of Boston. A new life of her own choosing!

The bitter taste of regret was like bile on her tongue. Look what her choices had brought her — no husband, no children, no belongings, no home. Her eyes flitted around the room, another of her choices. A windowless hovel with a dirt floor and a bed made of cut saplings, rope, and straw.

Should she break her agreement with Mr. Ollenburger and return to the hotel, then arrange to take a train to Boston? The answer came immediately: no.

Her children's graves required tending, and so did Thomas. He wasn't her boy, and she had no desire to make him her boy, yet he was a child on whom she could bestow affection and care. Her heart needed someone to care for.

Summer frowned, remembering the constant watchful gaze of the old grandmother today. As Mr. Ollenburger had indicated, the woman had not spoken to her at all throughout the afternoon. She had only watched Summer with an expression of worry in her faded wrinkled eyes. Summer had no idea what worry the woman held, but she hoped it would be set aside. It was unnerving to always be watched.

Her eyelids drooped, sleepiness taking hold. Although the *shariah* carried a perpetually musty odor, the fresh smell of straw beneath her head pleased her nostrils. She rolled to her side to bring her nose closer to the source of the smell, closed her eyes, and drifted off to sleep.

Thomas formed the letters to spell the word *beast.* Summer felt the grandmother's eyes on her from the rocking chair in the corner, but Summer kept her focus on the boy. He held the slate toward her, his eyebrows raised in query. She nodded, and he swept away the word with a rag and took up his slate pencil, ready for the next word.

"Instinctive." She watched the boy's brow furrow in concentration as he bent once more over the slate.

It had surprised Summer to discover the variety of books the Ollenburgers owned. After the breakfast dishes were cleared away, Thomas had proudly shown her his shelf containing reading and spelling primers, the most recent volume of Barnes's *United States History,* Reed and Kellogg's *Higher Grammar,* and Robinson's *Practical Arithmetic.* In addition to the instructional books, he had several volumes of Twain's work and *Uncle Tom's Cabin* by Harriet Beecher Stowe. When Summer had voiced her astonishment at the Stowe book, the boy confided that he didn't like it much.

"Not because it isn't good. It is a good story. But it makes me sad." He shrugged. "I'd rather laugh when I read than cry. Sometimes Twain makes me cry, too."

Thomas was so different from Vincent, although both boys enjoyed reading. Vincent would choose the saddest story, then read it aloud with great drama, bringing his audience to tears. Summer pushed aside thoughts of Vincent to ask, "Where did you get so many books?"

The boy answered in a matter-of-fact

tone. "Pa buys them for my birthdays and Christmas."

Summer would never have guessed the man would choose reading material as gifts for his son. Tools, yes. Perhaps even a rifle. But books? Summer asked, "Does your father read to you, then?"

Thomas frowned. "I read to Pa."

Summer turned the spelling primer to the page Thomas had indicated and began reviewing. But his statement repeated itself in her head: "I read to Pa." Although Thomas hadn't said it directly, Summer surmised Mr. Ollenburger couldn't read.

"Did I get it right?" Thomas held up the slate, bringing her back to the present.

Summer pointed. "All but one letter. Instinctive needs an *e* at the end."

The boy made a face. "You can't hear it. Why does it have to be there?"

"Well . . ." She blinked. "I don't know. But the word requires it, so put it on and then write it correctly five times. That way you'll remember it."

Thomas's scowl deepened, and she wondered if he would argue. Then, with a sigh, he followed her direction. She stifled her own sigh of relief at his acquiescence. She didn't care to grow stern with him while the grandmother observed her every move.

She rose and poured another cup of coffee while she waited for him to finish. Through the window, she observed Mr. Ollenburger at the chopping block, where he was turning logs into kindling. The thud of his ax had sounded for nearly an hour now. He had rolled up the sleeves of his plaid flannel shirt, and even from this distance, she could see the bulge of his muscles as he raised the tool over his head.

With a mighty thrust of the ax he split a sizable length of log into two halves, then *thunk! thunk!* — the halves became quarters. He lifted all four pieces and carried them to the woodpile, where they were added to a neat stack. He repeated the process with another log. Did the man never tire?

Every task Mr. Ollenburger performed was done with precision. His woodpile was as straight as a row of soldiers marching in parade. The grounds of his property were neatly kept. The house, though far from fancy, had a tidy appearance. She knew it could use an additional sweeping and dusting — those were things a woman would notice more than a man — but it was obvious the man took pride in everything he did. He also took pride in his son. The stack of books, purchased by an illiterate miller, were proof of that.

Turning from the window, she noticed the grandmother's expression had changed from worry to something else. Her thick brows hung so low her eyes were mere slits, and her jaw was firmly clamped. Her gnarled hands wrapped around the arms of the rocker, her posture stiff. Was she all right? Just as Summer prepared to ask, the old woman seemed to relax, easing back into the chair and putting her hands in her lap. Although her focus never wavered from Summer's face, the tense look disappeared. Puzzled, yet afraid to address the woman, Summer turned her attention back to the boy.

Thomas put down the pencil and held up the slate. She crossed to the table and examined the writing. "Well done. That's the last word on your list. Shall we move on to arithmetic?"

He wrinkled his nose. "Can't I take a break?"

She allowed her expression to answer. Although he blew out a breath of aggravation, he reached for his arithmetic book. They spent an hour on long division. Thomas's quick mind absorbed with ease the concept of remainders, and Summer discovered she didn't need to teach him but merely direct him.

When Mr. Ollenburger came in for lunch, she told him, "You were right. Thomas is a very bright boy. He'll be caught up with the studies he missed and perhaps even ahead of his classmates by the time he returns to school."

The man's eyes shone. "Oh, that boy takes after his mother, for sure. A very smart woman she was." He tapped his temple. Turning to the old woman, who had remained in her chair all morning, he said something in German. A wary smile flitted across her face. He turned back to Summer. "I tell her what you say about the boy."

He shrugged his massive shoulders. "It is a good thing two parents a boy has. From me he gets his big size and from his mother he gets his good head. Together he becomes a boy strong in body and mind. A good mix, for sure."

Summer sensed an undertone in his statement. Definitely she saw that he was proud of his son, but there was something else. A sense of inferiority, perhaps. Being illiterate must be difficult. How did he run a business if he hadn't the ability to read? A fleeting idea crossed her mind — should she offer to teach him? While Thomas undoubtedly read things for his father now, what would the man do if Thomas chose to leave Gaeddert when he came of age?

"Mr. Ollenburger, would you like to sit in on Thomas's reading lessons? I could teach you at the same time."

The man's face flooded with color and he reared back, his jaw clamped. He spun away from her, presenting his rigid profile. "The boy needs your teaching. I do not." All warmth was gone from his voice.

Guilt washed over Summer for creating his discomfort. "Very well. That-that's fine." She gathered up the papers and books strewn across the table. "I made sandwiches for lunch. You must be hungry."

He turned back, seeming to deliberately relax his stiff shoulders. "*Ja,* I am hungry. I will not wait to be asked twice."

While Peter sat at the table and consumed a pile of roast pork sandwiches, he observed the interactions between his son and *Frau* Steadman. Never did the woman smile, but she looked at the boy with attentiveness when he spoke, and the boy hung on her every response.

Grossmutter watched them, too. Occasionally she sent a look in his direction, and her brows would rise, as if communicating, *See what is happening here?* He sensed her

101

disapproval. He wished he had visited with her before bringing *Frau* Steadman to the house. Tonight he would take her aside and explain why he had chosen to invite the woman to their home. *Grossmutter*'s love for Thomas went deep. He knew she would accept the woman's presence once she understood how much good the teaching would do their boy.

Thomas and the woman discussed a book called *Ivanhoe.* The only hoe with which Peter was familiar was the one he used to eliminate weeds in his vegetable garden, but Thomas seemed to know of what the woman spoke. The boy contributed his thoughts, speaking of medieval castles and murderous maraudings and Robin Hood.

Medieval? Marauding? Peter's chest tightened with pride and anguish — pride in his son, anguish at his own inability to join in the conversation. When would his foolish head absorb all these words and meanings? Murder he knew, from the Good Book. But so many other ideas were beyond his limited vocabulary.

And the woman knew it. When she had offered to teach him, all shreds of pride had flown out the window. How horrible to be a grown man yet unable to grasp the meanings of words that came easily to others.

"I am finished. Please excuse me." Peter's voice boomed louder than he intended. When the woman startled and looked at him, he felt heat building in his neck. He cleared his throat and forced a softer tone. "I will spend most of the afternoon at the mill, readying it for winter. If you need me, ring the bell, Thomas."

"Sure, Pa."

Peter carried his plate to the sink as the two began discussing Sir Walter Scott. Peter's heels dragged as he headed toward the mill, his heart heavy. Peter's lack of education didn't matter to the boy now — Thomas was young and still saw his pa as all-knowing. But how might that change in another year or two? The boy's knowledge daily grew by leaps and bounds, while Peter probably would never know more than he did now.

He kicked at a dried tuft of grass. "I will not hold him back," he vowed aloud. "The boy will have all the education he wants. He will be more than me, for sure." Reaching the mill, he stood for a moment, his gaze following the path of the stilled paddles that caught the wind and turned the gears that powered the grinder. A simple concept, yet so necessary for the people of this area. The mill provided well for his family. All the farmers came to him at harvest time. With only one grinder, it took time to turn their wheat into flour, but the wind-powered mill had not disappointed anyone.

Peter boosted himself onto the platform and entered the mill. The area inside was snug, with just enough room for him to move around and see to operations. It was a one-man mill. Thomas wanted to one day be a miller, too. When that day came, they must either build another windmill or make a bigger mill and power it with something besides wind or water. Maybe they would use one of those steam engines that chugged locomotives across the land and pushed boats upstream.

From its spot in the corner, Peter retrieved a half-filled can of sheep tallow and a brush made of strips of cloth tied to a sturdy stick. He dipped the brush in the tallow and painstakingly coated each gear as his thoughts continued.

If Thomas gets an education, then he will know about such things as steam engines. What a team we will be, the boy and me. Peter knew allowing Thomas to become educated would be considered radical by many in town. Education beyond elementary school was not encouraged. The Mennonites stayed together, planted their fields, purchased their goods from one another, and tried to live in peaceful harmony. If their children were sent away for education, they might encounter evil influences or be coaxed into a different type of life.

Peter wondered about these threats as he pasted gears with tallow. The Bible said to train up a child in the way he should go and when he is old he will not depart from it. He and *Grossmutter* were training Thomas right. Should he worry about what the boy might encounter outside of Gaeddert? *But no, this is America, not Germany or Russia. No one will force him to join military. We have freedoms here, including freedom to learn more and more.*

But then his hands stilled, his brow furrowing with worry. If the boy got an education, would he still want to follow in his father's footsteps and become a miller? Peter's father and grandfather had been millers — three generations of Ollenburger millers in three different countries. *Grossvater* in Germany, *Vater* in Russia, and now Peter in America. Nothing else had Peter ever known. But the boy . . . In this land of many opportunities, what might await Thomas?

Peter put aside the can and brush and covered the can with a piece of oilcloth. Then he wrapped burlap sacks around the gears, his heart heavy. Giving his boy the education he deserved might lead him away from Kansas and this mill. Even so, though, Peter would not hold Thomas back.

He should ask the woman about institutions of learning. A learned woman such as herself would know which places were best. She would also know what kind of cost would be involved. The boy was already nearly ten years old. If, as *Frau* Steadman said, he would be ahead of his classmates, he might be ready for this higher education earlier than most. Peter must be prepared.

Whatever was best for Thomas would be done. Elsa would approve, and Peter would have it no other way.

7

When Peter returned to the house in late afternoon, *Grossmutter's* bedroom door was closed. Perhaps she was taking her afternoon nap. Thomas and *Frau* Steadman sat at the table, each with tablet paper in front of them. Thomas held a pencil, while *Frau* Steadman had a pen and inkpot.

He closed the door with a soft click. The woman glanced up, her gaze meeting his for only a moment before returning to her task. Her hand looked slender and graceful as it dipped the nib into the ink, then guided the pen across the surface of the paper. He shifted his attention to Thomas, who rose from the table and crossed the floor to press himself beneath his father's arm for a hug.

Peter savored the hug, holding the boy longer than usual, his hand cupping the back of his son's head. It saddened him to think of the day the boy would be too old to greet his papa with a hug at the end of a day.

"Mrs. Steadman is writing a letter. I gave her some of my tablet and your pen." The boy's eyes seemed to question whether he had done the right thing.

The woman paused for a moment, her back stiff.

"That is fine, son. You know welcome *Frau* Steadman is to use anything she needs while she helps you." To his gratification, her shoulders relaxed and her hand began to move again.

Thomas raised up on tiptoe, quirking a finger for his father to lean down. "Her husband's parents don't know her children are gone, Pa. She didn't have a way to let them know after her wagon was burned. Can you mail her letter for her?"

Peter straightened with a jerk. Why did he not think of such things? He needed to learn the important questions to ask. He gave Thomas a nod before crossing to the table, his hat in his hands, to stand beside the woman.

"*Frau* Steadman, a good host I have not been to you."

Her head came up, her dark eyes settling on him with an expression of puzzlement.

"Too long it has been only the boy, *Grossmutter,* and me. I forget what things are needed by others. Sorry I am that I did not ask you what things you could use." He rubbed his dry lips together as she continued to gaze at him silently. "You-you have paper and pen there. You make list of the things you need, and I will see they are gathered."

The woman finally nodded, the puzzlement fading. "Thank you. I have considered some things that would be helpful. I'll make a list." She raised her small chin in a defiant manner. "I don't expect you to purchase the items, however." She paused for a moment, her rebellion faltering. "But-but it will require your wagon for me to get into town."

The opportunity to visit with the woman about Thomas's education suddenly presented itself. Peter nodded, sweeping his hair with his hand. "*Ja,* a ride into town. I will take you. When will your list be done?"

Her narrow shoulders lifted and fell in a silent gesture of uncertainty. "Tomorrow morning, I suppose."

Peter nodded again, hoping he did not appear too eager. "Tomorrow will be fine. First thing after breakfast, we will go." He turned to hang up his hat and coat and paused when another idea struck. "*Frau* Steadman, would you like to stop at the graves? To put down some flowers for your family?"

Tears flooded the woman's eyes. The fervent gratitude shining there made Peter determined to take her to visit her family's headstones as often as she needed until her heart healed.

Thomas returned to the table. "There's still a whole passel of strawflowers growing behind the outhouse. I can pick some."

Peter sucked in his breath. Would the woman find offense in being offered flowers that grew in such a location? But warmth appeared in her eyes.

"Thank you, Thomas. Perhaps your father will find a jar for water. We'll put them in the jar so they'll still be fresh tomorrow."

Thomas peered up at his father. "May I go now, Pa? Supper's not fixed yet."

"Go, boy. But walk."

Thomas shot his father an impish grin, then walked toward the door as if slogging through cold molasses.

"Sie sind ein schelmischer junge!"

Thomas laughed, his arm protecting his ribs, and headed out the door.

Peter turned to find the woman staring at him in confusion.

"What did you say?"

Sympathy he felt for her then. How often he was confused when unfamiliar English words were spoken. He would not leave the woman wondering. "I tell the boy he has too much energy, and then I call him —" He scratched his head, searching for a word to convey his meaning. "What say you when someone is too playful for good sense?"

The woman's face puckered in thought. "Ornery? Or mischievous?"

"*Ach,* another *m* word." Peter shook his head. "Why are so many hard words starting with *m?*"

A muscle in *Frau* Steadman's cheek twitched, and Peter wondered if she was holding back a grin. "Hard words start with *m?*"

"*Ja.* You said one yesterday — manipulated. Today at lunch there were more." He frowned, trying to remember the correct pronunciations. "Medieval and marauding. I do not know these. Now mis-mismusvis." He struggled to make his tongue form the tricky word.

"Mischievous." Her expression and tone were kind.

"Mis-chie-vous," he repeated. "This means to be . . . ?"

"Ornery or silly. Playful."

Peter considered this. "Playful. *Ja,* that suits my Thomas." He pulled out a chair and sat down. The woman moved her tablet to give him room on the table. Half of the paper was covered with lines of ink, but he couldn't read any of it. Leaning his forearms on the table, he focused on the subject of Thomas. "My boy — he has not been . . . mischievous while with you, has he? I want him to not be silly when he works on studies."

"Oh no, he's very diligent." She must have read the confusion in his eyes, because she added, "He is serious about his studies. He doesn't play."

Peter breathed a sigh of relief. "This is good. *Ja,* this is good."

"He is particularly talented with arithmetic. He's well beyond the fourth grade level. I would say at least two years ahead." She leaned back. "It's good that he'll be in a classroom again before too long. I'm sure his teacher will have more knowledge of the advanced mathematics. My education was not strong in mathematics. I am not able to help Vincent in that subject as much as I

112

would like, either." Her face clouded. She lowered her head. "I must stop doing that."

"Doing what?"

"Speaking of my son as if he were still alive." Her voice was so soft, Peter nearly missed it. "I can't seem to accept that he and the others are gone. When I think of them, I think in the present tense. But I must begin thinking in the past tense."

Peter did not understand the word *tense,* but he understood past and present. "It takes time." It seemed as if he had said that frequently in the past days. "It was many weeks before I got up in the morning without thinking of what Elsa and I would do with the day. I wanted to keep her in the present, I think, so I would not forget her. Now I know how foolish that was. How could I forget someone so special as Elsa?"

"Do you think that's why I do it? Because I'm afraid I might forget them?"

Peter would not pretend to know all of what she felt. He only knew what he had felt. "I do not know, but I do know this: You will never forget them. They will live on in your heart forever. Forever young, forever yours. No matter how far in the past they become, a love for them will live on inside of you each day."

Summer sat in silence, digesting what Mr. Ollenburger had said. Having lost his wife, he could understand her own loss. Yet in her opinion, her own loss was deeper, harder. To have a child die was to lose not only the child but the adult the child would have become. While she never wanted to forget her children, she resented they would always be young. They should be able to grow up, to fulfill hopes and dreams. While Mr. Ollenburger would see that happen with Thomas, Summer would never be allowed that privilege with her children.

It was her own fault. She had uprooted her children from their safe, familiar home.

Swallowing, she took up the pen. "I must finish this letter, and then I will make my list. I appreciate your willingness to take me to town tomorrow."

The man rose. "*Bitte schoen* — you are welcome. Now supper I must think about. When the boy comes back, he will want to fill his belly. Always his mind is on food at this age."

Summer completed her letter and began her list while Mr. Ollenburger fried sausage, potatoes, and eggs for a simple supper.

Thomas came in, his arms laden with pale purple flowers that resembled bachelor's buttons. His beaming face above the thick bouquet brought tears to Summer's eyes. How often had Rose come in from play with her sticky hands holding frazzled clumps of flowers and her sweaty face wreathed in a smile? Oh, how she missed her children!

She swallowed her sadness. "Thank you so much, Thomas. Why, you must have picked every remaining flower."

"I didn't leave very many, but these straw-flowers come back every year. There'll be more in the spring. I'll pick you more then."

His guileless words pierced Summer's heart. She wouldn't be here in the spring. Thomas would be back in school, and she would no longer be needed.

Mr. Ollenburger produced an empty canning jar from beneath the dry sink and splashed a dipperful of water into it. Thomas placed the flowers in it, and Summer put the jar in the middle of the table. Blooms spilled over on all sides into a haphazard display of color.

As they stood admiring the bouquet, the middle bedroom door opened and the grandmother emerged, leaning heavily on her cane. She spotted the flowers and a smile broke across her face. She hobbled to the table to cup a drooping bloom with her bent fingers, turning her smile on Thomas.

"Die blumen sind für mich?"

It was the first time the old woman had spoken in Summer's presence. She looked at Thomas, who appeared shame-faced. He turned to Summer.

"Grandmother wonders if the flowers are for her."

The boy seemed so concerned about hurting his grandmother's feelings that Summer longed to smooth his cheek. She clutched her hands to her skirt. "Tell her they are for her. You can pick the remaining ones for me tomorrow morning for the graves."

The boy turned to his grandmother and nodded, his hair flopping with the motion. *"Ja, blumen für sie."*

The old woman clucked, stroking the blooms with her crippled hand, her eyes sparkling. Summer did not regret the decision. She turned to see Mr. Ollenburger watching her with approval shining in his eyes. He shifted his gaze to his son.

"Thomas, your hands must be washed. Then the table must be set so we can eat."

The boy rubbed his stomach as he moved toward the washbasin on the dry sink. "Oh good! I'm hungry!"

Mr. Ollenburger sent Summer a smile that

said, "I told you so." And Summer came very close to answering it with a smile of her own.

The next morning Mr. Ollenburger hitched up the oxen right after breakfast, as he had promised. Summer had donned her blue dress for the trip into town. It was the less dusty of her two remaining gowns. Her list included fabric — black muslin for two dresses. Her heart mourned; her attire may as well reflect it.

Mr. Ollenburger helped Summer into the wagon, his large hands retreating from her waist the moment her feet were secure. When she was seated, he handed her the jar of flowers Thomas had picked just minutes before. She cradled the jar with both hands, inhaling deeply of the wonderfully sweet scent that emanated from the blooms.

When he was aboard, he picked up a lap robe and draped it over her knees, his work-roughened hands careful to avoid contact with her skirts. He appeared coarse with his thick beard, shaggy hair, and simple work clothes, yet his behavior was always that of a gentleman. Summer appreciated his solicitousness.

In her reticule she carried the folded letter for Rodney's parents. As the wagon rolled down the dusty road toward Gaeddert, she wondered if Horace and Nadine would respond. In all likelihood, they would not. Furious with their only child's decision to leave, they had demanded Rodney at least leave Vincent with them so the boy could have a decent upbringing. How her heart had melted with relief when Rodney had declared they would all go. Now, however, guilt pricked her conscience. Had they left Vincent behind, he would still be alive. Horace and Nadine had lost their whole family, too, the day Rodney and Summer left Boston.

"*Frau* Steadman?"

She gave a little jump. Mr. Ollenburger pointed, and she twisted her head. The familiar stand of cottonwoods waited, the row of graves nearby. He leaped over the side of the wagon, took the flowers, and helped her down.

She took the jar and moved toward the graves, her skirts stirring dust. The ash pile was much smaller than the last time she had been here. The endlessly blowing wind had scattered the remnants of her belongings across the landscape. Her heart clutched with the thought. So much of her was here now, on this prairie called Kansas.

She stood for a moment, deciding at

which grave to place the flowers. Her gaze roved from Rodney's down to little Tillie's. Rodney's mound had lost its new appearance with the passing of weeks, but Tillie's grassless mound, so much smaller, seemed as new as the day she had been covered. Tears stung Summer's eyes as she looked at that tiny hill and imagined the sweet child lying beneath the hard sod.

The wind stirred the flowers; their scent filled Summer's nostrils. She buried her nose in their depths, inhaling, savoring, remembering. Deliberately she conjured a picture of each child: Vincent with a book in his hands, his eyes alight with pleasure; Rose pushing a needle through her embroidery hoop, her little brow furrowed and tongue touching her upper lip; Tod chasing fireflies, his endearing giggle filling the air; and Tillie asleep in her bed with her curling lashes throwing a shadow across her rosy cheeks. Always young, always hers, Mr. Ollenburger had said. She willed the memories to never fade.

After a long while she placed the jar between the graves of Rose and Tod, centered amongst her children. Of all the children, Rose would appreciate them most. The little girl had openly admired the wildflowers as their wagon lumbered across the land.

Summer tamped the ground around the jar to insure it wouldn't tip, then she turned back to the wagon. Mr. Ollenburger stood beside it, waiting. The sun touched his face, making his eyes appear even deeper in hue, and within their depths Summer recognized the sympathy that pooled there whenever he looked at her.

She allowed him to assist her back into the wagon, and he encouraged the oxen with a firm command. When they were well down the lane, she finally spoke. "Thank you for allowing me to visit the graves."

He cleared his throat, sending her a brief sidelong glance. "You are welcome. You tell me when again you want to come. I will bring you."

A gust of wind slapped her face, reminding Summer of the coming winter. Visits to the graves wouldn't be possible much longer. She had better visit often while she could. Observing Mr. Ollenburger's slouched position on the bouncing seat, she recalled he had no grave to visit when he missed his wife. That must be even more difficult. At least she had a place to go, to mourn and remember.

How did he manage to be so at peace with

the loss of his wife? He gave credit to God, which Summer didn't understand. Surely Mr. Ollenburger had prayed for his wife, yet she had died. How could a God who ignored pleas for help give comfort? She sighed. The faith she thought she'd possessed in Boston certainly paled when compared with that of Mr. Ollenburger.

"I would like to speak to you about Thomas."

She jumped and clutched her heart.

His thick brows came down. "I am sorry if I frighten you."

"It-it isn't you." She pressed her hands into her lap to steady their trembling. "So often I am lost in thought, not anticipating anyone talking. Then, when you speak with your deep voice . . . it startles me. Please don't apologize."

"You are thinking of your family." The words were a statement, not a question.

"Yes."

"You will think of them often. I will try to give warning when I am about to blurt out loudness."

"Blurt out loudly. Loudness is a noun; loudly is an adverb that describes how you blurt." She slapped a hand to her mouth. What was she thinking? He'd made it clear she was his son's teacher — not his!

He scowled but repeated, "Blurt out loudly." He cleared his throat, his fingers twisting the whip. "Now . . . about Thomas."

But the wagon turned the last curve that led to town. He released a sigh. "We will talk when home we drive. What things do you need?"

Summer consulted her list. "I need paper, envelopes, postage stamps, a pen and ink, material for dresses . . ." Next on the list was underclothes. Heat filled her cheeks.

Mr. Ollenburger didn't seem to notice her discomfort. "I will take you to Nickels' store. It has all things you said except the stamps."

"Thank you." Summer slipped the list back into her reticule.

He stopped the oxen in front of Nickels' Dry Goods, where the little camel coat still hung in the window. It served as a reminder of Summer's loss, and she froze momentarily, her fingers curled around the wooden seat. When she saw Mr. Ollenburger reaching to help her down, she made herself place her hands in his. He guided her onto the boardwalk and opened the door for her.

When she stepped inside, he paused in the doorway. "How long will you need?"

"Half an hour at most."

He nodded. "I will leave the wagon here

and will be back." He closed the door. Summer watched his tall frame move past the windows. She suddenly felt very alone.

8

Two women — one older, one fairly young — in plain dresses and bonnets stood near the fabrics, their curious faces aimed in Summer's direction. When she moved toward the bolts of cloth, both women skittered to the counter. They whispered in German to the man behind the counter. Summer raised her chin and ignored them even as her heart pounded and hands shook. Their low-voiced conversation continued as she selected a bolt of good quality black muslin, thread, and a packet of needles.

She walked to the counter, her feet echoing hollowly on the planked floor, and placed the items at the end of the tall wooden countertop. The conversation immediately ceased. "I need eight yards of the muslin," she told the clerk. She turned her back without waiting for an answer.

Her chest felt tight. Although she could

understand nothing of what was being said, she knew the women discussed her. And she didn't like it. How she wished Mr. Ollenburger had remained with her. Would these women behave so rudely if she were in the presence of that "bear of a man," a man the doctor said held the respect of the town?

She found paper, a pen, and an inkpot, but the selection of clothing was minimal at best. Shoes, stockings, and some children's items, but nothing of a personal nature for a woman. She had no desire to ask the location of such items with those two prune-faced women watching and whispering. Ordering from a catalog seemed her safest choice. Until she could order underclothes, she would have to continue to wash out her things each night as she'd been doing.

She selected a small tin washtub to replace the bucket she had borrowed from Mr. Ollenburger's barn. Picking up two chunky bars of soap from a shelf near the washtubs, she placed them inside the tub along with a new hairbrush and hairpins.

While she shopped, the clerk measured and cut the muslin, the snip of scissors an intrusion in the hushed atmosphere of the store. Her arms laden, Summer crossed to the counter, where the two women continued to stare unabashedly at her.

125

"Frau?" The older of the pair addressed Summer.

Summer looked at her, noticing the clerk's eyebrows quirk as his hands stilled in their task of folding the length of muslin. "Yes?"

The woman moved forward one step, her palm pressed to the counter as if to gather courage. "On miller Peter Ollenburger's place you are staying?"

Summer raised her chin a notch. Although she didn't see that this was their business, her silence would only create more questions. "I am providing tutoring for his son. Surely you're aware of his injury which keeps him from school?"

The two women exchanged glances, and the younger one gave a knowing nod. The older turned back to Summer. She pointed across the street. "You could not stay there, in the hotel?"

Summer took a deep breath. It seemed the doctor's indication that Mr. Ollenburger's reputation in town would protect her was incorrect. A cold sweat broke out across her back and shoulders as she faced the accusatory looks on these women's faces. "I could, but it would require Mr. Ollenburger to transport me each day. This would be inconvenient for him. Consequently, I have been given the privilege of residing in the

126

shariah on his property."

Summer used her best Boston voice and poise — learned from observing her sister-in-law, who could cause the haughtiest of women to cower — although inwardly she trembled from rage and humiliation. How dare these women question her morals?

The older woman's eyes narrowed. "If unable you are to pay a hotel bill, there is an orphans' home near Hillsboro, on other side of the Cottonwood River."

The younger woman stepped forward. "Allowed to stay at the orphans' home are also destitute adults."

Oh, how rude! Summer clenched her jaw as angry words fought for release. Destitute? These women saw her as destitute? Widowed? Yes. Homeless? Yes, that, too. But not destitute. She would make her own purchases here today. "I assure you there is no need for you to be concerned about my financial state." She raised her reticule. "I have funds to provide for myself. I have *chosen* to reside in the Ollenburgers' *shariah*. I have *chosen* to assist young Thomas in his studies. And *I* will choose at what time to change this arrangement."

The power Summer felt at that moment astounded her. Although a part of her wished to hide behind the apple barrel, her anger held her erect, giving her the courage to meet these adversaries without cringing. How she wished she had found this burst of angry courage when faced with the interference of Rodney's parents. Perhaps she would not have been forced to flee Boston and their critical disapproval.

The clerk crept behind the counter. "Please total my purchases," Summer told him. "I do have other stops to make, and Mr. Ollenburger will be calling for me soon. I don't wish to inconvenience him by making him wait for me."

The two women stood with gaping mouths, but Summer was sure she saw the clerk's lips twitch. He kept his eyes averted as he figured her bill on a pad of paper. She paid for her purchases, then turned toward the door. "Which direction to the post office? I must post a letter to my parents-in-law, informing them of my decision to remain in Gaeddert."

The clerk pointed mutely to the east. Summer swept from the store, her chin held high. Once outside, she wilted against the building. Then, hearing the door open behind her, she straightened and sent a glowering look over her shoulder at the two women. They sent looks back that were equally scathing before scuttling down the boardwalk in the opposite direction of Summer, their heads together and tongues wagging.

Summer sighed. The women's ill reception made it clear she was unwelcome in this town. But her love for her children outweighed the unease those two women had caused. As long as Mr. Ollenburger was willing to allow her to stay on his property, she would remain. She started toward the post office.

Peter opened the door to the barbershop and had to halt as *Frau* Schmidt and her daughter Malinda stormed past. The older woman spotted him and paused in her stride long enough to purse her lips in disapproval before grabbing Malinda's elbow and propelling her on down the boardwalk. The women's shoes clacked in an angry tempo.

What about his appearance had been displeasing to them? Before his haircut and trim, maybe the woman would have had reason to scowl in his direction. He needed to make this trip more often than he did — the mirror had almost frightened him when he had glimpsed his ragged image this morning. But now he looked presentable.

Shrugging, he walked to Nickels'. He called a greeting to Nick as he entered. "*Guten morgen.* Here I am to pick up *Frau* Steadman. She is ready?"

"Her things are ready," Nick responded in German as he pointed to a variety of items on the end of the counter. "She asked the direction to the post office."

"I will wait for her here, then."

Nick sucked in his lips. "So what *Frau* Schmidt said is true? The woman is living at your place?"

Peter pulled his brows downward. The tone used by Nick made his heart pound in uneasiness. "*Ja,* the woman is staying in my *shariah.* My boy is getting lessons from her while he mends."

"Did I hear she is a widow woman?" Nick asked as he swept a rag across the counter-top. He did not meet Peter's gaze.

Peter felt his neck hair prickle. "She is a woman with principles, and you know I am a godly man."

"I would not question that, Peter," he said, his shoulders rising in a shrug. "But others . . ."

"The hens are clucking?"

Nick's simple nod confirmed Peter's words.

Peter felt his chest tighten. That explained the cool reception he had received on the boardwalk a few minutes ago. "Was the woman badly treated by *Frau* Schmidt?"

Red appeared across Nick's cheeks. His dusting continued with nervous energy. "They suggested she go to live in the hotel or the orphans' home in Hillsboro."

The pressure in Peter's chest increased.

"Now, you cannot take *Frau* Schmidt too much to heart." Nick threw the rag beneath the counter. "You know she is a busybody."

"*Ja,* a noisy busybody. If she is saying this here, she is saying it elsewhere, too. And you know others will listen."

"Will you take the woman back to the hotel?" Nick's eyes were wide.

Peter would not allow one or two busy-bodies to dictate his actions. This town knew Peter was an honorable man, and they would need to trust him. "I promised the woman a home on my property for as long as she wants it. I will not go back on my word."

Nick nodded but worry appeared in his face. "I hope you will not be brought before council."

Peter rubbed his lips together. He had not thought of that. *Frau* Schmidt's clucking might result in council action. If brought before the council of church on the suspicion of immoral behavior, what would he say? His clumsy tongue would no doubt trip over itself if asked questions. *Mein Gott, I will need your presence if before council I must go.* Yet he had nothing to hide. Both Thomas and *Grossmutter* could verify that nothing untoward took place in his home.

He forced a confidence into his tone that he did not feel. "If brought before council I am, I will tell only the truth. The woman lives in my *shariah* and gives lessons to my boy. That is all. We have done nothing of which to be shamed before man or God."

Nick leaned across the counter, his lips twitching in sudden amusement. "The woman stood up to *Frau* Schmidt. She claimed she had chosen to live in the *shariah* and would continue to do so."

Peter's brows shot up in surprise. Although he knew it would create problems with *Frau* Schmidt, it pleased him that the woman had stood her ground. That showed spunk. She would need spunk to recover from her losses and to face possible censure from the town.

At that moment, the door to the store opened and *Frau* Steadman entered. Her lips were pinched, her face white. She had shown spunk to *Frau* Schmidt, but it had cost her. "*Frau* Steadman, you have finished your errands?" he asked.

She gave a brusque nod.

"You are ready then to return?"

Again, she nodded without speaking. Her stare lit upon the pile of purchases still resting on the counter. She moved to them, touching the washtub with a hand that quivered. She appeared deep in thought, her brow furrowed, her lower lip pulled between her teeth. Peter's heart began to pound. Would she ask Nick to return these items to the shelf and tell Peter to take her back to the hotel?

She turned to face Nick, and Peter saw determination in her dark eyes. "Sir, I would very much like a teapot and a box of tea leaves. Are these things available?"

Nick bustled around the end of the counter. *"Ja, Frau."*

The woman followed Nick to the small selection of china teapots. Her fingers caressed the roses painted on one pot, and Peter felt certain this was the one she would choose. But then she turned over the price tag hanging from the pot's handle. He saw her shoulders slump.

"Perhaps a teakettle would be better than a pot."

Peter heard the regret in her tone. Nick led her to the tin kettles, and she carried one to the counter. From a shelf behind the counter, Nick retrieved a box of tea leaves.

"A half pound of white sugar, too, please."

Nick measured out the sugar into a small paper bag. She paid for the tea, sugar, and kettle without another word. Her purchasing complete, she stepped out the door onto the boardwalk.

Nick placed the new purchases in the washtub and shoved it across the counter in Peter's direction.

Peter paused, his gaze drifting to the shelf that held the china teapots. Beside the pots stood dainty cups and saucers with similar painted patterns. Glancing over his shoulder to ensure the woman did not peek in the window, he crossed to the shelf and selected a cup with the same rose design as that on the teapot she had admired. How ridiculous the cup looked when held in his big callused hands. Yet it would suit the woman.

He handed the cup to Nick. "Wrap this and put it within her bundle."

"A gift, Peter?" Nick's eyes sparkled.

Peter felt his neck grow hot. "A . . . payment . . . for what she endured today with *Frau* Schmidt."

Nick nodded silently, but his face held a speculative expression as he wrapped the cup and saucer in newspaper and placed them in the washtub. Peter put the tub under his arm and joined the woman on the boardwalk. She stood with her shoulders hunched, her chin low. Peter felt sympathy swell again. She did not deserve scorn from *Frau* Schmidt. He touched her arm. "Come, *Frau* Steadman. Home we will get you."

She sent him a look that held both hurt and gratitude. "Yes." Her voice was small. "Thomas and I have much to do today."

It pleased Peter that she would think of the boy instead of herself. That spoke again of spunk and also a lack of selfishness. He felt certain *Frau* Schmidt and her wagging tongue would not defeat this woman despite her fragile appearance. He could not hold back the smile that tugged at his lips as he thumped to the wagon and placed the tub in the back. When he turned, he found her waiting beside the wagon.

She held out her hands, a silent request for his help in climbing into the wagon. As he assisted her, he noticed that Nick stood in the doorway of the dry goods store, watching them.

Well, he can look, Peter thought stubbornly. *He will see nothing to criticize.* He settled the woman, then rounded the wagon to climb into his own spot. As Peter urged the oxen to pull the wagon from town, he glimpsed eyes peering at him from behind windows of houses and businesses. Although his neck felt burned, he held his chin high and his shoulders back. They would not see him slink away in shame.

9

The woman sat so quietly on the seat as they traveled toward his home, Peter wondered if she'd fallen asleep. But when they passed the graves of her family, she suddenly straightened and looked toward the stones.

"Would you like to stop again?" he asked, sensing her desire.

"Can you spare the time?"

Although he had things to do at home, the stark longing in her voice made him decide to take the time. "Whoa." The oxen came to a halt, stamping the ground and nodding their heads at this interruption. He helped her down, then leaned his back against the wagon to wait for her.

But she peered up at him. "Would . . . would it be too much to ask for you to come to the graves, too?"

Visiting the gravesite of a loved one was a

private matter. Why would she want his intrusion?

"I could use a friend right now."

Ah . . . the treatment in town had left her feeling alone. Staring at those graves would heighten the feeling. He nodded that he would join her, took her elbow, and guided her across the dry grass. As they passed the ash pile, her gaze drifted over the sooty mess. She sighed, and he remembered her comment that ashes cannot be put back together again. For a moment he wished it were possible.

She crouched before the jar of flowers. Her skirt and coat became dust-laden as they swished the ground. She reached out and rearranged a few drooping blossoms, her slender hands appearing to weave the stems together, the movements of her fingers as graceful as a dance. Then she rose to stand beside the graves, her hands clasped in front of her, her scarf waving beneath her chin in the breeze.

Such a dismal picture she created as she stood, unmoving, beneath a cloudless sky, the sun glinting off her dark hair. Her shadow slanted across the two smallest graves, his own shadow appearing to bolster hers. That seemed appropriate, and he shifted forward to bring his shadow closer to hers. From the cottonwoods, a turtledove called, its mournful cry a fitting song for this setting.

He looked at her bent head, wondering why she avoided the grave of her husband. The husband was even buried slightly apart from the children, as if she tried to keep him away.

Suddenly she broke the stillness. "Am I doing the right thing, Mr. Ollenburger?"

"I . . . I do not know of what you ask."

She turned to face him. "Remaining in Gaeddert. Is it wrong of me to do so?"

Peter shrugged, his pulse pounding in his ears. "What makes you ask this?"

Her chin quivered and she set her jaw, stopping the trembling. "I don't wish to create problems for you, but . . . In town . . . some women . . ." She shook her head. "If my being here will cause strife, perhaps I should move on."

She stood close enough for him to touch, yet his hands remained in his pockets. "Strife." He pondered the word. "Do you speak of trouble?"

She nodded, her eyes meeting his. "Should I leave?"

"Where would you go?"

Her pained expression told him she did not know the answer.

"Have you prayed about what is best?"

She quickly spun away from him. "I don't pray anymore." The uncertain tone had turned harsh.

"I think maybe again you should."

He could see her dark eyes spark with anger as she whispered, "My prayers go unanswered."

"No prayers go unanswered."

She threw her right hand out toward the graves. "If all prayers are answered, then why am I standing here beside graves instead of beside living, breathing children?"

"The answer was no." He watched her face harden all the more. Before she could speak, he went on. "*Frau* Steadman, the God I love and serve hears all prayers. He answers all prayers. Sometimes it is yes. Sometimes it is wait awhile. Sometimes it is no. He knows best."

"*This* is best for me?" Her voice became shrill and loud. The turtledove's song ceased as she railed at him. "How can watching my children die one by one be what's best for me?"

Peter struggled to find an answer. "I know it is difficult to understand. Maybe . . . maybe it is what was best for them." He, too, pointed to the graves. "They are now

140

walking the streets of heaven. Their bodies are whole and strong. Their hearts are filled with joy."

"While my heart is empty."

From the trees, the dove began its hesitant song once more. Peter stepped forward, and the urge to touch her shoulder in a comforting manner was strong.

"*Frau* Steadman, I would like to speak to you as a friend. Will you listen?"

Though she held her shoulders stiff, she gave a little nod.

He offered a silent prayer for guidance before speaking. "For long weeks after my Elsa died, I questioned God, just as you are doing now. Why? Why did this woman who wanted so much to see America's soil and see her little boy grow up under America's freedoms have to die? Such a good woman she was. She deserved to see her dreams come true. Like you, I prayed very hard for my Elsa to be spared of the sickness. The day she was lowered into the sea was a day I want to forget."

The woman turned to look up at him. "Do you now know why she was allowed to die?"

Peter pressed his lips together as he sought the best way to answer her question. "I cannot know for sure, although I know I will understand all on the day I leave this earth and go to be in heaven with my Maker. All questions will find answers then. For now, though, I think many changes happened for me with Elsa's passing."

He swallowed. "Before Elsa died, I was a poor father. I allowed Elsa to care for Thomas while I only worked. I felt I had much to prove, and by being the hardest worker, I could find favor. But when she was gone, Thomas depended only on me. A bond was forged that is very strong. Being close with Thomas . . ." He smiled. "It is a good thing."

He shifted his feet, finding it harder to divulge these things than he had imagined. "Before Elsa died, I was not a man of strong faith. I go to church with my family, I say the mealtime prayers, but here, inside of me" — he touched his chest — "I do not feel the presence of the Lord. Then . . . Elsa is gone. I cannot rely on her. I had Thomas to look after, and Elsa's grandmother, who also mourned. I must be strong for them. I learned to lean on my heavenly Father for strength and wisdom to face the days. A bond with the Father was forged. This helped me be a better earthly father for Thomas, too. I could not make it through the days without God."

The woman turned her back once more

as she appeared to struggle with what he had said. He knew she was lonely — she needed someone on whom to depend. His heart swelled with the hope she would seek God to fill that longing.

"You ask me if you should move on. I cannot answer that for you, but I can tell you this. While Thomas was home and healing, I prayed for a way for him to get his schooling. He is a bright boy who deserves good education. So I prayed." *Frau* Steadman slowly raised her chin to look at him, her expression wistful. "And then I heard of you staying in the hotel, and I heard you might be a woman of learning. So I think, maybe this is my answer. I will ask this woman to teach my Thomas. And you say you will come. You are an answer to prayer for me." He followed his earlier instincts and reached out to touch her shoulder, his fingers barely grazing her coat. "Though I am sorry for the circumstances that make you able to teach my son, I am thankful you are here."

She stared at him silently for several moments before turning back to face the graves. His hand fell away from her shoulder.

"I want to stay in Gaeddert," she said. "I don't want to leave them."

Relief swept over him. "Then we will pray."

"You can pray. I'll remain with you until Thomas is ready to return to school. Maybe by then I will know what to do next." After one last lingering look at the graves, she turned toward the wagon. "I'm ready to go now."

Peter followed her to the wagon and lifted her up. As he moved to walk around the back of the wagon, he heard another team approaching. He shielded his eyes from the sun and looked down the road. His heart skipped a beat. Coming toward them was the husband of *Frau* Schmidt.

The *thud-thud* of horse hooves and the creak of wagon wheels captured Summer's attention. She twisted backward on the wagon seat to look down the road. A two-seat buggy rolled toward them, pulled by a single horse. She didn't recognize the driver — a man with a gray-streaked beard and dressed in the austere garb of a minister. Mr. Ollenburger remained at the tail of his wagon as the driver approached. A change in his bearing — a sudden straightening of his shoulders, a quick intake of breath — caused the fine hair on the back of her neck to prickle.

Summer squinted against the sun, her heart racing although she didn't understand why. Mr. Ollenburger removed his hat and held it in front of him. She couldn't see his hands, although she suspected he was twisting the plaid wool cap into a pretzel.

The other man brought his buggy to a halt behind the Ollenburger wagon, set the brake, and glared down at Mr. Ollenburger. He said something in German in a deep, accusing voice. Mr. Ollenburger answered, also using the German tongue, but he sounded as gentle as always.

The man on the buggy tugged his flat-brimmed black hat lower on his forehead. The scowl lines around his deep-set eyes became more pronounced as he harangued Mr. Ollenburger in rapid German. He jerked his chin in Summer's direction, and she instinctively shrank against the seat. Mr. Ollenburger flicked a glance toward her, frowned, and then took a step closer to the buggy, giving a low-toned response.

Summer's pulse increased as the men leaned toward each other, the conversation lively, both voices rising as if trying to out-do the other. The words flew back and forth so rapidly she would have had difficulty following even if they spoke in English.

Suddenly the man in the buggy reared back, his chin high, and grated out a stern question.

When Mr. Ollenburger answered *nein,* the man spoke again with angry tones, gesturing with one hand. His horse danced nervously, and Mr. Ollenburger reached out to stroke the animal's nose, bringing it back under control. He then stepped closer to the buggy and spoke earnestly in a soothing tone, his hand curled over the edge of the buggy seat. But the man in the buggy uttered another harsh statement and yanked the reins, forcing the horse to make a sharp turn. Summer gasped as Mr. Ollenburger jumped back to avoid being struck by the buggy.

Mr. Ollenburger remained in the road until the buggy and its driver rounded the curve, disappearing from sight. His shoulders wilted momentarily, then he squared them. Placing the hat on his head, he strode to the wagon and heaved himself onto the seat.

"Well, now we go home. Giddap!"

The bright note in his voice didn't fool her. The tightness of his lips betrayed his inner conflict. "Is everything all right?" Her voice quavered.

A chuckle sounded, but it lacked his usual enthusiasm. *"Ach,* that Schmidt. He *hellt fal fonn en kortet jebad onn ne lange wurst."*

Summer stared at him silently.

His expression turned repentant. "I apologize, *Frau* Steadman. I spoke an insult about the man. I say he thinks highly of short prayers and long sausages." He released a huff, his lips twitching into a lopsided grin. "An excitable man he is. So many problems with the hog butchering."

"Hog butchering?"

Mr. Ollenburger gave a firm nod. "*Ja.* It was to be at my home. Now . . ." He shrugged, his cheeks mottling with pink. "Now I am not so sure."

Her heart thudded against her ribs. It was because of her. She hadn't understood a word that was said between the men, but she knew the exchange had been made because of her.

"Mr. Ollenburger —"

"I have been wanting to ask you about schools." He kept his stare straight ahead. "My Thomas should have every opportunity for education. Can you tell me about higher education?"

She blinked twice, looking at his profile, then shook her head. Nothing ruffled this man. She envied his calm acceptance. If he was willing to set aside the angry exchange, she supposed she should be, too. She spent the remainder of their drive answering his questions about high schools and colleges — anticipated expense, types of courses offered, and requirements for entry. When they pulled into the yard, he set the brake then turned a serious expression in her direction. "And all of these school of which you speak . . . they are in the East?"

Summer nodded.

He heaved a sigh, his gaze somewhere past her shoulder. "Far from here." Then he straightened and gave her a bright smile. "My Thomas deserves the best, so if the best is in the East . . . well, then, I think he will get to do some traveling." He swung down from the seat and reached for her. "Come now, *Frau* Steadman. My boy will not be ready for these schools unless he is caught up on his studies. You go now and make him work hard."

Summer stood on the stoop and watched Mr. Ollenburger turn the oxen toward the shack to deliver her purchases. She noticed a slight droop in his shoulders, and sadness descended on her. Although college was years away, the man obviously already mourned the separation from his son.

10

Summer stepped through the front door and came to an abrupt halt. Her heart leaped into her throat.

On the floor, backlit by a shaft of sunlight streaming through the window, a boy kneeled, meticulously arranging a stack of wooden blocks into a tall tower. *Tod?* A rush of joy filled her. But then the boy turned his head, bringing his features into view. No, not Tod. Thomas. Tod was dead. A fresh wave of sorrow washed over her. Never again would she see her son building with blocks or playing with his soldiers.

"Hello, Mrs. Steadman. Did you get all the things on your list?"

"What?" She shook her head, clearing the images of her son. "Oh, my list . . . Yes, I was able to get most items." She forced her sluggish feet to move forward. "I see you're building." Bending down, she picked up a block. It was rough, obviously homemade, nothing like the fine painted set with pictures of animals and alphabet letters her children had owned.

"*Ja,* I like to build." The boy grinned, his hair falling across his eyes. "Maybe someday I'll build a mill even bigger than Pa's windmill."

"That's a fine aspiration." What might Tod have built if he had been given the chance to grow into maturity? Without thinking, she reached out in a tender gesture and brushed the heavy bangs away from the boy's eyebrows. She heard a gasp, and only then did she notice the grandmother erect in her chair, observing the two of them.

Realizing what she had just done, she jerked her hand back and pressed it to her hip, rising clumsily. She sent another quick glance in the old woman's direction, and the sharp scrutiny caused a lump to form in her throat. She turned back to Thomas. "But to learn all the tools of architecture, one must know mathematics. So come. Let's get to your schoolwork, shall we?"

The boy gave a halfhearted nod and scooped the blocks into a crate. He reached to lift the box.

"No, you'll hurt yourself." The maternal

care that filled Summer's breast surprised her. She picked up the box and carried it to his room, and then she retrieved his books from the shelf. When she returned to the kitchen, she found the boy waiting at the table.

Summer battled her emotions as she seated herself across the table. Spending time with Thomas increased her aching desire to spend time with her own children. Her fingers still tingled from the contact with his hair. She would not be able to touch this child without paying an emotional price. Or, apparently, upsetting the grandmother.

Thomas and she spent the next two hours on studies. Thomas fidgeted, but he followed every directive given. It was a relief when the supper hour came and she could move away from the table, away from the boy, away from the memories of working with Vincent. She put Thomas's books back on the shelf and reached for her coat.

"Mrs. Steadman, aren't you going to eat supper? Pa rolled *kjielkje* last night for our supper."

Summer paused at the door. "Your father rolled . . . what?"

"Kjielkje."

"Kee-ilk-yah." She wrinkled her nose. "Is

that some sort of fish?"

"Fish? No, fish is *fesch.* Why would Pa roll fish?" Thomas seemed to think this was a good joke. He chuckled in a way that reminded Summer of his father.

Despite her earlier despondence, his merriment created a lightness in her chest. She found herself teasing, "Well, does one not roll fish in cornmeal before frying?"

The boy shrugged, his face still holding a wide grin. "*Ja,* that does sound good." He rubbed his stomach. "You're making me feel hungry. Would you like to learn a German poem called *Mie Hungat?*"

Summer took a step back toward the center of the room. Thomas's twinkling eyes enticed her to join in his fun. "All right, Thomas. Teach it to me."

The grandmother's eyes sparkled as the boy assumed a pained pose — hands on stomach with back hunched. *"Mie hungat, mie schlungat."* He straightened and rubbed both hands up and down on the bib of his overalls as he announced, *"Mie schlackat de buck."* Throwing his hands outward and raising his eyebrows, he cried, *"Faudikje! Muttekje! Kome sei fluck!"*

Summer hid her smile behind her fingers.

"Very dramatic, Thomas. Now, what did you say?"

With a smirk, Thomas recited, "I'm hungry, I'm hungry, my belly is shaking. Papa, Mama! Come quick!"

Summer shook her head. "Well, I confess, it's much more poetic in German. In English it doesn't even rhyme."

"I guess that's why it's a German poem and not an English one." He went to stand beside the grandmother's chair. "You have to stay and have *kjielkje.*"

The grandmother nodded, as if confirming Thomas's words. *"Kjielke,"* she said in her wavery voice, smiling in apparent satisfaction as she took Thomas's hand.

Summer looked in surprise at the old woman. Had she just spoken to Summer? Yes, it seemed she had. But what had she meant? Only that *kjielkje* was planned for supper or that Summer should join them?

"Pa will be cooking them with potatoes and fried onions. I bet you've never had it before." Thomas's tone held a clear desire for her to stay.

Summer still had no idea what the dish was, so she was fairly certain she hadn't had it. She knew it would please the boy if she agreed. Yet she hesitated. Although she had enjoyed the playful moments with Thomas, she had a strong desire to be alone. And, unlike the poem Thomas had just recited, she was not hungry. Her belly was shaking, but not from hunger. From sadness. She knew food would not make the empty feeling go away. Sitting at the table with Thomas and his father and grandmother right now — remembering how it had felt to sit together with her family — would be too hard.

Her gaze fell to the joined hands — one young and wide and smooth, one old and thin and wrinkled — and the realization that she did not belong here swept over her. "I'm sorry, but I must return to the *shariah*. I still have my purchases to put away."

The boy's face drooped. "May I bring you a plate of food later? And see what you bought?"

"You want to see what I bought?"

"Yes, ma'am. I haven't been to town, except church on Sundays, since I fell out of the tree. Please?"

Summer could not deny this simple request when he looked at her with hopeful blue eyes. "That would be fine. You bring me some . . . kee-ilk-yah." Tipping her head and lowering her brows, she added, "Are you sure this is something edible?"

Another laugh burst from the boy. The grandmother tugged his hand, and he spoke to her in German. The old woman released a chuckle, then said something in response, shaking her head at Summer.

"Grandmother says to tell you Pa's *kjielkje* is much better than his bread."

Was the woman now teasing with her? Summer sent a hesitant smile to the grandmother, and to her surprise the woman's eyes softened. But she still kept her firm grip on Thomas's hand.

Summer was beginning to understand. The old woman had accepted her presence, but Summer must respect that there were boundaries. She looked at Thomas. "Very well, then." She reached for the doorknob again. "I will entertain you later in the *shariah.* You bring a couple of tin cups, and we'll have some tea together, also." Then she paused, looking back. "Thomas, what does *shariah* mean?"

The boy raised his shoulders and answered in a matter-of-fact tone. "*Shariah* is shack."

Shack. She sighed. She should have known.

"Boy, slow down. You will choke eating so fastly."

Thomas paused, spoon full of fried potatoes and noodles hovering midway to his mouth. "*Fastly* isn't a word."

The reprimand reminded Peter of the one given by the woman. His neck grew hot, and he spoke more gruffly than he intended. "Now I get lessons from you? Whether or not it is a word, you know the meaning. Slow down."

Grossmutter raised her gaze from her bowl, sending Peter a look of disapproval.

Thomas frowned for a moment but resumed eating at a slower pace.

Peter gave *Grossmutter* a repentant look, and to his relief she nodded, accepting his silent apology. She went back to eating. He sought to appease his own conscience for snapping at the boy. "What for are you hurrying tonight? Did *Frau* Steadman give you homework to get to?"

Thomas shook his head, swallowing. "No, sir. But she said I could bring her a plate of food and we would have tea together in the *shariah.* I want to go before it's dark."

The heat in Peter's neck increased. Tea together. She must have found the cup, then. Why had she not said anything to him? Could she feel offended that he bought her the cup? Or perhaps she misunderstood the

157

reason for the simple gift?

He considered once more why he had purchased the teacup, examining himself for hidden motives. Was he seeking to win her favor? No, he did not believe so. His concern for the woman increased as they became better acquainted — her deep pain and feelings of loneliness affected him more each time he spoke with her. Although most people would look at his size and assume he was a tough man inside and out, his heart was tender. It pained him to see her distress, and he wanted to ease it, if he could. The gift, while impulsive, might remind her of the pretty things she had no doubt possessed in her previous home. He hoped it might comfort her.

"Pa, I'm done." Thomas held up his empty plate. "May I take a plate to Mrs. Steadman now?"

Peter rose. "Yes. Heap it well with *kjielkje*. I will walk over with you to check her woodbox."

Grossmutter watched closely as Thomas filled a crockery bowl with the fried noodles, potatoes, and onions. When he turned from the pot, she instructed him to cover it with a piece of toweling. Thomas nodded and obeyed. He also took two tin cups from the shelf. "She asked me to bring cups for tea."

If she had asked for cups, she had not yet discovered she had one already. So she wasn't avoiding him at suppertime because of the gift. Peter's stomach unclenched. Turning to *Grossmutter,* he assured her he would return soon. At her nod, he opened the door and followed Thomas out.

At Peter's knock on the *shariah's* door, they heard her call, "Come in."

Peter gestured for Thomas to enter, then he ducked through the tunnel. When he stepped into the room, his heart set up a patter. Seated on the bed, the woman waited, her expression welcoming. She had tugged the blanket chest to the end of the bed and set the lamp and her teacup on it, creating a table. On the other side of the chest stood the small box he had left as a bedside table. This was obviously meant to be Thomas's chair as the two enjoyed tea together. The teakettle whistled softly from its spot on top of the tinners' stove. Peter felt like an intruder, and the feeling was reinforced when she leaped to her feet, her expression changing to surprise.

"Oh! Mr. Ollenburger, I didn't . . . I thought . . ." Her cheeks flooded with color, and she covered them with slim, trembling hands. Then she seemed to gain control of herself as she dropped her hands, straightened her shoulders, and tipped her chin into a proud angle. "Please forgive me. I did not prepare for two guests, but Thomas and I can sit on the bed here, and you may use the crate."

Peter snatched off his hat, shaking his head. "No, *Frau* Steadman. I only came to see that your woodbox was well filled. You and Thomas enjoy your tea as you planned." He strode to the woodbox, peered inside, and gave a nod. "*Ja,* it needs filling. I will be back." He headed for the door.

"Mr. Ollenburger?"

He stopped but did not turn around.

"Do I have you to thank for the teacup I found in my washtub?"

Slowly, he turned to peer at her across the short expanse separating them. Her dark eyes were wide, her cheeks wearing a becoming shade of pink. She cradled the cup in both slender hands. It took effort to force his head into a nod.

"Thank you. It's very lovely. I —" She dropped her gaze for a moment, the golden highlights in her hair shining as the lantern light graced the side of her head. Then she raised her eyes, an expression of self-

160

deprecation on her face. "It was kind of you to think of it and foolish of me to purchase a teakettle and no cups. It's very difficult to drink directly from a kettle."

Although she did not smile, her words seemed teasing, and Peter found himself sending her a quavering grin. "*Ja,* that would be messy, for sure."

"I brought tin cups, like you said," Thomas inserted.

She looked at him, a small smile playing at the corners of her lips. "Thank you for remembering." She turned back to Peter. "So we have three cups, if you'd like a cup of tea." Her cultured voice and her sweetly worded invitation seemed out of place in this dark, dank dwelling. Peter felt out of place, too.

He shook his head, holding up his hands — his big, callused, clumsy hands — and spoke with no small amount of regret. "I would only be a bumbler and create a mess of it. *Nein.* You two have your time. I will get that wood and leave you to talk." Shoving his hands into his pockets, he turned and hurried out of the shack.

Under the dusky sky, he let his head drop back. He inhaled deeply of the evening air, clearing the tumbling thoughts that had assailed him as he'd stood looking at the woman. What odd feelings had kindled within him at the sight of her in the lantern's glow, her graceful hands holding the fragile cup that did not fit in his *shariah* — or in his world.

Peter blew out his breath, creating a cloud that hovered around his beard briefly before disappearing. He spoke aloud as he moved toward the woodpile and began loading his arms. "*Lieber* Lord, I do not understand why the woman makes me feel so at once protecting and inadequate. How can I share your love with her when my tongue wants to turn into knots and refuses to spit out words? *Ach,* such a big stupid man I am. But you made me, and you love me, just as you love the woman. So somehow you find a way for me to make this all work out. Amen."

His arms full, he returned to the *shariah* and used the toe of his boot to knock. Thomas opened the door to him, and Peter dumped the wood into the woodbox with a series of clunks. "Well, I leave you to your tea. Thomas, not too late, *ja?* We have church tomorrow, and a bath you still need."

"Yes, sir." The boy seated himself on the crate and picked up his cup as if he had been to tea parties all his life.

Peter smiled. This woman truly was a godsend. She could teach the boy not only his studies, but how to be a gentleman in a world away from the Ollenburger mill. With her help, he would feel at ease in big cities and social gatherings. And although pain stabbed, a gratefulness filled his heart that Thomas would become more than his father ever hoped to be. He reached out and touched his son's hair. "Enjoy your tea." He turned to leave.

But once more, the woman's voice stopped him. "Mr. Ollenburger, before you go, may I ask a favor?"

"*Ja,* you can ask."

"I purchased fabric for new dresses, but as you can see" — she held out her hands to indicate the setting — "there is no place for me to lay the fabric for cutting. I also do not have scissors. May I borrow a pair of scissors and use your kitchen tomorrow to cut out my dresses?"

"While you are with us, you make yourself at home. You are doing us a favor. We will help you as much as we can."

"Thank you. I'll only use my free time for sewing. I won't take study time. Thomas needs my attention then."

"That will be fine. Well . . ." He fiddled

with a button on his shirt. "I go now." He waved at his son. "I will see you at the house soon, Thomas."

Thomas barely glanced up. "Sure, Pa. I'll be in soon."

The voices of the woman and his boy engaging in easy conversation filled his ears as he walked back through the darkness toward home.

11

Summer stepped out into a crisp fall breeze on Sunday morning. The sky still wore streaks of pink and yellow in the east, with gold-rimmed wisps of clouds hovering on the horizon, but overhead a proud robin's-egg blue promised a pleasant day. The landscape stretched endlessly in all directions, with no buildings in sight other than those belonging to the Ollenburgers.

For a moment she experienced a pang of melancholy — as if she were the only person left in the world. Then she heard a cardinal sing from one of the barren bushes beside the outhouse. The sound lifted her spirits, making her feel less alone. The grass beneath her feet crunched as she walked to the house, and the cold stung her nose as she inhaled. She hurried her steps.

She entered the pleasant warmth of the house. It seemed less welcoming without its occupants, who had rumbled away in the wagon a short time ago for church. For a moment she faltered. Did she want to spend her morning here alone? Then she spotted a square basket on the table.

She peered into it and found scissors, chalk, a tin thimble, a tape measure, a card of needles, two cards of buttons — one of brown, one of black — and several spools of thread. Her heart turned over. Had this been Elsa Ollenburger's or her grandmother's sewing basket? It was obviously laid out for her use. Immediately she hung up her coat, spread out her fabric, and got to work.

Although her sister-in-law had always purchased ready-made garments or visited a seamstress, Summer enjoyed sewing. Most of Rose's and Tillie's dresses had been made by Summer's hands. Rose, too, had displayed a knack for creating things from fabric and floss, and Summer had encouraged her fledgling efforts.

She felt sadness build as she thought of Rose, but she didn't try to push it aside. She wanted to remember everything about her children. As she slid her blue dress on top of the black muslin, using the finished dress as a pattern, she deliberately conjured images of Rose: Rose seated beside the parlor fireplace, stitching on a sampler; Rose on the swing Rodney had hung for the children from the apple tree in the backyard, her head hanging back, her dark braids nearly dragging on the ground; Rose in the flower garden, skipping in pursuit of a butterfly . . .

Before she knew it, she had all the pieces for both dresses cut, stacked, and ready to be stitched into a finished garment. Her stomach growled, reminding her that she hadn't eaten today. She set aside the fabric pieces and crossed to the stove. A pot rested on the rear burner, and she lifted the lid. Her nose twitched with appreciation. Fried potatoes and onions with scrambled eggs, still warm. Fried potatoes seemed to be a mainstay of the Ollenburgers' diet. She added another log to the stove to keep the fire going and dished up a serving of potatoes.

She ate, standing beside the stove, then placed her plate and fork in the wash pan that rested on the dry sink. She noticed three plates, forks, and cups already waiting to be washed. Without a second thought, she dipped hot water from the reservoir on the stove, washed and dried the few dishes, and stacked them back on their shelf.

She turned, and a trio of photographs hanging on the wall opposite the front door captured her attention. She went over to them, tipping her head to examine them one by one. In the largest photograph, which was oval-shaped, were the images of a serious-looking man and woman. She noted a similarity in physical appearance between the man in the picture and Mr. Ollenburger, although Mr. Ollenburger's eyes seemed to reflect more warmth. These must be his parents, she presumed.

The two smaller photographs were obviously of the same person, although the woman looked to be in her early teens in one and her mid-twenties in the other. She had a pretty face, Summer acknowledged, with eyes that seemed to harbor a pleasant secret. The woman's face was full and round, with dimpled cheeks and a sweetly upturned mouth. This must be Elsa. Suddenly Summer felt like an intruder, and she turned away.

She glanced around with a frown creasing her brow. The photographs, she observed, were the only personal items decorating the room. Although she thought the plain appearance should make the room feel cold, the memory of the warm, contented man and boy who lived here with the old woman kept the house from feeling bleak.

Turning to the photographs again, a wave of sorrow crashed against her heart. Just before leaving Boston, she and Rodney had taken the children to a photographer and had a family portrait made. She had carefully packed the gilt-framed picture within the folds of her grandmother's quilt. The fire had surely consumed it.

She touched the oval wood frame around the portrait of Mr. Ollenburger's parents. How she wished she still had the picture of her own family. She could hang it on the wall of the *shariah.* Then she almost laughed — a gilt-framed photograph hanging in that decidedly ungilded shack? The soot-stained bit of parchment from the Bible seemed to fit better. Perhaps she could frame that.

"I have things to do," she reminded herself sternly. She stomped back to the table and picked up the needles and thread she had purchased. She glanced at the grandmother's chair, draped with a heavy knitted blanket. It seemed the most comfortable place to sit, yet she hesitated. She had come to think of that chair as the old woman's throne.

Summer shook her head — she couldn't sit there. Settling into one of the straight-backed chairs instead, she threaded the needle and reached for the pieces that would form the skirt of one of her new dresses. But her hands stilled, her gaze drifting to the window, where sunlight streamed through, painting a golden path across the wood floor.

Despite the yellow sun lighting the panes, the window still appeared barren. What a difference a simple curtain would make. She looked at the blue dress crumpled on the floor beside her feet. The hem was ragged from dragging in the dust of the trail, the elbows shiny from repeated wear. Yet the skirt was still usable, although dusty. She held it up, shook it out, and measured it against the window. Her heart lifted. Yes, it would work.

She could sew simple panels in less than an hour. Mr. Ollenburger had done much for her — she would return the favor by creating window dressings for his house. Surely she could find a hammer, tacks, and some string to hang the curtains before he returned home. Eager to do this small deed, she picked up the scissors and began to snip.

Peter had never been given to anger, but he admitted the tightness in his chest was caused by pure righteous fury. He wished to strike out at something — someone. He didn't, though. *Grossmutter* sat in the wagon on a pile of old quilts, her chin drooping

170

toward her chest as she dozed, and the boy drowsed against Peter's shoulder. So he kept his fingers curled around the whip handle and called soft commands to the oxen, keeping the wagon on the smoothest parts of the road to avoid jarring either of his passengers too much.

Ach, Lord, it is good to have simple tasks on which to focus. It helps keep one's actions in check.

He could not understand people. In his village in Russia as a boy, he had often worried over the actions of some who lived in nearby houses. Why did they look down their noses at, or hold themselves aloof from, the fishmongers who peddled their wares in the early morning? Only because their clothing was different or they lived in another village? Why should this matter? He had assumed that when he was a man, when he had gained more wisdom, he would understand. Now he was a man, and still he questioned.

How he had relished his time in *Kleine Gemeinde.* Sitting in his familiar spot in the little church, Thomas attentive on the bench beside him, his ears filling with the verses of hymns sung when he was a boy in the comforting tongue of his beloved German, and then basking in the goodness of the Word of God read from the Holy Bible in Reverend Enns's strong voice — those had been pleasant moments.

But then the service had ended and his neighbors had approached, their expressions judgmental, their words harsh. Even as he, *Grossmutter,* and the boy had visited neighbors, as was their Sunday custom, partaking of *faspa* and sharing town news, it had seemed all the people were concerned about was this one woman. He had repeated, "She is only tutoring my boy," so many times that he feared he would be reciting it in his sleep tonight.

Why must the presence of one needy woman create such conflict? Peter sighed, his breath stirring his beard. Thomas twitched, his head slipping forward. Peter reached out his arm to keep the boy from falling. Thomas startled awake, his blue eyes blinking in the sunshine.

"Oh, I must have fallen asleep." His voice sounded croaky, as if he had been sleeping a long time, although it had only been a catnap.

Peter chuckled. "*Ja,* you have been sleeping. Not much company you are."

Thomas rubbed his eyes with both fists.

"I don't know why I'm so tired. I didn't even get to play this afternoon at the Penners'. When will I be able to play again?"

"When the doctor says the danger to your ribs is over. You follow what he says — he knows best."

Thomas sighed. "Yes, sir." He shifted in the seat. "Pa? I got mad at Rupert today."

Peter raised his brows at the boy's sheepish expression. "Oh?"

"He said we shouldn't let Mrs. Steadman stay at our place. He said she could cause trouble."

Peter's chest tightened. He wished the boy had been spared this discord. "Well, Rupert just repeats what he hears his parents say. He knows no better."

"But she's been real nice to me," Thomas said, puzzlement in his eyes. "She let me put as much sugar as I wanted in my tea last night, but when I said that to Rupert, he ran off and told everybody she was teaching me to be like a person from Boston."

Peter recognized the same confusion in his son as he had so often felt. He wished he had better answers for him. "*Ja,* she has been nice to you, and you remember that." He called, "Haw," guiding the oxen to the left as he sought words of explanation.

173

"Thomas, you remember last year when the men in fancy suits came to Gaeddert to talk about the railroad?"

"Yes, sir. They sure caused a ruckus." He smiled.

Peter chuckled ruefully. "*Ja,* they did, for sure. Do you know why?"

Thomas tipped his head. "People were scared if the railroad came through Gaeddert, it would bring strangers into town who didn't believe the way we do."

"That is right. Fear of strangers, of new thinking, of changes that might come, kept us from welcoming the railroad. So a station was made in Hillsboro instead. Now when someone from Gaeddert has goods to sell or he needs to order from the catalog, he must travel to Hillsboro to make use of that railroad train. Do you think we did the right thing?"

"I don't know." His brow was crinkled in thought. "It's an extra trouble to go to Hillsboro if you need the train, but maybe it kept trouble from coming to town. Was it the right thing?"

"I do not know the answer to the question, either, boy. I only know it was fear of change that made the town choose not to have the railroad here. And I think fear of change is what makes the town speak out against Mrs. Steadman."

"But she's only one lady! And she hasn't changed anything." He folded his arms across his chest, his lower lip trembling. "They're just being so . . . so . . ."

"So *mittel?*"

Thomas huffed. "Mean doesn't seem like a bad enough word. Rupert acted like Mrs. Steadman was going to make the whole town fall apart!" Worry showed in the pinch of his face. "Do you . . . do you think you shouldn't have asked her to help me?"

Peter clucked to the oxen, then quietly quoted a Bible passage he'd memorized long ago. " *'Und der König wird antworten und zu ihnen sagen . . .'* "

The boy sat in silence for several long minutes, working his jaw back and forth. "I know Jesus said whatever we do to people we meet is the same as doing it to Him. But what if Rupert is right? And as long as she's here, everybody is mad at us."

Peter gave his son's knee a squeeze. "Then we must pray for the people in town, that they will lose their fears. Prayer changes things, *ja?*"

Thomas didn't answer.

Peter's "whoa" brought the oxen to a stop

in front of the house, and he hopped down. He helped *Grossmutter* from the back and guided her to the stoop. Thomas sat scowling on the wagon seat. Peter sighed and returned to the wagon.

"Get down careful — do not jump. Change out of your good clothes. I will be in after the oxen I see to, and we will read together, *ja?*"

Thomas held to the sides of the wagon and lowered himself cautiously to the ground as Peter climbed in on the opposite side. Before the boy entered the house, Peter called, "Son?"

Thomas squinted up at his father.

He paused, finding it painful to share unhappy news with Thomas. "The butchering will be at the Josts', not here this year."

Thomas's face clouded. "But I can't ride the wagon every day, and I wanted the pigs' tails!"

Sorrow pressed Peter's chest at his son's obvious disappointment. "I am sorry, son. I tried to tell them still to come, but they would not listen. They will not come here while the woman lives in the *shariah.*"

Tears trembled on Thomas's lashes. He swallowed, his Adam's apple bobbing.

"Do you want me to send her back to town?"

Before Thomas could answer, the door to the house opened, capturing Peter's attention. The woman stood framed in the doorway as if she belonged there. Although she did not smile, Peter saw eagerness in her eyes.

"I'm glad you're back. I have a surprise for you." She licked her lips, glancing at *Grossmutter,* who stood on the stoop. "Come see the change I've made to your house."

Thomas looked at his father with fear in his eyes.

Thomas rolled to his side. He was tired, but sleep wouldn't come. Too many thoughts cluttered his mind.

That tea Mrs. Steadman had given him had sure been good. Grandmother and Pa didn't let him drink tea. Or coffee. Pa said it would stunt his growth. And Grandmother didn't let him have much sugar. But Mrs. Steadman had let him put three spoonfuls of sugar into his cup, just the way he liked it. He smacked his lips, remembering the sweetness of the warm liquid.

Mrs. Steadman was nice. Sometimes she wouldn't let him end his studies early, but

Pa said that meant she was a good teacher. He was probably right about that. She was a smart lady, for sure. And a good cook, too. Thomas released a long sigh, thinking about the supper she had cooked for them. She called it shepherd's pie, even though it wasn't like any pie he'd had before. Still, he'd liked it.

And her bread was good, too. Fluffy in the middle with a light brown crust, just the way Thomas liked it. Pa couldn't bake bread like that. Mrs. Steadman did lots of things right. But he thought about those curtains she'd made — changing how their windows looked — and his heart beat a little quicker when he thought about other things she might change around their house.

He scrunched up his face, remembering how riled he had gotten at Rupert today. When Rupert had talked mean about Mrs. Steadman, Thomas wanted to punch him good. Only Pa's warnings about not hurting his ribs had made him walk away instead of hitting Rupert. Now, thinking about how the hog butchering would be someplace else, he got mad all over again, and he punched the air.

A pain stabbed his side with the forceful motion, and he grimaced, rolling to his side and cradling his ribs. Tears pricked his eyelids. Mrs. Steadman had been nice to him. He wanted to like her. But she was making trouble, just like Rupert had said. Should he stand up for her or should he ask Pa to send her away? What was the right thing?

Pa seemed to think they should keep Mrs. Steadman here. Pa was usually right. Was he right this time? Thomas thought about it long and hard, shifting around on his bed in restlessness until his ribs ached and his covers were tangled around his legs. With a sigh, he wiggled his feet and managed to straighten out the sheets and quilt again. Then he lay still, staring at the ceiling.

He sure had liked that tea. But was it better than getting the pigs' tails? That was the last question that flitted through his mind before sleep took hold.

12

Summer, Thomas, and *Grossmutter* spent most of the following week alone. Mr. Ollenburger loaded the four hogs, which had been growing fat in their pen for the past six months, in the back of his wagon on Monday morning and headed to the Josts' place. Thomas explained to Summer that the whole community gathered together to butcher all of the hogs, turning the butchering into a week-long celebration. There were contests for which hog produced the most lard, which hog had the biggest ham hocks, and which man could cut the meat away from the bone the fastest with the least waste. Each evening the participants feasted on fresh pork and cracklings, a delicacy Thomas insisted was not to be missed.

The boy had seemed resentful for hours after he told Summer of the week's events, and it had taken some subtle coaxing from her before he finally admitted that he had been looking forward to hosting the hog butchering this year. "Pa said I'm big enough to watch the *meagrope*."

Summer recalled Mr. Ollenburger's comment about *m* words as she asked, "What is a *meagrope?*" Her *r* did not roll the way Thomas's did as she pronounced the word.

"It's a big boiling pot where you render the lard. You have to keep the fire hot, but not too hot, and keep stirring the fat. You have to make sure the cracklings don't swim, because that means the fire is too hot. It's an important job, watching the *meagrope*." His bright eyes snapped with an anger Summer didn't understand. "And whoever hosts the hog butchering gets the tails."

"The tails?"

"It's fun to sneak up and pin a tail on someone when he isn't looking." He scowled. "But now I have to wait until our turn comes around again."

Summer had questioned why the hog butchering had been moved, but the boy remained stubbornly silent. His refusal to answer gave her all the information she needed. The butchering had been moved so the townspeople would not be reminded of her presence. While she regretted that Thomas must suffer disappointment due to the town's ignorance, she had no desire to move on from this place. As long as her children were here, this is where she would remain.

She suspected her presence was creating more than just disappointment for Mr. Ollenburger. He hardly spoke when he returned each evening. Since he'd already eaten with the others who were butchering, he would greet his son and then retire to his bedroom. He gave the excuse of being tired from the work of butchering in addition to his regular chores, many of which Thomas still was unable to perform, but Summer suspected there was another reason he hid away.

Twice she had caught the big man fingering the hem of the curtains she had made from her blue dress, an unreadable expression on his face. Although he had thanked her for the kind gesture of dressing his windows, she wasn't convinced the change pleased him. She had approached him to ask if he would prefer she remove them, but before she could speak, he had begun asking questions about the boy and his studies, and her question had gone unasked.

As if worry about Mr. Ollenburger's

withdrawn behavior wasn't enough, she and Thomas entered a troubling time of hills and valleys. Although he had sometimes pouted, he had always followed her directions. Now he occasionally defied her, doing sloppy work or peering at her through narrowed eyes that made her feel like an intruder. She remembered Mr. Ollenburger telling her to let him know if the boy gave her trouble, but the man's distant behavior made her hesitant to approach him. Besides, there were also times when the boy was very cooperative, almost apologetic. Vincent had never behaved so erratically, and Summer simply did not understand Thomas's mercurial mood changes.

So the week dragged on with Summer attempting to follow their routine of study and conversation in hopes of turning Thomas around. She shared a bit of her past with him, avoiding speaking of her children but telling him about Boston. Thomas did express interest in the big city and how it differed from the small Kansas community in which he lived.

At the end of each day, Thomas read aloud from a novel called *Tattered Tom*. He seemed to find the idea of a girl named Tom amusing, and he openly admired the girl's spunk in caring for herself on the streets of

New York. Summer listened with an ache in her heart so intense she feared it would crush her. Thomas's animated reading of the story reminded her so much of Vincent. If she closed her eyes, she could almost hear her son's voice reading aloud.

While Thomas read, Summer finished her dresses and busied herself with baking bread and canning the last of the tomatoes from the Ollenburgers' garden. The grandmother did her part, as best as her crippled hands and slow-moving hips would allow. Although Summer still fought moments of uneasiness around the older woman, she felt she was slowly gaining favor. At least the woman's sharp eyes seemed to have lost their initial distrust, and a smile occasionally crinkled her face.

On Friday afternoon of the long week, Thomas closed *Tattered Tom* and sighed. "Pa will be finished with the butchering today. He'll bring home hams and sausages and bacon from the smokehouse. I put potatoes in the oven, so we'll have jacket potatoes for supper, and Pa will probably fry sausage." The boy rubbed his stomach. "Mmm, I can almost taste it already."

Summer set aside the history book she had been reviewing for next week's lessons.

"Don't forget the bread I baked. That will go well with your potatoes and sausage."

"Enne noot schmakt dee worscht uck one broot." Mischief sparkled in Thomas's eyes. *Grossmutter* chuckled from her chair.

Summer raised her brows and peered down her nose at the boy, pleased to see him in a playful rather than brooding mood. "Now, Thomas, you know I don't speak a word of German. What did you say?"

"I said sausage tastes good even without bread."

"Does that mean you don't want my fresh-baked bread with your potatoes and sausage?"

"Sure I do." He rose to his feet. "And we can make supper a real feast for Pa after his week away."

Thomas's enthusiasm encouraged Summer. Perhaps his misbehavior had been because he missed his father. "What did you have in mind?"

"Well, we've got the potatoes, you baked bread, Pa's bringing the sausage. For a treat, Pa loves sliced onions with vinegar, but he hasn't eaten any since you came. He didn't want to offend you with the smell of it."

The boy was probably right — the odor of onions and vinegar would no doubt singe her nostrils. Suddenly, though, it seemed

185

important that Mr. Ollenburger be given a hearty welcome. Perhaps it would improve his somber disposition.

She stood, cradling the history book against her chest. "If your father would consider onions and vinegar a feast, then he shall have it. I'll put your books away, and we can get started slicing."

She and Thomas were both raining tears, brought on by the strong fumes from the onions, when the door opened. Thomas dropped his knife and hop-skipped to the door with his arm tucked against his ribs. "Pa, you're early!"

Mr. Ollenburger gently pulled the boy against him in a hug, then cupped the boy's cheeks and looked at him, concern creasing his brow. "What for are you crying?" His gaze raised to meet Summer's, the furrow between his eyes deepening. "What has happened?" He looked to the chair, where the grandmother held up her gnarled hands and shook her head, apparently attempting to offer assurance.

"Nothing's wrong, Pa. It's onions."

Mr. Ollenburger seemed to wilt with relief. Summer felt a wave of sympathy for the real fear he had experienced. She swept away the tears with the backs of her wrists and held up a thick slice of onion. "Yes . . .

see? You grow powerful onions in your garden, Mr. Ollenburger."

"*Ach,* the greater the tears, the better the flavor, so you know these are good." The comment sounded more like the old Mr. Ollenburger, and Summer felt gratified to see the change. Shrugging out of his coat, he crossed the floor, took the slice from her hand, then ate it in one bite. He waggled his brows. "Only thing better than fresh onion is fresh onion in vinegar."

She held up the vinegar jar. "I have it here, ready to go." At his look of surprise, she added, "Thomas said you especially enjoy eating onions and vinegar."

"*Ja,* I do." He laced his fingers and pressed them to his stomach. "But I warn you, it will smell like a whole roomful of stout Germans when I am through."

Laughter bubbled upward, spilling out and filling the room. With a start, Summer realized the sound had come from her. She covered her mouth, a feeble attempt to gain control, but it was impossible. The size of the man belied the playfulness under the surface. He looked like a hairy oversized boy at the moment. Summer couldn't hold back her amusement.

"You laugh at me, *Frau* Steadman?" Mr.

Ollenburger touched his chest, his face twisting into an offended pout, yet his eyes sparkled merrily.

The laughter felt wonderful — cleansing. As it continued, though, she suddenly realized it was her first laughter since Rodney fell ill. Laughter poured forth, but her children weren't here to witness it, enjoy it, or join in.

Without warning, the sounds of mirth turned to choking sobs. Dropping the knife, she spun from the dry sink, from the onions, from the man who stood in shocked silence, and ran out the door without her coat. Halfway to the *shariah,* pounding steps caught up to her, and a large hand grasped her arm, bringing her to a halt.

"*Frau* Steadman, you must stop." Mr. Ollenburger's voice thundered through the evening calm. "What for do you run away like this?"

She pulled free of his grasp, hugging herself as the evening air chilled her limbs. "I-I had to get away. I had to leave the laughter."

The man's bushy brows lowered. "But laughter, it is good for the soul. It did my heart good to hear a laugh find its way from

188

your belly. Why must you leave the laughing?"

"How can I laugh when my children are dead?" Summer nearly choked on the words. Her body shook so badly her teeth rattled. "I shouldn't laugh. I shouldn't ever feel happiness again!"

"That is nonsense." Mr. Ollenburger took her shoulders and turned her toward the house, protecting her from the wind with a heavy arm across her back. "Why should you try to never have laughter again? Did you die? No, you are alive. So be alive! Laugh if you want to, cry if you must, let yourself *feel*."

They reached the stoop, and he guided her through the door and into a chair. She buried her face in her arms, trying to shut out the words that continued to fall in Mr. Ollenburger's deep authoritative voice.

"Our good Lord in heaven made us to feel. He gives us time to weep and time to laugh. But He does not want us to remain in weeping. In his book, in Psalms, He makes a promise. You stay here. I show you."

Her face still hidden, she listened to his footsteps thump away then return. The chair screeched against the floor, and a large hand touched her arm.

"Sit up here, *Frau* Steadman. You see these

words yourself."

Slowly she raised her head, focusing on the open Bible on the table in front of her. To her surprise, *Grossmutter* had left her chair and stood on the opposite side of the table, leaning forward to peer at the Bible, too.

Mr. Ollenburger pointed with his thick finger. "See here? You read it."

Summer frowned at the words. "I can't read this. It's German."

He grimaced, then turned the book to face him. "This is the book of Psalms, chapter 126, verse five. *'Die mit tränen säen, werden mit Jubel ernten.'* "

"Ja, ja." The grandmother tapped the page with a wizened finger.

Peter held his hand out to Thomas. "Son, come tell *Frau* Steadman what I read."

"You know the words." Thomas stood several feet away, as if afraid to approach.

"Ja, I know the words." A hint of impatience colored Mr. Ollenburger's tone. "But *Frau* Steadman wants them from you."

Summer realized he was asking the boy to translate so she wouldn't question his honesty with her. She also realized how foolish she had been, assuming Mr. Ollenburger was illiterate. Though the man couldn't read

English, he was obviously able to read German. How her assumption must have shamed him.

Thomas stepped forward and leaned against his father. His eyes on the Bible, he translated, "They that sow in tears shall reap in joy."

"Ja." The grandmother looked at Summer. Tears winked in the old woman's eyes, bringing a fresh rush to Summer's eyes.

"God keeps promises, *Frau* Steadman," Mr. Ollenburger said. "You must to believe the joy will come. But you must look for it."

"Look for it?" Summer let the question burst out. "And where do you suggest I look? Should I dig up the graves of my children?"

Mr. Ollenburger raised his head and thrust out his chin. "I find it in the teaching of this book." He placed his hand on the Bible, giving the worn pages a gentle caress. "And you will find it there, too."

The old woman also flattened her wrinkled hand on the pages of the Bible, her gaze boring into Summer's as if attempting to deliver a message. But Summer didn't understand it any more than she did the German lettering in Mr. Ollenburger's Bible.

Summer shook her head. She would never find joy there. She couldn't even read the words. The hopelessness of the situation struck her anew, and she lowered her head. "It's useless."

"You *will* find it," he insisted, misinterpreting her meaning, "if your heart is open. So a way must be made for your heart to be open. I must change part of our bargain."

Summer lowered her brows. "Are you planning to manipulate me again, Mr. Ollenburger?"

"No manipulate. Only say this — if you teach my son, you must go to church with us. Church, like laughter, is good for the soul."

13

Summer sat on a wooden bench — a hard, backless, uncomfortable bench — and waited for the service to begin. People filed in, filling the other benches. Mr. Ollenburger and Thomas didn't sit with her. Mr. Ollenburger had forewarned her that the men and women divided to sit on opposite sides of the church, so she wasn't surprised when the two Ollenburger men seated themselves across the aisle from her.

Although the grandmother sat beside her in her slumped-forward pose, the other women chose benches in front of or behind her. She found this arrangement acceptable. She had no desire to speak to people who had openly avoided her elsewhere in town. She recognized the two women from the store, but neither so much as looked in her direction.

Mr. Ollenburger had referred to the church as *Kleine Gemeinde* and then told her it meant "little church." His heritage believed a small congregation would become like family, so small congregations were encouraged. If a population outgrew the *Kleine Gemeinde,* the congregation would split and form a second church body.

Summer thought this sounded good in theory. She so needed a family. In reality, though, she knew it would never work for her in this place. How would these people become family when they were unwilling to reach out to her in friendship? They had ignored her needs while her children were ill. They had ignored her needs following her family's deaths. With the exception of Mr. Ollenburger, the community had made little effort to treat her with kindness. Family? Not with these people.

Then there was the church itself. Why, how could one even call this simple wood-slatted building a place of worship? The only thing that set it apart from the other buildings on the block was its small steeple — one that did not contain a bell but simply acted as a perch for the crude wooden cross pointing toward the heavens.

She compared the *Kleine Gemeinde*'s sanctuary to that of the towering two-story brick-and-mortar church she and Rodney had attended in Boston with his parents. Where were the stained-glass windows and carved woodwork? No highly-polished cherry lectern stood on a dais at the front of the sanctuary; only a plain, boxlike podium rested on the wide-planked floor. She scanned the bare walls, mindful of the absence of statues or paintings depicting the life of Christ. Summer could find no beauty on which to feast her hungry eyes. How could a sanctuary so devoid of beauty be good for the soul?

A minister wearing a simple black suit stepped behind the podium and raised his hands. A hush immediately fell, all eyes shifting to the front. He gestured, uttering a string of unintelligible words, and the congregation rose as a whole. Summer jumped to her feet, confusion making her heart pound.

Mouths opened in song, the tune unfamiliar to Summer and sung in a language she couldn't understand or speak. No piano or organ underscored the four-part harmony created by the congregants, yet she found the synchronization of voices pleasant to her ears. Her heartbeat slowed to a comfortable rhythm, the starkness of her surroundings melting away as she became lost in the beauty of the songs.

They sang three hymns with such majestic delivery that Summer fought tears. She recognized the melody of the third hymn as soon as they began singing. In her heart, she transposed the words to English — "Fairest Lord Jesus . . . Thee will I cherish, thee will I honor" — and despite an effort to stay silent, she hummed the soprano line along with those who knew the German pronunciations.

The minister gave a nod of permission for the congregation to sit, and the people settled in for the sermon. It turned out to be a lengthy one, none of which Summer could understand. What had Mr. Ollenburger been thinking to assume she could find meaning listening to gibberish? Although the music had been soul-stirring, now she simply felt lost.

Summer glanced at Mr. Ollenburger and Thomas often throughout the sermon. The big man's focus never wavered from the suited man in the front, although Thomas nodded off once or twice. Summer fought the impulse to close her eyes.

Her gaze drifted across the congregation. For the most part, the people seemed relaxed, interested, open to whatever was being shared from the pulpit. Frequently, the people referred to leather-bound books in their laps, nodding in agreement or smiling at the minister. Twice *Grossmutter* placed her gnarled hand on Summer's knee and patted, as if trying to encourage her to listen. Frustration welled — the woman knew Summer didn't understand the language!

Despite her discomfort, Summer had to acknowledge the people behaved much differently in this church than in her church at home. Even with the beautiful setting, she had never seen such intense concentration from the Boston parishioners. She wondered if it was the smaller number of people attending this service or the message that made the difference. She supposed she wouldn't know since the message remained a mystery.

She thought back to the hymns, the sincerity and nobility reflected in the *a cappella* singing. It had appeared that these people truly believed the words they sang. They weren't merely singing notes; they were sharing of their hearts. It had been both beautiful and tragic. Summer acknowledged she had never before felt the music the way it had touched her on this Sunday morning in this simple setting. What made the difference?

She looked again at Mr. Ollenburger. The man's lips were tipped into a gentle smile, his eyes warm. His entire bearing spoke of a peaceful spirit. The words from the hymn filtered through her mind — *"Thee will I cherish, thee will I honor"* — and a knot formed in her throat. When Mr. Ollenburger sang those words, he meant them. He meant them with the depth of his soul. But could Summer truly comprehend what it meant to honor and cherish the fair Lord Jesus?

Suddenly the congregation rose to its feet. Summer listened as the minister delivered a prayer, his hands clasped in reverence beneath his bearded chin. At the solemn amen, the congregation chanted a phrase together in closing, then people began filing outside, heads together in hushed conversations.

Mr. Ollenburger stepped between Summer and the grandmother, offering each woman an elbow. *Grossmutter* took hold and Summer did the same, more out of habit than a desire to cling to this man's arm. Although many people, some curious and others stoic, turned in her direction as she stepped into the sunshine of the brisk

November day, no one spoke to Summer except her giant escort.

"So, *Frau* Steadman, what did you think of *Kleine Gemeinde?*"

"How do you do it?"

He turned his startled face in her direction. "How . . . do what?"

"Sing like that." She tightened her fingers on his firm forearm, remembering the way the music had seemed to flow through her very soul. "The harmony, without any piano or organ . . . It was beautiful. But how is it done? Have you always sung without instruments?"

They reached the wagon, and Summer watched him gently lift *Grossmutter* into his arms and place her on the pile of quilts in the back. His tenderness with the old woman touched Summer's heart. He helped Summer onto the wagon seat and then lifted Thomas into the back, instructing the boy to use the stack of blankets to cushion his seat. Only when he had aimed the oxen for the road did he finally answer her question.

"As a boy, in the old country, I learned the notes. The leader would sing a phrase, then all worshipers would copy it. Slowly we learned the songs. Seldom was a piano or organ available. Our small congregations, and having to move much, made having such items not easy. But the music does not seem to suffer when the notes are sung right."

Summer agreed with that. "Why did you have to move too much?"

He gave a shrug. "People first welcomed us, but then later . . ." He sighed. "Much unkindness exists in the world. Many rules which are hard on the heart to follow. From Germany to Russia my family went to escape hard rules and unkindness. Then, after many years, the hard rules and unkindness finds us again. By then I am grown man with my own wife and son to think of. So to America we come. Here my Thomas and me follow our beliefs without problems."

"And the unkindness?" Summer thought of the way the people had ignored her presence, even in church. It hadn't seemed kind to her.

Again, the man sighed, and the sigh sounded heavy with sadness. "*Ach,* unkindness. Where people exist, unkindness will exist. I do not like it, but I do not know how to change it. I just pray. . . ."

Already the *shariah* was in view, which meant the house was just around the bend.

Something occurred to her. "Was the service longer last Sunday? You didn't return until late afternoon."

Mr. Ollenburger glanced back at Thomas, a warning frown creasing his brow. He turned to Summer, and his expression cleared. "Many times, after Sunday service, we visit with families. Last Sunday we visited the Penner family. They have boy same age as Thomas. This Sunday, though, we come home."

He called the oxen to a halt outside the house and hopped down. His feet hitting the ground seemed to bring a close to the topic, although Summer still had questions. Why hadn't they gone visiting today? Would no one welcome them with her in attendance? Why were the people so set against her? What had she done to them? The fear of the illness was past. What was wrong with her?

Mr. Ollenburger set *Grossmutter* safely on the ground, then reached for Thomas. The man looked up at her, his gentle blue eyes as kind as always. Raising his hands, he smiled. "Come, *Frau* Steadman. A nice lunch we will eat, and then a surprise I have for you."

■ ■ ■ ■

Peter watched Thomas clear the dishes from lunch and stack them on the dry sink. As soon as the table was clean, he would bring out the surprise he had prepared for the woman. He worried his lower lip between his teeth as he pondered what her reaction might be. Once more his intentions were honorable, but always he felt concern about how they would be understood. He only wished to make her feel less uncomfortable. Those in town did not make her feel welcome.

He remembered the warning thrown at him by *Herr* Schmidt — *"The Holy Book tells us not to be unequally yoked!"* Peter knew this. He wished he could make those in town understand he was not looking to be yoked with the woman — he only wanted to help her and allow her to help Thomas.

Looking at her pale face above the harsh black of her mourning gown, he wondered how anyone could treat her with anything but kindness. She was a picture of unhappy longing. He felt the need to compensate for the town's *abstand* — their unreasonable keeping of distance. Still, his heart pounded as he rose and smiled down at her.

"You stay here, *Frau* Steadman. I have something for you." He waved his hand at her, noticing a pink stain steal across her thin cheeks. As quickly as his big feet would allow, he darted to his bedroom.

There in the corner, it waited. A chair ordered from the Montgomery Ward and Company catalog and delivered to Nickels' Dry Goods store. It was not the most expensive chair from the catalog, but when he had seen the padded seat and back embroidered with a design of roses, he had thought it suited the woman. And its frame was made of oak — a good solid wood that would last.

Peter liked oak. He liked its grain and its warm honey color when touched with stain, and most of all he liked how the mighty tree grew from such a tiny acorn. He always thought of oak trees as one of God's miracles. But he would not say all this to the woman.

On the fabric seat of the chair rested a small square paper-wrapped package that was of more importance than even the oak chair. It, too, had been ordered from the catalog and had raised some eyebrows. The chair Nick could surmise was for Peter's home, but that second item . . . It could only be for the woman. Nick had been full of questions, for sure, about the little package.

A band of worry tightened Peter's chest as he remembered *Herr* Schmidt and *Herr* Penner watching him load the chair onto his wagon. *Herr* Schmidt had said, "I hear the mill in Hillsboro is now using a steam engine." *Herr* Penner had nodded, a smug look on his face, as *Herr* Schmidt continued, "Much faster it can grind the grain. Maybe I will go there next harvest, *ja?*"

Although neither man spoke to Peter, he understood the words were meant for him. It was a threat — send the woman away or risk the loss of his business. Peter did not respond but only latched the back of his wagon and headed home with the purchases.

Grossmutter's eyes were full of questions when she saw these things. Peter felt embarrassed, explaining to her why he had bought them, but when he finished she patted his hand and smiled approvingly. He could not decide whether *Grossmutter* truly liked *Frau* Steadman or only felt sorry for her.

He'd left the woman waiting too long already. He lifted the chair, careful not to tip the package from the seat, and stepped back into the living area. When Peter's feet scuffed the floor, she turned in his direction and her brown eyes widened.

"Oh my."

His heart lifted at her pleased tone.

She rose, rounded the table, and advanced on the chair, her fingers pressed to her lips. Tears shimmered in the corners of her eyes. "Oh, it's just beautiful. How could you possibly know . . . ?" A tear broke free and spilled down her cheek.

"I order it from the catalog." Peter thought his heart might burst through his chest, so heartily it pumped away as the woman circled the chair, her fingers tracing the curve of the armrest and following the line of the high, scrolled seatback. She pressed her palm to the rose design, and fresh tears made new tracks down her blushing face.

"The chair, it meets with your liking, then?"

"Oh yes." The words came out in a breathy whisper as she brought her steepled hands beneath her chin and stood in front of the chair, beaming down at it in pleasure.

"Well, sit in it!" Thomas's eager voice brought a smile to the woman's face.

Peter leaned over to remove the package from the seat, gesturing with his hand for her to make herself comfortable. With a girlish giggle, she turned and lowered herself into the padded seat. Draping her hands over the armrests, she leaned her head back, closed her eyes, and released a satisfied sigh.

"Does it sit good?" Thomas asked.

Her eyes opened, a smile crinkling their corners. "Does it sit *well*," she corrected. "Oh yes. It sits perfectly." She peered up at Peter with an expression of great appreciation. "It's a beautiful gift. I thank you."

Peter did not believe he had ever pleased someone as much as he had just pleased this woman. What a change the smile made in her appearance! His stomach felt fluttery, and he swallowed hard before speaking. "I promised you a chair so you need not always sit on the bed. I keep my promises."

Her eyes remained pinned to his. "Yes, you do. You are a good man."

The simple words sent another shot of warmth through his middle. This woman did not deserve the unkindness bestowed upon her by the townspeople. Somehow he must make them see the neediness, the loneliness that existed within her heart. Then maybe they would reach out to her instead of shunning her.

All during the butchering he had tried to tell them she was no threat to their humble existence, but they had not trusted his words. He must find some way to bring them together so the fear and worry could be set aside.

"Pa, aren't you going to give her the other present?" Thomas's words jarred their gazes apart.

The woman's face flooded with color, and she gripped the armrests. "Oh, please, the chair is present enough."

Peter had no choice but to give it to her. With awkward motions, he thrust the package at her. "You are the only one who can make use of this," he insisted when she didn't lift her hands to take it. "Please, *Frau* Steadman."

With a slight frown, the woman reached out her hands. When Peter released the package, her hands slipped downward, as if surprised by the weightiness. She placed the package in her lap and removed the string tie, then folded back the paper. A leather-covered book came into view. The black cover of the book was the same velvety color as the dress the woman wore.

"Holy Bible," she read aloud.

"Heilige Bibel," *Grossmutter* echoed, nodding her head.

Frau Steadman glanced up, acknowledging the woman's words, then touched the curling gold letters on the cover. Though she was still looking down, Peter heard her whisper, "Thank you, Mr. Ollenburger."

He knelt next to the chair, his big hand on the armrest beside her elbow. "This morning in *Kleine Gemeinde,* you could not know the lesson because you could not understand the language. I keep the verses our Reverend Enns spoke in here." He tapped his forehead. "I will write down where to find them, and Thomas will tell you in English. I do not know the English spelling." He regretted that so many steps were necessary for this woman to receive the message. "Then you read the verses in your English. We can talk about them afterward."

To his great relief, the woman did not push the Bible back at him. Her chin raised and lowered in a gentle nod of agreement.

He rose to his feet, clapped his hands, and then rubbed his palms together. "And there is no better time to start than now. Thomas, get my tablet and inkpot, please. Before my mind forgets, I must to write down the verses for our *Frau* Steadman."

14

"Our Frau Steadman . . ." Often over the next week, the impulsively spoken words came back to haunt Peter. Why had he let those words slip out? He had been feeling tender because he knew he, *Grossmutter,* and Thomas were her only friends. But the word *our* spoke of possession. He did not want to give her the wrong idea.

Yet, there were two things he did each day that were only for the woman. Every afternoon, while Thomas washed lunch dishes and *Grossmutter* napped, he took her to visit the little spot where her family was buried. Every evening after supper, with heads together and Bibles open, he spent an hour with her in study. It was a peaceful time for Peter, a pleasant end to the day.

During the past week they had moved beyond the preacher's sermon to other parts of the Bible. Peter tried to stay in the New

Testament, turning the woman's attention to others who had suffered so she would know she was not alone. Tonight, as he sat across the table and guided the woman in reading about the apostle Paul, he felt her quizzical expression, and he squirmed in his seat.

Her eyes seemed to ask of things that went beyond the subject they studied, and his foolish words *"our Frau Steadman"* tickled his mind. Thank goodness for Thomas's presence at the table and *Grossmutter*'s chaperonage from her chair in the corner.

"Philippians, chapter four, verse eleven." Thomas glanced at the verse his father indicated. "I know that one by memory. 'Not that I speak in respect of want: for I have learned, in whatsoever state I am, therewith to be content.' "

Frau Steadman's dark-eyed gaze turned toward Thomas. Peter noticed that the woman's eyes had lost their haggard look. Eating regularly had done her some good. And, he admitted to himself, it did not hurt that much of the time she ate her own cooking rather than his attempts. They were all eating flavorful meals thanks to the woman's willingness to assume the cooking chores.

"Thomas, how did you learn all of these

verses?" she asked. "This is the third time this week you've quoted a verse from memory."

He shrugged. "I don't know. Things just stick with me. Especially things I like. And I like that verse. It helps me remember that even though I don't have all the things I want, I can still be happy."

Peter tousled the boy's hair. "And what do you want that you do not already have?"

"A bicycle."

The answer came so quickly that both Peter and *Frau* Steadman released a laugh. How good it was to hear laughter from her lips.

"*Ach,* boy, I think you misunderstand. When Paul writes these words, he is in much physical discomfort. In prison, alone, and far from everyone he holds dear. Yet he found contentment in the knowledge of God's presence. I do not think Paul was meaning bicycles."

The boy shrugged. "Oh, I know. Bicycles hadn't been invented yet." He turned to the woman. "But it still reminds me to be happy with what I have, and I think Paul might have meant that, too."

"Yes, I suppose he could have." The woman closed her Bible. "Mr. Ollenburger, you have a commendable grasp of Scripture. You obviously paid attention in church all of your growing-up years."

A warmth flooded Peter's chest as he remembered the church of his childhood. "*Ach, ja.* A treat it was each Sunday to put on my nicest clothes, to smell the chicken simmering in the pot. My belly would growl at the good smell. Then I walk with *Vater, Mutter,* and *Grossvater* to *Kleine Gemeinde.* The singing, the preaching . . . *Ja,* it was good feeling, but mostly I think of that chicken waiting at home for me to eat it."

He pinched his brows as other memories crowded in. "Then, later, we are told we cannot gather to worship. We must to go somewhere else if we wish to meet together and learn from Scripture. So we go. And when we meet again, I never take lightly listening to the Word. I think less of the good chicken dinner and more of the food of the spirit. I listen close. I remember. I hide the words in my heart." He rested his hand against his chest. The familiar rhythm of his heartbeat served as a reminder of the knowledge of his faith.

A pained expression crossed the woman's face. He smiled to reassure her. "But here in America, no one comes and says you cannot study — you cannot learn. Still I listen. I feel glad that I can listen."

To Peter's amazement, tears appeared in her eyes. Then she blinked rapidly, and the tears disappeared. She rose. "I believe I'm ready to turn in."

He stood, too. "Then I will walk you to *shariah*." He reached for her coat, and a sudden whistling blast shook the windows in the house. "Hear the wind! Winter is upon us when we hear the howl."

He held her coat for her, then put on his own coat, buttoning it to the collar before opening the door. The sharp wind nearly took his breath away, and worry struck. "A storm must be brewing. We go quickly."

Neither spoke as he guided her with a hand on her back to the *shariah* and helped her inside. It felt good to close the door on the wind, but the tiny abode was far from warm. He lit her stove. "You get another blanket from the chest tonight. This shelter is not airtight. I —" He scratched his beard. He wished he had more to offer her than this flimsy shelter.

"I'll pile the blankets on my bed. I'll be fine." She stood, her fingers woven together and pressed to her stomach. "You go ahead and return to your home before the wind

213

gets any stronger."

Summer nearly wilted with relief when he finally stepped out of the shanty. For days, his offhanded wording, calling her *"our Frau Steadman,"* had niggled in the back of her mind, teasing her dreams and worrying her heart. Did he truly see her as "their" *Frau* Steadman? It was much too early for her to become involved with someone. Rodney had only been gone four months. The convention of mourning dictated at least a year must pass.

Summer had heard that on the prairie, convention was often replaced with practicality, survival dependent upon having a partner with whom to share the work load. But Mr. Ollenburger had already proven he was capable of caring for himself and his son with the help of the grandmother. He obviously didn't *need* a wife.

But did she need a husband? She nibbled her lower lip and contemplated that question. The town might view her more favorably if she became Mrs. Peter Ollenburger, and it would certainly solve her problem of not having a permanent home. It would ensure her placement in Gaeddert, near her children's graves. Yet she had no desire to engage herself in a marriage of convenience.

Her marriage to Rodney, she admitted with a deep regret, had not been the result of steadfast love. She had married him for security, and she suspected he chose her to spite his father, who had wanted him to marry into a family equal to theirs in wealth and social status. How Summer had longed for Rodney to cherish her. But when he seemed to care about other things more than he cared about her, she had shut him away — sealed her emotions tight to protect herself. And, she knew, had not allowed herself to truly love him.

Mr. Ollenburger's words, spoken at the gravesite, came back: *"My Elsa . . ."* The tenderness in his voice and his eyes as he'd spoken those words had brought tears to Summer's eyes. Would anyone ever look at her and say with such tender feeling, "My Summer . . ."? Would she ever care for someone else in that same way?

Another gust of wind shook the entire shack, and small particles of grit blew between the planks of the north wall. She hurried to the blanket chest and retrieved the last two blankets. She spread the blankets on the bed and, fully dressed, slipped beneath them. But sleep eluded her.

While shadows danced on the beamed ceiling, the wind howled, and bits of grit sifted onto her blanket, she thought about the passage she and Mr. Ollenburger had studied this evening. Throwing back the covers, she reached for the Bible she had placed on top of the little crate. Perched on the edge of the bed, she turned the pages toward the stove for light, searching the Scriptures until she located the fourth chapter of Philippians again.

In verses six and seven she found the reference she wanted: *"Be careful for nothing; but in every thing by prayer and supplication with thanksgiving let your requests be made known unto God. And the peace of God, which passeth all understanding, shall keep your hearts and minds through Christ Jesus."* She read the verses twice, leaning over the Bible with great concentration. She underlined a few words with her finger: *". . . let your requests be made known unto God. . . . The peace of God . . . shall keep your hearts and minds . . ."*

Straightening, she remembered something Mr. Ollenburger had said when at the graves of her family. *"God is a God who knows."* She shivered as the wind took up a howl that threatened to pierce her eardrums. She hugged herself, the words of her host echoing like a chorus with the wind.

Did God know her secret longing? Did He recognize the coldness of her heart? Did He know how to melt the icy exterior and bring warmth to her soul? She set the Bible aside and leaped to her feet, walking to the center of the floor. There she stopped, her arms held tight across her middle, her heart pounding with the desire for God to make Himself known to her in a way she couldn't misunderstand. How she needed peace for her heart! She strained, listening, waiting for a voice from above to allay her fears and insecurities and give her the peace she'd seen in Mr. Ollenburger's eyes.

Wind. Only wind.

Her head dropped, disappointment sagging her shoulders. What did she think would happen? Love would strike like a bolt of lightning from the sky? The only people who had truly loved her were her children, and they were dead. Summer's heart had died with them. Her ability to love had died with them. Her heart was surely a shriveled thing, incapable of offering anything of value to anyone.

Which must make her valueless to anyone else, as well.

She raised her chin, determination

straightening her spine. Valueless, perhaps, to all but one: Thomas. He needed her — at least until winter's end. And if she were to be her best for him, she needed rest. She set the Bible on the crate and climbed back into her bed.

With a deep sigh, she pulled the blankets to her chin, hugging herself for warmth. The wind continued to howl. Her thoughts continued to tumble. But eventually, despite the noise of the wind, she fell into a restless, dreamless sleep.

A fierce, relentless howl pushed aside the curtain of sleep, forcing Summer's eyes open. She squinted into the dark, scowling. Would the wind never cease? She closed her eyes again, determined to ignore the wind, but a mighty gust yanked her into full wakefulness. Only a feeble orange glow of coals showed in the belly of the stove.

Perhaps the wind waking her was a blessing. The stove needed wood. She crept from beneath the covers, shivering from the cold. She crossed her arms over her chest as she moved stiffly to the woodbox. As she turned toward the stove, two logs in her arms, she heard a creaking noise.

Her heart pounded as an unnamed fear took hold. She stared in horror as the frame of the *shariah* seemed to lean, the shuddering sound increasing as boards groaned in protest against the force of the wind. Realization struck, and she broke out in a sweat despite the frigid room.

With a gasp, she threw the logs aside, snatched up her Bible, and dove under the bed. She had barely pulled her feet under when the shack gave way, pressed beyond its limits by the wind. Summer hugged the Bible, her eyes squinted tight, as the roof folded in on itself and fell across the pit with a resounding crash. Dust filled the air. She choked, her nose burning. She curled tighter, pressing her face into the crook of her elbow. Would she be buried alive?

At least, came the fleeting thought, *I will once more be with my children.*

15

Peter jolted awake. He rolled out of the bed, shivering as his feet touched the icy floor, and hurried to the main room.

Grossmutter stood in her doorway, rubbing her eyes in confusion. She spoke to him, and Peter nodded. A sound had awakened him, too.

Thomas appeared in his doorway, his eyes wide with fright. "Pa, I heard a crash."

The whistle of wind told Peter the storm still raged. Had it been the voice of the wind that had awakened them? Peter pressed his memory, trying to determine what had roused him from a sound sleep.

Another strong gust slammed against the house. The window panes rattled. "Did you hear the wind, do you think, son?"

"It wasn't wind. It was a crash. Like something broke."

These strong winds could do much damage. Peter did not like the idea of having to go out in a storm, yet he must find out what his son had heard. He returned to his bedroom and pulled on his shirt and pants over his long johns. As he tugged on his boots, Thomas appeared in his doorway with *Grossmutter* behind him.

"Pa, should I get dressed, too?"

"*Nein,* you and *Grossmutter* stay here in the warmth. I will go find out if something broke." He moved through the doorway and went to the woodbox. "Do not worry. Go get back under your covers."

Both Thomas and *Grossmutter* returned to their rooms. Peter made sure the fire was well stoked and then lit a lantern. He put on his coat, gloves, and hat before lifting the lantern and heading outside.

The wind slapped Peter hard, stealing his breath. It had even put out the stars, he noted — the night was very black. He shrugged deeper into his coat as he held the lantern well in front of him and moved across the yard, the clump of his boots against the hard ground matching the thump of his heartbeat.

"*Ach,* Lord, unpleasant it is out here." The wind blew the lantern back and forth, creating shadows that turned trees and bushes into wild things that leaped and danced in the feeble moonlight. He wished to return to the warmth and security of the house.

A sweep of the grounds closest to the house told Peter the barn and chicken coop were unharmed, the animals restless but safe. He started toward the mill, but something turned his feet in the opposite direction.

He squinted, his eyes burning from the force of the wind, as he moved toward the little spot of ground where the *shariah* stood. The meager lantern glow only allowed Peter to see a few feet in front of him, so when his foot encountered the crumbled roof, he gasped in surprise.

He stared, disbelieving, at the spot of ground where a wooden A-frame had once stood. Now it lay on the ground, folded like a great ragged wooden sheet, covering the pit. His heart pounded in his ears, louder even than the blowing wind, and he lurched forward. Thrusting the lantern over the flattened roof, he searched for an opening. At the north end, he noticed a narrow slice, not more than twelve inches wide, where the pit was exposed.

He stumbled to the opening and knelt, peering into the black cavity. *"Frau* Steadman! *Frau* Steadman! *Wo sind sie?"* He shook his head, forcing his tongue to form English words. "Where are you, *Frau* Steadman?"

He strained, his heart in his throat, listening for the reply. Finally, nearly masked by the wailing wind, he heard a weak voice.

"I'm trapped. Under the bed."

"You are hurt?"

It seemed a long time before her answer came. "No. But I'm afraid the roof might fall in. And I don't want to bump the stove."

The stove! Peter's limbs quivered with fear. If the roof had collapsed on top of the stove, a fire could start. He must get her out — there was no time to waste.

"You stay still, *Frau* Steadman! I will get you. Do not worry." Still on his knees next to the tumbled building, he prayed aloud, "*Lieber* Lord, help me!" He considered ways to remove the roof. Miraculously, it seemed to lie on top of the pit. Should he yoke Gaert and Roth and use them to slide the roof from the pit?

The wind tore the hat from his head. He let it roll away into the darkness, his thoughts fixed on freeing *Frau* Steadman. Sliding the roof could knock the stove sideways. His chest constricted. No, he would not use the oxen to slide it. Somehow he must lift the roof without making it fall into the pit. He prayed for enough strength to do the task alone.

He pushed his face next to the opening. "*Frau* Steadman, I must go to get wood and a stump for a lever. You will be all right for little longer?"

Gusts of wind tried to cover her voice, but he heard her reply. "Yes . . . hurry, please. It's hard to breathe."

The cough that followed her words spurred Peter into action.

Summer kept her eyes tightly closed. The wind whipped through an opening somewhere and drove more dust into the pit. Fear made her want to take gasping breaths, but she forced herself to remain calm. Swallowing more dust wouldn't benefit her. Mr. Ollenburger was coming. He had said he would free her, and he was a man who kept his word.

It seemed as though hours had passed since she'd heard his voice, yet it couldn't have been more than thirty minutes. The Bible pressed against her chest. What had possessed her to grab it before seeking refuge beneath the bed? She had done it without conscious thought, but now, cradling it in her arms, she felt a comfort from its presence.

She shivered. Her dress had shifted up around her thighs, exposing her lower legs. Her stockings didn't provide much protection from the biting cold. Could she pull a blanket from the bed? She considered trying, but fear of accidentally bumping the stove kept her from reaching for it. If the roof caught fire, it would mean certain death. She swallowed the panic that rose from her belly. Surely Mr. Ollenburger would return soon. She could hold on.

"*Frau* Steadman?"

The voice came as if from a great distance. She opened her eyes, blinking against the sting of dust. She could see nothing.

"*Frau* Steadman, you can hear me?"

She took a great gulp of air, battling not to cough against the grit that filled her throat. "Yes!"

"You listen to me now careful." He pronounced the words slowly, precisely, the sound of his voice competing with the furious howl of the wind. "I will lift the roof. When you hear me say it is safe, you must come out to the north end. Come quickly — I do not know how long I can hold up the roof."

Hold up the roof? He was planning to lift

225

it on his own? Her heart pounded. Even a strong man like Peter Ollenburger would be incapable of such a feat.

"You hear me, *Frau* Steadman?"

"I hear you!" she choked out.

"Stay under the bed until I say it is safe!" The stern tone made her coil into a tighter ball. "If the roof drops . . ." He didn't finish the sentence.

The wail of wind, the sound of splintering wood, the groans of her benefactor — all blended into a nightmare of fearsome sound. Fresh air whooshed into the pit — cold and clean. Summer gulped the air. It stung her lungs, but she didn't care.

"Now, *Frau* Steadman!"

Mr. Ollenburger's voice sounded strained. Summer rolled from beneath the bed and blinked rapidly, clearing her vision. A pale band of yellow beckoned her. She held the Bible to her chest with one arm and crawled awkwardly toward the source of light. The crack and moan of the roof made her wish to hurry, but her trembling limbs and tangled skirt refused to cooperate. The journey might have been miles in length for the time it took for her to struggle across the short expanse of floor on knees and elbows. Finally she reached the edge of the pit.

Mr. Ollenburger had created an opening nearly two feet high. She scrambled up the side of the pit to freedom, falling face first onto the ground. The moment she was free, a mighty crash sounded behind her. She released a shudder with the fall of the roof. Then Mr. Ollenburger knelt beside her on the dried grass, his hands touching her head, her shoulder, her back.

"You are unhurt, *Frau* Steadman?"

The genuine concern in his voice brought tears to her eyes. "I'm unhurt. Thank you, Mr. Ollenburger." A sob of relief broke the last word in half.

"You get up now." In the dim glow of a single lantern, she watched him remove his coat. He wrapped it around her as he helped her to her feet. "We get you to the house."

"Your *shariah* . . . The chair, my teacup . . ." She muttered nonsensically as he guided her across the ground. Her teeth chattered despite the comforting warmth of his coat and his heavy arm around her shoulders. "I'm so sorry."

"You have no need for sorry." His calm voice was incongruous to the storm that continued to rage. Snowflakes danced on the wind, stinging her cheeks. "You are safe now. That is all that matters."

They reached the house, and he guided her over the stoop. The wind slammed the door into its frame, the sound bringing *Grossmutter* and Thomas from their bedrooms.

Thomas, his eyes wide, crossed to his father. "Pa, what — ?"

Mr. Ollenburger's large hand cupped the boy's head. "You did hear something break, son. The *shariah* no longer stands."

The child's wild eyes spun to Summer. "You're all right?"

Blinking back tears, she took his hand. "I'm fine, Thomas. Please, you go on back to bed. It's late — you need your sleep."

"Ja." Mr. Ollenburger gave his son a pat. "We talk more in the morning. To bed with you."

Thomas hesitated, but at his father's firm nod, he returned to his bedroom, closing the door behind him.

The grandmother clucked at Summer, her gnarled hands reaching to pluck bits of grit and dried grass from Summer's hair.

Mr. Ollenburger murmured something to the old woman in German, and she scuttled to the stove to pour a cup of coffee. Mr. Ollenburger pressed Summer into a chair, leaving his coat wrapped around her shoulders. "You sit, *Frau* Steadman. An ordeal you have been through."

The grandmother held the cup of steaming brew out to Summer, and she took it, gulping eagerly. She felt the warmth fill her middle, and she sighed. Here, in the cozy house, with the big man and his grandmother seeing to her needs, the last frightening hour seemed to fade into the distance. It took on a dreamlike quality. If she pinched herself, would she awaken to find herself lying on the rope bed in the shack?

"I'm so grateful for the sturdy bed you built," she told Mr. Ollenburger. "And your strength in raising that roof."

"*Ach,* with a well-placed lever and fulcrum much is possible."

She shook her head, amazement at his abilities making her gape at him in wonder. "Is there nothing you can't do?"

The man sank into a kitchen chair, his shaggy head drooping. "A flimsy *shariah* I built, for it to fall in the wind." The windows rattled against another mighty blast, and he cringed. "I should have bolstered it before allowing you to live there. Many years it has stood, many winds it has faced. It became weakened with time, I am sure. I am sorry for the fear you experienced this night."

The grandmother made soothing noises and stroked his shoulder. He took her hand, offering her a weak smile. His face looked pale, drawn. Exhaustion sagged his features.

Concern for him welled in her breast. "I'm fine, but you've had a rough night. Please, get your rest. I'll . . . I'll curl up . . ." Suddenly she didn't know where to go or what to do.

Mr. Ollenburger drew himself up in the chair, releasing a big sigh. "You will curl up in my bed."

"W-what?" The room spun.

His face flooded with color. *"Ach! Nein. Sie verstehen mich nicht!"*

The grandmother reared back as Summer stared at Mr. Ollenburger in mute horror.

He shook his head, growling as he repeated his words in English. "You do not understand my meaning." He gestured wildly as he spoke. "I will go sleep in the barn tonight. Then, tomorrow, I build you another bed, which we will put in *Grossmutter*'s room." He turned to the old woman and spoke in rapid German.

"I appreciate your kindness," Summer argued, "but I don't wish to inconvenience you any further than my presence already has. I can go to the barn."

230

Another gust of wind shook the entire house. "*Nein,* I cannot leave you to the barn. It is too cold."

She opened her mouth to protest, and he spoke again, his expression stern. "Woman, you cannot go to the barn. You will freeze, and then what use will you be to the boy?"

He called her *woman* in a tone that spoke of deep familiarity. She wished to run outside into the biting wind to cool the heat that filled her face. Before he could say anything that would embarrass her further, she stammered, "All-all right, Mr. Ollenburger. I-I will sleep in your bed tonight."

He nodded in satisfaction and removed his coat from her shoulders. "Clean sheets are in the *schrank* in the corner. Morning will be here soon, so do not tarry. You sleep well." He shrugged into his coat and disappeared into his room, returning a few moments later with a blanket draped over his arm. Kissing the grandmother's wrinkled cheek, he murmured something in German. She nodded, then toddled back to her room.

Summer watched Mr. Ollenburger head to the door. His hand on the doorknob, he looked at her and repeated, "You sleep well."

Although she nodded, she knew she wouldn't sleep. Not with her head on the pillow that normally cradled his head. She went to his room, pulled quilts and a feather pillow from the large cupboard in the corner, and made a pallet on the floor. Sleep claimed her the moment her head touched the pillow.

16

"Pa! Pa, come quick!"

Summer awakened with a start. She jerked to a seated position, a cramp catching in her lower back. Pressing a hand to the offending spot, she struggled to her feet and staggered to the bedroom door. Thomas stood in the kitchen with the front door open, allowing in a stream of sunshine and a large portion of the cold morning air.

"What is it? What's wrong?"

At her voice he spun to face her. "What're you doing in there? Where's Pa?"

"Your father slept in the barn last night." She crossed to the door. The wind, at last, had blown itself away, but the cold remained. Chilly air swirled around her, and she shivered. "Close the door, please. It's cold."

"But look!" The boy pointed. "It snowed last night!"

Summer squinted into the bright morning

sunshine. Thomas was right — the flurry of snow had left behind a light dusting of powdery flakes.

"First snow of the year!" Thomas beamed. "Not enough to play in, but it's a start. Whoopee!"

Summer didn't echo Thomas's joy at this harbinger of winter. She shivered again. "Yes, it's snow. Now please close the door. You're sending all our warmth outside."

He heaved a great sigh as he closed the door. "Why'd Pa stay in the barn?"

She opened the door of the stove. "He was concerned about it being too cold out there for me." Using the poker, she turned over the glowing coals. "We need to get the fire going again." She chose two logs from the woodbox and placed them on top of the coals.

Thomas stood close, watching as she blew into the coals, encouraging a flame. "Can't be much colder in the barn than it is in here."

Summer released a chuckle. "Well, I'm sure that's because you left the door standing wide open for so long, gawking at the snow!"

The boy shrugged, grinning. "Guess so."

"Once the fire is roaring, we'll get break-fast started, hmm?" She realized she had enjoyed waking to the sound of the boy's voice. It was certainly preferable to the lonely silence of the *shariah.*

The far door opened, revealing the grandmother, who stood with a shawl draped over her nightgown. Her long gray hair lay in tangled strands on top of the woven shawl. She blinked at Summer, as if puzzled, then her expression cleared. Her focus bounced to the stove, where a cheery blaze crackled, then returned to Summer. A smile surfaced in her eyes.

"Thomas, will you tell your grandmother I will prepare breakfast?" She listened to Thomas's German words, watching the old woman's face for her reaction. To her relief, the woman merely nodded, giving her approval, and then went back into her bedroom. Summer said, "If I allow you to bundle up and visit the henhouse, do you promise to walk slowly and not hurt yourself?"

The boy's face lit up. "I promise!" He donned his hat, coat, and gloves, then stepped out into the snow-covered morning with a basket on his arm. Summer watched through the frosty window as he took slow steps across the yard; every once in a while he turned back to look at the imprint of his boots in the sparse snow.

She turned from the window, a smile tugging at her lips. How could one remain gloomy with Thomas nearby? The boy's excitement and bright eyes lit the room, his cheerful nature so much like her own little Tod's. Her heart clutched with remembrance, but she deliberately pushed aside the sorrow, focusing instead on the living, breathing boy who required her attention.

By the time Thomas returned, Summer had her bedding put away and the table set for breakfast. The grandmother came out, fully clothed, her hair twisted into its familiar bun, and ambled to her chair. Thomas handed the basket to Summer.

She peered into it, her eyebrows rising. "What? Only three eggs?"

He shrugged. "Must be too cold to lay. That's all there was."

"Well, that will hardly make enough eggs to feed your father." She huffed. "What's wrong with those hens? Don't they know a growing boy also lives in this house?"

Thomas giggled, responding to her teasing tone. "Should I go tell them what you said? Maybe they'll lay some more."

Summer smiled at his red cheeks and nose. "I think one excursion into the snow is enough for this morning. Unbundle and we'll think of something else to do with these three lonely eggs."

Less than half an hour later, Mr. Ollen-burger stomped through the door. His nose and ears glowed red from the cold, and a huge smile brightened his face. *"Die wind-schläge und wir haben schnee!"* As *Grossmut-ter* chuckled, he turned to Summer and said, "The wind, she does blow, and we shall have snow!"

Summer felt another grin tug her cheeks. How ruddy he looked with his cold-reddened features and beard bristling in all directions. Even the recent haircut and trim couldn't completely tame his bearlike appearance. The morning breeze had teased his wheat-colored hair, causing it to stick out in uncontrolled tufts over his sparkling blue eyes. "You look no older than Thomas, standing there with your mussed hair, red nose, and snowy feet."

His eyes widened in surprise, and she clapped a hand to her mouth. How could she have spoken to him so casually? But then he opened his mouth and laughed, his eyes crinkling with delight.

"Ah, *Frau* Steadman, a bit of the Old Nick you are feeling. The first snow will do that to a person." He reached up with a broad hand to smooth his hair. "I have been choring, so mussed I probably am. And hungry as a spring-wakened bear. Is that *pankuake* I smell?"

"What?"

"*Pankuake* — what you call pancake."

The smell of scorched batter reached Summer's nose. She spun back to the stove, lifting the iron skillet from the burner. "I was going to make scrambled eggs, but Thomas said the hens were too cold to lay, so there were only three, and that wasn't even enough to feed *you,* so —"

She was prattling. What on earth was wrong with her this morning? Obviously she hadn't gotten enough sleep last night. Her cheeks burned, and she considered running outside to thrust her face into the snow and stay there until the spring thaw. But Mr. Ollenburger's laughter rang again.

"Well known you have become with my appetite." He removed his outerwear. "Pancakes are good choice to make the eggs stretch. Many times as a boy, my family had *pankuake* for an evening meal. They will surely fill this bear's stomach.

"Thomas, have you fetched the molasses jar? No? Then get it, boy. Ready I am to eat a mountain of pancakes."

Breakfast passed with cheerful camaraderie that calmed Summer's unsettled nerves. It was difficult to stay on edge around the Ollenburgers. Their easy acceptance of her and their loving relationship with each other made her heart patter with the desire to be more than just Thomas's tutor, to actually be a member of this family. And at the same time, her heart lurched in fear of where her thoughts were leading.

As Summer rose to clear the dishes, the crunch of wagon wheels sounded from the front yard, and a voice called, "Hello in the house! Peter Ollenburger, are you home?"

Mr. Ollenburger rose to open the door. "*Guten morgen, Herr* Penner. Good morning, Rupert. What for do you come out this Saturday morning?"

"Last night's wind storm has brought down a tree at the Ratzlaffs'. Through the barn roof it fell. We need oxen to move the tree and strong arms to rebuild the barn. Are you able to help?"

Without hesitating, Mr. Ollenburger reached for his coat. "I will come." He paused, his apologetic gaze resting on Summer. "I will not be able to make a bed for you today."

She shook her head. "Don't worry about my bed. Take care of your neighbor."

Thomas tugged at his father's sleeve. "Pa,

239

can Rupert stay here and play? We'll stay in the house, and I promise not to be rough. Please?"

Mr. Ollenburger turned to the grandmother. *"Mag der junge einen besucher heute haben?"*

To Summer's surprise, the woman lifted a hand to point with a gnarled finger in Summer's direction.

Mr. Ollenburger nodded and shifted his focus to Summer. "*Frau* Steadman, do you mind if a friend the boy has here today?"

She shook her head. Although she would prefer only Thomas's company, she knew the boy missed spending time with his classmates. "No. That's fine."

"Hurray!" Thomas yelped. He hollered out the open door, "Rupert, can you stay here today while our fathers work at the Ratzlaff place?"

A brief consultation took place between the father and son on the wagon, and then Rupert bounded into the house. His red hair, freckles, and pale amber eyes contrasted with Thomas's ruddy complexion and bright blue eyes. Thomas was a much more handsome lad, Summer thought with pride, startling herself with her sense of ownership of the boy.

"Good-bye now, *Frau* Steadman." Mr. Ollenburger spoke from the doorway, pulling her attention from the boys who huddled in the corner, obviously planning their day. "Do not worry about chores — I will tend to the chickens and horses when I return."

She nodded, and the man turned to his son.

"Thomas?"

"Yes, Pa?"

"Mind *Frau* Steadman, and do not get wild. And Rupert," he said to the red-haired boy, "remember Thomas cannot get wild or his ribs may be hurt."

Both boys nodded, but grins split their faces.

The door closed, and Summer offered a trembling smile. "Rupert, have you had breakfast?"

The boy's grin faded and disapproval shone in his eyes. "*Ja.* My mother fed me."

"Very well then." Summer faltered, twisting her hands in the apron that still hung around her waist. Realizing what she was doing, she pulled her hands loose and began clearing dishes. Would she let this little boy intimidate her in her own home? Then her hands froze. Home? This wasn't her home.

Looking directly at Thomas, she sug-

241

gested, "Why don't you boys go to your room and play? I would imagine Rupert enjoys building towers and bridges with blocks as much as you do."

Thomas turned his eager grin in Rupert's direction. "Want to?"

The other boy shrugged. "*Ja,* I suppose."

As the boys walked to the bedroom, Summer could feel Rupert's narrowed eyes watching her.

Thomas hummed as he grabbed a handful of blocks and dumped them in the middle of the floor. He really wanted to go outside and tramp through the first snow of the season, but having Rupert visit was almost as good. With his friend helping, they could probably build a better tower than he'd ever made by himself. The click of the door latch startled him, and he looked over his shoulder to see Rupert leaning against the closed door. His friend's face twisted into a scowl.

"How come *she's* in your house, cooking breakfast for you?"

The question caught Thomas by surprise. A funny feeling crept into his stomach. "Because she's a better cook than Pa."

Rupert crossed his arms. "She shouldn't be cooking for you."

"Why not?"

Rupert stalked to Thomas and knelt in front of him. "Thomas, you have to be careful."

Even though Rupert's face was serious and the whispered words were clearly a warning, Thomas couldn't stop the giggle that rose from his throat. Rupert had no idea how silly he sounded. "Careful about what?"

Rupert punched Thomas's shoulder. "Thomas, I'm not making fun. My pa says letting her stay here is just like letting a Russian soldier stay in your house. My pa says every time somebody different comes to stay, problems start. That's why your pa and my pa had to leave Russia. Because different people came to the village and caused problems."

Thomas resisted rolling his eyes. "Rupert, we talked about this before. Mrs. Steadman is only one lady. She isn't going to cause problems. Besides, she's just teaching me."

"Teaching you what? That's what my pa wants to know. Is she teaching you things that aren't of the church?"

"Of course not!" Indignation rose in Thomas's chest. "She's learning *about* our church. She and my pa study every night."

To Thomas's amazement, Rupert's face turned white. His freckles looked like tiny pennies swimming in milk. "He's telling her about our church?"

Thomas frowned. "Sure he is."

Rupert shook his head, his eyes wide. "He shouldn't be doing that."

"But why?"

"If she knows about our church, then she can *really* cause problems!"

Thomas huffed. Now he wished he hadn't asked Rupert to stay. "Rupert, you don't make any sense. You say she can cause problems because she isn't part of our church. Then you say she can cause problems because she's learning about our church. And I say you're full of sauerkraut!" He pushed two blocks toward his friend and crossed his arms.

"And I say *you're* asking for trouble." Rupert pushed the blocks back. "You shouldn't be letting some fancy lady stay in your *shariah.*"

Without thinking, Thomas blurted, "She's staying in the house."

Rupert's eyes grew so wide Thomas was afraid they might pop out of his head. "In the *house?*"

Thomas leaned forward, his heart pounding as he realized his mistake. "Yes, but it's okay. She stays in Pa's room, and —"

Rupert leaped to his feet. "In your pa's room?"

Thomas struggled to his feet and reached out to Rupert. "But it's okay! Pa's staying —"

"I don't wanna hear anything else, Thomas," Rupert said, putting his hands over his ears.

Thomas grabbed Rupert's hands and pulled them down. "It's okay, I told you!" Leaning close, Thomas whispered, "I think she's gonna be my new ma." Even though Thomas had never dared to think such a thing, now that he'd said it, it sounded like a good idea. Even though sometimes she got bossy, he knew that's what ma's did — told children what to do. But most of the time she was nice, and he really liked Mrs. Steadman. He knew she liked him, too.

Rupert stared at Thomas, bug-eyed. "Your new ma? But . . . but she can't!"

"Why can't she?" He shrugged. "She doesn't have a husband, and she and my pa get along real good. She can be my new ma if she wants to."

Rupert shook his head. "My pa's a deacon, and I know the rules. Your pa can't marry her because she's not part of our church."

"But she's going to be." Thomas stuck out his chin. "You'll see."

Rupert shook his head, a gloomy look in his eyes. "If your pa marries her, there's going to be big trouble, Thomas."

"I don't think so." Thomas sat beside the pile of blocks. "Now, are we going to build or not?"

Rupert stood for several long seconds, chewing on his lip and staring at Thomas. Finally, he sighed and sat down, too. "Okay, let's build."

Even though he and Rupert built the best, highest, most elaborate block tower ever, Thomas found no joy in the creation. All the shine of a friend's visit and the first snow was lost with Rupert's ominous statement, *"There's going to be big trouble."*

17

Summer turned from the window and blinked blearily at the boys, who sat together at the table creating a picture of a lamb with the pieces of a jigsaw puzzle. Although the boys had been well behaved, her nerves felt frayed by the red-haired boy's constant scrutiny. The tension had worn her out. "Thomas?"

"Yes, ma'am?" Thomas looked up, but his friend's focus never wavered from the puzzle.

"Do you suppose you boys will be all right if I turn in early? I can hardly keep my eyes open."

"Sure, we'll be fine."

The other boy lifted his face just enough to send Summer another look full of suspicion. She shivered and forced a weak smile. "It's dark, so I'm sure your fathers will be here soon." She pointed to the stove. "I left some salt pork and potatoes in the skillet.

Remind your father to eat, will you?" She felt a blush build as she remembered the boy's father prodding her to eat.

A secretive smile tipped up Thomas's lips, and he sent Rupert a knowing look that gave Summer an uneasy feeling. "Yes, ma'am, I'll tell him you said so."

"Thank you." She hesitated. Was it negligent to leave the boys unattended? The grandmother had toddled off to bed nearly an hour ago. A yawn pressed at her throat, and she knew she wouldn't be able to stay awake much longer. Thomas was a responsible boy — surely they would be fine. She crossed to the table and touched his shoulder. "You sleep well tonight, Thomas."

"I will, ma'am. *Schlop die gesunt.*"

"Thank you." She looked at Rupert. "Good night, Rupert."

He didn't respond.

Summer closed herself in the bedroom and leaned against the door, her eyes closed. Thomas's good-night message echoed in her ears. How much the boy was like his father in appearance and mannerisms. Yet, with the typical openness of children, he was much less restrained than his father.

She smiled, remembering the brief conversation they had shared when Rupert had visited the outhouse.

"Mrs. Steadman, do you have a first name?"

The question had taken her aback, and she had stammered out, "Well, of course I do. It's Summer."

The boy's eyes had widened. "Summer? I like that name."

She had shared the reason for her unusual name, watching his eyebrows rise. When she was finished, he had exclaimed, "You're like me, then. You don't have a ma, either."

She had shaken her head. "No, I don't."

Abruptly, he had turned the conversation back to her name. "May I call you Summer? When it's just us, I mean? Not in front of Rupert."

It had pleased her to think of the boy using her name, so she had given permission. Now she wondered if she'd done the right thing. Would his father approve? Even now, after a month with the family, he still referred to her formally as *Frau* Steadman, except that one time he had called her *woman.* Her face flamed with the remembrance. What would her name sound like spoken by his deep voice?

When her thoughts ran in those kinds of directions, she knew she needed rest. She made a pallet of blankets on the floor, lay down, and quickly fell asleep.

Ach, it had been a long day. But the Ratzlaff barn was rebuilt, the offending tree now lay stacked as firewood, and his own animals munched hay in their stalls. Peter could turn in. He entered the house as quietly as his big feet would allow so he would not wake anyone. He was surprised to find Thomas at the table.

"Son, you still are awake?"

"I was waiting for you. Rupert went home over an hour ago." The boy went to the stove and raised the lid on a skillet. A good smell greeted Peter's nostrils. "You're supposed to eat. Summer went to bed, but she left this for you."

Peter frowned. "Summer?" He hung up his coat. "Of what do you speak?"

The boy blinked, his expression innocent. "Mrs. Steadman. She said I could call her Summer."

"But why?" He plodded to the table and seated himself heavily.

Thomas shrugged as he scooped food onto a plate. "It's her name."

The woman's name was Summer? The word brought images of blooming flowers and golden wheat, of cottony clouds and

250

whispered breezes. Summer . . . Ah yes, the name suited the woman. "How did a woman get an unusual name as that?"

"She told me how." Thomas placed the plate and a fork in front of Peter. Pressing the heels of his hands on the edge of the table, he explained. "Her folks had a boy — Summer's brother, William — but after him, they lost four babies in a row. So when Summer was born in early summer, her mother said they maybe shouldn't name her since she probably wouldn't live. They called her Summer for the season."

Peter thought about this explanation. It did not seem as though the parents cared a great deal if they had no hopes of her living. But perhaps they only shielded their own hearts from possible pain. He knew the woman did this — tried to shield herself from Thomas. The boy had weaseled his way into her heart anyway. He suspected *Grossmutter* had found a spot there, too. The thought warmed him.

"Summer's Ma died when Summer was ten years old, almost the same age I am now," Thomas went on, bringing Peter's attention back. "Her pa, too. Both of them died in a carriage accident."

She was an orphan? The thought pained Peter. She had lost her husband and children after losing parents? What a great deal of sadness she had borne.

"Her brother and his wife took care of her after that." Thomas scowled. "And even though she didn't say so, I felt like she wasn't very happy with them." He shrugged. "Sometimes I don't think she's very happy with us, either, but she did smile today. Twice."

A smile was still rare on the woman's face. If she had smiled twice today, Thomas was working miracles. "I think your friend is just careful, Thomas." Peter paused. How should he word his thoughts? "People who have lost much are always worried about losing more. So they guard their hearts. It is not that she does not feel the happiness; she only wishes to hide it so as not to be hurt should she lose something more."

Thomas seemed to consider what his father had said. Finally he nodded, his expression somber. "I think I understand. Is . . . is that why you haven't found another wife?"

Peter felt his lips twitch. The boy was growing up fast. "What is this? You want to be matchmaker for your father?"

"No." Thomas grimaced. "But Stuart and Fannie Jacobs got a new ma when their pa married Martin Hett's ma. So Martin got a new pa, too." He gave another shrug. "Grown-ups just seem to get married. Why don't you?"

Peter chewed his lower lip thoughtfully as he examined his son. "Do you want a new mother, boy?"

A blush stole across Thomas's cheeks. "Sometimes." His voice was so soft, Peter nearly missed the single word answer.

Peter did something he had not done for many years. He lifted his son onto his knee. The boy had to curl his back to nestle his head on his father's shoulder. Peter wrapped his arms around him.

"*Ach,* boy, you are almost too big for this, but I think for now we both need it." Peter kissed the top of Thomas's head. "You know I love you, and I want to give you the things that will make you happy. But a mother . . ." He chuckled. "Well, that is not something I can order from Nickels' Dry Goods, for sure."

"I know." The boy's breath stirred Peter's beard.

"The Hett woman and Jacobs married for good reason. *Frau* Hett had a farm she could not run by herself. Jacobs has fine strapping boys to help. By their marriage, they solved problems. But . . ." How much could the boy understand? Although he was growing up, he was still very much a boy inside. The way he curled on his father's lap proved that.

"But . . . ?" Thomas lifted his head.

"But to me, son, if a man proposes marriage to a woman, he should feel about her like he feels for no other. God means for a man and a woman to cleave to one another. How can they do this if love does not exist between them?" Peter looked intently into his son's face. "Do you understand this, Thomas?"

"Yes. I know how much you loved Ma."

Peter swallowed. Elsa had been his light, his God-chosen love. No other light would ever shine as bright for him again. "*Ja,* my love for her went deep. I still feel it inside my heart. Until I feel for someone else the way I felt for your dear mother, I cannot think of proposing marriage."

Thomas twiddled with the buttons on his father's shirt. "Do you think it'll ever happen?"

Peter answered honestly. "I do not know, son. I know God gives gifts, and love is one of them. If He wishes for me to have a wife, He will let the love to bloom again." Peter took Thomas's chin in his hand. "But no matter if I marry again or I do not, one thing does not change, and that is my love for you, boy." His voice turned gruff with emotion. "You are one of my God-given loves."

"I love you, too, Pa." Thomas threw his arms around Peter's neck and clung.

Peter clasped the back of Thomas's head, his fingers in the boy's coarse hair. "I know, Thomas. I know."

They sat together for several minutes, until Thomas's hold loosened and his arms slid from Peter's shoulders. The boy had fallen asleep. Peter carried him to his bed, threw back the blankets, and laid him on the sheet. After untying the boy's boots and tugging them from his feet, Peter covered his son's snoring frame, kissed his forehead, and tiptoed from the room.

He returned to the chair, staring thoughtfully out the dark window. His bedroom door was closed. Behind it, the woman no doubt slumbered. What kept her here? She had family. He had mailed two letters for her to the parents-in-law who lived in Boston. Why did she choose to remain in this town rather than return to them? She said it was her children's graves, but there must be more.

Peter thought he knew. Love for the boy.

He had watched it blossom between the pair. The boy's questions tonight were not idle ones. Thomas looked at this woman — Summer — and saw her as more than his teacher.

Peter thought back on the years since Elsa's death. Having Elsa's grandmother here had always seemed to be enough. The woman had mothered Elsa through her childhood and young adulthood. She had done the same for Thomas. Peter had never considered that the boy needed anything more than his father and great-grandmother to care for him. Now, though, Thomas's words made Peter realize the boy longed for a mother.

Peter searched his own heart, bringing forth an image of *Frau* Steadman. There was much about her to admire. Her way with the boy, her kindness toward *Grossmutter,* her willingness to help in his house and assume chores that were not part of their bargain. Her appearance was also pleasing. Now that she was eating and filling out, she had lost the gaunt look. *Frau* Steadman was an attractive woman.

Peter rubbed the back of his neck. He wished to give his boy all the things that would make him happy, but on this one thing, should he not think of himself? While marriages of convenience were not uncommon, a marriage of convenience was not for Peter Ollenburger. Marriage for love — the same as he'd had for his dear Elsa — was all he could accept.

On Sunday morning, Summer awakened before dawn lit the room. She frowned, trying to determine what had pulled her from sleep, and then she heard it — the sound of a cough. She rose to her feet and left the bedroom. With her ear pressed against Thomas's door, she waited. The sound came again.

Alarm filled her breast, and she entered the room without knocking. She touched the boy's forehead. "Thomas? Are you sick?"

The boy opened his eyes and squinted upward. "Oh . . . Summer, I don't feel good." He coughed again.

"I'll get your father." She pulled on shoes, but she didn't take the time to button her coat — just slipped it on over her night-clothes and dashed through the frost-laden predawn to the barn. Pushing through the door, she called, "Mr. Ollenburger, come quickly!"

A scuffle sounded from a stall in the shadowed corner, then the man stepped into the murky light. He was attired in pants with suspenders over long johns, and his hair stood on end; his eyes appeared wild. *"Was? Was ist es?"*

"It's Thomas — he's sick." Summer choked back a sob as fear pressed like a weight on her chest.

Mr. Ollenburger turned back into the shadows. Summer danced with impatience beside the door. It seemed ages before he emerged with untied boots covering his feet and his coat flapping. "Come." He took her arm, and together they ran back to the house. When they entered Thomas's bedroom, *Grossmutter* was there, stroking the boy's hair and murmuring to him in low tones.

Whispering to her, Peter took the old woman by the shoulders and gently shifted her to the side. He leaned over his son. "What is wrong, boy?"

"My throat," he croaked. "It hurts."

The man sat on the edge of the bed. "Only your throat?"

The boy nodded.

Mr. Ollenburger looked up at Summer. "It is only his throat. Sore throats he gets when chilled he has been. He will be fine." He covered Thomas to the chin. "I will fix you a gargle, son. You rest."

The grandmother resumed her spot and continued to stroke Thomas's hair as Mr. Ollenburger guided Summer out of the room. Looking down at her, he smiled. "Come now, Summer Steadman, you must not look so troubled. Boys get sore throats. There is no need for such worry."

The sound of her name on his lips, delivered in the deep, gentle roll of thunder, touched Summer in a way she hadn't expected. She felt tears spurt into her eyes, and she covered her face, abashed by the reaction. His large hand touched her back, guiding her to the table, where he pulled out a chair and pressed her into it. Sitting across from her, he took her wrist.

"*Frau* Steadman, you must not worry so. Thomas will be fine."

She nodded but found she couldn't speak. A large knot of emotion blocked her voice box. She stared at his hand, which continued to hold her wrist. Could he feel the beat of her pulse pounding faster and faster?

"I must fix the boy a gargle, but first I think we pray together, *ja?* This will make you feel better?"

His concern for her brought a fresh rush of tears. What a good man he was — a good, gentle, caring man. She raised her gaze and gave another wordless nod.

A slight smile tipped his lips, then he lowered his head, closing his eyes. The prayer, delivered in German, washed over Summer like a healing balm. Although she understood not one word, the reverence and familiarity of the tone reached deep into her soul. *I want this for myself. I want the relationship with God Mr. Ollenburger has.*

At his amen, she opened her eyes. Giving her wrist a pat, he rose. "I fix Thomas his gargle now. You . . . go dress." Pink appeared on the tops of his ears. "We will not attend *Kleine Gemeinde* this morning, but I think we study together, *ja?*"

Summer pulled her coat snug across her chest, suddenly realizing she was still in her nightclothes. As she dashed to the bedroom, though, her heart tripped faster for a reason other than embarrassment. They would study together. Summer would ask him how she could form a relationship with his God.

18

The promised Bible study was delayed since Mr. Ollenburger spent the morning with Thomas. The boy, cranky from his fever and sore throat, wanted his father close. So the man sat on the bed and read aloud from his Bible while the boy drowsed. *Grossmutter* sat in her chair, her familiar shawl over her shoulders and her Bible in her lap. Occasionally the old woman's eyes slipped closed and her lips moved in silent communication. Praying, Summer assumed, and her heart caught each time. Oh, she longed to feel able to speak so freely with God!

As she sliced cabbage, potatoes, and onions for soup, Summer listened to the gentle flow of words from the bedroom, but to her frustration, she couldn't understand what was said. If she was going to stay in Gaeddert, perhaps she should learn to speak their language.

When the soup simmered on the stove, steaming the room with pleasant aromas, Summer retrieved her own Bible. She sat at the table and opened the Bible to the last place she had studied with Mr. Ollenburger. As she reread the passages from Philippians, she discovered her repeated readings had committed several verses to memory. She particularly liked verse thirteen of chapter four: *"I can do all things through Christ which strengtheneth me."* She wondered if that knowledge was what helped Mr. Ollenburger maintain his positive attitude in the face of discouragement.

The sound of a wagon intruded in her thoughts. *Grossmutter* looked up and sent Summer a look of puzzlement. Summer raised her shoulders in silent response, then rose and peered out the window. Mr. Penner and the man who had argued with Mr. Ollenburger on the road after her visit to town — Mr. Schmidt — pulled into the yard. What were they doing here?

Both men got down, stood for a moment beside the wagon in conversation, and then started toward the house.

"Mr. Ollenburger?" Summer moved to open the door. "You have visitors."

Mr. Ollenburger appeared in the boy's

doorway as Summer opened the door to the two men. Both men froze when they found Summer waiting inside the house. Their faces wore twin frowns of displeasure.

"Hello." Summer stepped back. "Won't you come in?"

The men entered, removing their hats.

"To what do I owe the honor of this visit?" Mr. Ollenburger asked as he shook their hands. Although he usually used German when addressing those from town, today he spoke in English.

"Ollenburger, we need to speak with you." Penner also used English. "But outside. Out of the hearing of . . . *her.*"

Mr. Ollenburger frowned. *"Frau* Steadman is guest in my home. Rude it would be to exclude her. Especially since my thought is this visit concerns her, *ja?"*

The two pursed their lips, and for a moment Summer wondered if they would leave without speaking. But then the one who had argued stepped forward, his eyes snapping.

"All right, *Herr* Ollenburger. I speak in front of . . . your guest." The way he said *guest* sent a chill down Summer's spine. "We hear that this woman now stays in your home, not in the *shariah.* We hear that she stays" — the man's face turned red — "in your sleeping room."

Summer's mind raced. Who would have said these things? Thomas stepped into the doorway of his bedroom, his bare feet sticking out below the hem of his nightshirt. The boy looked frightened. *Grossmutter* pushed herself from her chair and went to stand with an arm around his shoulders.

Mr. Ollenburger spoke. "*Ja,* this is true. But I think you misunderstand. The *shariah* was toppled in the same storm that destroyed *Herr* Ratzlaff's barn roof. So she stays here, and I stay in my barn."

Summer was proud of the way he stood up to the men with kind yet firm responses.

Thomas shivered, and *Grossmutter* leaned down to whisper in his ear. The boy shook his head, defiance sparking in his eyes. He pulled away, crossing to stand beside his father. "We're not doing anything wrong."

Peter looked down at him. "Boy, return to your bed."

"No, Pa." Thomas glared at the two men.

Summer took hold of Thomas's shoulders to turn him back to the bedroom, but the boy jerked free, his back stiff. "Summer — Mrs. Steadman is our friend. She's helping me with my studies. And she studies the

Bible with Pa. We're not doing anything wrong."

"*Junge,* return to your bed!"

Summer had never heard Mr. Ollenburger use that tone of voice. It startled her, and it was clear it startled Thomas, too. He looked up with wide eyes, then tears flooded. Without a word he turned and walked on stiff legs back to his bedroom. He slammed the door. *Grossmutter* opened the door, slipped inside, then closed it again much more softly than Thomas had.

Mr. Ollenburger turned to the men. "*Herr* Schmidt, *Herr* Penner, say what you came to say." The man's deep voice held no animosity.

Mr. Schmidt lifted his chin and glared at Mr. Ollenburger with narrowed eyes. "The church council asks you to send this woman from your home. If you do not follow this direction, there will be a meeting to discuss your removal from membership."

Summer gasped. She stepped forward, holding out her hands in entreaty. "Please, gentlemen, I don't wish to create problems for Mr. Ollenburger. I-I'll stay in the barn."

The two men nodded in satisfaction, but Mr. Ollenburger raised one of his hands. "Wait. Does the Bible not instruct us to love

265

our neighbors as ourselves? How am I showing Christian love by sending this woman to a cold barn? Is it not more neighborly to give her my room, the warmth of my fire?"

"You cause your brother to stumble!" Schmidt's eyes blazed.

"This I will consider," Mr. Ollenburger countered. "But the needs of this woman were placed on my heart by the God I serve. I must follow His guidance, not the counsel of men."

Mr. Penner released a snort. "You are a foolish man, Peter Ollenburger. Will you allow this woman to ruin your standing in our community?"

Mr. Ollenburger shook his head, and Summer read sadness in his expression. "More concerned I am with my standing with my Maker, *Herr* Penner. Now I ask you to leave. My boy is not feeling well, and your visit has upset him." He reached out with his large hand. "I thank you for your concern, and I will pray for God's guidance."

Neither Schmidt nor Penner reached to shake Mr. Ollenburger's hand. Instead, they slapped their hats back onto their heads and left without another word.

The moment the door closed behind

them, Thomas's door flew open and the boy cried, "I hate them, Pa! I hate them both!"

Peter's heart felt heavy in his chest. Regret, sadness, and frustration mingled, all fighting for release. He felt the woman's gaze follow him as he moved to the woodbox and chose two thick logs to add to the fire. When the task was done, he took a deep breath, which calmed him. Then he sat down at the table and gestured to the other chairs.

"Come here, boy. You, too, *Frau* Steadman. A talk we must have." *Grossmutter* stood in Thomas's bedroom doorway. With a smile, he invited her to come, too.

All three approached the table and seated themselves, *Grossmutter* between the boy and the woman. The old woman's gnarled hands crept out, palms up, and both Thomas and *Frau* Steadman placed their hands in hers. It gave Peter a good feeling to see the three of them united in such a way. Thomas thrust his chin out in a stubborn gesture, but the woman looked more sad than angry. Peter sighed. He hoped these words would help ease the aching hearts around this table.

"Thomas, you tell me — why do we not

have a dog on the property like so many others?"

The boy exchanged his sullen look for one of surprise. "Pa, you know why. I —" He glanced at the woman, then dropped his chin — "I'm scared of dogs."

"Why?"

Pink appeared in Thomas's cheeks. "Because one bit me when I was little."

"*Ja*, you carry the marks on your leg where you were bit. How many dogs have bit you, boy?"

Thomas lowered his brows. "Only one."

Peter turned to the woman. "*Frau* Steadman, when you find Thomas sick in bed, why do you run to me with fear in your eyes?"

The woman looked as confused as Thomas. "Because . . . because I —" She closed her jaw and tears appeared in the corners of her eyes.

Peter offered gently, "Because when you looked at the boy, you did not see a sore throat, you saw typhoid?"

Silently, the woman nodded.

Peter nodded, too. "Things from before make a difference in the now. Thomas, your scar reminds you dogs can bite. *Frau* Steadman, your memory reminds you fevers can bring death. You forget that not all dogs bite and not all sickness results in death. You know this here" — he tapped his forehead — "but in your heart, when faced with a dog or a fever, you forget."

He prayed inwardly for guidance. "It is the same way with people in town. They are not bad people, only frightened people who carry scars. Is good for Thomas to know these things as well as you, *Frau* Steadman. So please, both listen to me."

His heart twisted as he looked into *Grossmutter*'s faded eyes and forced himself to recall unpleasant bits of his past. "For many years, our people — the Mennonites — suffer much persecution. We are peaceful people. We do not want to fight in wars. But in Germany, the rule is if you are man, you do military duty. Our people say no, God does not wish us to take up a gun and point it at another human being. The government say if you live here, you must. And it makes things hard for us."

He shrugged. "So we go from our country. We go to Russia, where the leader says we can live and grow our wheat and not fight in their wars. For many years, this is allowed, but then things change. The Mennonites do too good with their farming, and the government becomes jealous. Soldiers come into our villages. They burn and they steal and they . . ." He swallowed hard, shaking his head to dispel the memories. "They make things very hard. And we know we can no longer stay."

Peter laced his fingers together and rested his hands on the table edge. A glance at his audience found attentive serious faces on both the boy and the woman. Even *Grossmutter* seemed to absorb his words, although he knew she understood little of what he said. He went on. "By God's grace, we are able to make it to this country — to America, land of many freedoms. Here we can worship as we please. Here we are not forced to be part of military. We make our village — our town Gaeddert — and no one comes to burn things or take things from us. We have peace. But —"

"But you can't forget," the woman's quiet voice interrupted.

Peter nodded. "We cannot forget what has been before. What we have lived has left its mark as surely as the dog's teeth left its mark on Thomas's leg."

Thomas tipped his head, his brow furrowed. "So the people in town aren't really mad at Summer. They're just scared?"

Peter cupped his son's head with his hand.

"That is right, son. They are scared of what she reminds them, and this makes them act as if angry."

Thomas chewed his lower lip. He released a sigh. "I don't really hate them. I was just mad at Rupert for telling his pa things he shouldn't have and at his pa for coming here and making me feel like I was bad."

Peter tousled the boy's hair. "*Ach,* I know this, boy. Your heart is too pure to allow hatred to grow there. You are good boy. And you must stay that way. Hatred hardens a heart. A hard heart is a bitter thing. We must to feel sorrow for these people, for the pain they have borne, rather than hate them. Can you do this?"

Thomas's chin quivered. "But they're going to make Summer go away."

"Would that be best, Mr. Ollenburger?" *Frau* Steadman spoke in a low tone.

Peter shook his head. "We cannot allow hatred and fear to have its way. You will help to show that we need not mistrust all people who are not of our heritage. God sent you here to teach us this lesson. Of that I am sure."

The woman's eyes filled with tears. Her face glowed with some emotion Peter could not recognize, but he knew she felt pleased by his words.

"Thank you." Her words quavered.

"And since that is settled, my stomach rumbles. I will slice bread. *Frau* Steadman, you dish soup. We will eat, *ja?* Together. Just like always." In his heart, Peter knew it was right. For now, it would be the four of them.

19

Thomas's fever and sore throat were much better by Monday morning, but Summer decided to allow him another day of rest. She wanted to take no chances with his full recovery. A fear still quivered in her chest regarding any type of illness. Mr. Ollenburger's words about the "before" impacting the "now" helped her understand her own fears and those of the people in town. They weren't bad people, only cautious. She would try to reflect on that if she had another less-than-pleasant encounter with one of them.

Grossmutter observed the mixing of pancake batter. She nodded her approval and murmured words Summer didn't understand. Even with the language barrier, it was nice to have the woman nearby. Summer chuckled to herself as she remembered her first impression of the grandmother and her worry at whether the old woman would resent her intrusion. The light of God that lit Mr. Ollenburger's heart also existed within the soul of *Grossmutter*. Although it had taken a few weeks for the old woman to trust her, Summer felt she had a friend in Thomas's great-grandmother.

Mr. Ollenburger came in for breakfast, his cheeks rosy with cold and blue eyes bright beneath his bushy brows. He smiled when he saw the stack of pancakes waiting. "*Frau* Steadman, I must tell you *danke schoen* for the cooking you do. I did not expect you to do this when I say come and teach my boy, but how nice it is to not be cooking all the time."

Summer felt a rush of pleasure at his words. "You're very welcome. I enjoy the cooking, so please don't consider it an inconvenience."

The man nodded, then turned away to hang up his coat. When he faced her again, his brow was furrowed. "Many days it has been since the graves you visited. When winter comes full force, visiting will be hard. Would you like to go today? It is cold, but the sun shines bright and the wind is not so strong."

"Yes, please," she said eagerly.

After breakfast, Mr. Ollenburger helped Summer into the wagon, and they headed toward the gravesites. The yellow sun did shine brightly, as the man had said, although it didn't produce much warmth.

The graves came into view, a stark row of gray stones against a backdrop of leafless growth. Small mounds of snow remained at the base of each headstone, with brown stalks of grass sticking through in careless clumps. Summer immediately knelt beside Tillie's grave and tugged at the tough grass. Mr. Ollenburger crouched nearby and helped. She sent him a grateful smile.

When the area was clear again, he got up. His tall form blocked the sun as he looked down at her. "I will go walk by the river for a while. You visit as long as you like." He turned and strode away, leaving her alone with her memories.

Summer shifted her attention to the headstones. One by one, she stroked the rough top of each stone, from little Tillie's up to Rodney's. When she reached his, she sat down on the ground and released a heavy sigh.

"Sometimes I envy you, Rodney." She stretched out her hand to touch the carved letters that formed his name on the cold sandstone. "Here you are, the children close by, while I'm far away from all of you. At first I wanted to die, too, so I could be with you. I had the same thought when I feared I might be buried in the shack." She swallowed hard and dared to admit, "Now I'm glad I'm not dead, although I do wish we were still all together."

She shifted her position, pulling her coat more snugly around her chin to better block the cool air. "Winter's coming, Rodney, and I don't know how many more times I'll be able to visit, so there is much I want to say to you today. First, I want to apologize. You and I didn't really have a loving marriage, did we? Oh, we got along well — we never fought or were unkind to each other. But since I've lived with Mr. Ollenburger and his family, I've become aware of what we lacked."

Closing her eyes, she remembered Mr. Ollenburger's face as he spoke of his Elsa. Tears stung her eyes. "It's too late for us to share an abiding love — a love that comes from the very depth of one's heart and fills the person with warmth and joy. If what Mr. Ollenburger says is true and you are in heaven, you must be feeling that kind of love there. Heaven must overflow with that kind of love."

Summer glanced over her shoulder toward

the river. Mr. Ollenburger was nowhere in sight. She turned back to Rodney's headstone. "Mr. Ollenburger speaks of God as if they share a friendship. You often spoke of God, and I'm sure you believed in His presence, but somehow it was . . . different."

She scowled as she tried to sort out her thoughts. "Even when we attended church, God always seemed distant to me — out of reach. When you and the children fell ill and I prayed to God to save you, it seemed He stayed away. Mr. Ollenburger assures me God was listening and cared, but He answered no. Mr. Ollenburger seems to find peace even when the answer he gets from God is no, but I . . ."

Biting on her lip, she paused. So many different emotions jumbled her mind. "Since I've been with the Ollenburgers, I've witnessed God close enough to touch. I want to know Him on a personal level — not in my head, like I did in Boston, but in my heart. I want to know without any doubt that He is here, that He cares, that He listens when I speak to Him."

Leaning forward, her voice dropped to a raspy whisper. "I want to experience joy, Rodney. *Real* joy. I'm sorry I didn't allow myself to find it with you. I'm sorry if by holding myself from you I kept you from finding it. Maybe we would have found it in Oklahoma, there on our own with no one but the Lord and each other to rely on. I'm sorry we didn't get a chance to find out. And I hope you'll forgive me if . . . if I find joy now, on my own, without you."

Her gaze drifted across the headstones carved with her children's names. Guilt washed over her as she realized what she had just said. She covered her face, releasing a groan. Oh, how she wanted the joy she had seen shining in the eyes of her benefactor! But did she deserve to feel joy if her children and husband were no longer here?

The crunch of feet on dry grass startled her, and she looked back to see Mr. Ollenburger slowly approach. His hands were thrust deep into his pockets, his shoulders hunched as if afraid to intrude. He offered a half smile and lifted one shoulder in a shy shrug. "I do not mean to rush you. Just checking on you I am, to see if you are ready to go back to a fire's warmth."

Summer rose and brushed off her skirts. She wasn't quite ready to go, but she could see the sense of returning to the house. Mr. Ollenburger had work to catch up on since he had spent Saturday at the Ratzlaffs' place. She gave one last lingering look at the headstones before allowing herself to take in the expanse of landscape that surrounded them. "They look so lonely here."

Mr. Ollenburger nodded. "*Ja.* With so much nothing all around, lonely they do seem."

Summer's heart rate increased with a sudden thought. "Mr. Ollenburger, do you know who owns the land in this area?"

He stepped closer. "Why you ask this?"

"I was thinking — you said it would be good for the people of Gaeddert to learn they need not fear all non-Mennonites. And I want to be near my . . . my family. If I were to purchase this little plot of ground, build a house here and live in it instead of your home, then your problems with the town would be solved."

"You wish to stay in Gaeddert for good? Not return to Boston?" He seemed surprised.

She hugged herself. "I need a fresh start, and Gaeddert is as good a place as any." She felt a small smile tug at her lips. "At least I have friends here — Thomas, your grandmother . . . and you."

The big man nodded, his expression serious. "*Ja,* your friends we are." He scratched his chin and his brow furrowed in thought. "This land, so close to the town, is owned by *Herr* Gaeddert's sons Heinrich and Bernard."

Summer looked again toward the graves. How easily she could envision a white-washed cottage. It would have green shutters, a wraparound porch, and a picket fence to surround the yard. She would build it to the right of the headstones, tucked between the two largest cottonwoods, where she could walk down the rise and visit the stones easily. If she planted some flowers in front of the porch, and perhaps a lilac bush under the windows, it would be a cheery place to live. Yes, she could be happy here.

"*Herr* Gaeddert. Is that the person who founded the town?"

"*Ja,* he bought all land from what you call land developer. Then he sold pieces to people to settle in town. Very wealthy businessman he was in Russia. Only two years in America and he dies, but his sons carry on in his name."

Summer considered this information. Surely the sons would be interested in selling the land. Keeping it gained them nothing. Would they sell to an outsider? She licked her dry lips as fear tumbled through her chest. What would she do if they re-fused?

Mr. Ollenburger touched her shoulder, bringing her attention back around. "*Frau* Steadman, you must pray. You must find out if this is what God would choose for you. If Gaeddert is in your plan, then a way will be made for your purchase of land. But prayer must to come first."

Fear slammed against her breast. She wanted so much to *belong* somewhere. Had she ever felt as if she belonged? Never — not with her parents, who had always seemed afraid to embrace her; not with her brother, whose wife viewed her as an intrusion; and not with Rodney, since his parents had never accepted her as part of their family.

All she loved was buried here on this little plot of land. She wanted to be near them. Her only prayers had concerned her family — *save them, save them,* she had begged — and God had taken them away. If she prayed now, might He take away this possibility, too? A war took place in her heart. The desire to draw close to Him — to trust Him the way Mr. Ollenburger did — battled with the fear of allowing Him to guide her if it could mean leaving this land and her family.

Peter watched the woman's face as she stared into the distance. She seemed pained — even tormented. An ache filled his chest. How hard she sought joy. She tried to find it here, on this barren land, where headstones proved she once had children and a husband. If she would only turn these hurts over to the Lord, her soul could find peace.

He took hold of her elbow and turned her to face him. "*Frau* Steadman, come here with me, please." She came without hesitation as he led her to the largest headstone, the one of her husband. He knelt on the flattened stalks of brown grass and gestured for her to join him.

Her face looked pinched as she knelt beside him in a graceful sweeping aside of skirts. She clasped her hands together beneath her chin, and he waited until her eyes slid closed.

"Dear Father . . ." Peter was so accustomed to praying in German, he found it difficult to form English words. Yet it was important the woman understand this prayer. He offered a silent plea in his native tongue for God to guide him, then went on haltingly. "This woman . . . has lost much.

Her heart aches with missing those who are no longer here. She wishes . . . she wishes to remain close to them. She wishes to buy this piece of land and stay in Gaeddert."

He paused, his eyes still tightly closed. "Your Book tells us that all days ordained for us were written before they came to be. You have a perfect plan for all lives who are born. You have perfect plan for Summer Steadman, too. I ask you to speak to her, to share your plan with her, so she might find peace and joy. You are a God who listens and a God who speaks. Listen to the longing of her heart, and answer what is your will for her.

"And, my dear Father, if your will is for her to stay, then I ask you to soften the hearts of those in town. Let them make her feel welcome. You are the God of miracles. I fear that is what it will take. But I trust you. I thank you for your loving care for us. In your Son's name I pray. Amen."

He opened his eyes to find the woman staring at him. Her dark eyes were bright with tears, her knuckles pressed to the underside of her chin. He rose, offering her his hand. "Come now. We go back and see how Thomas fares, *ja?* And today I build you a new bed."

20

Summer spent the afternoon baking bread while Thomas sat in the grandmother's rocking chair with a book. Just as she removed the last crusty, aromatic loaf from the oven, the door banged open and Mr. Ollenburger entered, carrying the chair he had purchased for her. Summer put down the loaf, turning toward the smiling man in surprise. "My chair!"

"*Ja,* your chair. It took some doing, but the pieces are together again." He pushed the door closed with his foot, then set the chair on the floor. His smile grew wider as Summer approached to circle the chair in wonder.

"But . . . but the roof must have broken it into pieces."

The man chuckled. "*Ja,* it did, for sure. But broken things are sometimes fixed. This time it worked."

Thomas approached and examined the back of the chair. "Did you make new back legs?"

Mr. Ollenburger shook his head. "*Nein,* boy. The back legs are the same. But broken in half they were from the weight of the roof. See here is what I did — this is good thing for you to know."

He crouched behind the chair, and Thomas imitated him. Summer watched over their shoulders as Mr. Ollenburger pointed to a ragged seam where the seat and back met. "See here? How the leg goes from the floor to the top of the chair? The leg snapped in the middle. So I take each half and drill a hole into the center of the wood. Then I carve dowels and fit the pieces around the dowel. This strengthens the pieces and holds them together again. After that, I put all pieces together like a big puzzle and use more dowels underneath" — he tipped the chair forward so Thomas could peek — "to give strength there, too."

He rose, his apologetic smile aimed at Summer. "It is not so pretty as it was. Some of the wood splintered, but I fill the spots with spackling and stain over it. From the front, you cannot tell. Even if it is not so pretty, it is strong. It will not collapse when you sit in it. You need not worry."

"I'm not worried." And to prove it, she sat in the chair and smiled up at both Thomas and Mr. Ollenburger.

The man laughed. "But this is not good place for you, right in front of the door. When your bed I bring in, I will knock into you."

She rose, her mouth dropping open in surprise. "You fixed my bed, too?"

"*Ja*. It did not take as much work as the chair, I tell you. Only replace one leg and pound all the dust from the mattress. An easy job." He lifted her chair and carried it to the corner, placing it next to the grandmother's rocking chair. "I will bring it in now if you and my son will go out of my way."

Summer and Thomas stepped well away from the door as Mr. Ollenburger struggled through with his burden. He leaned the bed's frame against the wall next to the grandmother's door rather than disturb her rest, then carried in the mattress and bedding. Last, he came with a rag-wrapped package, which he placed in Summer's hands.

"I think this will please you." The smile in his eyes made Summer's heart lurch.

"What is it?"

"Open and see."

She peeled back the layers of rag. "My teacup!"

He touched the delicate rim of the cup with one rough finger. "Surprised I was to find it all in one piece. The saucer was broken in two, but not even a chip does the cup have." He pushed his hands into his pockets. "I save the pieces from the plate, and I will glue them for you."

Tears filled her eyes. There were so many things this man had put back together for her. She looked up at him and found him watching her with a secretive smile on his lips, visible behind the bushiness of his beard.

"Is that bread I smell? Hungry it makes me. I will clean up for supper." He headed back outside.

That evening, after the Ollenburgers had retired to bed, Summer lit a lamp and sat in her chair with her Bible in her lap. She stumbled upon Second Corinthians, chapter four. As she read, her heart set up such a clamor it filled her ears. Bits and pieces seemed to leap from the page and fill her searching soul.

"For God, who commanded the light to shine

out of darkness, hath shined in our hearts, to give the light of the knowledge of the glory of God in the face of Jesus Christ . . ." How Summer wanted the darkness to slip away — for God to bring light to her heart.

"We are troubled on every side, yet not distressed; we are perplexed, but not in despair. . . ." She didn't understand why her family was gone — she would always feel perplexed by their abrupt departure — yet she wished to throw away the cloak of despair.

She read on to chapter five, and the first verse made her catch her breath. "We have a building of God, an house not made with hands, eternal in the heavens."

She straightened in her chair, remembering what Mr. Ollenburger had said about her children — they now lived eternally with God in heaven. Summer's heart pounded ever harder. How she wanted a building of God, too. She wanted to know that, someday, she would also reside eternally with Him.

"I want faith in you, God," she whispered into the quiet room. A peace settled around her heart. She felt a smile tug at her lips even as tears pricked her eyes. "You're here, aren't you? You're right here, waiting for me to invite you in."

Closing her eyes, she dropped to her knees. "Dear God, my heavenly Father, I believe in your Son. Let Him enter my heart. Flood my soul with His presence. Fill me with your joy."

As she opened her eyes to the simple room lit by flickering lantern glow, Summer's heart sang with the knowledge of God's love for her. For an instant, she thought she heard Him murmur, with great tenderness, "*My* Summer . . ."

The joy had come.

Grossmutter tapped Peter's coat sleeve and tipped her head toward *Frau* Steadman, who walked on his other side. The old woman's eyes shone with pleasure. Peter looked again at the woman, so straight and proud beside him. He shook his head with wonder, giving *Grossmutter* a smile to acknowledge he understood her silent message.

Not once throughout the church service had the woman cringed with shame or prickled with anger when the people in town stared or whispered. Now, walking out, she smiled and nodded silent greetings, even though few responded with more than looks of distrust. Something had changed her.

He knew what. There was a new light shining in her eyes, an awareness of her own value he had not seen before. In the past days Summer Steadman had discovered her God. Although eager to ask her about it, he hesitated. New faith could be a private thing, and she seemed to be a private woman. He would not push her, much as he longed to celebrate this victory with her. In a way, he believed it to be his victory, too.

Thomas peeked around *Grossmutter* at his father. "Pa, are we going anywhere today for *faspa?*"

Before Peter could answer, *Herr* Schmidt approached and took hold of Peter's coat sleeve. "Ollenburger, a word we will have with you," *Herr* Schmidt nearly snarled in German. "Inside." He released Peter's sleeve and strode away, his back stiff.

Peter glanced at the woman, who simply raised her eyebrows and offered a nervous smile. *Grossmutter* patted his arm, offering silent reassurance. He turned to his son. "I will answer when done I am inside."

His feet felt heavy as he plodded back to the church. He passed through the door, which *Herr* Schmidt had left open, and stepped into the almost empty sanctuary.

The deacons and Reverend Enns waited in a forbidding row on the front pew. Peter swallowed the uneasiness that filled his throat and stood in the front of the church facing them.

"What is it you want of me?" He spoke in German.

Herr Schmidt opened his mouth, but Reverend Enns put out his hand, addressing Peter himself. "Peter, the council has heard that you allow the woman whom you hired to provide teaching for your son to live in your house and reside in —" the older man's voice cracked — "to reside in your own sleeping room. I ask you to either refute or confirm this claim."

Peter clasped his hands together behind his back, praying silently for courage. "As I told *Herr* Schmidt and *Herr* Penner, my *shariah* was destroyed in the storm. So the woman does reside beneath my roof. She was using my sleeping room at the time of their visit."

Herr Schmidt and *Herr* Penner exchanged looks of satisfaction.

"And also I told them," Peter continued calmly although his stomach quivered in tension, "that no longer do I reside in the house. I have taken residence in the barn."

Reverend Enns shot each of the deacons a stern glance. "He speaks the truth? This is what he told you?"

"*Ja,* it is what he said, but —"

The reverend cut off Herr Schmidt's words with a raised hand. "This part should have also been expressed to the council."

Peter added, "The woman has a bed now in the room of my wife's grandmother. But still, I stay in the barn."

The two men exchanged another look that seemed to show disgust more than satisfaction. He waited while Reverend Enns stroked his beard and appeared to study the ceiling beams. The deacons, waiting on the bench, stared at their own feet and examined their fingernails while waiting for their leader to speak again.

At last the reverend addressed Peter. "For many years you have lived and worked in Gaeddert. You have proven yourself to be a man of integrity. Having this woman reside in your home casts suspicion and creates concern. Yet I am aware, from having spoken with Dr. Wiebe, that this woman was offered no other alternatives. You have fulfilled a biblical admonition of feeding the widowed by providing a home for her in her time of need. Yet, a widowed woman and a widower . . ." He shook his head. "I face a dilemma."

"Reverend, may I speak?" Peter requested.

A wave of the man's hand granted permission.

"This woman is a widow and an orphan. All of her family is buried on land owned by the Gaeddert family. She desires to purchase the land and build a small home of her own. She desires to remain in Gaeddert."

"But she is not Mennonite!" *Herr* Penner burst out.

Reverend Enns shot him a silencing look before turning back to Peter. "Continue, Peter."

"If the Gaedderts are willing to sell her the land, she will have a home of her own as soon as one can be built. That will, no doubt, be spring. In the meantime, she must have a place to live for the winter. My Thomas needs her. A very good teacher she is to him, and convenient it is to have her so near."

"But in your *home*," *Herr* Schmidt spluttered, his face red.

"In my home with a chaperone," Peter corrected.

Herr Schmidt waved his hand. "Bah! A

293

chaperone! A woman who is old, who sleeps much, and whose eyesight is failing."

"I cannot change the age or eyesight of *Frau* Suderman. Old she may be, but alert. She sees what needs seeing with her eyes." Peter could tell his words did not relieve either Schmidt or Penner. He squared his shoulders. "If you have concerns, I suggest this. You come to my place, you visit without warning, you see if anything improper goes on. If ever you find something that is against my Maker's commandments, I will move myself into the hotel until the woman's home is built. This is my vow to you."

A whispered consultation took place among the men while Peter stood silently and waited. He felt sweat tickle between his shoulder blades, and his heart seemed to beat at twice its normal rhythm. A silent prayer repeated in his head — *Your will, Lord. Let this be according to your will.*

Suddenly *Herr* Schmidt shot to his feet and stormed from the church. Reverend Enns waited until the door had slammed behind the man before facing Peter once more.

"Peter, we feel you have been honest today, and you are sincere in your desire to do what is right. We will do as you have suggested — make visits to your place without notice." He paused for a moment, tugging at the end of his thick beard. "It saddens me that others will not approve of this decision. There may be conflict among our membership. But we will pray for hearts to accept even in disagreement. Thank you, Peter. You may go."

He held in his sigh of relief until he was outside the church. Then he let it go with a huge dispelling of breath. He looked around, surprised to see few people had left the churchyard. Heat built in the back of his neck. They must have waited to hear what the council had decided. Well, they would not hear it from him. He turned toward the wagon, where Thomas, *Grossmutter,* and *Frau* Steadman waited.

Thomas crossed the yard to meet him. "So, Pa, can we? Can we go to *faspa* at the Penners'?"

Peter felt certain they would not be welcome at the Penners' home. He ushered the boy to the wagon. "Thomas, I think we go home and eat there."

Thomas's shoulders deflated. "But I never get to see my friends." Then he brightened. "May I invite the Krafts to our place for *faspa?* It's only Toby and his folks — it wouldn't take much to feed them. And maybe Toby and I could play in the barn?"

Peter looked to *Frau* Steadman. He did not wish to put her in an uncomfortable position.

"I think it would be good for Thomas to have time with his friends," she said. "You invite them. I can stay in the bedroom if they'd rather not spend time with me. I'll take Thomas's books with me and plan his lessons for next week."

The boy made a sour face, and she laughed, reaching out to tousle his hair. Peter noticed *Frau* Schmidt, Malinda, and *Frau* Penner scowling in their direction. He shifted his position to block them from the woman's view. "If you are sure . . ."

"I'm quite sure. Invite your friends, Thomas. Please don't allow me to disrupt your normal routines." She smiled. "Truly, I'll be fine."

Peter looked into Thomas's eager face. "Go and ask them. But walk slow, and do not be disappointed if other plans they already have."

Thomas gave him an innocent grin. "I won't be, Pa. I'll be right back."

The woman's eyes followed the boy, fondness in their depths. When she looked up to find Peter watching her, her cheeks took on a pink hue that he believed was not related to the cold.

Peter gestured toward the wagon. "Come. If company we are to have, we must hurry home and prepare."

He had just settled *Grossmutter* and the woman when Thomas returned. The boy's breath came out in little puffs with his effort to keep from running.

"They're coming, Pa!" Thomas reached for his father, and Peter hefted him into the back of the wagon. The boy leaned forward to touch the woman's shoulder. "Summer, Mrs. Kraft said she'd like to get to know you."

Peter watched the woman's fine eyebrows shoot upward. "She did?"

Thomas nodded. "So you won't have to hide in the bedroom."

Peter sucked in his breath. The boy's outspokenness could be hard to bear.

But Summer merely released a light laugh. "You don't want me working on too many lessons for next week, I'm thinking." Her voice held a teasing lilt.

Peter couldn't help but grin as he pulled himself into the wagon. Yes, the woman had changed. He picked up the whip. "Giddap! A *faspa* we must prepare."

21

Peter had almost forgotten how pleasant *faspa* could be. The last ones he and the boy had attended had been tense affairs, with people giving warnings about the woman. This time, though, only happy conversation took place around the table. After the simple lunch of cold sausage, *zweibach,* and sand plum *moos* had been consumed, the two boys went to the barn to play in the hay. *Grossmutter* murmured her farewells and toddled to her bedroom to rest. Peter, Summer, and the Krafts remained at the table to chat.

Out of the corner of his eye, Peter watched *Frau* Steadman with *Frau* Kraft as he talked shipping prices with *Herr* Kraft. He had always thought Katherine Kraft a kind woman, and his heart swelled in gratefulness as he saw the stirrings of friendship develop between the two very different women.

Where *Frau* Steadman was dark in hair and eyes, *Frau* Kraft was nearly white haired with pale green eyes. *Frau* Steadman, although heavier than when she had arrived, still seemed very thin when compared to *Frau* Kraft's sturdy frame. But it became clear they had found common ground as the two visited and laughed as if known to one another for many years. It was good to see this happen. If *Frau* Steadman were to stay, she would need friends to help her feel at ease.

Although Peter would not have minded visiting longer, after an hour of talk *Herr* Kraft rose. "Come, wife. Long enough we have stayed here. We must get you home now for some rest."

Frau Steadman looked up sharply, concern in her eyes. "Rest? Are you ill?"

Frau Kraft shook her head, a smile lighting her features. "*Nein,* Summer — not ill. Another child I expect in the spring. Many I have lost. We are being very careful."

Peter was surprised that Katherine Kraft would share something so personal with someone she had just met. How would *Frau*

Steadman respond to this news? Having lost her own children, would this send her to despair? He watched *Frau* Steadman's reaction, his chest constricting.

"Oh, Katherine, a baby is happy news. I will be praying for you."

Peter nearly reeled. Although no happy light shone in her eyes, her words were soft, empathetic. He knew she meant them. This woman surely had changed!

Frau Kraft rose, reaching to take *Frau* Steadman's hands. "I have enjoyed my time with you, Summer." Her gaze swept to include Peter. "You come for Thanksgiving dinner on Thursday."

The invitation was issued as if for a family. Peter felt heat on the back of his neck. *Frau* Steadman looked to him, and he stammered an answer. "Y-you are very kind, *Frau* Kraft. I had forgotten Thanksgiving was so near." He swallowed. Should he accept the invitation or would it be best to refuse? What was proper? He saw longing in *Frau* Steadman's eyes, and his answer came without thought. "We will come. I bring you some dried apple pies, *ja?*"

Frau Kraft gave a happy nod and released *Frau* Steadman's hands. "Good. Summer, I will see you very soon, hmm? Take care."

Peter followed the Krafts to the door, where *Herr* Kraft bellowed for Toby. The boy came running. Thomas followed more slowly. By their smiles, it seemed the boys had enjoyed their time together.

Thomas pressed himself beneath Peter's arm, lifting his hand to wave at his friend as the Krafts' wagon neared the road. Peter smiled down at the boy, and then he froze. Very near his elbow stood the woman, watching the wagon, her expression serene. His heart took up a mighty thumping. He suddenly felt very much as if they were a family — child, father . . . and mother.

As if sensing his scrutiny, the woman looked up. A soft smile tipped up the corners of her lips. "They are nice people."

He nodded silently. His breathing felt irregular. He was not sure he would find words if he tried to speak. Finally he managed to croak, "*Ja.* Fine people, for sure."

"I'd be glad to make those pies for you. I've never baked with dried apples, but I can't imagine it would be much different than fresh apple pie."

So easily she accepted the invitation to attend the Thanksgiving meal. So comfortable she seemed about going visiting with him and his family.

"*Ja.* Not much different it is. My crusts, sometimes they do not hold together so good."

Thomas laughed, peering up at his father. "Your pie crusts are better than your bread."

The woman laughed, too. Her eyes crinkled into a smile as she looked at Thomas — the way a mother might look with fondness at her own child.

Peter swallowed hard. "If you want to make pies, *Frau* Steadman, you are welcome to make pies." He gave Thomas a little push toward the house. "Go in now, boy, and rest. Look at a book if you like, but rest your ribs."

Thomas sighed but obeyed.

The woman stepped back into the house and Peter followed, closing the door behind them. Suddenly he felt uneasy in the house with her. Being invited to attend a holiday meal together, standing together on the porch waving good-bye to guests . . . All had felt too much like they belonged together.

What should he say to her now? He was not sure what she expected from him. He wanted to go to the barn and sort out these odd feelings, but before he could voice that thought, the woman spoke.

"Mr. Ollenburger, will you please sit down? I'd like to speak with you."

Stars glimmered in a sky of deep gray. The moon hung heavy and full, the shadows of craters clearly discernible. The air was so cold and crisp that Summer's eyes felt as if they froze between blinks, but she kept them open as long as possible to absorb the beautiful November night. She sighed skyward. "What a perfect end to the day."

Mr. Ollenburger's head turned in her direction. Though the shadows hid his expression, she suspected a smile lingered on his face. "*Ja,* it has been good day. Good food, good company, good time."

From the back of the wagon, Thomas inserted, "My belly hurts. I ate too much pie."

Summer and Mr. Ollenburger shared a soft laugh. Summer was amazed at how easily she had fit in at the Kraft house today. Two other families had also attended, both headed by widows, so the house had been quite full. When Summer had walked in and seen the number of people, she had wanted to get in the wagon and go back to the Ollenburger place. All those children running around had nearly turned her heart inside out with desire for Vincent, Rose, Tod, and Tillie.

But Mr. Ollenburger's warm hand on her back had assured her all would be fine, and it had been. She'd had a wonderful time visiting again with Katherine Kraft. How she prayed this new baby would arrive healthy and strong! She also enjoyed getting to know Bertha Klein and Martha Jost. While at first Mrs. Klein and Mrs. Jost had been reticent, by the middle of the day they had relaxed, treating her with friendliness. She still felt the warmth of their kindness even in the cold night air.

"Did you have an opportunity to visit with Mr. Kraft?" Summer asked.

Mr. Ollenburger cleared his throat. "*Ja,* I visit plenty with *Herr* Kraft since we were only two men there."

Summer scowled in his direction, even though she knew he couldn't read her expression. "Stop teasing me, Mr. Ollenburger. I meant about what we had discussed earlier." She glanced over her shoulder at Thomas, then lowered her voice. "About the land?"

His head nodded twice.

"And what did he say?"

"He say . . ." His voice sound tight, and Summer's heart picked up its tempo. "The

305

Gaeddert boys will probably ask council's advice before agreeing to sell land to someone not of our sect. But he did not say right off he thought they would refuse you."

It wasn't the answer she hoped for. She had been on tenterhooks since Sunday, when she had asked Mr. Ollenburger to inquire about the land she wished to purchase. She had hoped having him ask would eliminate an immediate negative response. "Did he have any idea when the council might meet?"

Mr. Ollenburger's broad shoulders raised in a shrug. "He did not say. First the Gaedderts must be talked to. *Herr* Kraft says he will do this for you."

Summer's eyebrows shot upward. "He will?"

"*Ja.* Tobias Kraft is fair man. He does not wish for you to be mistreated."

Summer wondered if Mr. Ollenburger's prayers for the town to accept her were already at work. The day truly had been a pleasant one. If these few people had decided not to fear her, surely others would soon follow suit. She became even more determined to purchase that piece of land and remain in Gaeddert. And if that were possible, it would become a day of thanksgiving for her in the truest sense.

A light snore sounded from the wagon bed, and Summer glanced back. Thomas lay stretched out in the hay beside *Grossmutter*'s hip, his arm curled beneath his head. She smiled, remembering how Tod had often slept that way, using his elbow as a pillow. It surprised and pleased her that pain did not stab with the memory. There was only a coil of remembrance coupled with a sense of regret that those days were over. She was healing, she realized, thanks to God's intervention.

The wagon rumbled into the yard, and Thomas sat up, yawning. Mr. Ollenburger lifted out Thomas and the grandmother before helping Summer down. "Since late it is, I will put away the oxen and stay in the barn. Thomas, you can tuck yourself in tonight?"

"Sure, Pa. If I need something, *Grossmutter* and Summer will be here."

Summer put her arm around the boy's shoulders. "I've learned to say *schlop die gesunt.* I'll see that he's properly tucked in."

Mr. Ollenburger gave a nod, then urged the oxen into moving. Summer opened the door and followed Thomas and his great-grandmother inside. The boy yawned as he took off his coat and hung it up.

"I'm sure you're ready for sleep," Summer said.

"Yes, but I had fun today. Did you?" Thomas's hair stood on end with bits of straw stuck in the thick strands.

Summer plucked the straw out as she answered. "I had a very enjoyable day."

"Felt good," the boy said, his gaze never wavering from Summer's face, "to have you there with Pa and *Grossmutter* and me. I . . . I like you a lot, Summer."

For the first time Summer opened her arms and embraced the boy. His arms wrapped around her waist as if he'd never let go. She felt tears prick her eyes as she breathed in the dusty little-boy smell. How good it felt to hold the child.

"I like you, too, Thomas." She swallowed against tears that threatened to burst forth. With effort, she removed herself from his hug. Smiling down at him, she added, "It was a special Thanksgiving for me. Thank you for including me."

"Our first Thanksgiving together . . ." Thomas tipped his head, peering at her with bright eyes. "Do you figure we'll always remember it?"

Summer considered the question. It was her first Thanksgiving without her children, her first Thanksgiving away from Boston, her first Thanksgiving as one of God's children. Her first Thanksgiving with Peter and Thomas Ollenburger. "Yes." Her lips trembled as she formed a smile. "I will always remember it."

"Good." Thomas gave her another impulsive hug, then he headed toward his bedroom. He paused at the door to call back, "*Schlop die gesunt,* Summer."

"*Schlop die gesunt,* Thomas."

He said good-night to his grandmother and then closed the door.

Summer turned to find *Grossmutter* behind her. She had forgotten the other woman was in the room, she'd been so caught up with Thomas. The old woman's gaze seemed to penetrate to Summer's very soul. Summer held her breath. Would the grandmother be angry with her for hugging the boy?

The grandmother stepped closer, cupped Summer's cheek with her hand, and spoke soft German words. The gentle wrinkled fingers patted Summer's face before she removed her hand, clasped it to her shawl, and hobbled into her bedroom.

Summer stared at the woman's retreating back, replaying the words in her mind. The grandmother was pleased, she realized. The thought brought a rush of gratefulness.

Summer stood in the kitchen for long minutes while images of the day swept over her. Although she would carry many pleasant memories of this day, none could compare with the remembrance of the hug from Thomas at day's end, followed by the old woman's open acceptance.

She pressed a hand to her chest. Although she had repeated Thomas's words — had said, "I like you, Thomas" — she knew her feelings were deeper. She loved the boy. Somehow, in these past weeks, her heart had opened to loving Thomas Ollenburger.

Her breath caught. When she purchased her land and moved into her own little house, she would no longer have this daily contact with Thomas. She knew she didn't want to leave the boy. But she couldn't have the boy without the father.

Slowly she removed her coat and hung it up. She stoked the stove, listened briefly at Thomas's door, smiling when she heard his snore, then entered the room she shared with the grandmother. She slipped into her nightclothes, then climbed between the sheets, her thoughts drifting once more to the father.

She had found her comfort in being in

the father's home. Was she meant to belong in the father's heart, as well?

Peter lay on the blanket-covered mound of straw, his hands beneath his head, staring at the dark ceiling. A few dancing shadows entertained his tired eyes as his thoughts drifted back over the day.

He could still see Tobias Kraft's eyebrows rise in surprise when Peter asked whether he thought the Gaedderts would sell *Frau* Steadman some land on which to build a house. Tobias's response had caused Peter's eyebrows to shoot downward: *"Her own house she is building? But we thought you intended to have her be with you."*

With him. Married to him, he knew Tobias meant. His face burned with the memory. He had watched the woman all day, staying close in case she needed a friend. She had fit in well with the women — they had seemed to accept her. Was their willingness to do so because they thought she would soon be Mrs. Peter Ollenburger?

He struggled again with figuring out people's thoughts. At first all were opposed to the woman being at his home. *"She is an outsider." "She is not of our faith." "She should go back to her own people."* Their comments rang in his head. What had made the change? Had they recognized, as he had, the light of God's presence shining on her face? Had the visits from the deacons — visits that usually came after the supper hour when he, *Grossmutter,* the woman, and the boy were all together in the house — finally proven that nothing unseemly occurred beneath his roof? Or were they opening themselves to her out of consideration for him, believing he would make her his wife?

How he wished to be wise enough to understand all things, to be able to say, "Ah, that is so," and *know* things.

Summer Steadman was a good woman, that much he did know. She had proven herself a good mother in her kindness toward Thomas. She had proven herself a good wife in her assuming of household duties. But *his* wife? Did he *want* her to be his wife?

Images of Elsa played through his mind. So many there were to remember. Elsa the child, with impish grin and dimpled cheeks, flowers in the braids that fell sweetly across her shoulders. Elsa the teenager, peeking at him with fluttering lashes, letting him know she found him pleasing despite his big size and clumsy hands. Elsa the young wife, smiling from the stove or across the table — always smiling. Elsa the new mother, cradling a sleeping Thomas, an expression of tenderness on her face.

How he had loved his Elsa. Even now his heart beat with the memory of the love they had shared. Could he even consider taking another wife? Could he ever love another woman the way he had loved his Elsa?

"*Lieber* Lord, for sure it would solve problems if we were to wed. Summer Steadman would have a home. Thomas would have a mother. The people in town who point fingers and accuse would have no more grounds to suspect wrongdoing. But I do not know what is your will." He brought down his hands, thumping the covers in disgust. "And I am too tired to think on it tonight. I give it to you, Lord. You work things out according to what is best for the boy, for the woman, and for me. I sleep."

Still, it was many hours before Peter was able to sleep. In his mind, images of his dear Elsa kept playing, along with those of Summer Steadman.

22

On a morning in mid-December, Summer stood at the window and peered out between delicate whorls of hoarfrost. Fresh snowfalls had coated the ground with meringue. The frosty scene made her shiver, and she cupped her hands around the steaming cup of coffee. She whispered a prayer, thanking God for the sturdy roof over her head and the warmth of the Ollenburgers' stove.

Mr. Ollenburger must have been cold in the barn. Yet what else could they do? The *shariah* had been turned into kindling, and he couldn't live in the house while she was in it. Although he'd never shared what had taken place in the church the Sunday *Herr* Schmidt had summoned him, she suspected the evening visits from various townsmen were a result of that meeting. Often she prayed that whatever the men were seeking when they tapped on the door and spent a few minutes surveying the room and carrying on stilted conversations with Mr. Ollenburger, the finding would please them.

Releasing a sigh that steamed the windowpane, she turned and seated herself at the table. She traced her finger along the pattern in the table's wood grain and imagined the house she hoped to build. Would the Gaeddert brothers allow her to buy the land? Her house needed to be started as soon as possible.

Thomas was doing well. If the weather were less frigid, he could make the trek to school each day. School would close down for a lengthy Christmas break soon, but once the break was over in late January, Mr. Ollenburger would surely allow Thomas to go back. What would she do then? Mr. Ollenburger had promised she could stay at his place as long as she needed to, yet she felt bad about displacing him to the barn. The man should be able to reside in his own home.

As if thoughts of him could make him appear, the door swung open and he entered, allowing in a gust of cold air teased with snowflakes. She leaped from the table and rushed to close the door as he stomped snow from his boots.

"Brr!" He shook his head, sending more snowflakes into the room. "It is cold this morning! And the sky looks very gray and threatening in the east. More snow is coming, I predict."

"Well, we don't need any more than we've got now on this floor." She grabbed a rag and stooped to clean up the mess. "I just scrubbed the floor yesterday. Couldn't you stomp off outside?"

"Cranky you are this morning, *Frau* Steadman."

At his calmly given statement, warmth flooded her cheeks. Had she really scolded him for mucking up his own floor? If she was being territorial, it was definitely time to move into her own place. She shot to her feet and turned her back on him.

"I-I apologize for snapping at you. It was foolish of me."

He chuckled — a deep, soothing sound. "*Ach,* nothing foolish about wishing to keep floors clean. Scrubbing is not pleasant. Grateful I am that you do it. I will stomp off outside next time."

She peeked at him. He grinned, his eyes sparkling, his nose brighter red than his cheeks. His beard bore tiny droplets of melting ice. He looked very appealing. She managed to squeak, "Thank you."

"The wind bites this morning." He hung his coat, and she scurried to the stove to pour him a cup of coffee. "To town I must go to —" He looked toward Thomas's door and lowered his voice. "Where is the boy?"

Summer handed him the cup. "He's still asleep. He stayed up late last night reading, so I let him sleep in this morning."

"And *Grossmutter?*"

"I haven't heard a sound from her, either. The cold seems to bother her in the morning. Perhaps she's decided to stay beneath the warmth of her covers a bit longer."

"That is fine." He took a noisy slurp of coffee. "I must go to town to pick up packages from Nickels'. Will you see to the boy while I am gone?"

"Of course I will." It was no chore to see to Thomas.

"I pick up the things I order for Christmas." A grin spread across his face, crinkling his eyes. "Not much longer till Christmas is here."

"I was hoping you were going to town today," she said. "Will you see if my order has come in at Nickels'?" He nodded, and she reached into Elsa Ollenburger's apron pocket to withdraw an envelope and two pennies. "And would you mail this for me?"

He took it, looking at the address with his brow furrowed.

"It's to my parents-in-law," she explained. "I want them to know I'm still in Gaeddert should they choose to contact me."

"You write, but they do not write back." Mr. Ollenburger's face reflected his concern.

She shrugged, feeling a pang of loneliness. "I didn't expect them to. Things were strained between Rodney and his parents even before we left. His father made it clear that Rodney was no longer considered a part of his family when we announced our decision to leave. They never cared for me, although I know they loved the children. So I feel obligated to keep in touch with them."

"What about your brother? Why do you not write to him, too?" Mr. Ollenburger slid her letter into one of the big front pockets of his coat.

On the stove, the lid of a pot began to jiggle. Summer returned to the stove and scooped cornmeal into the boiling water. "My brother and his wife took me in after my parents died, but with great reluctance. William was fourteen when I was born, and he married young. We really didn't know each other. He and his wife had two children

318

by the time my parents died. At first his wife thought I would be helpful with the children, but apparently I didn't meet her expectations, because I was with them less than a year before they sent me to boarding school. I stayed there until I was sixteen."

Mr. Ollenburger leaned against the wall and held his hands out to the stove. "What is this — boarding school?"

"A school where you live. You don't just go to class and come home, you stay there."

"And this is a good thing?"

Summer released a brief huff of humorless laughter. "It was better than living with my brother's wife. But I think it's a sad thing for children to be away from their families." *Just as it's a sad thing for parents to be away from their children,* her thoughts continued. Were Rodney's parents finding comfort while missing their son? She wished she knew. Perhaps the contents of her letter — the lesson she had learned by putting her faith in God and giving Him her heartache — would help them.

She swallowed and went on. "I did receive a very good education, and I'm thankful for that. Education is an important thing."

"As important as family?"

"Nothing is more important than family."

Summer was surprised by the vehemence in her voice.

"*Ja.*" Mr. Ollenburger stroked his beard as he peered at her with a thoughtful expression. "How alone you must have felt, away from your parents and brother at that school."

Summer stirred the pot. She felt tears pricking at his kind understanding, but she held them at bay. "Less alone than I felt after Rodney and the children died."

He touched her arm. "*Frau* Steadman, how old are you?"

"I am twenty-nine." She looked up at him, puzzled by the question. "Why?"

He removed his hand and slid it into his trouser pocket. "You were a young bride, then."

She tipped her head. "Yes, I suppose I was. No one seemed to think I was too young, however. My sister-in-law was very eager to see me wed. She could be rid of me then, you see." She offered a weak smile.

"You are still a young woman. Do you —" his ears turned bright red — "do you ever wish to have another family?"

Immediately she turned her attention to the pot of bubbling cornmeal mush. "I don't know." Why was he asking this?

He moved to the table and sat down, drawing his hand down his beard. "If the Gaeddert boys do not choose to sell you the land, what will you do?"

The question had plagued her for days, but she hadn't come up with an answer. She answered the same as she had his previous question. "I don't know."

"*Ja,* well, not many options are available in Gaeddert, for sure. Let us hope for the best."

Summer scooped servings of the mush into bowls and carried them to the table. Mr. Ollenburger offered a brief prayer of thanks, and they picked up spoons and ate in silence. Summer replayed the conversation they had shared. It was more personal than any other. How far their friendship had developed.

Halfway through breakfast, Mr. Ollenburger said, "I will go see the Gaedderts when in town I am today. Spring will be here before long, and plans you need to be making."

A rock settled in her stomach at his words. His questions about her age and her future plans suddenly painted an unpleasant picture. They seemed to indicate an eagerness to see her off on her own. She supposed she shouldn't be surprised. The townspeople had certainly put pressure on him to send her from his property. To be truthful, she hadn't met many people who desired to keep her close. Yet it hurt more, coming from this man who'd always been so kind. She closed her eyes for a moment, breathing a silent prayer for God to remind her she was wanted by Him.

Peter lowered the flaps on his new cap to cover his ears, then hunched his shoulders to bring the jacket up around his neck. The wind still managed to sneak beneath the fabric and send chills down his body. Inside his gloves, his fingers felt stiff, and he could hardly wait to reach Gaeddert and Nickels' Dry Goods, where he could stand beside the fire and thaw out.

All the woman had shared with him this morning burdened his heart. His childhood had not always been easy — people taunted his big size and clumsiness, and often unkindness touched his family because their beliefs were different. Nevertheless, he had been loved and wanted. First by his parents, then by his Elsa, and now by his dear son and community. And of course he had known always of God's love for him, which touched him deep below the skin.

This woman, though . . .

"Why, dear Lord, did you take her husband and children when so little she had to love her?" he wondered aloud. His breath created a steamy cloud of moisture that clung to his beard and froze, making his face feel stiff. "Was it the only way you had to reach her? I do not understand your ways, Lord, but I trust you have plan in mind for her. She is special woman."

His heart tripped at his own words. So often he found himself admiring her. He clenched his fist around the whip. "But do I love her?" His breath came faster, stinging his nose as he sucked in frigid air. "I do not even know my own heart, God. You must help me."

In town, he stopped the team in front of Nickels' and pushed himself from the seat. Stiff from the cold, he moved slower than usual as he entered the store. The warmth enveloped him, and he drew a grateful breath to be out of the weather. Nick was helping another customer, so Peter went to the stove to warm his hands and wait his turn. The heat sent needles of pain through his fingers, and he rubbed his palms together, clenching his teeth against the discomfort. By the time Nick joined him, his hands had adjusted and no longer prickled.

"*Guten morgen,* Peter," Nick greeted. "You have come for your Christmas packages?"

"*Ja.* The bicycle, it has come?"

Nick crooked a finger. "Come see." He guided Peter to the storeroom.

Peter admired the shiny metal of the bicycle. Jet black and sleek, with nickel-plated handlebars and a soft leather seat, it was sized for a boy. Peter could not stop the smile from building as he imagined Thomas's joy on Christmas morning. He patted the seat, nodding. "*Ja,* this is fine one."

"I ordered some rubber tires in the size to fit the bicycle, in case the pneumatic tires do not hold up to our rough roads," Nick said. "They are here if you need them."

"That is kind of you. *Danke.*" Peter rolled the bicycle to the counter and put down the little kickstand to hold it in place. "The other things, they are all here?"

Nick nodded. He hefted a package from behind the counter, thumping it onto the countertop. He disappeared again, then emerged with a second bundle. "This is *Frau* Steadman's order. You will take it, as well?"

"*Ja,* I will do that." He patted the brown-paper-wrapped bundle. What was inside? Things for the boy, probably. "I thank you for your help in making it a happy Christmas for my boy." Peter paused, biting the inside of his lip. He wished it to be a happy Christmas for the woman, too. If the Gaedderts said yes on the land, knowing she would have a place of her own would be gift enough. But if they said no . . .

"I want to see picture frames," Peter said.

Nick strode to a shelf at the front of the store. "Standing or hanging?"

"I think . . . hanging," Peter decided, looking at the selection. "But size I do not know." It had been too long since he'd held that scrap of paper that had blown down by the river, but he knew the woman kept it between the pages of the Bible he had given her. He wished he had sneaked a look at it before coming to town.

He examined the variety of frames and finally eliminated some as too small and others as too large. Finally he picked up one made of stained oak with roses carved into the corners. It reminded him of the design on her chair. And it was oak — a good, solid choice.

He held it up to Nick. "If this is not right size, can I bring it back and choose another?"

"Of course." Nick took it from him. "Do you want me to wrap it?"

"*Ja.* Do you have pretty paper? Something red or with flowers?"

Nick rummaged beneath the counter and emerged with a piece of pale green paper bearing red roses. "How is this?"

Peter beamed. "That is perfect." He watched as Nick flattened the paper on the countertop and laid the frame on it. "I have errand to run." He would visit Heinrich Gaeddert and see if a decision had been made. "I will pick these things up before I leave town. That will be all right?"

"Of course. I'll have it all by the door, ready to go. I would not dally, though, Peter. *Frau* Nickels' knee tells her a storm is brewing, and she has never been wrong."

"I will not dally. *Danke.*" Buttoning his coat and putting on his hat and gloves, he prayed silently that this next errand would be as successful as the first one. He wanted the woman's future to be better than her past. As he reached for the door, it suddenly swung inward, knocking Peter's hand aside.

A youngster charged into the store. "There is trouble!" His cheeks and ears were red with cold, his eyes watery.

Nick rounded the counter. "What is it?"

The boy leaned forward, taking great heaving breaths. "*Herr* Schmidt — that

326

fancy buggy of his — it slid off the road and is caught in a snowbank. His horse cannot free it. The animal — we fear it will harm itself trying."

Peter's heart turned over as he considered the plight of the poor horse. He tugged his hat more securely over his ears, then took the boy by the arm. "You show me where the buggy is. My oxen can pull it free."

The boy looked at him in surprise. "You will help *Herr* Schmidt? After all he has —"

"Show me." Peter shook the boy's arm. "I will not allow the animal to work itself to death."

The boy nodded and led Peter out the door.

23

The wind screamed like a wild animal and made the house tremble. The walls seemed to groan against the pressure of the wind until Summer was certain they would collapse like the walls of the *shariah*. She shivered even near the cookstove, although she knew it wasn't the cold that caused her to shake. It was fear.

Where was he? More than enough time had passed for Mr. Ollenburger to make it to town and back. What if he'd lost his way in that violently blowing snow? She'd heard of such things happening. After having been in the raging storm herself only long enough to go to the henhouse and secure the door, she understood how it could happen. What relief had washed over her when she'd stumbled into the back corner of the house. Another few feet to the left and . . . She shuddered. She didn't want to consider what might have happened.

If the storm claimed him, what would happen to Thomas? *Grossmutter* couldn't care for him alone. Another shudder shook her, and she hugged herself. She turned her attention to Thomas, who stood by the window, his nose pressed to the frosty pane. He had shoved the curtains aside and scratched a tiny peephole in the frost.

Summer crossed the floor, boards squeaking beneath her feet, and stopped behind him. She gave his shoulders — surprisingly solid for one so young — a firm squeeze and smiled down at him. "Don't worry. Your father is a strong, intelligent man. He knows how to take care of himself. He'll be in soon, hungry as a bear. Which reminds me . . . shouldn't we start supper?"

The boy kept staring out the window. Summer looked, too, but she could see nothing beyond the swirl of white frost.

"Come, Thomas. The smell of supper will surely entice your father to come in."

From her chair, *Grossmutter* murmured something, holding her hand toward Thomas. The boy sighed and went to her, taking her hand. He looked at Summer. "What will we make?" His voice held little interest.

Somehow she had to get Thomas focused on something besides his father. She remembered a game she'd played with Vincent and Rose. "I know what we can do. We can make a surprise supper."

The boy tipped his head. "What's that?"

"Go down in the cellar and stand in front of the shelves. Close your eyes, then reach out until you touch two jars. Whatever your fingers find, bring up. Then we'll use it to make a surprise supper."

If she thought this game would bring a smile to Thomas's face, she was wrong.

"All right, Summer." He pulled his hand from *Grossmutter's* grasp and spoke in German to her. She nodded, and the boy moved to the trapdoor that led to the cellar.

Summer took hold of the metal pull ring and, with a grunt, heaved the door open. Thomas headed down the steep stairs. "Remember," she warned, "no peeking!"

From the depths of the cellar, she heard his reply. "Yes, ma'am." There was no enthusiasm in his voice.

Summer moved to the window, scratched away a larger area with her fingernail, and peeked through the glass. The light was fading as evening approached, but the brightness of the blowing snow hid the late hour. *Oh, Peter, where are you?*

"You're worried, too, aren't you?"

Summer spun to find Thomas beside the cellar door, two quart jars in his hands. Had she spoken the words aloud? She forced a smile and rushed toward him, hands outstretched. "Let me see what you found. Oh! Carrots and tomatoes. Why, that's the start of a wonderful soup, Thomas. Can you go back down once more and bring me some potatoes and an onion? The bin up here is empty. I'll stoke the fire."

Thomas nodded and disappeared into the cellar again. Summer pulled three more logs from the woodbox and laid them atop the snapping blaze. She was glad Mr. Ollenburger had filled the box before leaving for town. There was enough wood to last through tomorrow and into the next day, if necessary. How long could a Kansas blizzard last? She retrieved a kettle from the shelf above the stove and dipped water from the bucket. Another thought struck — the water bucket was nearly empty. What would they do when it was gone? There wasn't time to dwell on it, for Thomas reappeared, struggling up the cellar steps with his burden.

He cradled several potatoes and one onion, its long tail of greens now brown and dry. He dropped the vegetables on the table and brushed off the front of his overalls.

Summer closed the cellar door. "Thank you, Thomas. Let's rub these potatoes well with a rag" — she dared not waste water washing them — "and get them boiling with the onion. We'll have a fine surprise soup for supper!"

The boy's eyes appeared much older than his not-quite-ten years. "You're not fooling me, Summer. I know you're thinking Pa's stuck out in that storm, too." Tears filled his eyes and spilled over, trailing down his round cheeks in two thin rivulets. "Will you pray for Pa? I'm really scared."

Summer pointed inanely at the potatoes. "Why-why don't you and your grandmother pray while I get the soup started?"

The boy shook his head, a thick shock of hair falling across his forehead. It made him look even more like his father. "I can't eat anything. My stomach feels funny — like there's rocks inside it. I won't be able to eat until I feel better." He took a step toward her, the tears still wet on his cheeks. "Please, Summer?"

An ache filled Summer's chest. So far all her prayers had been met with a resounding no. Only the one for God to enter her heart had been answered with a yes. What if she prayed and God said no this time, too? Could she bear the hurt this child would feel if her prayers were as useless as those she'd uttered for her own family? Still, looking into Thomas's pleading face, she couldn't deny his request.

She guided him to Grandmother's corner, where they knelt together on the braided rug, facing each other. *Grossmutter* held out her hands from her seat in her chair, and they formed a circle by joining hands.

Though her stomach churned, Summer closed her eyes and began. "Dear God . . ." Her voice trembled. She clung to Thomas and *Grossmutter.* Their grips tightened, encouraging her. "Dear God, we come to you today because . . . because we are worried. Mr. Ollenburger — Peter — is somewhere in the storm. We don't know where. But . . . but you do." A feeling of peace crept through her heart as she realized what she'd just said. *"God is a God who knows."*

Squeezing Thomas's cold hand, she heard her voice gain strength. "Wherever he is, please keep him safe and warm. Let no harm come to him. And let him find his way to the house again. In your name we pray. Amen."

"Amen," the grandmother echoed.

Summer opened her eyes. Thomas's eyes still glittered with tears. He used the backs of his wrists to remove the moisture.

"Thank you, Summer."

"You're welcome. We've done all we can. Now, let's get that soup started."

She and the boy worked in silence as they scrubbed potatoes with clean rags and cut them into bite-sized pieces. Soon the boiling water steamed the kitchen, leaving a fine mist of moisture hanging in the air. Still the wind blew, causing the house to creak and moan in protest. Summer found herself silently praying the walls would hold. Even as she prayed, her heart begged, *Don't say no! Please, God, don't say no!*

While the potatoes boiled, Thomas roamed from window to window. Summer finally decided something must be done to distract the boy.

"Thomas, what games do you have in your bedroom?"

"Games?" He turned a quizzical look in her direction. "I have blocks, and an iron horse and wagon, two puzzles, and books."

"No jacks? Or a checkerboard?"

He shook his head.

Summer had ordered the card game Authors, a tiddledywinks set, and a new shirt in addition to a fine dictionary for Thomas for Christmas. These items were with Mr. Ollenburger right now, wherever he was.

"Do you have colored chalk crayons?"

The boy nodded.

"Get your paper tablet and chalks. We'll make a checkerboard. A boy your age should know how to play checkers."

"Did your son know how to play checkers?"

Summer's heart constricted, but she smiled, remembering sitting on the opposite side of the wooden checkerboard in their parlor in Boston with Vincent. "Yes, my son was a champion checkers player."

"Then I reckon I can do it, too." His voice finally held a hint of interest.

It took the better part of an hour to create a paper checkerboard, colored with squares of brown and red, and cut out enough circles to play the game. They used the crayons to make a red *R* or brown *B* on the front of the circles to denote the difference between the two, then put a red or brown *K* on the backs in case the checker made it all the way across and became kinged.

Grandmother seemed especially interested in the process, leaning forward and asking questions of Thomas, which he in turn asked Summer. When she replied, he translated the answer into German. It made for a lengthy conversation, but Summer didn't mind. It cheered her to have the old woman pay so much attention and speak more frequently than she had since Summer's arrival.

Although the homemade game was simple, it worked. She and Thomas played checkers until the soup was finished. She dished up steaming bowls for the three of them, and they ate in companionable conversation, continuing the question-translate-answer-translate pattern. When they were finished eating, Summer washed the few dishes, and then she and the boy played checkers again.

Thomas picked up the strategies quickly, as Summer had expected he would, and he beat her as many times as he lost. She feigned great disgust when he won, vowing to get him next time. To her relief, the boy laughed and teased, apparently forgetting the worry about his father.

Grossmutter laughed, too, smiling in pleasure from her chair. Her smiles gradually faded to wide yawns, and at last she rose, releasing a sigh. Thomas gave her a good-night hug, and the two engaged in a whispered conversation before the woman kissed his cheek and headed to her bedroom.

Thomas set up the checkerboard again,

grinning across the table. "I'm gonna get at least three kings this time!" But when the hour of bedtime slipped past and still Mr. Ollenburger hadn't returned, not even winning checkers could ease the boy's fears. He shifted from his chair across the table and sat down next to her. "Summer, do you *really* think Pa is safe?"

Summer gave a wayward lock of his hair a gentle tug. "I believe your father will come tramping through that door any minute, his beard covered with icicles and his nose as red as a ripe cherry. He'll demand a bowl of soup and a big chunk of bread, and he'll scold us all for worrying even one minute about him." Her heart pounded. She hoped the words had sounded more certain than she felt.

"You like my pa, don't you?" A tentative smile appeared on the corners of Thomas's lips.

Summer gave his hair brief tousle before curling her hand into her lap. "He's a fine man. You should be proud of him."

"I am." The boy scooted closer to her, resting his head on her shoulder. "If . . . if Pa doesn't make it home, will you stay and take care of me, Summer?"

She shrugged her shoulder, dislodging the boy. "You listen to me, Thomas Ollenburger. Don't you give up on your father. Didn't we pray for God to keep him safe? Don't you think your father is praying the same thing? I don't want you to even ask questions like that. They aren't needed." Her surety surprised her. When had she stopped worrying God might answer this prayer with a no?

The boy looked at her with wide, hurt eyes.

"Besides," she finished in a kinder tone, "I promised your pa I would see to you. You have nothing to worry about. You'll be cared for."

He nodded solemnly and then rose. "There's a chamber pot under my bed. Don't reckon we'll be going to the outhouse tonight."

Summer listened to the wind, which continued to howl like a hundred hungry wolves. "No, we won't. I'm glad you're resourceful enough to have a chamber pot available."

"*Grossmutter* has one, too."

"Good. We'll be taken care of, then." It amazed her she could carry on a conversation about chamber pots without blushing in shame. Her sister-in-law would be appalled, but it made Summer want to giggle.

Thomas disappeared into his room. When

338

he emerged several minutes later, he was in his nightshirt. He leaned forward, wrapping his arms around her neck. "*Schlop die gesunt,* Summer."

She hugged him back, even delivering a kiss above his ear. "You, too. Have good dreams. No worrying, all right?"

He nodded, yawned, and padded back to the bedroom. Before going in, he paused. "May I leave the door open? That way I'll hear Pa when he comes back."

Summer sent him a smile. He was thinking positively now. "That's a fine idea. You'll also be warmer."

Thomas gave a little wave and stepped into his room. Summer heard his bed squeak as he settled himself, and then there was silence inside the house. She poured a cup of coffee. By now it had steeped for several hours and was strong enough to make her tongue tingle, but it would keep her awake. She didn't intend to sleep until Mr. Ollenburger was safely home.

She retrieved the woven blanket from her bed and draped it around her shoulders. Turning her chair to face the door, she seated herself and lifted the cup of coffee to her lips. She blew on the thick brew before taking a sip. Grimacing, she lowered the cup to her lap. The warmth from the mug felt good against her hands.

She kept her gaze on the window, which was completely coated with frost, as she listened to the complaints of the wind and let her thoughts drift to Mr. Ollenburger. While worry still pinched her heart, she knew if anyone could survive this storm, he could. Besides, who was to say he wasn't still in Gaeddert, snug and warm at someone's house, worrying about her, Grandmother, and Thomas? She smiled, imagining him pacing back and forth, his thundering voice repeating, "I must to get home. My son will be worryful."

She let her eyes slide closed, and she whispered to the empty room. "Dear God, I'm new at praying. I'm probably not very good at it, either. But Mr. Ollenburger has convinced me you hear my every prayer. For Thomas's sake, let his father come home again. Losing those you love hurts so much. . . ." Her throat tightened. "So please, God, if at all possible, spare Thomas that pain. I trust you to do what's best. Thank you. Amen."

It felt good to give it to God — to trust Him to meet her needs. She rested her head against the padded back of the chair and closed her eyes. A soft snore came from Thomas's bedroom, and she smiled. "*Schlop die gesunt,* Thomas," she whispered. "And *schlop die gesunt,* Mr. Ollenburger, wher-ever you are."

24

Summer woke with a jerk. The half-empty mug in her lap tipped, spilling the remainder of the coffee across her dress and the blanket. She grabbed the cup and sucked in her breath as the cold liquid soaked through to her skin. Morning sunlight backlit the thick swirling feathers of frost on the window, the bright white stabbing her eyes. A dull pain throbbed in the back of her skull. She released a light moan as she struggled out of the chair and deposited the cup on the table.

Squinting against the light, one hand pressed to her temple and the other holding her wet skirt away from her thighs, she approached the window. Thomas's peephole was completely sealed over, the frost layer there less thick than elsewhere on the window. She scraped that area clean again and peered outside.

The bright sun made her grimace as the

throbbing in her temples increased in intensity. The snowfall had stopped, but the fiercely blowing wind whipped snow into little cyclones of white crystals. Steep drifts that resembled raging ocean waves slanted against the sides of buildings and appeared to climb tree trunks. Although it hurt to look out into the overwhelming brightness of sun on snow, she forced herself to search for some evidence of life.

But there was no wagon, no oxen. No big bear of a man.

She sighed, turning from the window, and rubbed both temples.

Thomas appeared in his doorway, hugging himself, hunched forward. "Morning, Summer." His voice sounded raspy from sleep. "Has the snow stopped?"

"It's stopped coming down," she answered, "but it's still blowing. I've never seen so much snow. Take a look."

Thomas tiptoed across the cold floor and peeked out the hole. He spun, turning to her with excited eyes. "I bet it's higher than my head in some places! Pa and me could build a really good snow cave." Then his expression clouded over. "Except Pa's not here, is he?"

Summer squeezed his shoulder. "Not yet. But since the snow has stopped falling, he

343

should be able to come home now."

"How?" Thomas pointed out the window. "Look at all that! Roth and Gaert can't pull the wagon through it. Wherever he is, he's stuck, for sure."

"Well, then, we'll just have to pray for the snow to melt so he can come home," she said firmly. "Should we do that before or after we get dressed for the day and start breakfast?"

"Let's pray first." He clasped his hands beneath his chin, closed his eyes, and dove directly into a prayer. "Dear God, Pa's stuck away from us, and we miss him. I don't see how he can get through that snow. There's sure a lot of it. Would you please make enough of it go away for Pa to get home? Thanks, God. Amen."

The innocence of children, Summer thought. "That was a perfect prayer, Thomas. Now, put on your warmest pants and shirt. Then we'll see what we can scrounge up for breakfast. Cornmeal mush, probably, since I won't have to go to the henhouse for eggs to make it."

"And some fried potatoes?" The boy looked hopeful. "Pa likes fried potatoes and onions for breakfast. We should have it ready for him."

Summer nodded, even though she was

afraid it would be well past breakfast before the man arrived. Cold fried potatoes and onions didn't seem appealing, but if it would make Thomas feel better, she would fry a panful. "Of course. Now get dressed."

He padded back to his bedroom as the grandmother entered the kitchen, her shawl held around her shoulders. She pointed at Summer's coffee-stained clothes, her eyebrows raised high in question. Summer nodded, acknowledging she knew she should change her dress. First, though, she took time to stoke the fire.

When Summer returned to the kitchen after changing her clothes, *Grossmutter* was picking potatoes from the bin in the corner. Summer gave the old woman a smile as she took the potatoes and began scrubbing them for frying. As she worked, her thoughts drifted outside. How had the hens fared against last night's storm? And Thomas's poor Daisy. She would need to be fed and watered. Thomas couldn't see to those chores — the last time he'd gotten chilled, he'd become ill. Mr. Ollenburger would probably not be back until late. The only person left to see to the animals was her.

Well, she told herself firmly as she thumped the scrubbed potatoes into a bowl,

345

*if I'm going to live on this prairie from now on,
I've got to learn to take care of things for
myself. Now is as good a time to learn as any.*

What had she heard about precautions for
snowstorms? Rope . . . Rope leading from
the house to outbuildings.

"Thomas! Might there be a length of rope
in this cellar of yours?"

"*Herr* Gaeddert, to home I must go. My boy,
he will be very much worried about me."

By the time Peter's oxen had managed to
pull the Schmidts' horse and buggy from
the snowbank, the storm *Frau* Nickels's
knee had predicted had struck with force,
preventing Peter from going home. He appreciated Heinrich Gaeddert's kindness in
putting him up for the night, but he did not
wish to remain any longer than necessary.
He paced across the sitting room of *Herr*
Gaeddert's home, his hands deep in his
pockets for lack of something better to do
with them. Always his hands were busy —
they were working hands — and idleness
was not easy to bear.

"Now, Peter, I understand you do not
want to worry your boy, but you said yourself the boy's great-grandmother and the
Steadman woman are with him. He is cared

346

for. Going out in that snow would be foolhardy at best."

Herr Gaeddert's calm voice did nothing to alleviate Peter's worry. It was not only the boy that concerned him, although Thomas was first on his list. There were the animals, the woodbox, the water bucket. So many things he saw to each day.

"Sit down here, Peter, and let us look at this map of Gaeddert land holdings." Heinrich held up a roll of parchment as he gestured to the sofa. "If the Steadman woman plans to purchase a plot, I need to make sure I understand which plot."

Peter blew out his breath. He reminded himself this was an errand he needed to complete. If he could not make it home right away, at least he could do this for the woman. "All right, *Herr* Gaeddert. I show you where the graves are found."

Peter traced the Cottonwood River to the location of the Steadman gravesites. The two men drew a box on the map that would include the graves and one more plot, giving the woman enough space for a house, a garden, and a henhouse, as well as a small barn. Peter was glad the plot was near the river. Water would not be difficult to find, and perhaps it could even be pumped to the house to make things easier for her. A woman faring alone would need as many conveniences as possible.

"Now, this I must ask you," Heinrich said when the land decisions had been made, "does the woman intend to become a member of *Kleine Gemeinde?*"

Peter nodded solemnly. "She has prayed the prayer of accepting salvation. I have seen evidence of it. She will be baptized and ask to be admitted as member."

Heinrich leaned back and stroked his graying beard. "This is good. It was important to my father that Gaeddert be a haven for our people. He would not welcome outsiders with new ideas. If she is willing to accept our values and our doctrine, then I do not see that my brother Bernard would argue against it."

"Then you will sell the woman this land?" Peter wanted a clear answer.

"*Ja,* I think we will." Heinrich rolled the map and put it on the desk that stood in the corner of the room. "How will she care for herself there? There is not enough land to farm. Does she have other skills?"

"A good teacher she is," Peter said, "and she sews. We are praying she will find the means to support herself. She is strong woman — stronger than she looks. God will make a way for her, for sure." He rose and went back to the window. He slid his hands back into his pockets. "And I must trust God to make a way home for me. Very soon."

Summer's ears had stung so much for the first half hour she thought she might cry out. But now they were numb, like her hands, which made it hard to finish her tasks. She set her jaw, prayed for strength, and continued. Daisy had plenty of fresh water and hay, the chickens were fed and watered, and she had even laid out hay in the oxen's stalls to save Mr. Ollenburger the trouble when he finally returned.

The rope Thomas had retrieved from the cellar proved to be too short to reach clear to the barn, but she found a full bale of rope in the barn and rolled it out to meet the shorter piece, tying the ends together in a clumsy knot she prayed would hold. She looped the rope behind the henhouse so a person could follow it to both outbuildings. She smiled with pride at her ingenuity.

After caring for the animals, she carried in the essentials. Her fingers, layered in Thomas's gloves under her mittens, were uncooperative, and it took much longer than she wanted, but it had to be done. Thomas had found two extra buckets in the cellar, and she filled them with water from the well. Then she hauled in firewood — three to four pieces at a time — until the woodbox heaped once more. Only one thing left to do.

"Thomas, fetch the chamber pots, please."

The boy handed them to her with his face puckered in distaste. She wasn't keen on this task, either, but who else would do it? She trudged through the snow, following the trail she had already broken to get to the barn, then broke fresh ground to the outhouse.

Her thighs burned with the effort it took to create a pathway. The wind came in bursts, stealing her breath. Her arms ached with the effort of holding the pots away from her body — she did not want to spill any of the contents on her clothing! The snow reached her hips at times. Her dragging skirts made progress nearly impossible.

Panting with exertion, her body screaming in protest at what she forced it to do, she considered just tossing the vile contents onto the snow. Her stomach turned in revulsion. No! She would dump it down the outhouse portal no matter how hard it was to get there. Her skirts caught again, and she put down the pots long enough to tug the tangled fabric free.

She groaned. "Maybe I should have borrowed some of Mr. Ollenburger's pants." Then she laughed, imagining trying to keep the pants up. The laughter, in an odd way, revived her.

Gritting her teeth, she forced her numb feet to carry her the last twenty feet. Planting her shoulder against the outhouse door, she forced it open and stumbled through. With a huge sigh of relief, she disposed of both pots' contents.

She dropped the pots and sank onto the outhouse seat to catch her breath. But after only a few minutes the cold encouraged her to get back to the house and warmth. Besides, the sun was waning — nightfall would soon be upon her. She had no desire to be in the snow-covered yard in the dark.

When she tried to pick up the pots by their handles, she discovered her numb fingers wouldn't grasp the handles anymore. Fear gripped her — were her fingers frozen? Surely they would unstiffen once they were warm again. She bent her elbows and looped a pot over each arm. They banged against her hips as she struggled back to the house.

The door opened as she heaved herself

onto the stoop, and Thomas reached for her. She gave him the pots, then fell through the door in a flurry of snow and sodden clothing. She sat on the floor, her back against the wall, and huffed for several minutes while Grandmother hovered, watching her with wide, worried eyes.

Thomas crouched beside her. "Are you okay?"

"I'll be fine. It was just harder moving through the snow than I expected. But everything is taken care of for today." She managed a weak laugh. "If I have to do this year after year, I'm going to purchase some sturdy work pants. Long skirts catch the snow and bring it with you." To her amazement, steam rose off her snow-coated skirt. She needed to get out of these clothes, but at the moment it felt good to sit still and rest.

Grossmutter scuttled to the stove and poured a cup of coffee. Summer tried to remove her mittens and found her fingers still wouldn't work. Thomas tugged her mittens free, pulling the gloves underneath off at the same time. She scowled at her own hands. Her fingers looked strange — blotched with pink and white. Bloodless. They didn't bend at all, and when *Grossmut-*

ter placed the hot mug between her palms, they stung with such intensity Summer cried out.

Thomas took the cup and reared backward, spattering coffee across her crusty skirts. They hissed as steam rose.

She cradled her hands against her chest. "It hurt." Her fingers pricked as if stung by dozens of bees.

Grossmutter reached toward Summer, her voice wavering as she spoke.

"What is she saying?" Summer asked Thomas.

"She says you must warm your hands slowly," he translated.

Summer nodded. Her head felt weighted. She looked again at her hands, scowling as she tried to decide what to do next.

"How can I help?" the boy asked.

She looked into Thomas's frightened face. Summer remembered that same question asked by another child, Vincent, kneeling beside his father's sleeping mat, his face white with worry. *"How can I help, Mama?"* She'd been helpless then. She wouldn't be helpless this time.

"I've got to get into dry clothes and warm myself. I don't know, but I might have frostbite. Your grandmother is right. I seem to remember reading that frozen limbs need to be warmed slowly." She rolled onto one hip and, with some difficulty, got to her feet. Clumps of snow fell from her clothing as she made her way to the bedroom.

"Do you . . . do you need my help with . . ." Thomas paused beside the bedroom door. His fingers twitched on her arm. *Grossmutter* stood behind him, and her pale blue eyes never wavered from Summer's face.

She managed a small smile although it hurt her dry lips. "No thank you, Thomas. *Grossmutter* can help me."

Sealed inside the bedroom with the old woman, she prayed for strength as she fought her way out of the snow-encrusted dress. *Grossmutter* murmured softly, clucking her tongue against her teeth, as she painstakingly fastened the buttons on Summer's dry dress with gnarled fingers. When the last button was hooked, Summer turned and offered the old woman a grateful smile. The grandmother touched Summer's cheek and smiled back. How wonderful that gentle touch felt. It warmed her from the inside out.

"Come," Summer said, although she knew the woman didn't understand. "Let's go back to the fire."

Together they stepped out of the bedroom and found Thomas waiting, his hands pushed inside the bib of his overalls. "What can I do for you?"

Summer checked the stove, where the wood she had hauled in lay in a disorderly heap. Mr. Ollenburger would not be pleased with the appearance of his usually organized woodbox. "Thomas, perhaps you could —"

Her words were interrupted by a mighty crash. It took Summer a moment to recognize the sound — the door banging against the wall. The wind must have blown it open. Cold air slammed through the room, and Thomas shrank back, wrapping his arms around Summer.

Summer took hold of the boy's arms. "Close the door again, Thomas!"

"Woman, please do not shut me out." The deep voice carried over the whine of the wind. Although weaker than she'd ever heard it, the voice was easily recognized. Peter was home!

25

Stunned, Summer froze in place as Thomas stumbled across the floor. She watched the snow-covered man push the door closed and turn with opened arms.

"Pa! We were so worried!" Thomas sobbed against his father's coat while the man's great paws stroked the boy's hair.

"I worried, too," the man admitted. "This was a storm the likes of which I have not seen since leaving Russia."

"Where have you been?"

"I will answer your question, boy, but I am dripping on the clean floor." The calm tone seemed to pacify Thomas. The boy released his hold, and his father moved away from the door, removing his jacket. Foot-sized puddles of melting snow marked his pathway. "Sorry for the mess, I am, *Frau* Steadman."

What was one more mess when her heart pounded so hard it could surely be seen?

He was here. How heart lifting to know prayers sometimes were answered with a yes — even her prayers. They had prayed for him to come, and he was here.

And he'd arrived right after she had finished all his chores.

"*Now* you come." Summer laughed with the irony of the situation. "Peter Ollenburger, couldn't you have been just a few hours sooner? You could have saved me trekking all over the place out there, taking care of your duties!"

His red-rimmed eyes sparkled. "So that was your little pathway all over my yard? I wondered who . . . And you put out the rope?"

She nodded. "Just in case it snowed again, I wanted to be able to find my way to the outbuildings and back again."

"That was very wise thing to do."

"I think it would have been wiser to trust our prayers that you would return and leave the work for you!" Such pleasure she found in sparring with him. The twinkle in his eyes and the playful grin that twitched his cheeks took her mind off the needles shooting through her hands, feet, and ears.

Suddenly he scowled. "How long were you out in the cold?"

She shrugged. "I'm really not sure."

"How long, boy?" Peter glared down at Thomas.

The boy shrugged, too, his eyes wide. "I don't know, Pa. She went out after we cleaned up from lunch, and the sun was setting when she came back in."

Peter stomped across the floor. "Let me see your hands."

She held up her hands, too surprised to do otherwise.

"Do you feel pain in them?"

She cringed. His large fingers pressing her flesh created a new rush of discomfort. "Oh, yes. In my feet and ears, too."

He cupped her cheeks and tipped her head, looking at her ears, then guided her to the table. He placed her in a chair and lifted her feet in turn. Finally he sat back on his haunches and grinned at her. "You will be in world of hurt, but that is good thing. The pain tells you nothing will be lost." He shook his head. "You are amazing woman, Summer Steadman."

Despite her discomfort, Summer couldn't stop smiling as she looked at the gentle bear of a man.

Peter had expected to return to three people fretting and wringing their hands in worry.

Instead, he came home to no chores, a woman's laugh, and an aromatic pot bubbling on the stove. This woman was full of surprises. And now he held a surprise for her.

He rose. "I must change. Summer Steadman, you stay away from the stove. Too close to the heat is not good for you as your skin thaws out. Thomas can stir whatever it is that smells so good on the stove."

"Leftover soup," she reported.

"Surprise soup," Thomas added.

Peter's eyebrows rose. "Surprise soup?" It seemed there were many surprises in this room.

"We'll explain later," the woman said. "You go get changed."

He dressed quickly, then sat at the table and let Thomas bring him a cup of strong coffee while *Grossmutter* clucked at the stove.

"Pa, how'd you get the wagon through the snow?" Thomas seated himself across the table. The woman sat in her chair with her hands lying palms up in her lap. From the look on her face, her hands gave her pain, but she did not complain.

"The wagon is still safe in Gaeddert, behind Heinrich Gaeddert's house. Our oxen are snug in his barn." He turned to the woman. "Heinrich Gaeddert's father had good sense to build Russian house and barn. They stick together — you step right from house into barn. No need for rope to find the way through snow at his place."

A brief smile upturned her cracked lips. "In the summer, I can't imagine it's pleasant to have the animals so near."

He let loose a hearty laugh. He was enjoying this humorous side of her. *"Ja,* you are right, for sure. Still, it is convenient, *ja?"*

Thomas tugged his arm. "Did you walk home?"

"Nein, boy." Peter tweaked his son's hair. "I brought *Herr* Gaeddert's two-seater sleigh pulled by his gelding Pat. So your Daisy has a new friend in the barn."

Thomas jerked upright. "His two-seater sleigh? Will you give me a ride in it before you take it back?"

"I tell you what we do. When time it is to return it, you ride with me to town. You must make a promise not to peek in wagon, though, for Christmas is coming and peeking is not a good thing to be doing, for sure."

The boy pulled a face. "Ah, it's hard not to peek."

"I will not take you unless you promise."

Thomas shrugged, blowing out his breath.

"All right, I promise." A grin flashed across his face. "I guess it's no fun to ruin surprises anyway."

"*Ja,* this is true." Peter chewed the inside of his mouth for a moment, thinking of the news he had not yet shared with the woman. Then something else crossed his mind and he turned again to her. "*Frau* Steadman, an apology I owe you."

She raised her eyebrows in question.

"Before I could go to post office, the storm came up." He did not mention the time helping *Herr* Schmidt. "I did not have chance to go to post office and send your letter. It is still in my pocket. So wet I got coming back, it is now ruined."

"Please, don't concern yourself about it. I can rewrite it. It's far more important to have you safely home, Peter." She jerked, her eyes widening and her cheeks blazing pink. "I mean, M-Mr. Ollenburger."

He sat back in his chair, a lopsided grin tugging at his face. "I think it is all right for you to call me by my name. We do not need to be always formal. You call me Peter. And . . . and I call you Summer." He enjoyed the taste of her name on his tongue.

She licked her lips. Would she agree?

"All right, Peter. You're right. We're

friends, aren't we? So from now on, I'll call you Peter."

"And I call you Summer."

From the stove, *Grossmutter* suddenly interjected, "Lena."

Summer's startled eyes bounced from Peter to *Grossmutter.* The old woman tapped her bodice with bent fingers. "Lena."

"Lena," Summer repeated. "I will call you Lena."

The old woman nodded in satisfaction, her wrinkled face wreathed in a smile. She went back to stirring the pot on the stove, and Peter and Summer smiled in each other's direction. Peter felt a warmth fill him as he celebrated the open acceptance of Elsa's grandmother toward the woman. They sat for a few minutes in easy quiet. Finally the woman sighed, leaned her head back, and closed her eyes.

"You are tired, Summer?" He wondered if she had slept at all the night he was away.

"Yes. I didn't rest well." Her face flooded with pink, and she stammered, "Th-the wind kept me up."

He suspected it was more than the wind, but it would not be proper for her to admit it. "Then come." Peter crossed to the chair and very gently took her elbow. "You go lie

362

down. We will save you a bowl of your surprise soup." He walked her across the room, his own chest constricting as she winced with every step. To take her mind from her discomfort, he teased, "The surprise is not shoes or socks floating in that broth, is it?"

A light laugh tripped from her lips. "No. Everything in it comes from your cellar."

"Hmm." He helped her sit on the edge of the bed and fluffed the pillow for her. "In my cellar are tools and ropes and all sorts of things. Maybe no soup I eat after all."

She awarded him with another tired smile as she leaned back against the pillow, her hands cradled against her chest. He placed a quilt over her. "You rest now, Summer. *Schlop die gesunt.*"

A smile crept across her lips as her eyelids closed with a flutter of lashes. "I said that to you last night," she told him in an airy voice, already drifting off.

"That is probably why I slept so well in a strange house."

Without touching her skin, he traced the outline of her cheek with one rough finger. Then he tiptoed from the room, leaving her to sleep.

It was two days before Summer could pick

up a hot cup of coffee without her fingers hurting. She couldn't imagine how people saw to chores day after day in that kind of cold. Peter had indicated this storm wasn't typical for Kansas, but having happened once, it could happen again, she reasoned. Every prickle of her fingers reminded her that she would have her own chores to see to when she built her own house, and there were moments she wondered if she was doing the right thing. But then she would think of the graves, now covered with snow on the lonely landscape, and her resolve would return to be near her family in a place of her own.

On the third day following the storm, Peter announced at breakfast that he would be returning *Herr* Gaeddert's sleigh and horse. "If you are coming, boy, you bundle up good. A second pair of long johns, your thickest wool pants, and a sweater over your shirt."

"I won't hardly be able to move!"

"Bundle or stay here," his father returned calmly. "It is your choice."

"I'll bundle." Thomas headed to his bedroom, grumbling under his breath.

"I think the boy has what they call cabin

fever," Peter told Summer. "Cranky he has been."

She sipped the last of her coffee. "One can hardly blame him. Even before the winter storm hit, he'd spent weeks here with only you, Lena, and then me for company most of the time. A trip to town will do him good."

"I would be glad if you could come, too." She heard the regret in his tone. "But the sleigh, it only seats two. If all people were slight like you, three could go, but me? I fill most of the seat myself."

His large size did not intimidate her, nor could she imagine him any other way. "I'll be fine here," she assured him, "and you can mail the letter I rewrote to Nadine and Horace." She glanced toward Thomas's closed door then leaned forward to whisper, "Did my order come in?"

Peter whispered, too. "*Ja,* in the wagon are your things, all bound in brown paper. The boy will not peek."

She leaned back and smiled. "Good. It will be fun to watch him open his gifts." She felt her smile fade as memories of past Christmases pressed in. She pictured the towering nine-foot tree bedecked with glass balls, gold foil stars, candles, and ropes of popcorn and cranberries the children always helped her string. Beneath the tree, piles of gifts awaited opening. Tears threatened as the sound of feet on the stairs, happy squeals, and cries of *"Oh, Mama! Thank you!"* replayed in her heart.

What happy moments those had been, almost sweeter in memory than in living them, for now she knew what a priceless gift her family had been. Her heart swelled. She also knew — personally — who she needed to thank for the privilege of loving them.

"Summer?"

Peter's voice intruded, dispelling the memories. She turned to face him. "Yes?"

"Deeply thinking you are."

She smiled at his homey phrase. "I was thinking about Christmas and how special this one will be."

His expression changed from interest to puzzlement. "Special? Away from . . . your dear children?"

Summer considered how to answer. Would it make sense to him? "Yes, special. You see, Peter, when I lived in Boston, I had much — a husband who provided well for me, children to love who loved me back, a beautiful home full of fine belongings. Then typhoid and a fire took that all away. I thought I had nothing — no reason to live, no reason to be." She swallowed as tears flooded her eyes. "But I was so wrong. It is *now* that I have everything, because God has filled me."

She felt warm tears spill down her cheeks, and she allowed them to flow. "This Christmas is my first to truly understand the gift of God's Son to the world and what that gift means to each of us. Yes, I miss my children. The ache is still here" — she touched her chest — "and I am sure it always will be. But that ache no longer consumes me. The joy of God's love fills me, taking up all the empty places. It's the gift He's given me, and I will always remember this Christmas as special because of what I have learned."

Peter sat back, his fingers convulsing on the handle of his cup. Tears glinted in the corners of his eyes. "You are wise woman, Summer Steadman."

Thomas's door opened, bringing their conversation to a close. They both laughed as the boy waddled to the table, his arms held from his body, his wide-legged stance exaggerated for his father's benefit. In addition to the articles of clothing Peter had dictated must be worn, he had wrapped woolen socks around his neck and pulled them over his arms, hiding his hands.

Another thick gray sock, tied around his head, covered his ears with the knot standing up like a bow on his mussed blond hair.

"Am I bundled enough?" His eyes sparkled.

Peter chuckled in Summer's direction. "What is that *m* word you teach me? Mismus-vis?"

Summer shook her head, her fingers hiding her grin. "Mischievous."

"*Ja,* that is it. This boy is too mis-chievous for his good, for sure. But I think I keep him anyway." He rose, still chuckling. "Boy, can you put your coat on over all that gear?"

Thomas waddled to the hooks and pulled his coat down. With some struggling — which he played up for his audience — he wrestled himself into his coat, but his sock-covered fingers couldn't manage the buttons. He turned a winsome expression on Summer. "Summer, will you do my buttons?"

She released a laugh as she crossed the floor. "I suppose I can do that." Finished, she gave him a pat. "There you are, ready to ride in the sleigh."

"I wish you could come, too."

"Oh, I have a busy morning planned." She

placed her hands on her hips. "Lena and I are going to bake cookies — lots of cookies — and sprinkle them with sugar so they'll sparkle like stars." Looking over her shoulder at Peter, she added, "I'd like to give them as Christmas gifts to those who have been kind to me."

Peter joined them by the door, reaching for his coat and hat. "That is fine idea. I will bring extra sugar. Do you have need for anything else from town?"

Summer thought about it for a moment. "No, I believe I have everything I need. I do have one more request, though."

"What is that?"

She quirked a brow and pointed a warning finger at him. "About those packages — you don't peek, either, Peter Ollenburger."

26

The pain Summer worried might plague her thankfully remained at bay Christmas morning. Watching Thomas open his gifts one by one brought bittersweet memories of watching her children on former Christmases, although the sweet outweighed the bitter.

Thomas grinned at her as he held up the Authors game. "The next time Pa's snowed in somewhere, we'll be able to play something besides checkers. But I'll still beat you!"

Summer held up the fine fur-lined leather gloves from Peter. "The next time your pa's snowed in somewhere, I'll be able to do his chores without freezing my fingers."

Peter patted the flannel shirt that lay across his knees. "I like this, too. Warm, and a color that is pleasing. It reminds me of the night sky full with stars."

Summer smiled. When she'd seen the deep blue flannel bearing specks of yellow and white, she had thought the same thing. How many times had she observed this man standing in his yard on widespread legs, hands in pockets, gazing upward? She had known the pattern would please him.

Lena leaned forward from her chair to pat Summer's knee. *"Danke,"* she murmured, cradling the handkerchief Summer had embroidered.

Summer replied in her limited German. *"Bitte schoen."*

Lena laughed, her eyes crinkling.

Peter shook his head. *"Grossmutter* finds your German amusing, I think."

"I don't blame her." Summer's heart felt light, seeing the smiles on the faces around her. "And I don't mind her laughing at me. I enjoy her laughter."

"As do I." Peter's warm tone matched the expression in his eyes.

Thomas pointed to a small square package under the tree. "Who is that for?"

Peter plucked it out and turned a grin in Summer's direction. "It is for Summer."

She took it, unable to contain a smile. "Another one?" She admired the roses on a pale green background before peeling back the paper to reveal a beautifully carved oak frame. Her fingers traced over the delicate rose pattern. "Oh, it's lovely, Peter. Roses have so many meanings for me. My daughter's name, the flowers she loved to stitch with floss, the blossoming vines that covered the trellis in my childhood yard . . . Roses bring good memories." She caught Peter's eye. "Thank you so much."

"You are welcome. That frame is to hold the page with your children's names on it."

Summer thought her chest would burst from emotion. This man's sensitivity went beyond anything she'd known before. He truly was a man who followed God in every way.

"Nick tells me if it is wrong size, it can go back."

Even if the page didn't fit, she would never part with this frame. "It will be fine, I'm sure." She let her smile beam on all of the Ollenburgers. "What a wonderful Christmas I've had!"

"But we are not done. There is one more gift for you." A secretive smile played at the corners of Peter's lips. "Wrapping it was not possible. So . . . I just have to tell you."

His boyish appearance made her heart skip a beat. She released a breathy laugh and held out her hands in silent inquiry.

"*Herr* Heinrich Gaeddert says the land is yours."

Summer reared backward so sharply the legs of her chair screeched against the floor. She hugged the frame to her chest as her pulse raced. "Oh, Peter! Really? The land — I can build my house there? And I can stay?"

Thomas looked back and forth from his father to Summer. "You'll stay in Gaeddert *forever*, Summer?"

"Forever!" Summer declared. She bounced from the chair, put the frame on the seat, then caught Thomas's hands and spun him in a happy circle. Releasing Thomas, she turned to his father. "Peter, you've been so kind. I can't believe how much you've done for me."

He shrugged and gave her a shy smile. "Is not so much."

She snorted — a very unladylike sound. "It *is* much. And I thank you."

"You are welcome." Their eyes remained locked for long seconds.

"But, Summer," Thomas interrupted, "if you have your own house, you won't be living here anymore."

Summer pulled her attention away from Peter. "No, but I was only staying until you were caught up on your studies and could return to school. You're all caught up and even ahead, I would wager. Your ribs have healed enough for you to ride Daisy to school when the winter break is over. So my time here is nearly done."

"But-but . . ." the boy sputtered.

"What is troubling you, boy?" Peter asked.

Thomas looked at the floor. "I wanted Summer to . . . always stay here. I wanted her to . . . be . . . my ma." His words ended on a hoarse whisper.

Summer felt as though her heart turned over in her chest. She looked at Peter, uncertain how to answer the boy. By Peter's expression, he was lost, too. Maternal instinct took over, and she pulled Thomas into her embrace. As he had the night Peter didn't return, the boy clung, burying his face against her shoulder.

"Thomas, what a wonderful gift you just gave me. It would be an honor to call a boy like you my son."

He raised his head to look at her. "Because I remind you of Vincent?"

Summer closed her eyes for a moment, picturing her son. Dark-haired, slender, with thick curling eyelashes and deep brown eyes. A pensive face, curiosity in his expression. She opened her eyes and looked at the sturdy blond boy who coiled his arms around her waist. The same pensive, curious, want-to-learn desire burned in Thomas's eyes.

She answered honestly. "Because you are you."

Thomas burrowed again.

Peter rose and touched the boy's shoulder. "Thomas, we talked about this, *ja?* That man and woman must love each other to make a union?"

Thomas loosened his grip to step back and peer up at his father. "Yes, but don't you love Summer?" He swiveled his face to look at Summer. "And don't you love my pa?"

Peter's cheeks and ears were turning deep red. Her cheeks burned, and she wondered if she was glowing more brightly than Peter.

"If Summer's staying, I don't know why she can't stay right here." Thomas's tone turned stubborn.

Peter gave his son's shoulder a shake. "You are talking of things that are best left to grownups, boy." While he spoke firmly, the gentleness Summer had grown to appreciate was still very much in place.

Thomas turned a pleading look on Summer. "Will you talk about it, please?"

She couldn't bear to deny the boy. "We'll talk about it, Thomas." Did she love this man? What she'd felt for Rodney had been acceptable — a feeling of security, but no real passion. If she married again, she knew she wanted more than she'd had before. She wanted her husband to feel for her what Peter had felt for his wife. Was it possible for him to feel for someone new what he had felt for Elsa? Could *she* feel that way about *him?* "We'll talk about it," she repeated, "and we'll pray about it. Whatever happens must be God's will, Thomas."

The big man nodded, approving her words. "But now we must finish with gifts."

Thomas's brow crinkled. "But there's nothing left to open."

"Wait here." Peter winked at Summer and put on his coat. He headed outside while Thomas stood at the window, his nose pressed to the glass. Summer, knowing what had been hidden in the hay, could hardly wait to see Thomas's reaction. Watching someone else's joy was as good as feeling it herself. She felt someone touch her elbow, and she turned to find Lena beside her, her own focus aimed toward the door in anticipation. Summer put her arm around the old woman's shoulders as they waited together for Thomas's surprise.

Summer knew the moment Peter came into sight with the new bicycle. Thomas leaped from the window and flew out the door. He remained on the stoop, his arms crossed over himself, feet dancing in excitement. "You got me a bicycle, Pa? Really? My own bicycle?"

"*Ja,* boy, your own bicycle." Peter slogged through the mushy, leftover snow. He thumped his feet clean on the stoop and then brought the ungainly machine into the house. Leaning it against the wall next to the tree hung with paper streamers and cookies, he said, "You cannot ride it until the snow melts and the ground dries hard again, but here it is for you to look at."

"Can I sit on it?"

Peter laughed and obligingly held up the bike. The boy clambered onto the seat and put his feet on the pedals. Summer, witnessing the joy on Thomas's face, couldn't hold back her own grin. Lena, too, beamed and murmured something Summer was sure were words of approval.

"Thomas, you look quite sporty atop that bicycle," Summer said.

"I can't wait to ride it! I bet it goes faster than Daisy!"

"It goes as fast as your feet pedal, but I am trusting you to use good judgment," his father said with a touch of warning in his tone.

"Sure, Pa. I'll be careful." Thomas balanced on the seat, his arms out to his sides.

"More careful than in trees? Two hands you will use?"

He wrapped his hands around the handlebars, a sheepish grin on his face. "Two hands, Pa. Honest."

"Good boy," Peter said. "Now hop off there and let us clean up all this mess so dinner we can have. I cannot go on smelling the good smells any more without tasting."

As Summer washed the dishes and carefully stacked them away, she listened to the evening sounds of her temporary home: a gentle wind outside the window, the fire crackling from the stove, Lena's rumbling snore, and voices. She tipped her head, trying to hear better the voices of Peter and Thomas from Thomas's bedroom. She couldn't make out the words, but the tone indicated a serious discussion was taking place. Her face flushed again as she remembered her promise to speak to Peter about the possibility of becoming Thomas's mother.

Confusion filled her as completely as the lye soap smell filled her nostrils. She wrinkled her nose. The earlier smells of the day had been much more pleasant. She dwelled on those — roast pork, fried potatoes and onions, dried cherry moos, and spicy *pfeffernuesse,* a gift from the Kraft family. She must have eaten a dozen handfuls of the richly spiced nickel-sized cookies. She sighed. What a lovely day it had been.

There was a time she would have thought the happiness of Christmas was wrapped up in a huge gaily decorated tree laden with beribboned gifts and a four-course feast, with dozens of people flooding the house to create a cacophony of merriment. But this day — with only the boy, his great-grandmother, and his father — had been happy in its simplicity.

Christmas, she realized, was recognizing one's blessings. So much Summer had learned in the short time she had spent with the Ollenburgers. Her heart pattered. Was she meant to be more than their neighbor and friend?

"Summer?"

She jumped, splattering the front of her dress and apron with suds. Turning, she spotted Peter standing just behind her left shoulder. "You did it again. One would think feet as large as yours incapable of moving soundlessly."

He gave the expected chuckle. Then,

without warning, he took the corner of the apron and brushed it across her chin. She felt her face go hot at the butterfly touch.

"Mark of your surprise was sitting on your chin," he said as he dropped the apron.

"W-what?"

"Soap sud." He chuckled again. "The dishwater must be too hot. Red your face is."

She spun back to face the dishpan.

"Would you like help?"

She glanced at him. The eagerness in his eyes reminded her of his son. Without speaking, she nodded.

He took up a length of toweling and reached for the plate she held out. "And when we are finished, we will sit and talk, *ja?*"

27

Peter linked his fingers together and rested his hands on the clean tabletop. Everything sparkled in the house since the woman moved in. A fine wife she would make. But *his* wife? He cleared his throat as she seated herself across from him. "Summer, we must talk about the boy."

The woman's gaze dropped to her lap, then bounced upward. Her eyes appeared wide and apprehensive. She was not making this easy for him, but he would proceed for Thomas's sake.

"I think I cause this problem with the boy. I do not consider that bringing you here would show the boy what he has missed by not having a mother. Someone to cook for him, read to him, see to his needs."

"But you and Lena have —"

He raised one hand, silencing her protest. "*Ja,* caring for the boy we have done. But it is somehow different when you do it. A mother's care is very different than a father's, or even a great-grandmother's. Now the boy knows this, and he has decided he wants the care of a mother, too." He shrugged, searching for the words to explain his thoughts. "You are first woman to spend long times with him since his mother dies, so only natural it is for him to grow close to you."

"So you don't think it's *me* he wants, it's just that I'm the only one available."

Did he hear defensiveness in her tone? He leaned forward. "*Nein,* Summer, you — you are the one he loves. He loves you because he knows you."

A slight frown appeared on her face, but she nodded. "I think I understand what you're saying. Thomas now realizes what it means to have a mother. I am here, he knows me, he trusts me, so I am the logical choice."

Logical. This word puzzled Peter, but the other things she'd said made sense. "*Ja,* for the boy, you are his choice for mother."

She nibbled her lower lip, her brow deeply furrowed. He waited in silence for her to gather her thoughts. "Peter, may I be honest with you?"

"For sure. I want you to be honest with me."

Pink stained her cheeks as she admitted, "I have considered what problems would be solved if I were to marry you. I would have a home, security, a standing in the community. You are a good man, and I admire you." She drew in a deep breath. "How-how can one be sure the decisions we make are ones God wants us to make and not only our own selfish desires?"

Peter felt proud that this educated woman would ask him — just a common miller, not a scholar or preacher — such an important question. He gave it much consideration before forming an answer. "I think God speaks in many ways. Inside of us, when we let God's Son in, lives the Holy Spirit, who helps guide and direct our thoughts. The Holy Spirit prompts us. When decision is right one, you will know deep in your heart."

"So my heart will tell me whom I should marry, if anyone?"

"That is right. You follow your heart."

"Then . . . it is all right that . . . for now . . ." The pink in her cheeks deepened to red.

Peter gave a slow nod. "Is okay. We are friends, and that is enough, *ja?*"

A smile broke across her face. "Yes. Thank you." Unexpectedly, she reached across the table and placed her hand over his. How small hers appeared next to his thick, rough hands. "It's good having you for a friend, Peter Ollenburger. I don't know that I've ever had a better one."

He released a chuckle, partly from pleasure, partly from embarrassment. "*Ja.* Well, never have I called a woman my friend — other than my Elsa, of course. But I think it is good, too."

"Would you like another cup of coffee?" She removed her hand from his.

"*Ja.* Coffee would be good."

Is peaceful ending for a pleasureful day, Peter thought as he and the woman sipped coffee at the table together. The woman had been right — their marriage could solve problems. It would mean security for her, and it would make the boy happy, for sure. But God-ordained marriage was what they both wanted. It was good to agree on that. He would pray for Thomas's acceptance.

Thomas pulled the covers over his head.

"*Sie stoppen sich zu verstecken.*" Pa's voice sounded stern.

Thomas obeyed his pa's order, emerging

384

from his hiding place by lowering the blankets until his eyes were uncovered. His pa's hand moved toward his face. He didn't flinch when Pa took hold of the blankets — Pa never hit him — but he cringed when his pa pulled the covers down far enough so his chin showed. He felt better when he was all covered up.

"I know how you feel about the woman." Pa put his hand on Thomas's chest. "But is important for you to know how I feel, too. We talked, Summer and me, and we agree on this. We care for each other as very good friends, but it would be wrong to marry without love."

Thomas blinked as fast as he could. He didn't want to cry in front of his father. "But, Pa, I know Summer likes you. She likes you a lot. And you like her, too."

"*Ja,* of course we like each other. I said we are good friends. But like and love are two very different things, boy."

Thomas felt his chin begin to quiver. He clamped his teeth together as hard as he could to make it stop.

"When you are grown up, you will understand better that some things cannot be forced. Love is one of them. Love must grow on its own, planted in gentleness and watered with God's hand." Pa patted Thomas's chest. "You feel love growing here for the woman. There is nothing wrong with that. It is good to find love in your heart. Love makes the heart softer, makes you think more of others, makes you want to do good instead of evil. Be thankful love is there, son. Let it be enough that you love her."

The tears Thomas had tried so hard to hold back spilled from his eyes. Embarrassed, he turned his face away from his father. He sucked in air, but one sob came out anyway. "I don't want to talk anymore."

He closed his eyes as tight as he could and felt his father's hand slide away. The bed creaked as his pa stood up. Thomas kept his eyes shut and jammed his chin against his shoulder. Pa wouldn't be hearing any more baby noises!

The door clicked shut, and Thomas opened one eye to peek. The room was empty. He threw back the covers and lunged forward, bringing up his knees to bury his face against them. Why couldn't they love each other? It wasn't hard to love. He loved Summer, and it was easy. She loved him, too. He knew she did. If she could love him, why couldn't she love his pa? It didn't make sense!

He cried against his knees, making no

noise but getting his nightshirt soggy with tears. The crying made his head hurt. He needed to stop. He raised his head, sniffing hard until he felt under control. After rubbing his eyes, he looked around.

The room was shadowed, but he could see the shapes of the gifts Summer had given him, lined up on his bureau. He thrust out his chin. Well, if she wasn't going to be his ma, he sure wasn't going to leave those things up there like a row of trophies.

He kicked the covers down and climbed out of his bed. Barefoot, he marched across the drafty floor and scooped everything into his arms. The dictionary dug into his ribs, and he winced as he carried the load back to the bed, knelt, and shoved it all underneath.

"There," he murmured through gritted teeth, "that's better. Won't have to look at that stuff." He threw himself back into the bed and yanked the covers up. But after a while he realized having those presents under the bed didn't make him feel better. In fact, it made him feel worse, knowing how roughly he had treated them.

What had Pa said? Loving people makes you want to do good instead of evil. He sighed. Well, then, he must love Summer something fierce, because it made him feel awful to have treated her presents like that. He swung out of the bed and got down on his hands and knees beside it, reaching under the bed to retrieve every item.

He put the gifts back on the bureau top, placing them all just so. He remembered how he'd felt when he'd opened the games, thinking about evenings when he and Summer would play and laugh like they had with that silly checkers game. It felt like he had a ma when she played with him. He wanted that. He wanted a ma *so bad.* Sadness pressed at him now instead of anger, and it was harder to hold in.

Thomas shivered. Whenever he felt sad, his pa had taught him, you should talk to God and let Him share it. The way he figured it, God had already taken one ma away from him. It wouldn't be fair if He took this one, too. He would just have to let God know that.

Summer stood on the stoop and watched Daisy trot down the road toward school with Thomas bouncing on her broad back. She felt a pang at the boy's departure. The past couple of weeks since Christmas had been strained between them. She had sensed his pulling away, as if separating himself emotionally from her before he had to be separated physically. She understood, and she tried to treat him no differently so he would see her feelings toward him hadn't changed, yet she knew things were changing.

Thomas's ribs were completely healed. There would be no more long days together, teaching him and learning from him. No longer did she have an excuse to reside beneath Peter's roof. But Peter had insisted she stay until her house was built. Even though it was too cold to begin construction yet, she had made the first move toward building the house: she had gone to town the past Saturday to pay for her land.

Her land. What a wonderful feeling that thought evoked! Her own place, a place no one could take away from her or talk her into leaving. Even if it meant being away from Thomas, she eagerly anticipated having her very own house.

"Summer, the boy is gone. Will you stand there looking until home he rides?"

Peter's voice from the kitchen brought a stop to her musings. She turned, a sheepish smile tugging at her cheeks. "Of course not. I was just —"

"Thinking." He sent her a broad grin. "Always you are thinking. What is it now that makes your forehead wrinkle like a sand plum left in the sun?"

Summer laughed as she closed the door, sealing out the cold. The things this man said! But she enjoyed their easy camaraderie. She would miss that as much as the boy when she moved into her own house. She began clearing dishes as she answered him. "I was thinking of my house and how soon it could be built. I have big plans for it. A porch, and a flower garden, and a picket fence . . ."

"Picket?" Peter's forehead now crinkled like a plum left in the sun. "What is picket?"

"You know — a fence made of narrow boards set with space between them. A decorative fence rather than a practical one."

He nodded, his expression clearing. "*Ja,* I think I know. There is one around *Frau* Schmidt's flower garden. So high" — he gestured — "and painted white, standing like a row of snaggled teeth."

Again, her laughter bubbled. "Well, I'd prefer my fence didn't resemble snaggled teeth, but you have the height and color right." She ladled water from the reservoir to wash dishes. "When do you suppose construction can begin?"

Peter carried his coffee mug to the dry

sink and leaned against the wall, facing her. Many of their conversations took place over the washing of dishes, Summer realized. She heard a light chuckle, and she turned to see Lena in her bedroom doorway, smiling at the two of them. Heat filled her face as she realized what a homey picture they must paint, standing together this way. The heat seemed to extend to her chest, and she swallowed hard in an attempt to calm her suddenly jangled nerves.

"Late February at earliest, for sure, on the building," he answered as Lena padded forward and poured herself a cup of coffee. The old woman stayed beside them as Peter continued. "But there is much to do before building can begin. Rock must be collected for the foundation. Lumber and glass panes must be ordered. We must to dig a well for you. A cellar must be dug in case of bad storms and also for storing of vegetables. Land must be cleared for the garden. And, of course, those little boards must be cut for your snaggle-tooth fence." He grinned.

"Picket fence." Her discomfort faded away. It was so easy to respond to his playfulness.

"Will you have animals? Chickens? Pigs? A horse? This must be planned for, too." He downed the last drop of his coffee and dropped the mug into the dishpan.

Summer sighed. "There is much to think about. I suppose it's good I still have a few weeks to sort everything out. I hope my money will stretch far enough to cover everything. I still have no job."

"If it is God's will, a job will come," he said. "Think of all things that have worked out so far. You bought the land without problems from the Gaeddert brothers. The council considers your acceptance into church membership. Some women from town choose to be your friend."

Summer smiled as she remembered times of coffee and cinnamon cake with Katherine Kraft, Bertha Klein, or Martha Jost. Most of the women still kept their distance, but now that Summer understood their reason for holding themselves aloof, she had confidence they would eventually come to accept her. Long-held hurts took time to heal.

"Yes, God has been good to me," she agreed. "So I'll trust Him in the acquiring of a job." She carefully stacked two plates, her thoughts on the months ahead and all the changes in store. "I'm so glad you bought Thomas that bicycle. He should be able to visit me regularly."

"You will miss the boy."

"Yes." Her throat caught on the single-word answer.

Peter pushed off from the wall. "You need distraction today. When the dishes are done, you put on your coat. I will take you to visit *Frau* Kraft. She cannot get out much now with the burden of the baby she carries, but she will welcome your company."

Summer immediately perked up with this idea. "Are you sure it wouldn't be an inconvenience?"

"Her boy, too, is gone now after a long break from school. She will be looking for a distraction, for sure."

Summer liked the way he'd said "her boy, too," as if Summer had a right to claim Thomas as a little bit her own. "Thank you. I'll be ready in less than half an hour."

"I will be in barn. Come out when ready you are."

28

Peter's heart had lifted when Katherine welcomed Summer with a warm hug and invited her to stay for tea. Summer bid him farewell, and he rolled on toward town, his mind on the morning's conversation with the woman.

She wanted a house, but he suspected she had little knowledge of how a house was built. Left to herself, it would be a sorry house, ill planned. But he knew how to build, and planning he could do for her.

First he would stop at the sawmill and get prices for lumber. While there, he would also ask Lundy Wismer about rock for the foundation and about digging a cellar. The man was handy when it came to such things. At the General Merchandise he would find out how much windows were priced these days — prices went up all the time. The woman would need to follow a tight budget.

At Nickels' he would ask to borrow the Montgomery Ward and Company catalog for a few days so the woman could look at furniture. All she had was a chair and a handmade rope bed. She would need much to fill even a small house. Also he could ask about jobs. Maybe the hotel could use her to do cleaning or dishwashing. There must be something a woman could do to support herself. He did not think it was wise to begin building the house until she had a job, but he would not tell her what to do. He would only pray for her wisdom, which he did even while he drove to town.

The sound of the steam-powered sawmill engine filled his ears before he made the final curve into town. Good that even in the winter, *Herr* Wismer could continue to cut lumber. Peter had to save carefully through the months to make sure his and the boy's needs were met all year. The bicycle had been an extravagance, but Peter did not regret it. Giving the boy delight now and then would not spoil him.

He ordered the oxen to halt outside the sawmill, hopped down, and entered the noisy building. Two men worked at the saw, guiding logs through the great teeth and turning them into boards. Peter thrilled to the vibration of the saw and the pungent smell of fresh-cut wood.

Herr Wismer gestured for Peter to come into the small office at the front of the mill. It was slightly quieter there. Peter had to yell to make himself heard, but he left assured the mill could provide the woman with what she needed to build her house. *Herr* Wismer promised to loan Peter some floor plans from which the woman could choose. He also said he would make a list of the needed lumber and its cost when she'd chosen a plan. The men shook hands, and Peter started to leave.

Then he remembered something else and turned back. After a brief consultation, Peter left with a smile on his face. He did enjoy giving other people surprises.

He left the oxen nosing the ground in front of the sawmill and walked to Nickels', where Nick agreed to let him take the catalog with the assurance it would come back with no missing pages.

"Why would I tear out pages? In the house I will use it, not the outhouse," Peter teased.

Nick shook his head. "Some customers tear out the pages so they remember what they want to order. What use is a catalog with missing pages? I trust you to bring it back whole, Peter."

Peter tucked the catalog into the large pocket inside his jacket and moved on to the General Merchandise. As he had feared, windowpanes would be pricey.

"It is the railroad, Peter. I have to raise my prices to allow for the shipping." *Herr* Brunk sounded apologetic. "The more fragile the good, the higher the price to ship it."

"I understand," Peter answered. "But I know the woman has limited means."

"Then tell her to get the smallest panes and put them together to make a bigger window," the man encouraged. "Four little panes together make a good bedroom window. Three little panes over three more make a good parlor window. Of course, there will be sashes between the panes, but they should not block too much of a view."

"This is good to know. I will tell her." Peter wished he had brought some paper to write on.

"Why is the woman building a house?" *Herr* Brunk asked.

Peter smiled. "I cannot stay forever in my barn."

"I did not expect you to." The man pulled his lips sideways and bit down on his mustache. "My *frau* tells me marriage is probable between you."

Heat built in Peter's neck. He forced a smile. "Your *frau* tells you wrongly."

"*Ach*. Women!" Brunk waved his hand. "Always they have marriage on their minds. She meant nothing, I am sure."

"I am sure," Peter answered. "Thank you for helping with the windows. I will be back after the woman has picked her house design."

Peter left the General Merchandise and headed for his wagon. Although he had intended to check into jobs for the woman, the hour was growing late and Thomas would be out of school soon. He did not want to miss the boy's arrival on his first day back. He would hurry and pick up Summer from the Kraft farm, then together they would greet the boy.

Thomas pulled back on Daisy's reins to slow her from a canter to a walk as he came upon the lane that led to his house. Would Summer still be there when he came home? Ever since Christmas, when Pa had said he didn't love Summer, Thomas had worried. If he was back in school, Summer might go away. He didn't want her to go away. She needed to be with him so Pa could grow to love her and she could grow to love Pa.

A funny weight sat in his tummy. It had been there all day. At first it was a little rock, nervousness about being back in school after his long time away. But over the day it had gotten bigger with Rupert's teasing, some of the other boys' questions, and Belinda Schmidt's snooty faces. Those Schmidt women could make a snooty face better than anybody. Belinda had never turned it on him before, but today she had picked him out and made it hard for him to focus on the first ten amendments to the Constitution.

Only Toby Kraft had stood beside him. At recess Toby had told Rupert to quit his jokes about Summer unless he wanted to never play with Toby's erector set again. That had made Rupert and all the other boys shut up. Everybody liked to play with Toby's erector set, which was the only one in town. Toby was his new best friend, Thomas decided. Toby had kept the rock from turning into a boulder. But Thomas's stomach still didn't feel right.

How come God had let him grow to love Summer if she wasn't going to be his ma? All his life, he'd been taught God gave good gifts, God knew what was best, God answered prayers. But now Thomas wasn't sure. That feeling scared him even more than the rock in his belly.

The house came into view.

"Whoa, Daisy." Thomas brought the animal to a halt. He shielded his eyes with his hand and waited, watching. Was she there?

The door opened and Pa stepped onto the stoop. Even from here, Thomas could see Pa's smile. Like everything else on him, Pa's smile was big. Thomas waved when his pa waved, but he couldn't smile back. Not yet. Where was she?

And then a shadow appeared behind Pa. The shadow moved beside Pa, and Thomas saw that it was Summer in her black dress. The smile he'd held in burst over his face. She hadn't left him. Not yet. There was still a chance. . . .

"C'mon, Daisy!" He dug in his heels and Daisy obeyed, carrying him briskly the final yards to the house.

"Well, boy," his pa greeted, his big hands rolled into fists on his hips. "A good day did you have at school?"

Thomas decided it wasn't important anymore what everyone had said and done. All that mattered was Summer was still here. "It was a good day."

Summer tipped her head in that way she

did when she was ready to listen. "Were you all caught up or do we have some extra homework tonight?"

The rock shrank when he heard the word *we.* She was still willing to help him. Just like a ma would be. "I am all caught up, and Mr. Funk said I am near the sixth grade level in arithmetic. He said I made good use of my time at home, and he is proud of me." Thomas didn't tell them Rupert had called him "teacher's pet."

"That's wonderful, Thomas." Summer smiled at him with her eyes all crinkly. "I'm proud of you, too."

Thomas finally allowed himself to feel proud. "Uh-huh."

"Well, you put that animal in the corral and let her run. She needs to stretch her legs after being tethered all day," Pa instructed. "Then come inside. *Gruznikje* are on the table."

Ammonia cookies! His favorite. Thomas's mouth watered at the thought of biting into one of the big soft peppermint-flavored cookies. "Yes, sir!"

He stayed still long enough to watch his father turn to Summer and gesture toward the kitchen. Summer smiled up at Pa, and

Pa touched her back as he followed her into the house.

Thomas's heart pounded hard in his chest. They had looked just like Toby's parents there on the stoop side-by-side and then going into the house together. He'd keep praying. Didn't his Bible say the prayers of a righteous man availeth much? Maybe he wasn't a man yet, but Pa had always told him God looked on a person's heart. Thomas was righteous. His prayers would avail much, too.

"Let's go, Daisy." Thomas clicked his tongue and turned Daisy toward the corral. As long as Summer was here, there was still hope.

"Today, Peter? Really?"

Summer could hardly believe what she'd just heard. Her house could be started!

"*Ja,* today. Enough rock has been collected. *Herr* Kraft, *Herr* Ratzlaff, and *Herr* Hett have all said today they will help. So the foundation will be laid. You come so you show how you want the house to sit on the land."

Summer dashed across the room to retrieve her coat. "It will face west so I can sit on the porch in the evening and watch the sunset. Kansas has the most beautiful sunsets." Fastening her buttons, she turned to him eagerly. "Will we be ready to start building it tomorrow, then?"

Peter laughed, his eyes sparkling. "The wood is yet to be cut. This takes time. But in two weeks or so, by end of February? *Ja,* I think building will start. So ready you are to be out of my house?"

"I must sound like an impatient child." She hugged herself. "Oh, I can hardly believe — my own house!" She removed his coat from its hook and pushed it at him. "Put this on and let's go!" She dashed out the door with Peter behind her.

On the way to her land, she examined the house plan again. It was a small house, she acknowledged — nothing like the two-story Queen Anne in Boston — but it had a nice floor plan. If it faced west, as she desired, the south half would have the sitting room, dining room, and kitchen all arranged shotgun style from front to back. The north half would have two bedrooms with a small bathing room between them.

Summer had insisted on two things when choosing a plan — a dining room and a wraparound porch. Since the plan had three larger rooms on one side and three smaller rooms on the other, she would have her wraparound porch in front and also a small stoop leading to the kitchen at the rear of the house. The cellar would be outside the kitchen door. It was a good arrangement. Summer was pleased with her choice.

When the wagon rolled to a stop near the gravesites, the other men were waiting. Peter jumped down and then reached for her. The moment her feet touched the ground, she hurried to the others and beamed at each in turn. "Thank you so much for helping."

Tobias Kraft removed his hat when speaking to her. "Helping neighbors is an easy thing. My Katherine sent a basket lunch for us, and she said to tell you the jar of pickled beets is to go home for your supper."

Summer smiled her thanks as Peter came up behind her. He held several wooden stakes and a roll of twine in his large hands.

"*Frau* Steadman" — he always used her proper name when with people from town — "you show us now how far from the graves you want the house. Then we will begin digging to set the rocks."

Summer scurried around, pointing to her choice of location. She listened to the men discuss why it should be shifted six feet to the north, nodded in agreement, then stood to the side with her hands clasped beneath her chin as the real work began. The men measured for the foundation using *Herr* Kraft's measuring rule. They set the stakes and twine to show where the foundation must go, then *Herr* Ratzlaff and *Herr* Hett dug a gully in which Peter and *Herr* Kraft could set the rocks.

Summer trotted alongside Peter as he carried a large rock from a pile near the road. "Where did all these rocks come from?"

"Fields," he huffed. "When farmers plow, they find them. Every farm has a rock pile. Then, when one is preparing to build, the rocks are collected for foundation. Works well."

She nodded, turning with him back toward the rock pile. But he put his hand on her coat sleeve.

"*Frau* Steadman, I do not wish for you to be injured. Please sit off to the side for your watching."

Although disappointed, she understood the sense of his direction. She sat near the graves and watched. Slowly, rock by rock, they laid the foundation for the house and porch. As the morning progressed, despite the chill air, the men shed their coats and worked in shirtsleeves beneath the azure sky. When the sun shone straight overhead, she brought out the basket lunch from the Kraft wagon and served the men. They ate quickly and returned to work.

By the time school was letting out, they were finished. The sweaty men loaded up the tools they had brought and donned their coats. Summer thanked them all again and told them their families would be welcome to visit anytime. After good-byes were exchanged, Peter and Summer were left alone.

Summer walked around the periphery of the foundation, imagining the inside rooms and the porches. With the rocks outlining the house, it was all so much more real than it had been on paper. She hugged herself, smiling.

"Summer, may I ask you a question?" Peter stood behind her right shoulder.

She squinted against the sun and gave a slight nod.

"That big space" — he pointed toward the graves — "between your husband's grave and the grave of your oldest girl. Why is it there?"

"I left room for myself, of course. It seemed appropriate, considering I didn't really want to live." She squatted down, running her hand over the row of rocks by her feet.

Peter hunkered next to her, his forearms on his bent knees. "You wished to die?"

She plucked at a blade of brown grass caught between stones. "I could see no reason for living. My children were gone, Rodney was gone, I knew neither my brother nor Rodney's parents would welcome me and so . . ." She raised her shoulders in a brief shrug. "So death seemed the best choice."

"Is that why you would not eat?"

She considered his question. Though it hadn't been a conscious thought, perhaps unconsciously she had hoped the lack of food would lead to her death. "Yes." She felt a small smile tug at her lips. "But you manipulated me."

He raised his chin and laughed. "*Nein,* I prayed for way to get you to eat. God manipulated you."

She shook her head. "No, He simply reached out to me in the form of a big tender-hearted man and a dear little boy who offered me a reason to live." She touched his arm with her gloved hand. "Thank you, Peter."

His Adam's apple bobbed up and down in a big swallow. "To be the bringer of God's love to a person is a humbling thing. Thank you for telling me this."

"You're welcome."

He added, "You have done much for us, too. I say thank you."

She took in a deep breath through her nose as her gaze swung across the grounds that would be her new home. "And I can't believe how much God has done for me." She patted a rock and stood up, brushing off her skirt. "But now we'd better head back so we're there when Thomas returns home."

Peter rose, and they walked toward the wagon. She asked, "Will we be able to bring him back out and let him see where the house will be?"

Peter shook his head, regret in his eyes. "The days are still too short. Evening will be upon us. But on Saturday, when school he does not have, we will bring him. *Herr* Kraft said he would be available that day to help dig. Much must be dug — a well, a pit for the outhouse, a cellar. I do not much care for digging."

Summer laughed at the face he made. "I'll help as much as I can."

His eyes twinkled. "A little colt like you could not break the soil. Even for me, who is used to heavy labor, it is hard." He helped her into the wagon. "The ground is still hard from the cold. We set fires to soften the ground first, then dig."

At the mention of fires, Summer's stomach quivered. Although no evidence of the ash pile that was once her wagon and belongings still existed, the memories were still in her mind. It was difficult for her to walk past that spot without experiencing a pang of loss.

Peter heaved himself into the wagon. He looked at her, and his brow furrowed. "You are troubled again."

She tried to relax her expression. "No, I was just thinking of . . ."

Understanding dawned across his face. "Fires."

She nodded, biting down on her lip. "I'm sure that seems child—"

"Not childish." His firm tone cut her off. "Maybe it would be better if you did not come for the burning."

"No. Right now only bad memories are associated with the idea of a fire. But the fire you're planning is to build something, to put something together." She stopped as an idea entered her mind. "Oh, Peter. Ashes . . ." She touched her lips with her fingers. "Ashes can't be put back together again, remember?"

"*Ja,* I remember."

"But these ashes — these ashes will be *building* ashes." Peace flooded through her at the realization. "They are needed to build the home of my new beginning."

He smiled at her, unspeaking, but she sensed he understood her jumbled thoughts.

She pressed her hands together, pushing them between her knees as he started the oxen in motion. "As soon as the house is finished, the very first thing I will hang on the wall is the frame you gave me, with the page from Rodney's Bible inside. It will be my reminder that with God, ashes *can* be put back together again. Not in the same form they were before the fire, but refined."

29

Summer waited outside the church, her coat pulled tight across her chest. Inside, the congregation voted. If the majority voted yes, Summer would become an official member of the Gaeddert *Kleine Gemeinde.* If the majority voted no, she could attend services but not be an active participant. How she wanted to belong! Her heart ached with the desire for the vote to be yes.

The door squeaked, and she spun. Tobias Kraft stood in the doorway. Her heart pounded. He offered a smile and nod. The vote had gone in her favor. She was a member! With light steps she returned to the sanctuary, where Mr. Kraft escorted her to the front of the church. It was easier to face the congregation now than it had been earlier, when she'd shared her conversion and her reasons for desiring membership.

Reverend Enns shook her hand, welcoming her into the fold. He turned to the members. "*Frau* Summer Steadman, a member of our flock."

How the words warmed her. She allowed herself to search each face. A few still held frowns — those of the Schmidt and Penner families — but most smiled as she made eye contact, offering support. She looked at Peter and Thomas, and she couldn't stop the smile that rounded her cheeks at the glowing expressions on those two dear faces.

As they left the church, Peter and Thomas on one side and Lena on the other, Summer laughed. "Well, Mr. Ollenburger, I am now a member of a church whose language I do not speak." She shrugged within the confines of her coat. "But I trust I can still depend on you to share the Bible references from the sermons with me. I'll continue to study on my own."

"That will not be necessary, *Frau* Steadman." The deep voice came from behind them. Peter and Summer turned to find the minister on their heels. "In addition to the vote we took for your membership, other business we did, too. We voted to give sermons in English so you could understand what is spoken. The congregation held long talk on this, but they agree your growth is more important than hearing the words in German."

Summer's heart turned over in gratefulness. The fact that these people were willing to make this change for her spoke deeply of their loosening of fears. She thought of Lena, who did not understand English. Had she voted to use English so Summer would understand?

She took the old woman's bony hand. Lena smiled, squeezing her hand in response. Summer turned back to the minister. "Thank you so much, Reverend Enns. I appreciate your kindness."

The man's eyes twinkled. "Still we will sing our hymns in German and read the Bible verses in German. But I will give reference in English so you can follow the reading."

"A perfect compromise."

Thomas tugged her sleeve. "Summer, the Krafts want to know if we'll come for *faspa*." He pointed across the yard. Katherine and Tobias waited with expectant faces. She gave a nod. "If it's all right with your father, I would be delighted."

"Is it okay, Pa?"

"*Ja.* It is fine."

Thomas scampered off.

The warmth of acceptance carried Summer through the remainder of the week. Peter took her to the building site every afternoon so she could watch the progress of her house. It delighted her to walk across the sturdy planked floor, giggling as she slipped between the studs that would support the lath-and-plaster walls rather than using openings that would eventually be doorways.

On Wednesday she insisted on taking cookies and tea to the structure. She, Peter, and Thomas sat on the porch and enjoyed an after-school snack. Peter teased her about using a porch that was only a floor, but she merely laughed.

"It won't always be only a floor, and I want to remember each moment of this home's creation. It's my very first, you know."

Thomas gave her a puzzled look. "You've had houses before."

"Yes," she agreed, tweaking his nose. "But this is the first that's been truly mine. Every other house has belonged to someone else — my parents, my brother, my husband, you and your father." She threw her arms out and drew in a breath, reveling in the smell of new wood, musty earth, and clean

414

air. "This one is really, truly mine in every sense."

As Saturday neared, Summer vacillated between two desires. Although she wanted to be at the house when her cellar and outhouse were dug, she had an errand to tend — a secret she hoped would be well received. But it would require time away from the Ollenburgers. She knew it wouldn't be troublesome for Peter to drop her at the Kraft farm when he headed to her land Saturday morning, yet she feared he would worry she was still troubled by seeing fire.

She tossed the ideas back and forth in her mind all day Friday, finding herself biting down on her lower lip in consternation so many times she created a sore spot. Finally, after supper, she gathered her courage and brought up the subject as she and Thomas cleared the table.

"Peter, it has been a week since I've visited with Katherine Kraft. Do you suppose I could spend Saturday with her rather than going to the house?"

Peter raised his head, his face showing surprise. "You do not wish to see the digging?"

Summer lowered a stack of plates into the dishpan. "I suppose I prefer to see the finished product this time." She glanced at

415

him, her tongue finding the sore spot on her lip. "Will that be all right?"

He gave a slow nod. "*Ja,* I think fine that will be."

Summer nearly wilted with relief. He seemed puzzled but not concerned. And he'd agreed so readily. *Well,* she thought as she dipped hot water from the reservoir, *I guess it was meant to be.*

Peter hollered, "Giddap! Haw," directing the oxen toward the road. He gave one last wave to the woman, who stood on the Krafts' porch, as the wagon lumbered away. A grin climbed his cheeks, and he did nothing to hold it back. He could scarce believe his good fortune.

He had needed a day without the woman at the house-building site, but he had not known how to keep her away. When she had expressed the desire to not go on this Saturday, he had found himself wanting to shout with glee. How difficult it had been to keep a sober expression and simply agree. Now, though, his heart pounded hard in his chest. One day — only one day he would have to prepare his surprise for her.

Thomas sat on the wagon seat beside him, squinting up at the sun. Peter felt his smile

416

growing broader. How much the boy had grown in the past months. And since his ribs had healed, he could work again. This was a blessing. With the boy's help, surely they would finish the job.

He gave Thomas a light nudge with his elbow. "How would you like to pound nails today instead of carry dirt?"

Thomas brought up a hand to shield his eyes. "You gonna have me build the outhouse or something?"

"*Nein,* not the outhouse. Something else. Something special. You can help me?"

"Sure, Pa!"

The boy's eagerness matched Peter's. He coaxed the oxen, willing them to move faster than their normal sedate pace. A day only had so many hours.

"Pa, that looks real pretty." Thomas's words came out in a breathy sigh.

Peter clamped a hand around the back of Thomas's neck and gave a gentle squeeze. "I could not have done it without you, boy. A good team we make, *ja?*"

The boy nodded as the two beamed at the crisp white picket fence that proudly guarded the graves of Summer's family members. It had been a good day's work, and it had felt good to work side-by-side with the boy, their bare heads receiving the heat of the sun, their muscles flexing with the swing of a hammer or the push of a saw, their brows furrowing as they sought to keep each picket in alignment with the last.

Many times Peter had fought a desire to reach out and hug the boy against his chest, so good the feeling had been. A day only had so many hours, and a boy's childhood only so many years. Then he would be a man — a man who would find his own way. Peter swallowed the lump in his throat and gave Thomas's neck another slight squeeze before dropping his hand.

"A fine fence it is, boy. A fence of which to be proud."

"Summer's gonna love it. Won't she be surprised?"

"*Ja,* surprised for sure. She was expecting an outhouse and cellar today. And she gets an outhouse, a cellar, *and* a white picket fence."

Thomas stretched a finger toward one of the pickets, but Peter admonished, "That paint is not yet dry, son. You will leave a smudge."

Thomas stuck the offending hand into his jacket pocket and shrugged. "Can we go get her now and show it to her?"

Peter shook his head. "I think we wait till tomorrow." He leaned forward and finished in a whisper. "More fun it will be to let her discover it herself. Let us stay silent, and tomorrow, as we pass by to go to church, she will see it then. *Ja?*"

Thomas grinned. "I won't say anything."

Peter and the boy strode to the other men who were loading their tools in the back of *Herr* Jost's wagon. They complimented one another on the accomplishment of their tasks and agreed to meet again each afternoon of the next week to finish the roof and put in the windows.

"Surely the windowpanes are in at Brunk's General Merchandise by now," Peter said. "I will go and see before I come here on Monday."

"Fine, Peter," Tobias Kraft agreed. "And with one more week of working, the house will be ready for the woman." He stroked his chin. "Peter, I wonder if she would accept used furniture?"

Peter offered a shrug. "I do not see that she would reject used furniture. Why do you ask?"

"My Katherine is concerned for her. Would it not be good if, when the woman moved in, she had some things in place?"

He looked at the other men. "A table we have that is not being used. Maybe a trunk, too. Do you think others in town might offer some household furnishings?"

Thomas tugged at Peter's jacket. "Pa, you could give her a housewarming."

Herr Kraft slapped Thomas's shoulder. "That is a fine idea, boy! A housewarming. My Katherine can organize it. Will your wives help?"

The men all nodded or spoke their agreement. Peter felt his chest tighten. Summer had been truly accepted. How good for her to finally belong. And how good for the town to finally reach out. God had worked a miracle here.

Everyone went in his separate direction, calling back good-byes and plans for Sunday's *faspa*. Peter and Thomas were the last to leave. They stood long moments, admiring their picket fence. The woman would be pleased, for sure. Peter sighed and wrapped an arm around Thomas's shoulders.

"Come on, boy. Chores wait at home. Let us fetch your Summer, and then home we go."

Thomas scampered to the wagon and climbed aboard. Peter sat beside Thomas and picked up the whip. Then, with a smirk, he put the whip in his son's hand. "Well, boy, let us see if you are as good a driver as you are a fence builder, *ja?*"

"Really, Pa?" Thomas raised the whip.

Peter put his hand over the boy's. "Really. But only your calls are needed to direct them."

Thomas relaxed his hold.

"Now, you know how to start them."

Thomas took in a great breath. "Giddap!"

With a jerk, the oxen moved forward. When they reached the bend in the road, the boy yelped, "Haw! Haw!"

"Only once, son, or too sharp they will turn," Peter warned.

"Okay, Pa." The boy held his shoulders straight and angled his chin upward, his expression serious.

Peter hid his smile. "You are doing fine." The boy seemed to puff with pride. Peter scooted down in the seat and propped his boots on the footboard. "A little nap I think I take. Wake me when to Krafts' we are."

"B-but," Thomas protested, "how'll I turn onto their road?"

"A gentle call to gee, and the oxen will turn. They know what to do." He gave Thomas a little nudge with his elbow. "Relax and let the beasts do their work." He pulled his hat over his eyes and leaned back. "Stay on the road, boy."

Peter drowsed with the crunch of wagon wheels against dirt and Thomas's breathing competing for attention in his ears. It seemed little time passed before the boy's voice quavered, "Gee!" Obediently, the oxen turned into the Krafts' lane. Peter sat up, rubbing his eyes.

Thomas beamed at him. "I did it, Pa!"

"*Ja,* you did it, boy. A teamster we will make of you yet, for sure."

When they reached the yard, the door to the house opened and Summer stepped onto the porch. Thomas called in a deep voice, "Who-o-o-oa." The oxen drew to a halt. Thomas raised his hand to wave at Summer, but she didn't wave back. She cradled something in her arms.

Peter squinted, trying to identify the fuzzy lump. A rug? Or a bundle of rags? Then the lump shifted, one part rising up, with two floppy ears perking on either side of a furry face, and Peter knew what she had.

Thomas must have recognized it at the same time, because he stiffened on the seat. "S-Summer?" The one-word query came out in a whisper.

Summer walked to the side of the wagon, her smile on Thomas. "Look here, Thomas." She held the furry bundle up to him. The puppy hung from her hands, his ears flopping and front paws drooping. "The Krafts' dog had a litter — eight in all — but this one is the runt, and no one has claimed him. So I decided to give him a home. Do you want to hold him?"

Thomas drew back, leaning against Peter's chest. "No, you go ahead."

Summer pulled the puppy against her own chest and stroked its head, her eyes down. Peter sensed her disappointment. But when she spoke, he heard no rancor. "Well, he'll need a name, and I'm afraid I'm not very good at naming things." She peered up again, her expression hopeful. "Will you help me choose one?"

Thomas still leaned against his father, examining the pup with narrowed eyes. "He's got that brown around his eye, kind of like a pirate's patch, and another brown spot on his side. Maybe you could call him Patches?"

Summer released a light laugh, causing Peter to smile, too. "Patches." She spoke the name to the puppy, and the little thing wagged its tail and licked her chin. She laughed again. "Yes, I think he likes it. Patches it is." She held the pup toward Thomas. "Take him now, so I can climb in."

Thomas's hands shot out, and then the

puppy was in his lap. Peter's admiration for the woman expanded. He understood what she was doing. The town was setting aside its fears. Now it was time for Thomas to do the same. Peter hopped down and trotted around the wagon to help her up. Once she was seated, he sat on the other side of the boy. It was a tight fit three across, but he didn't mind.

"Boy, do you want to drive home?" he asked.

Thomas looked at him, the pup wiggling in his arms. "I'm scared to turn the wagon around."

Peter sent Summer a smile over the top of Thomas's head. "I will drive, then." Once they were headed straight again, he leaned forward and addressed the woman. "Full of surprises, you are."

She gave a graceful shrug. "What is a house without a dog scurrying underfoot? He'll keep me from becoming too lonely in my fine new house."

Peter hid a smile. A fine new house she had, with a white picket fence. He could hardly wait until morning, when she would be the one who was surprised.

30

Summer's delight at the sight of the picket fence gave Peter his first taste of enjoyment Sunday morning. More followed at the Krafts' *faspa* as he listened to his fellow townspeople make plans for the woman's housewarming the following Saturday. Of course, this planning was all done in German, so she understood none of it. He watched her face, noticing that although she appeared puzzled, no anger or resentment flashed in her eyes. This pleased him, too. It showed her changed heart. He remembered a time when she would have sparked at conversations that did not make sense to her ears.

The secret of the housewarming left him feeling smug and warm inside. Picturing her pleasure at the things the town had gathered for her use, knowing how it would tell her of their acceptance, made Peter eager for

Saturday to hurry and arrive. Yet the week crept by at its usual pace.

Wednesday morning Peter hitched the oxen to the wagon while Thomas climbed onto Daisy's back, and then he followed the boy toward town. When the bend in the road that led to the school appeared, Thomas called out, "Bye, Pa! Have a good day!"

"*Danke,* son. You have good day, too." He whistled the rest of the way into town. As he rolled past the post office, he heard someone call him. He stopped the team and turned to see postman *Herr* Hiebert on the sidewalk. The man waved an envelope in the air.

"A letter for that woman whose house is being built has come. It is marked from Boston."

"This must be from her husband's parents." Peter took the envelope and tucked it into his pocket. "She has hoped to hear from them."

"Well, now she has." *Herr* Hiebert headed back inside the post office.

Peter aimed the team toward Brunk's General Merchandise. The woman's panes of glass had arrived, and he and *Herr* Brunk sandwiched them between layers of burlap in the back of the wagon. *Herr* Brunk latched the gate while commenting, "The *frau* and I are bringing a bureau to the housewarming. Some silverware and a serving dish, too."

Peter gave the man a hearty clap on the shoulder. "This will be appreciated. Thank you."

"Welcome you are." He waved as Peter climbed back onto the wagon. "Now go finish that house so there will be someplace to put the things we have gathered!"

Peter laughed as he headed out of town. As he rolled past the post office, his laughter faded. While he wanted to go directly to the building site, he knew Summer would want to read the letter from Boston. Although it meant lost working time, he decided to take the letter to Summer first.

He found her in the kitchen, surrounded by mixing bowls, flour, and eggs. As he had expected, she reached eagerly for the envelope. "It's from Nadine. I'm so pleased she wrote." She removed the letter and scanned the text as she continued, "I feared they would ignore my — Oh!" At the gasp, she covered her mouth with one hand and stared up at Peter in horror.

He took a step toward her. *Grossmutter*

rose up in her chair, her worried eyes on Summer.

Summer held the letter out to Peter. He looked at it although he could not read the script. "My father-in-law died on Christmas Day," she said.

Peter thought back to the Christmas he had shared with *Grossmutter,* Thomas, and Summer. A happy day, with smiles and joy. This news put a pall over the memories. And how much worse it must be for her, who had known the man. He touched her arm. "Sorry I am that you hear this." He turned to *Grossmutter* and translated Summer's words. The old woman clucked in sympathy.

Summer gave them a quavering smile of thanks. She slumped into a kitchen chair and finished reading, then tucked the letter into her apron pocket. Rising, she reached for the flour. "Busy hands are good medicine." She set her jaw.

"Ja . . ." Peter backed toward the door. "Well, I go get my hands busy, too."

She didn't even glance up as he left.

Peter closed the barn door and moved slowly across the dark yard. He scowled as he thought back on the evening. Supper had been a tense time. Summer appeared troubled, which in turn troubled him. Thomas had barely spoken, preferring to sneak to his room when the meal was done, and *Grossmutter* had followed. He wondered if by now Summer, too, had turned in. Part of him hoped she had — he was not sure what to say to her.

When he opened the door and found Summer sitting at the table, his heart leaped into his throat. How at home she seemed in her work apron, a cup of steaming coffee held beneath her chin. The wispy strands of hair tucked behind her ears gave her a girlish appearance, but the worried expression in her dark eyes made Peter think of a much older woman.

At the click of the door closing, she looked up. "Peter. I was waiting for you."

The welcoming words warmed him more than the heat from the stove. He shrugged out of his coat and hung it up while she rose and poured him a cup of coffee.

"It's about the letter."

He sat, holding the cup of coffee between his palms without drinking. "*Ja.* I know you are troubled."

"My mother-in-law — she's asked me to return to Boston." She blinked rapidly, her expression strained. "She wishes for me to live with her."

Peter leaned back, his thoughts racing but his mouth silent. He considered saying, "But we have built you a house." Or, "The town is making you a housewarming." Or, "This will be very hard on Thomas." But he said nothing, only sat, staring at the part in her dark hair as she looked at the coffee cup on the table.

Finally she lifted her chin again, and he saw tears glittering in the corners of her velvet eyes. "I've prayed all afternoon about the right thing to do. And I believe . . . I have to go, Peter. I'm all she has now."

He pulled his brows into a stern frown. "Are you doing this because you feel guilty?"

She pursed her lips for a moment as if carefully choosing her words. When she spoke, her voice was quiet, wistful, yet full of confidence. "At first, yes — I did feel guilt. If we had remained in Boston, perhaps Horace wouldn't have worked so hard. If we had remained in Boston, even if Horace had died, Nadine would still have her son and grandchildren. But we didn't." A breathy sigh underscored the final words, but she continued in a strong voice. "I can't look back. I have to think about now. You said the Holy Spirit would prompt me, and He has. The sermon from last week keeps playing in my mind. The biblical example of Naomi and Ruth — 'Whither thou goest, I will go.' Remember? She needs me, Peter. I must go."

A lump formed in his throat. He pushed his voice past it. "*Ja,* you must go, for sure."

Her face crumpled. "Oh, Peter. It will be so hard . . . to go."

He reached out and took her hand. It lay limply against his rough palm, small and warm and moist. He gave it a gentle squeeze. "You must not worry about the graves. I will care for them. They will not fall into poor condition."

"Thank you, Peter." Gratitude shone in her eyes.

Other things would need to be discussed, but now was not the time. Now was the time to mourn. So, silently, with Summer's hand in his, Peter mourned.

On Saturday — the day when the towns-people had planned to give Summer a housewarming — she stood on the familiar stoop with Peter and Lena and said good-bye. The old woman's eyes were moist, and Summer thought her heart might break at the grandmother's expression of sorrow.

"Auf wiedersehen, leibes." Lena's voice trembled. She stroked Summer's cheek with her wrinkled hand.

Summer closed her eyes for a moment, swallowing. "What did she say besides good-bye?"

Peter's Adam's apple bobbed up and down once. "She called you *dear one.*"

A strangled sob found its way from Summer's breast. Dear one . . . This woman was the dear one. She had allowed Summer into her home and loved her despite long-held apprehension toward non-Mennonites. Summer embraced Lena, kissing the wrinkled cheek now damp with tears.

Peter helped Summer onto the wagon seat for the last time. In the back of the wagon, Thomas leaned against her plump carpetbag. Patches sat with his front legs draped over Thomas's knee. She twisted around backward in the seat to give the boy a smile, but he stroked the pup's head and ignored her. With a heavy heart, Summer turned forward again.

Peter's weight on the seat caused the springs to squeak and the seat to shift. She planted her feet against the floor to keep herself from sliding sideways. What a big man he was. A big, gentle, caring man. A lump formed in her throat. She would miss him. Oh, how she would miss him.

They didn't talk as they drove to Hillsboro, where Summer would board the train that would eventually take her to Boston. She and Peter had done their talking last night, discussing everything of importance: the house, the care of the gravesite, and Thomas.

The finished house would be put on the market and, she hoped, sold to a newcomer to Gaeddert. Summer was grateful she'd had an opportunity to stand on the spindled wraparound porch and watch the sun set behind the silhouette created by the picket fence and sandstone headstones. She was also grateful the townspeople were willing to allow her to sell the house to the next newcomer. Peter had expressed his joy at this indication that non-Mennonites would be welcomed to Gaeddert. Summer's presence had opened their hearts to trusting.

Peter had promised to care for the graves, and Summer knew he would do so. He was a man of his word. She sent a sidelong glance at him now, memorizing the full sweep of his beard, the crease between his eyes from squinting into the sun, the thick lashes, the breadth of his hand on the whip, and the tautness of his sleeve against his forearm. A strange constriction grabbed her heart, a desire to cry welling with it.

She sneaked another look into the back. Thomas cradled Patches, his cheek against the top of the puppy's head. A smile tugged at her lips at the sight — afraid of dogs? Not anymore.

She and Peter had discussed Thomas, too. For long hours, late last night, they had discussed Thomas. Peter had lofty dreams for the boy. If Summer was in Boston, she could help see those dreams become reality. That thought gave a small lift to her heart. In another few years, when the boy had finished eighth grade, he would be given the opportunity to come to Boston for high school and possibly college. Summer knew this decision might cause dissension in town, but Peter was determined Thomas have every opportunity this country provided. "He will be educated man, with choices before him," Peter had said in a solemn tone while his beard quivered. "He will be better man than me."

At that Summer had squeezed his arm and assured him, "There are no better men than you, Peter Ollenburger." She remembered those words now, the way he had flushed and turned away, but she had sensed his pleasure. She also remembered the way his reaction had set her heart to pattering high in her chest. She was glad she had found the courage to say the words her heart felt. He had introduced her to God. He had shown her how to release her bitterness and find joy. She would be forever grateful to this bear of a man.

The wagon wheels squeaked a steady rhythm. The wind teased her hair. Along the side of the road, a few brave stalks of green pushed through the dried brown grass that rustled in the wind and added to the unique melody of the countryside. Summer listened, looked, and tasted the air. Now that her time here was nearing its end, it seemed important to savor every detail of the Kansas landscape.

They heard the train well before they reached the town. At the first blast of the whistle, Thomas stood and held the back of the wagon seat, leaning in between Summer and Peter.

"Are we too late, Pa? Did it already leave?"

Summer heard the hopefulness beneath the question, and she swallowed the lump of sorrow that formed in her throat.

Peter answered in a gruff tone, "It is only a warning blast, boy. We will have Summer on the train, for sure."

The boy turned and sat again, presenting

his back to Summer. She patted his shoulder, but he grunted and pulled away. She removed her hand, battling tears.

All too soon her bags were loaded, her ticket was in hand, and it was time to board. Summer hovered on the boardwalk with the two men who were so dear to her.

Peter cleared his throat. "Well, Summer Steadman —"

"Are you sure you have to go?" The question burst out from Thomas, as if against his will. Tears quivered on his thick lashes.

She brushed the glistening moisture away with the gloved end of her finger, feeling her smile quaver with the effort of not breaking down herself. "Yes, sweetheart, I must. Nadine has no one now — not even God. She needs me."

"But I need you, too!" Thomas held Patches across his chest as he glared upward.

Summer wished she could hug his hurt away, although she knew a hug wouldn't fix the ache in Thomas's heart. Time would have to heal the wound. Time and prayer. She told him gently, "It makes me feel so special, Thomas, that you need me. But think of all the people you have right here who love you — your father, your great-grandmother, your teacher, your friends.

And I expect to hear from you. Will you write to me?"

The boy scowled, staring off to the side, but when she touched his chin, he lifted his gaze to meet hers. Remorse filled his eyes. He threw himself against her, burying his face against her shoulder as Patches squirmed between them. "I'll write to you, Summer. I'm sorry I've been mean. I'll miss you. I . . . I love you, Summer."

"Oh, Thomas . . ." Summer rested her cheek against his hair as tears flooded her eyes and distorted her vision. "I love you, too." She glanced up at Peter, who stood to the side, twisting his hat in his large hands, much the way he had the first time she'd met him. She reached one hand toward him, and he took it, linking her with both father and son.

A deep feeling welled up inside of her — a feeling that seemed to have been hiding beneath the surface, waiting for its opportunity to present itself. It chose to rear up, strong and sure, at a time when she should not speak of it. Tears pricked behind her eyes, and she swallowed hard. She loved the boy, yes. She also loved the man. The notion caught beneath her breastbone and held with an intensity that nearly took her breath away. Why, oh why did her heart tell her this now? Now, when she was leaving?

They stood together — one hand held tightly in Peter's grip, the other arm wrapped securely around Thomas's sturdy back — until the conductor called, "Last call! Bo-o-o-ard!"

Peter gave her hand a final squeeze before releasing it. Thomas stepped back, his face blotchy with the effort of holding back tears. Summer watched as Peter cupped his hand around Thomas's neck and the boy leaned against his father's bulk.

"Ma'am, are you boarding?"

Summer glanced at the conductor as the train's stack belched a great billow of smoke and the ground beneath their feet vibrated with the mighty heaves of the engine. "I . . . I . . ." She pointed stupidly toward the car.

Peter nodded, his eyes unnaturally bright. His image blurred as tears filled her eyes, but still she didn't turn aside. Thomas cried silently, his shoulders shaking. Summer brought her hand upward, reaching for Peter. He reached back, nearly lunging.

He took her hand and pulled her against his chest in a hug that stole her breath and sent her heart winging somewhere in the clouds. The embrace lasted only a few seconds — a few glorious seconds — and then his strong hands caught her shoulders and set her in front of him. He peered into her face, his thick brows low, his expression serious. His tongue sneaked out to moisten his lips, and then his voice came — his gentle voice of distant thunder. "My prayers go with you."

"And mine will be with you." The words choked out on a sob.

The tenderness in his blue eyes nearly melted Summer. Never had anyone looked at her with such an expression of adoration. She read in his eyes the same feeling that filled her own heart, yet neither of them spoke of it. How she longed to hear the words from his lips — to hear him say, "I love you, Summer." At the same time she realized leaving would be impossible if he gave voice to the thought.

She must say good-bye and get on board that train before her traitorous tongue gave her away. Her lips parted, the words formed, but —

"Go now." Peter spoke the words in a low, harsh growl. Taking her by the arm, he marched her to the train and helped her onto the step. Tears glinted in his eyes as he looked up at her. "You have safe trip, Summer Steadman. God be with you."

The train jerked, a *chug-chug* sounding, then it vibrated as it started to roll. Gritty gray smoke hung over Peter's head, and Summer blinked, needing one last glimpse of this dear man. Thomas trotted up next to his father and waved.

The train picked up speed. Wind tossed her hair and tangled her skirt around her ankles. She clung to the railing with one hand and waved. Tears distorted her vision, but she waved. And waved. The train turned a bend, and the man and boy disappeared from sight. Even then, she remained on the top step, her hand raised in farewell, as the rushing wind carried away the sounds of her mourning.

31

Peter heaved a sigh and looked down at his son. Tears rolled down Thomas's cheeks, just as they had Summer's. His memory would always carry the picture of Summer, clinging to the railing, a silver trail of tears staining her cheeks. He hugged the boy tight against his side. An emptiness sat in his chest. Summer's leave-taking had left a hole. A lump pressed in his throat, but he swallowed hard against it. Crying would do him no good. She was gone, and now they must accept it.

His arm around Thomas's shoulders, he turned toward their waiting wagon. "Come, boy. Let us go home." As he and Thomas plodded across the ground, heads low, he prayed for relief for the boy's aching heart.

And for his, too.

"Boston, Massachusetts! Next stop, Boston!"

The conductor's call startled Summer out of drowsing. She straightened in her seat to peer out the window at the landscape. A rush of familiarity filled her. Yes, she was nearly there. A knot of apprehension tightened her belly. Boston. The place where she was born and raised. The place where she met and married Rodney. The place where her children were born. Her home.

And yet no longer her home.

Through communication with God in prayer during this journey, she had reached peace about returning to Boston and assisting Nadine. Yet a part of her still longed for Gaeddert, where Peter and Thomas were probably sitting down to breakfast with Lena, while Patches hid beneath the table, waiting for Thomas to "accidentally" drop a morsel or two. She felt a smile tug at her lips as she envisioned it. In her heart, she was with them.

She closed her eyes, reliving that all-too-brief moment when Peter had pulled her into his arms. She felt the scratchy shirt beneath her cheek, his hard arms around her back, the tickle of his beard against her forehead. Taking in a deep breath, she tried to capture the essence of the man, but all she could smell was sweat and acrid coal smoke.

The reminder brought her eyes open again. Peter was in Gaeddert, and she was in Boston. *Dear Lord, how my heart misses him. Please remind me that you are enough. I have my joy in you.* The simple prayer revived her, and she resolved to not allow despair to bring her down.

The train whistle blasted as the mighty locomotive slowed its pace. The whistle, screeching brakes, and huffing steam created a cacophony of sound that nearly pierced Summer's eardrums. The train lurched in its attempt to come to a stop, and she braced herself against the back of the seat in front of her to keep from tumbling to the floor. With one final blast of the whistle and a great release of steam, the locomotive came to a heaving halt in front of the Old Colony Railroad Station.

Passengers filed past her as Summer pressed her face to the window, scanning the crowds for a glimpse of her mother-in-law. She spotted Nadine alone and searching beneath the center bricked archway of the depot's entryway. Summer could read sorrow in the slope of Nadine's shoulder and the droop of her chin. For the first time since the train had pulled out from Hillsboro five days ago, she was truly glad she had come. She jostled her way off the train, waving as she called, "Nadine! Nadine, I'm here!"

Nadine pushed through the crowd to meet Summer in the center of the wide concrete sidewalk. Summer found herself embraced by Nadine for the first time in her memory, but the hug lasted only a moment. Her mother-in-law pulled back sharply, distaste on her face.

"Phew, Summer. You are as unpleasant as the mule that pulls the milk wagon." She took hold of Summer's arm and tugged her toward the street. "Come, let's move away from the others before your odor offends. We'll get you home and into a bath."

Summer released a brief laugh. Nadine hadn't changed. "A bath sounds heavenly. The only washing I've been able to do since I left Kansas has been in sinks in depots where we made water and coal stops. There wasn't even a place to change my clothes."

Nadine's eyes swept from Summer's head to her feet, and her scowl deepened. "I should think the uncleanliness would be unbearable. And wherever did you get that dress?" She herded Summer to a waiting carriage. "Did you lose all sense of decorum while living on the Kansas plain?"

Summer had no answer. She merely shrugged.

"Well," Nadine went on in a brisk tone, "you're back now. All vestiges of that uncivilized prairie will soon be erased."

Summer intended to retain her memories of the prairie town and its people, but she made no argument.

Nadine's servant, Clarence, waited to help the ladies aboard the carriage. He took Summer's hand as Nadine's strident voice continued. "Climb well over on your own side, please." Summer obeyed, and Nadine seated herself. The carriage door closed behind them, and within moments a jerk indicated forward motion. The steady *click-click* of wagon wheels rolling over cobblestone filled Summer's ears, nearly covering the deep sigh Nadine released.

"Ah, Summer, I admit I'm relieved to have you here."

In all the years of marriage with Rodney, Summer had never engaged in a conversation with Nadine. She wasn't sure how to proceed now. Praying silently for wisdom, she offered, "I'm pleased you asked."

Nadine looked out the window. "Of course, it would be lovely if all of you were —" She stopped abruptly.

Impulsively, Summer scooted so she could touch Nadine's knee. "It's all right to mourn. You've suffered a tremendous loss. But the mourning will not last forever. There is a time to mourn and a time to laugh. I'm here now, and I promise I will help you find the laughter again."

Nadine shook her head. "Never again will I find laughter."

Summer leaned back, her heart twisting in sympathy. "You'll find laughter, but it will take time. Trust me."

As Nadine continued to stare out the window, Summer's resolve strengthened. Peter had taught her the meaning of joy. Summer would now teach it to Nadine.

"Schlop die gesunt." Peter paused in Thomas's bedroom doorway. The slanted shaft of yellow light from the lamp on the table did not reach the boy's face, but Peter sensed the frown that rested there. "Are . . . are you thinking of Summer?"

A long silence followed the question and then finally a soft answer. "I miss her, Pa."

Peter crossed the shadowy floor to sit on the edge of Thomas's bed and put his hand on the boy's chest. The heaving told Peter his son fought tears. He blinked to hold back his own tears. "She is a special friend. It is fine for you to miss her, but do not let your missing her make you bitter." Peter spoke to himself as well as his son. He remembered the bitter days following Elsa's death. Summer was not dead — but that almost made it harder. Knowing she was alive and not with them was somehow more painful than a death.

"I keep wondering what she's doing. If she thinks of us at all." Thomas's voice seemed almost eerie in the gray room. "Her letter didn't say she missed us."

No, the letter that had come did not say she missed them. Peter knew, though, she did — that she thought of them as often as they thought of her, that her heart ached as much as theirs did.

"Words on a page are not always the best at sharing what one feels." Peter felt Thomas's chest rise and fall. He found comfort in his son's steady breathing. "But you remember how Summer treated you when she was here. You remember the way she took care of you and taught you with such kindness. Do you think she has forgotten that?"

A soft swish of movement against the starched pillowcase told Peter the boy shook his head.

"She has not forgotten. She thinks of us."

"How do you *know*, Pa?"

He smiled. "I know because I know Summer. And I know she loves you. Love does not drift away, son, like leaves falling from a tree. Love endures. You do not need to worry that she has forgotten you."

A sigh came from the bed. "I hope you're right."

Peter leaned forward and placed a kiss on his son's forehead. "I am right. I am your pa. Am I not always right?" He heard the soft answering chuckle, and he smiled again. "You sleep now. Tomorrow you write Summer a letter. You will feel better once you have told her how you feel."

"All right, Pa." The boy yawned. "Good night."

Peter left the room, closing Thomas's door behind him. He should go to bed, too, and sleep like the rest of his family. But his restlessness sent him to the stove, where he poured a cup of coffee. He crossed to the window and peered into the inky night. Across the country, did Summer stand at a window, peering outward, her thoughts on Gaeddert?

"*Ach,* Lord, a foolish man I am, standing here heartsick. All the blessings you have given me, and I think only of what I do not have." Somewhere in the distance a coyote howled. Patches raised his head from the rug by the stove and growled. Peter crouched next to the pup and gave his ears a reassuring scratch. The coyote called again, its mournful cry causing the hairs on Peter's neck to stand up. Patches whined.

"Shh, now," Peter soothed the dog. "A coyote is nothing to fear. He is only lonely and calls for someone to listen. So we listen, *ja?* It hurts us not at all."

Peter ran his hand down the pup's back with long, firm strokes, and finally Patches rested his chin on his paws. His ears remained perked, listening, but he stayed quiet. Peter rose and returned to the window. He caught a glimpse of his reflection in the glass, and despite himself a grin found its way to his face.

He clasped his beard with one hand and thought about the last evening when he and Summer sat at the table well into the night and talked. She had told him there were no better men than he. The words warmed him as much now as they had then. Other things she had said — admiring his mill, asking him questions as if he should know the answers. She had made him feel clever and strong and . . . yes, even handsome. She had touched his heart.

Turning from the window, his focus went to Thomas's bedroom door, and more memories crowded in. Summer with Thomas at the table as they studied together. At the sink as they washed dishes and talked. And at the grave site, inside the picket fence, their hands clasped, as Summer shared memories of her children. How motherly she had been toward his boy. She did not have to love Thomas, only to teach him — that had been their agreement — but how much more she had given.

If Peter was honest with himself, he knew part of the reason he had not sought a new wife was concern that a woman could not love another woman's child as her own. He would not take someone as his wife who did not care as deeply for his son as he did. But Summer had dispelled those fears. He knew Summer loved Thomas. Maybe as much as she had loved her own children. How many times he had wondered if he wanted her as his wife. Now he wondered why he had questioned it. Summer had been the perfect choice.

A deep sigh found its way from his soul. Summer was gone now. She had made her choice, and it was the right choice. Nadine needed her. Summer had much to teach

Nadine. She had come into his life and she had taught him, but then she had said good-bye. This was the way of life, with seasons coming and going.

Summer had belonged to them for a season. But the season had ended. He must let her go.

32

Summer stared at her reflection in the oval mirror above the sink. Her hair clung in damp coils around her face, and she smoothed the strands behind her ears. She tipped her head, examining her firm chin, then traced the tiny lines at her eyes with one finger. *Still a young woman,* Peter had said. Well, yes, she was. The sorrow of the past year, which she had felt aged her beyond her years, hardly showed anymore. That was surely one of God's miracles.

The sorrow still sat heavily on Nadine. Six weeks had passed since Summer's return to Boston. Summer had tried many times to visit with Nadine about the joy one could possess by trusting God to take the sorrow. Each attempt was met with firm rebuttal. Summer shook her head, smiling sadly at her image in the mirror. She now understood what she had put Peter through with her stubborn refusal to believe a heart could heal. But Peter hadn't given up on her, and she wouldn't give up on Nadine. God was faithful — healing would come.

A swirl of steam fogged the lower edge of the mirror. She turned the spigot, stopping the flow of hot water, and turned from the sink. Her gaze drifted from the rolled edge sink basin to the oversized claw-footed porcelain tub, and finally to the door of the water closet.

Nadine had every known convenience available here. If Summer stayed, she would never tote a chamber pot through drifting snow to dump its unpleasant contents down the outhouse portal. She would never have to draw water from a well, heat it on the stove, and fill an iron washtub to take a bath. Life was much simpler under Nadine's roof, enjoying the many conveniences.

So why did Summer long for Gaeddert? Moving down the hallway toward the lavish bedroom that was now hers, Summer reflected on her longing for Gaeddert. It wasn't the town. It was the people — Peter, Thomas, and Lena; Katherine Kraft and Bertha Harms; even red-headed Rupert Penner. She missed them.

A wave of homesickness washed over her, and she hurried to the dresser. She paused for a moment to touch the framed page from Rodney's Bible that bore the names of her children. She smiled, touching each name in turn, her children's faces appearing in her memory. She looked at the letter that rested next to the frame. It lay open, as if in invitation. Although she nearly had it memorized from repeated readings, she picked it up and read it again.

Dear Summer,
  Pa and me sure miss you. We talk about you all the time. Grandmother misses you to. I know becuz she doesn't talk about you but she looks at your chair and her eyes are sad. I bet you miss your chair.
  Patches is getting bigger. Pa and me are going to bild him his own house. I can help because I bilt that ~~pikit~~ pickit fence and did all right. I got a 100 on my math test. Mrs. Kraft had her baby, a girl named Hannah. Toby thinks she's better than Patches but I don't think so.
  I miss you Summer. Do you miss me and pa? I hope you write to me again. Pa said to tell you hello and he hopes you are happy in Boston. I hope you are happy to but I still wish you were here. I got to go. I love you Summer.
  Sincerely, Thomas.

Summer held the letter to her chest for a moment, closing her eyes and picturing the little boy with his tousled hair and broad grin. She could imagine him at the table, inkpot in front of him, forehead creased in concentration as he penned his letter. She looked at the letter again, and a chuckle vibrated through her.

How he jumped from topic to topic! He also could make use of the dictionary she'd purchased for him, but she treasured the letter despite its errors. She placed it back on the dresser, still open, so she could look at the lines of writing while she twisted her hair into its familiar knot.

She wondered if Thomas kept the letters she had sent him in a place of honor. Or did Peter have them? Of course, Peter couldn't read them since they were written in English. She wished she could receive a letter from him. She wished she could send a letter that would only be read by his eyes. Sending messages through Thomas was ineffectual at least and frustrating at most. How could she pour out her heart to Peter knowing his ten-year-old son would be reading it aloud? Color filled her cheeks at the thought. No, it wouldn't do. Communicating with Thomas — and hoping Peter was able to read between the lines of her simple messages — would have to be enough.

Her eyes drifted to Thomas's words *"Pa . . . hopes you are happy in Boston."* She understood the question behind his message. She could almost hear Peter's rumbling voice asking, "Have you learned the lesson of Paul, to be content in whatever state you are?" She smiled. Yes, she had learned that lesson. Despite the ache in her heart, which spoke of a longing for Peter, she was not discontented. God's joy remained with her. Her smile faded. If only she could help Nadine capture that joy.

A light knock sounded on her door, ending her reverie. She stabbed the last hairpin into place and crossed to the door.

Nadine's maid, Mildred, stood in the hallway. "Miss Summer, Missus Nadine is ready to go. She asks are you ready?"

Summer picked up her Bible and reticule from the table beside the door. "Yes, Mildred. I'm ready." Before Summer passed through the doorway, Mildred put out her hand.

"Missus Nadine," Mildred whispered, her brow creased tightly, "she's in a sour mood this morning. Step careful, you hear?"

Summer patted the older woman's hand,

giving her a smile. "I'll step careful, Mildred. Thank you."

Mildred's words proved to be accurate. Nadine grumbled all the way to church, first about the lack of sugar in her morning oatmeal, then about the bumps in the road that Clarence *chose* not to avoid, and finally about Summer's simple mourning dress.

"Now, Nadine, I won't be wearing mourning attire forever," Summer said kindly, smoothing the skirt of one of the dresses she had sewn in Gaeddert. She couldn't stop the smile of remembrance of that day, of finding a basket of notions waiting for her and sewing the curtains to surprise Peter.

"Why are you smiling?" Nadine snapped. "You sit there in your ugly black dress which tells the world you've suffered the death of someone dear, and yet you smile! What is wrong with you, Summer Steadman? Have you taken leave of your senses?"

The carriage rolled to a halt. Summer opened her mouth to answer Nadine, but Clarence interrupted.

"Mind your footing, Missus," he said, reaching to take Nadine's arm. "The rain last night left the road slippery."

Nadine slapped his hand away. "I'm not a doddering old woman who requires your assistance. Step back."

The servant obeyed as he shot Summer a look of worry. She offered a reassuring smile as she stepped out of the carriage.

"Be back here sharply at noon," Nadine instructed in a strident tone. "And tell Mildred I expect a decent dinner after that deplorable breakfast. Come along, Summer." Nadine swept toward the church in her elegant black gown.

Summer followed Nadine's swirling skirts. What had the woman in such a dither this morning? While she had never been one to demonstrate great warmth, the extent of her irritation today seemed out of character. Something was bothering her — but what? Not until Summer was standing, adding her voice to the hymn "Come, Christian, Let Us Sing," did she remember the significance of today's date. Her heart sank to her stomach, her hands fumbled the hymnal, and she fought the need to embrace Nadine right in church in the middle of singing.

Today Rodney would have turned thirty-one years old. And no one had remembered. Except Nadine.

The congregation sat, and Summer peeked sideways. Nadine's chin quivered, her lips pursed into a grimace. Should Summer touch her? Whisper something? She prayed inwardly for guidance. Nadine must be in excruciating pain, remembering the day of her son's birth.

Even as Summer sought a means to comfort her mother-in-law, the minister stepped behind the polished lectern and said, "Please turn in your Bibles to the first chapter of Ruth."

Summer's breath caught. It was reading from this chapter in church that had convinced her she must return to Nadine. She followed along in her Bible as the minister read straight through the first chapter. Summer felt Nadine stiffen on the seat next to her. Summer's heart turned over in her chest. How difficult these words, of a mother's loss of her sons, must be for Nadine today.

She gave Nadine a small smile, an attempt to offer understanding and comfort. Nadine ignored her, but as the minister read verses twenty and twenty-one — "And she said unto them, Call me not Naomi, call me Mara: for the Almighty hath dealt very bitterly with me. I went out full and the Lord hath brought me home again empty" — Summer heard Nadine gasp.

Without thinking, Summer reached out and took hold of Nadine's hand. Nadine clung, her icy fingers digging into Summer's palm. Summer held tight, expressing through physical touch her support for her mother-in-law.

During the remainder of the service, Summer held Nadine's hand. Though the hand trembled within Summer's grasp, Nadine made no effort to pull loose. When they rose for the final hymn, Nadine still held on. She did not release her hold even as they left the sanctuary and walked to the carriage, which waited beside the curb as Clarence had been directed.

Summer removed her hand long enough to allow Nadine's entry into the carriage, but as soon as both women were settled, Nadine reached out again. Although she spoke no words, her fierce hold on Summer's hand spoke volumes. Summer prayed silently all the way to the house that she would find words to ease Nadine's pain.

They sat at opposite ends of the dining room table and ate their roast beef, boiled potatoes and carrots, and crusty rolls in silence. Although Summer longed to talk, she sensed Nadine was deep in thought. Remembering the times Peter had allowed her to reflect in silence, she allowed Nadine that freedom now, waiting until she showed signs of readiness to discuss whatever was on her heart.

Finally, as Mildred cleared away the dishes and presented a dessert of cherry tarts, Nadine let Summer know she was ready.

"Today is my son's birthday." The words were uttered in a low tone, almost a groan.

Summer nodded.

"Never have I been away from him on his birthday. Do you remember, Summer? Do you remember how you and Rodney would come here for dinner and cake? Even after the children arrived, always you came here for dinner and cake."

Again, Summer nodded. The pain in Nadine's voice made her heart ache.

Nadine lowered her gaze. "How I miss him. . . ."

Summer rose and went around the table to kneel beside Nadine's chair. She took Nadine's limp hand. It was as cold as it had been in the church. "I know you miss him. I do, too."

Nadine searched Summer's eyes. "Do you? I've wondered. I've watched you. You don't seem lonely. You don't seem sad." She closed her eyes, leaning her head back. "How do you bear it? I feel very much like the woman in the Bible. Naomi, who said the Lord had dealt bitterly with her. Taking Horace . . . and Rodney . . . and the children. I . . . I fear I cannot bear it, Sum-

461

mer." Tears rolled down Nadine's cheeks.

"Shh, Mother." Summer rested her cheek against Nadine's shoulder. "You don't have to bear it alone. I am here. And God is here, too."

Nadine opened her eyes. "Why did you return to me? Horace and I — we never treated you like family. I admit that. We gave you no reason to care about us. It can't be love that brought you here. I do not see loneliness in your bearing. Surely you don't need me as desperately as I need you. So why are you here?"

Summer cupped Nadine's cheek. "I am here because you asked me. You needed me." She swallowed, lowering her hand. "After Rodney and the children were gone, I felt just as you said — as if God had dealt bitterly with me. I didn't feel as if I could return to Boston, to my brother's house. I didn't feel as if I could come here to you and Horace. I felt so very lost and alone. But someone needed me — Peter Ollenburger's son, Thomas."

Just saying Peter's and Thomas's names brought a new rush of longing through Summer's chest. She paused, envisioning their dear faces, before continuing. "Giving of myself to Thomas kept my heart from becoming hard with bitterness. Loving softens the heart. A soft heart is open to new love. And I found it." She felt tears gather in her eyes. "I found it with Thomas and Peter and Lena. I found it with the God who is so very real to Peter. Having God with me has brought me joy despite the pain."

"Joy despite the pain?" Nadine released a huff of disbelief. "The two are opposites, Summer. Both cannot reside simultaneously within the same breast."

"Ah, but they can, Nadine." Summer rose. "You wait here. I will get my Bible. May I show you what I've discovered?"

Nadine stared at Summer with narrowed eyes for long seconds, her lips pursed tight into a scowl of indecision.

Summer held her breath, waiting, praying, hoping.

At last Nadine sighed. She raised her hand in a tired gesture, as if it weighed more than she could comfortably lift. "Yes, Summer. You may show me."

Summer deposited a kiss on Nadine's soft cheek and then ran upstairs to retrieve the Bible Peter had given her.

God, give me the words to turn Nadine's sorrow into joy.

33

Thomas held tiny Hannah Kraft and beamed up at his father. As soon as the *faspa* meal had been consumed, Thomas had begged to hold the baby. "Look, Pa. She's smiling. I think she likes me."

Peter looked into the baby's face. A smile curved the infant's lips, and she waved a tiny fist. "*Ja,* she does like you."

Thomas bounced Hannah as he made silly nonsense noises. The baby let out a squawk, and Thomas's eyebrows flew upward.

Katherine Kraft clucked and removed the baby from Thomas's arms. She smiled at the boy's crestfallen expression. "It is not that Hannah dislikes you, Thomas. She likes to be held like this." She cradled the baby against her shoulder. "Would you like to try again?"

The boy backed away. "No. You keep her. I'll go play with Toby. I *know* what Toby likes." He trotted toward Toby's bedroom, but before moving through the doorway he called back, "Bet Summer would sure like her."

At Summer's name, Peter's heart lifted. He turned to find Katherine Kraft fixing him with a look of interest. The back of his neck heated up. He forced a casual tone. "*Ja,* the boy is right. Summer would like Hannah very much. Have you sent letter to tell her your baby is here?"

"We had Toby send a postcard," Katherine replied. "You know I do not write in the English." She carried the infant to a cradle in the corner of the kitchen and gently laid her in it. "Have you sent letters to Summer?"

"I . . . I do not write in the English either, Katherine."

Katherine patted the baby as she spoke. "Has Thomas sent her letters then, with words from you inside?"

Seated at the table, Tobias cleared his throat. "Woman, maybe Peter wishes to talk of something else."

Katherine shook her head. "When the name Summer was said, his face changed. He wishes to speak of Summer. He wishes to speak of little else." She turned back to Peter. "Am I right, Peter?"

The heat crept from Peter's neck to his ears. Katherine was right. He wished to speak of little else. Often he and the boy spoke of Summer, but with the boy, he felt limited in what he could say. Thomas missed her so much. His own words of longing would only add to the boy's loneliness for his friend.

He hung his head. "You are right, Katherine, that I wish to speak of the woman. I wish to do more than speak of her. I wish to speak *to* her. But I cannot do that. So it is best not to speak at all. It makes it easier on my heart, for sure."

Katherine carried the coffeepot to the table and poured fresh cups. After putting the pot back on the stove, she seated herself between the men and sighed. "*Ach,* Peter, I do not try to make things uncomfortable for you. But in Summer I found a friend, and I miss her, too. I wonder how she is doing. I am sorry if sad I have made you by speaking of her today."

Peter raised his head. "You have not made me sad. It is good that others remember her and miss her. It makes me feel not so alone."

Tobias asked, "Have any people given interest in the house we built for her?"

Peter scratched his beard. "*Nein.* Not yet.

I see to it — and to the graves. I am sure, when time is right, God will send a person to live in the house."

"Maybe," Katherine said in a bright tone, "it will be Summer who comes back to live in the house."

"I do not know," Peter said. "Her last letter to us said her mother-in-law liked having her near." He remembered the message Thomas had read to him from Summer's last letter — *Tell your father I have joy where I am.* Peter felt he understood her meaning. Her happiness was found in caring for the mother-in-law, just as Ruth had done for Naomi. "I think she will stay there."

Katherine nodded, her eyes sad.

"So why was *Frau* Suderman not at *Kleine Gemeinde* this morning?" Tobias picked up his cup and slurped his coffee.

Peter's brows pinched. "Our *grossmutter* has been under the weather. When she chooses to miss a Sunday service, I know she is feeling poorly."

Katherine patted his arm. "I will take her some soup this week. She is probably working too hard now that Summer is gone. Are you letting her to do the household chores?"

"It is not that I let her. She does what she will do. The boy is at school; I am away working. I come home to find her very tired. So, *ja,* she is working too hard. But how do you tell her to stop? It makes her feel . . . useless. Useless is not something I wish on anyone."

"She has earned a rest." Katherine's staunch words made Peter smile. "Many years she has taken care of others — first her own child, then her granddaughter, and now you and your son. You tell her she is not useless, but she deserves a rest."

Despite the worry he felt when he thought of how much *Grossmutter* had slowed down in the past weeks, how silent she had become again, he could not stop the chuckle that came from his chest. "She is a stubborn woman. I do not think she would take kindly to my telling her to rest. Her eyes, they snap at me when I say she does too much."

"Well, we are your closest neighbor," Katherine said. "I will try to come by once or twice a week with Hannah and let her hold the baby while I do some of the chores."

Peter's heart warmed at Katherine's concern. "That is kind of you. I know she would enjoy the chance to hold a baby again."

"I will do it, then." Katherine leaned back;

her expression turned speculative. "Did *Frau* Suderman allow Summer to do the chores in your house?"

"*Ja-a-a.*" Peter drew out the word. Had they not decided to let talk of Summer end?

"So *Frau* Suderman would not resent another woman living in your house . . ."

Tobias frowned at his wife. "Woman, what are you leading to now?"

Katherine offered a sly smile. "*Ach,* I am not leading to anything, husband. I am just thinking. Peter could benefit from someone who would give his grandmother help during the day. And in our community are two widows who would be able to help. Maybe he should —"

Peter held up his hand. "What you are thinking I already know." He shook his head, his ears hot. "A widow in my house I do not need. Ideas it would give her."

"*Ja,*" Katherine agreed, "and ideas it might give you."

"Katherine!" Tobias's tone held reproach. "Too bold you are being."

"Boldness is not a bad thing," the woman insisted. "To mend a broken heart sometimes takes turning attention to someone else."

Peter knew Katherine meant well, so he

answered her kindly. "I thank you for your concern. But I tell you my heart has no desire to look to someone else. It is fine just the way it is."

Katherine nodded slowly. "Fine it might be, but do not let it grow closed, Peter. Let it stay open. It may be that God brought Summer to open you to the idea of taking a wife again."

Tobias slurped his coffee noisily. His wife shot him an impatient look. "Men! You cannot allow a serious conversation to happen." She turned back to Peter and touched his forearm. "I keep her in my prayers, for God's will to be done in her life. And yours, too, Peter."

He swallowed the lump that formed in his throat. *God's will is best,* he told himself. *I pray I can accept it if it means never seeing my Summer again.*

Peter stood in the doorway to *Grossmutter's* room, peering in as the doctor leaned over the bed. He could hear each labored breath the old woman made, and his heart constricted in worry and fear. Was she dying? He knew if her life slipped away, her soul would be winged to a better place, yet the selfish part of him longed for her to remain here with him and the boy. How they would miss her steadfast presence should she leave them.

As if sensing his father's thoughts, Thomas tugged at Peter's sleeve. "Grandmother isn't going to . . . die . . . is she, Pa?" The question came out in a harsh whisper.

Peter put his arm around the boy and pulled him hard against his side. "Sick she is, son, and old and tired. It may be God is ready to let her come home to Him, where she will be healthy and whole once more."

The boy's eyes flooded with tears. "But I don't want her to go."

"Nor do I, for sure," Peter agreed, "but we must think what is best for our dear *Grossmutter, ja?*"

The boy nodded, his chin low. Then he looked up. "Pa, do I have to go to school today? I want to stay here with you and Grandmother."

Peter could not refuse his son when the boy begged so with his eyes. He gave Thomas a pat. "You read to her, *ja?* She likes that. She will enjoy having you near."

"I'll read Summer's letters to her again," Thomas said. "She always smiles when I tell her what Summer says in her letters."

The boy scampered to his room as Dr.

Wiebe moved toward the doorway. Peter stepped out of his way, and the doctor closed *Grossmutter's* door before addressing Peter.

"She has some congestion in her chest," the man said, rubbing his chin, "but I do not think it is serious. I think she is just worn out. Too old she is to be working herself so hard. She needs much rest."

"*Ja,* rest. I will see she gets it."

"You cannot sit beside her all day and watch her," the doctor said. "As soon as you leave, she will be up and doing. She told me as much. The housework must be done, she says."

"Katherine Kraft said she will come once or twice a week."

"Once or twice a week is not enough. If you want *Frau* Suderman to recover, she must not work so hard ever again." Dr. Wiebe fixed his eyes firmly on Peter. "Peter, have you considered —"

"I got them, Pa!" Thomas bounced beside the men, a cluster of pages in his hand. "I'll go read to Grandmother now."

The doctor put his hand on the boy's shoulder. "You go in, Thomas, but do not keep her awake if she tries to sleep. Sleep is good medicine."

The boy nodded, his expression serious. "I won't. But I know these letters will be good medicine, too. She likes hearing from Summer." He closed the bedroom door behind him.

Dr. Wiebe looked at the door for long moments, his forehead creased in thought. Finally he turned back to Peter. "While *Frau* Steadman was here, *Frau* Suderman need not work so hard. She did better then, *ja?*"

Peter thought about how *Grossmutter* had spoken more, been more lively, when Summer was with them. "*Ja,* she did better then."

The doctor touched Peter's arm. "Another woman in the house to do the work every day would be good for your grandmother."

Peter's neck grew hot with the doctor's insinuation. Was everyone going to push him to marry again?

The doctor gave his arm another pat, then turned away. "You think about it, Peter. God did not intend for man to be alone. Maybe you have been alone long enough now. Another wife would be good for you, good for the boy, good for *Frau* Suderman. It could solve many problems."

Peter saw the doctor to the door and thanked him for coming. Then he crossed to the stove and poured himself a cup of strong coffee.

What had Katherine said? That God had brought Summer to open his heart to the idea of loving again. Even the doctor, a very wise man, thought taking a wife would be good. Peter shook his head. He did not want to think of this now. A wife was not to be taken to be a housekeeper. A wife must be a helpmate — a partner in life and in love.

The sound of Thomas's voice drifted out to him, Summer's name in the midst of what the boy said. Peter lowered his head and closed his eyes. When he thought *wife*, he thought *Summer*. Until the word *wife* did not bring to mind a slender woman with dark hair and eyes, he would not think of it. But he did not find it so easy to set aside.

34

The rising morning can't insure
That we shall end the day;
For death stands ready at the door
To snatch our lives away

How appropriate the message etched on the ornate granite tombstone Nadine had chosen for Horace, Summer thought as she stood beside the gravesite with her mother-in-law.

"You know," Nadine said softly, "when I chose this spot for Horace's final resting place, I thought I would bring the children here to picnic and visit."

Summer glanced around, drinking in the beauty of the surrounding landscape. The Bennington Street Cemetery's shaded grounds, which received ocean breezes from the Harbor, was a lovely spot to picnic. She took Nadine's hand, giving it a reassuring squeeze.

"I'm sorry the children aren't here, but I'm here, Mother."

Nadine sighed. "Yes, you are. And I appreciate your company, Summer."

Summer relished those words. Who would have thought that she and Nadine would ever share a loving relationship? Yet, over the past months, Nadine had grown in her knowledge of God's love and had, in turn, bestowed tender care on Summer. Nadine had come to mean a great deal to Summer, and she knew the woman loved her, too.

"Summer, I wish to make a trip to Kansas."

Summer jerked her hand away and turned a startled gaze on Nadine. "You — you want to *what?*"

Nadine pursed her lips. "Summer, kindly do not raise your voice to me in this somber surrounding."

"I apologize." Summer took a deep breath to calm her racing heart. "But you took me by surprise."

"I assumed my idea would meet with your approval," Nadine said. "You've spoken of the friendships you forged in that Kansas town." She pursed her lips. "I can never recall the name . . ."

"Gaeddert." Summer pressed her hand to her throat.

"Gaeddert," Nadine repeated. "There is even a house in which we could stay while visiting. The boy's last letter indicated the house still sits empty, so perhaps we could stay in it rather than share a hotel room." She tipped her head. "Do you not want to see the people again?"

Faces paraded through Summer's mind, coupled with a fierce longing. Her eyes slipped closed, her lips tipped into a smile, her breathing increased. Oh yes, Summer desired to see the people again . . .

"Summer?"

Nadine's soft voice brought Summer's eyes open.

"What are your thoughts?"

For long moments Summer stood silent, her gaze beyond Horace's headstone. She sucked on her lower lip, organizing her thoughts. It had taken weeks for the deep ache of missing Peter and Thomas to lessen. Wouldn't a visit reactivate the pain? "It — it is a lengthy journey. Are you sure you want to go?"

Nadine lifted her chin. "I wish to visit the graves of my son and my grandchildren. I wish to say my final good-byes to them. Will you deny me that?"

Summer's shoulders slumped. How could she refuse? "When — when do you wish to go?"

Nadine looped her hand through Summer's arm and began moving toward the carriage. "Train schedules need to be checked and tickets purchased. I must make arrangements for Clarence and Mildred to be in charge of the house during our absence. I would think a week of preparation would be enough."

Summer watched the toes of her shoes move across the grass. "We'd be there in two weeks . . ." Her breath came in little spurts.

"However," Nadine considered, pausing in her walk, "perhaps we need to give those in Gaeddert a bit more notice. You'll want to send a letter, and that will take several days to reach them. They will probably need to give the little house a cleaning. Let's try to arrive the first week of June."

Nearly a month instead of two weeks. Summer's gaze bounced upward. An entire month? The anticipation might drive her mad!

Nadine asked, "Do you find that agreeable?"

In slow motion, Summer nodded. "Yes. Yes, I find that agreeable."

"Good." Nadine put her arm around Summer's waist and gave her a brief hug. A cunning look crossed the woman's face. "Oh, and before we go, you will visit a dress shop. You must set aside those black gowns. The time of mourning is over."

"Look what I have, boy," Peter announced as he stepped through the front door. It did his heart good to see *Grossmutter* in her chair, watching as Thomas stirred something on the stove. He was glad the old woman had not complained when he'd hired the oldest Schmidt girl, Malinda, to do household chores each afternoon. The slowing down on work — and the prayers offered by him and the boy — had helped her regain her strength.

Thomas set aside the wooden spoon and moved toward his father. "What is it?"

Peter held out the envelope. "A letter from Summer."

Grossmutter sat up straight. A smile broke across her face. "Summer."

"Summer!" Thomas reached for it with both hands. "Let me see, Pa! I'll read it to us!"

Peter chuckled as he placed the letter in Thomas's outstretched hands. "This eager

479

you should be to do your schoolwork, *ja?*"

Thomas grinned as he tore the envelope open and pulled out the letter. Peter peeked at the neat lines of script covering both sides of the single sheet of paper. Just the sight of the words, penned by Summer's graceful hand, made his heart beat in a happy rhythm.

Thomas plopped down at the table and read aloud.

"Dear Thomas, Peter, and Lena,

I have a surprise for you. I hope it will be a happy surprise. Nadine has decided she would like to visit the graves of her son and grandchildren, to say good-bye to them, so she will be traveling to Gaeddert. Of course, I will be traveling with her. This means I will be seeing you soon. I am looking forward to visiting with you. I have missed you. I want to see how tall Thomas has grown. I want to taste Lena's good borscht. I want to hear Peter's loud laugh that makes me want to laugh, too."

Peter's eyebrows shot up. His laugh made her feel happy inside? He had not known this. But when he interrupted, it was to ask a different question. "It says she comes for a visit, is that right, boy?"

Thomas scanned the letter. "Yes, Pa — she looks forward to visiting with us."

Peter's heart fell, but he still smiled. "Ah, good. We all will enjoy to have a visit with Summer."

Grossmutter waved her gnarled hand and demanded in German to know what the letter said.

Peter obliged her by translating it. The woman's face lit in a happy smile.

Thomas lifted the letter again and continued.

"Nadine and I will arrive by Marion and McPherson Railway at the depot in Hillsboro on the fourth of June. The stationmaster indicated the train's arrival time to be two o'clock in the afternoon. I sincerely hope Peter will be available to pick us up and transport us to Gaeddert."

Peter's heart increased its tempo. He would set aside anything else to go meet the train.

"Pa? Can I go, too? I'll be out of school."

Although Peter would rather meet the woman alone, he knew it was selfish to ask the boy to stay behind. "If Malinda will come stay with *Grossmutter,* you may go."

Thomas beamed. "Thank you!" He bent his head back to the letter.

"If it would not be too much trouble, Nadine and I would like to stay in the house you built near the graves. I am assuming, of course, that it has not been purchased. If it is unavailable, we will take rooms at the hotel. If we are able to stay at the house, it will no doubt require a cleaning prior to our arrival. Could you hire someone from town to take care of this? Nadine and I will pay them when we arrive. You are familiar with young people who might appreciate earning a little extra pocket money, so I trust you to find someone reliable."

"Summer sure uses big words, Pa," Thomas said. "Kind of hard to read sometimes."

"You are doing fine," Peter praised. "Big words are good to learn. Someday you may need to know them and use them." Especially if Thomas went away to a school in a big city, as he and the woman had discussed. "So you pay attention, *ja?*"

The boy scratched his head. "Okay, Pa."

"Is that all she says?"

"No. There's more." Thomas turned back

482

to the letter.

"I am so happy to tell you Nadine has accepted God's love for herself. You are all very good teachers. What I learned from you I was able to share with Nadine. I believe the angels in heaven sang when Nadine made the decision to accept Jesus into her heart, just as they must have sung for me. Thank you for your kind teaching. Your lessons are reaching eternity."

Thomas frowned. "What does that mean?"

"It is like when you throw a pebble in the water, and the circles keep getting bigger and bigger, and finally they touch the bank. All from one little pebble. When you tell one person about God, and he tells somebody else, it adds another circle."

Thomas gave an eager nod. "And all the circles will touch heaven someday, right, Pa?"

The boy's grasp of the idea of spreading God's word made Peter's chest expand in pride. What a smart boy. What a good boy. Peter reached out and pulled his son close in a hug. "You are right, boy. And you remember to share God's love just the way you did with Summer. God's love is not something to be kept hidden, for sure."

A scraping noise captured Peter's attention. He released the boy to look toward his bedroom. There, through the open doorway, he saw *Grossmutter's* backside. She bent forward, and by her slow motions, he knew she tugged at something.

Crossing to the doorway, he peered in. He had moved Summer's chair into the corner of his bedroom so Thomas and *Grossmutter* would not have to be always reminded of her absence. Now *Grossmutter* was attempting to drag the chair from the room. He jumped in front of her and took the chair from her.

Her eyes sparked. She pointed to the main room. *"Setzen sie den stuhl in die küche ein!"*

Peter nodded as a smile tugged at his face. He would put the chair in the kitchen, as she wished if she would move aside and allow him to do it. She waddled back to the kitchen and sat in her rocking chair, watching as he carried Summer's chair into the room. He started to put it down, but she snapped, *"Nein!"* and pointed where she wanted it. He obeyed.

Once the chair was in position next to *Grossmutter's*, the old woman smiled in satisfaction. She patted the armrest of Summer's chair and murmured to herself.

Thomas sighed. "June fourth. Only three more weeks and Summer will be here." Then he burst out laughing. "I made a joke, Pa! Summer the lady and summer the season will both be here at the same time."

Ja, Peter thought, tousling his son's hair. *Both bring a welcome warmth to my heart. But I wish my Summer was staying longer than a season.*

35

Summer smoothed the skirt of her new twill dress. Her white gloves appeared to glow against the vivid color of the fabric. She grimaced. Had she made the wrong choice in her attire?

When she had spotted the gown in the window of Miss Fannie's Dress Shop on Boylston Street, she had fallen in love on the spot. After wearing black for so many months, the bold reddish purple dress had thrilled her eyes. The moment she slipped it over her head, Nadine declared it a perfect choice. Never had Summer paid more than six dollars for a dress, but Nadine had insisted on that, too. She admitted she felt feminine and attractive in the gown with its pleated front and velvet butterfly half belt. The dress was beautiful and flattering — there was no doubt.

But was it appropriate for Gaeddert?

In less than an hour they would reach

Hillsboro. Peter would be waiting — in his chambray work shirt, tan trousers, and thick boots, with his little plaid hat in his big gentle hands. What would he think when she stepped off the train? Would he disapprove of her city finery? She touched her traveling hat — a purple velvet bowler with a raven's wing sweeping back on its right side — and she wished again she had chosen something more demure. Not so blatantly *Boston.*

Her mother-in-law's attire was nearly as flashy as Summer's. Although Nadine had chosen a more matronly shade of deep myrtle green, her dress was styled in the latest fashion, with leg-of-mutton sleeves and gold braid trim. Nadine had insisted on a thorough washing and a change of clothes at the last stop, so Summer felt as fresh as was possible given the heat of this early June day. Yet she was certain neither Hillsboro nor Gaeddert had ever witnessed such gowns. She sighed.

Nadine turned from the window. "Sleepy?"

"No. I was just thinking."

"About?" Nadine prompted.

Summer bit down on the inside of her lip. Would Nadine understand her concern even if she voiced it? Probably not. Nadine had never lived anywhere but Boston. She had always moved in the circles of high society. Gaeddert's simplicity would be alien to her. Summer sighed again.

Nadine took her hand. "Are you worried you'll find the people changed from when you were here before? The friendships perhaps not as important as they once were?"

Although that wasn't Summer's biggest concern at the moment, she did admit to wondering whether Peter's feelings had changed. She had seen love shine in his eyes that day at the train station, had felt it in his hug and heard it in his gruff, pained voice. The old adage that absence makes the heart grow fonder had certainly proved true for her. Her love for Peter had continued to blossom despite the distance between them. But what of Peter's love for her? Had it dimmed with the passage of time?

She finally answered. "I suppose there's always that fear when one has been away for a while. Nothing stays the same, does it?"

A soft smile tipped up Nadine's lips. "No, my dear, life does not stay the same. But are you not the one who keeps telling me God has good plans for His children? Perhaps you should relax and allow Him to be in control, hmm?"

Summer released a light laugh. "Oh, how wonderful it is to hear you speak of God so easily!"

Nadine gave Summer's knee a brisk pat. "Everything will be fine, I promise you."

Summer remembered making a promise to Nadine the day she arrived in Boston. Her promise to help Nadine find joy again had come to fruition. What a wonderful change had occurred in her mother-in-law's outlook on life. Summer sighed. She could take any change save one — a change in Peter's feelings toward her. *Please, Lord, prepare my heart. If his love has changed, let me accept it as your will. But, heavenly Father, I do still love him so. . . .*

Peter pulled his watch from the little pocket inside his suit jacket and peered at the numbers again. Only three minutes had passed since the last time he had checked it. With a huff of disgust at his own impatience, he replaced the watch and tugged the hem of his jacket back into place.

Thomas stood beside his father, also dressed in his Sunday clothes. The boy shifted his shoulders and pulled a face. "My shirt's scratching me, Pa. Why did we have to get dressed up, anyway?" The boy's cranky tone told of his impatience at the waiting.

"We are dressed for a special occasion," Peter reminded his son. "Summer coming back for a visit is special, so we dress to tell her how pleased we are."

Thomas released a breath of disgust. "Well, it's too hot in the sun."

Beads of sweat dribbled down Peter's forehead and his underarms felt moist. He hoped the dark spots would not show on his good black suit jacket. He touched the little knot of his ribbon tie and wished he could loosen it. Uncomfortable he felt, too. Yet, as much as he agreed with the boy, he would not move from this spot until the train arrived. He pointed to some trees on the east side of Ash Street. "If you are too hot, go stand in the shade over there. Just take care you do not get your clothes dirty."

"Okay, Pa." The boy trotted across the street and circled one of the tree trunks in slow motion, as if examining the ground. His circle complete, he leaned against the trunk and scraped his toe in the dirt.

Peter watched for a few minutes until he felt sure the boy would not start playing. Then he turned his attention back to the silver lines of track. The sun bounced off the rails in glaring rays. Peter squinted, his eyes watering, but he did not avert his attention. Soon, around that bend, would come an M and M Railway engine. Behind that engine would be passenger cars. And in one of those cars would be Summer.

His heart picked up its pace at the thought of her name. In his mind he held a picture from the last moments he had spent with her on this very boardwalk. Her face had been pale, her dark eyes sad and glittering with tears. Their good-bye had been rushed, unsatisfying. After this visit, he would make sure they had a chance for a decent leave-taking. No more rushing and lost words and unfinished thoughts. This time they would do it right.

From the distance, a whistle came — a hollow sound, like an echo. He straightened his shoulders and tipped forward as if fighting against a brisk wind. His breath caught in his throat as his eyes strained for the first glimpse of the engine. Then his heart flew into his throat. Around the bend — smoke streaming from its stack, wheels gliding along the track, whistle calling its warning — here it came!

"Here she comes, Pa!" Thomas huffed up beside his father's elbow.

Peter was not sure if the boy referred to

the train or Summer. "*Ja,* she comes, for sure!"

They stood together, eyes pinned to the train. The vibration beneath Peter's feet sent shivers of awareness to the roots of his hair. He yanked off his hat and held it against his left thigh. The wind touched his newly trimmed hair and dried his eyes, but he did not blink. He feared he would miss his first glimpse of her if he closed his eyes for even a second.

"Come on, Pa!" Thomas grabbed his father's hand and pulled.

Peter's feet would not move. He stayed in place, his body tense, his heart thumping in anticipation. A porter hopped down from the first passenger car to place a small wooden stool on the ground beneath the single metal step.

"Let's go meet her, Pa!"

Thomas's tone sounded fretful now, but still Peter remained rooted in place. Fresh sweat broke out between his shoulder blades and across his forehead. His eyes hurt from forcing them open against the wind and sun.

The porter assisted a young woman from the train to the ground. She wore a fancy dress the same color as the blooms on ironweed that grew wild on the prairie. Another woman — older, her dress the color of the top side of ironweed leaves — followed the first woman. Peter swallowed hard as his focus jerked toward the train again, waiting for more people to disembark. Where was Summer?

"Pa, that's her!" Thomas nearly yanked Peter's arm from its socket. "Come on!"

Peter blinked twice before squinting hard at the two women. The younger one . . . could it be? Then she turned to face him, and he recognized the delicate chin and dark eyes of his Summer. He felt his heart catch. Summer . . . how different she appeared.

He knew when she saw him. A smile lit her face, and she left the side of the older woman to rush forward, her bright skirts swirling, her hands outstretched. Thomas released his father's arm and raced to meet her. The two embraced, their laughter ringing out, with Summer's slender arms around the boy. But her gaze remained on Peter's face. She whispered something in the boy's ear, and Thomas scampered toward the back of the train.

And still Peter did not move.

Time seemed to stand still while Summer approached him. Slowly. As if gliding. Her skirts swept the wooden walkway. Her gloved hands, with fingertips touching, rested against her waist. She stopped — the distance of one pace between them — and peered upward. The brim of her funny little hat shaded her forehead, but he could see her eyes. Dark, hopeful eyes.

"Hello, Peter."

How could such a simple greeting cause such a big reaction? Peter took a shuddering breath to calm his jumbled nerves. He felt his lips quiver with his smile. Finally he managed to answer. "Hello, Summer. It is . . . it is good to see you again."

He did not wish to be formal. He wished to sweep her into his arms and welcome her with a kiss that would speak all the things his heart felt. But here in the sun with people nearby and her in a hat with a bird's wing on it? His lips felt dry. He licked them and asked, "A good trip you had?" His voice sounded odd to his ears.

"Yes." Her stilted speech did not match the warmth in her eyes. "Yes, we had a good trip." Then her eyes flew wide and one hand rose to grasp her slender neck. "Oh!" She spun away from him, her hand reaching toward the older woman, who remained alone beside the passenger car. "Nadine, I'm so sorry. Please join us."

The older woman took hold of her skirts and walked gingerly across the dusty ground toward them. When she reached Summer's side, Summer placed her arm around the other woman's waist and smiled up at Peter. "Peter Ollenburger, please meet my mother-in-law, Mrs. Nadine Steadman."

The woman extended her hand, and Peter took it briefly, nodding. "It is good to meet you, *Frau* Steadman."

"Likewise, Mr. Ollenburger."

The older woman seemed to take stock of him, and he felt his neck grow hot. He did not know what to say. His clumsy brain fumbled for words, but before he could find any, Thomas struggled onto the walkway, weighted down by two large bags. The women had planned a lengthy visit, it appeared.

"I got your bags, Summer! Can we go now, Pa?"

"*Ja. Ja,* we will go. The wagon" — he gestured toward the street — "it is over there. Come." He reached for the bags.

"I can get 'em," Thomas insisted. "C'mon! Summer, wait'll you see Patches!"

The boy led the way, still jabbering. The women fell into step behind him, and Peter followed. He remembered how he had first wanted to come alone to get Summer and her mother-in-law. Now he felt grateful he had brought his son. Thomas's cheerful chatter would fill the uncomfortable silence between the adults.

Even as he lifted Summer into the wagon — his heart pattering with remembrance of other times of performing this courtesy — he wondered at the awkwardness between them. She appeared so . . . different. Elegant. Her dark eyes were the same, but they seemed to now reside within a stranger's form.

"Pa, let's go!"

Thomas's call reminded him he had been standing beside the wagon staring upward for too long. He felt heat climb his cheeks — a heat not brought on by the summer sun. Slapping his hat onto his head, he gave a brusque nod and headed around to his side of the wagon. He looked at the seat and realized there would not be room for him with both Summer and her mother-in-law there. He hesitated, unsure what to do.

Then Summer solved the problem herself. "I'll sit in the back with Thomas." She rose, looking expectantly at Peter. "Will you assist me, please?"

He scurried to the side of the wagon and lifted her out. When he set her feet on the ground, she did not move her hands from his shoulders right away, but looked at him with a winsome expression. His breath came fast and hard, and he wished once more they could be alone and he could just kiss her and see what happened. Her hands slipped away, and she moved to the rear of the wagon. He removed the tailgate so she could climb in. He offered her his hand, his heart thrumming at the feel of her slender fingers clasping his. She settled beside Thomas with her legs bent to the side and her skirts sweeping to cover her feet. Even sitting in the back of wagon she looked graceful.

And very out of place.

Summer stood on the porch of her Gaeddert house and watched Nadine. Her mother-in-law had insisted on visiting the little gravesite alone, and now she stood inside the picket fence in front of the row of headstones with her hands clasped behind her back. Summer could imagine Nadine's sorrow as she faced the sandstone markers that served as a visual reminder of all she had lost.

On the way from Hillsboro, Thomas had jabbered nonstop, and Nadine had whispered how like Tod he was with his cheerful spirit. Yes, Thomas had talked, but Peter had not uttered a word. Although his face had shown joy at her arrival, it seemed only moments later he shut himself away from her. The air nearly crackled with tension despite the boy's happy prattle.

Lena thrilled to her arrival, though. At the Ollenburgers' home, Lena hugged her and then guided her to her chair, demanding she be seated. Slipping into the chair embroidered with roses was like coming home, and Summer closed her eyes, basking in the warmth of that feeling. When she opened her eyes, though, she saw Peter watching her with some unfathomable expression on his face.

She opened her mouth to question him, but he said in a tight voice, "I must to change out of these clothes. Excuse me, please." Then he disappeared into his bedroom.

Now she and Peter stood side-by-side on the spindled porch of her little house. She sensed his gaze drifting toward her, and she turned to meet it, but he turned his head sharply to avoid making eye contact. Only a few porch boards separated them, yet it might as well have been a mighty chasm.

Nadine opened the little gate and walked slowly toward the porch. Thomas ran from the opposite direction, a fistful of tiny orange blossoms in his hand. He came to a stop directly below Summer and thrust the flowers toward her.

"Here, Summer! Picked you some milk-weed."

She forced a smile to her face. "Why, Thomas, thank you." She took the limp bouquet and sniffed it. "Mm, they smell so good. I'll put them in a little cup on the table inside."

The boy beamed. "Butterflies like those flowers, so I figured you would, too."

Nadine hurried the last few feet of ground to reach the porch. "Thomas, those are lovely. Are they the only wild flower growing nearby?"

He crinkled his forehead. "No, ma'am. I've seen some leadplant, and there's wild indigo by the road. Do you want some flowers, too?"

"Yes. I want a cluster for each grave." The boy turned as if to dart away, and she put her hand on his shoulder. "But I would like to gather them myself. Would you show me where they grow?"

Thomas looked at his father for approval.

The big man stroked his chin. "*Frau* Steadman, the ground is not always smooth. And your fine dress — dusty it will become if you go traipsing."

"Dust brushes off," Nadine replied, "and I prefer to choose my own bouquet. I can go myself if you'd rather the boy stayed here."

Immediately Peter waved his large hand. "*Nein,* the boy need not stay behind. He will go and show you where the flowers grow. Boy, you mind *Frau* Steadman and stay close to her, you hear?"

"I hear, Pa."

Nadine informed Thomas, "I want to find some sort of receptacle with which to carry the flowers. Wait just a moment, Thomas." She climbed the two steps leading to the porch, sending a stern look in Summer's direction. "Summer, will you help me find something suitable?"

Summer looked at Peter. His Adam's apple bobbed in a swallow, but he didn't look at her. "Certainly." She followed Nadine into the house.

The moment Summer closed the door, Nadine took hold of her upper arms. "Young woman, I don't know what game you're playing, but it must stop right now."

Summer's eyes flew wide. "G-game? I don't understand."

"Nor do I." Nadine leaned close and spoke in a firm whisper. "That man out

500

there loves you, and you're playing cat and mouse. I don't understand the reason."

Heat flooded Summer's cheeks. She flapped her jaw, but no words came out.

"For months I've watched you finger the letters from the little boy, and each time you mentioned the father's name, your expression changed."

Summer was amazed by Nadine's observations. Had she really been so transparent?

"Do you love him?" Nadine demanded.

Summer dropped her chin, and Nadine gave her a little shake. "I said, do you love him?"

Summer gave her a brief, painful nod.

"Then why are you holding yourself aloof?"

"I . . . I . . ."

"Well? What!"

"I'm afraid."

Nadine pulled back and lowered her brows. "Afraid? Of what?"

Tears filled Summer's eyes. "Oh, Nadine, he's hardly spoken two words to me. We used to talk so easily, Peter and I. But now . . . He's different. And I don't know why." She swallowed, and one tear spilled down her cheek. "I'm afraid his heart has changed."

"Nonsense." Though the word was curt,

Nadine's tone was gentle. "He loves you — I could see it on his face at the train depot, and I saw it on his face at his house. His heart hasn't changed — not one bit. Something is making him keep his distance, and you must find out what it is. I'll take the boy away for a while. You talk. You work things out."

"B-but, Nadine, if we work things out, that means —"

"Yes, that means you'll remain here while I return alone to Boston."

"And . . . and you don't mind?"

"Of course I mind!" Nadine embraced Summer briefly. Sternly. Then she gave Summer's shoulders a firm pat and pulled away. "But you must follow the pathway God planned for you. And I believe wholeheartedly your pathway includes Gaeddert and Peter Ollenburger." Nadine took a step backward. "Clean your face and get back out there. I won't go flower seeking for more than half an hour. By the time I return, I want things worked out between the two of you. Do you understand?"

Summer smiled through her tears. She pulled a handkerchief from the pocket of her dress. "I understand. And thank you, Mother."

Nadine cupped Summer's cheek. "You are

welcome, daughter. Now hurry. Love is not something to squander."

Summer put her flowers in the kitchen, then watched through the window until Nadine and Thomas disappeared around the back of the house. When they were gone, she took a deep breath, offered a silent prayer for guidance, and stepped outside. Peter jumped at the sound of the door opening. His blue-eyed gaze swept from her head to her toes, and his expression turned grim. He spun away from her once more, his hands clamping on the porch railing. She wished those hands would hold her as tightly as they held that painted length of wood.

"Peter?"

At the single word, he turned his head, but he did not release the railing. *"Ja?"*

"Are —" Her voice sounded unnaturally high. She swallowed and began again. "Are you pleased to see me?"

His brow furrowed. "*Ja.* I tell you at the depot how good it is to see you again."

Despite herself, she smiled. "And then you stopped speaking to me. That doesn't denote pleasure, Peter."

"Denote . . ." He frowned. "I do not understand what you are meaning."

"Denote. Indicate." His expression didn't clear. "Not speaking to me means you are *dis*pleased, not pleased."

"But I am not displeased. Good it is to see you. It is just that —" He turned toward the graves once more.

She moved beside him and touched his hard forearm. His muscles twitched beneath her fingers. "Peter? May I ask you a question?"

Still looking away, he nodded.

Her heart began beating double time. Although she feared his answer, Nadine's comments still rang in Summer's ears. "Have . . . have you changed your mind . . . about loving me?"

His fingers convulsed on the wood; his whole body tensed. "How . . . how did you know this is what I feel?"

She allowed her grip on his arm to tighten. "I saw it in your eyes the day I left Gaeddert. Did you not see it in mine?"

A brusque nod, and still he wouldn't look at her. "*Ja. Ja,* I hoped, but . . ."

Fear made her heart pound in her throat. "Have your feelings changed?"

He spun so fast her hand flew from his arm. In less than two seconds she was wrapped in his embrace, his arms around her back, his cheek pressed to the top of her head. His answer was clear. She wiggled her arms loose to coil them around his neck and cling, letting him feel her heartbeat against his firm chest.

He spoke gently. "My heart has not changed. It is full of love for you."

Still nestled within his arms, she whispered, "Then why have you been so silent? So distant? I thought —"

He released her abruptly and she stumbled backward. He caught her, then cupped her cheeks and raised her face to him. "I look at you in your dress the same color as the wild flowers, and I listen to your speech which is so *gezuchtet.*"

She laughed softly. "What?"

He shook his head, scowling. "*Gezuchtet.* I mean you are much educated, and you have such fine speech. How can I measure up to you?"

"Oh, Peter." The words came out in a regret-filled sigh. "How could you even think for one minute you don't measure up to me? When I saw you today, standing on that walkway, in your black suit with your hair lifting in the breeze . . ." She ran her fingers through the thick locks the way she'd always wanted to. "You are a very appealing man, Peter Ollenburger."

"I am a big, clumsy man."

"Big? Yes, but clumsy? Oh no, Peter. I've watched you chop wood. There is a grace to the rhythm of the swinging ax. Your arms are strong, as are your convictions of right and wrong. A person can depend on you. You are a man who fixes things instead of tearing things apart. Within your chest beats a big, gentle heart."

He shook his head, his eyes holding disbelief, and she tugged a strand of hair. "You *are* appealing. Most important is your love for God, Peter. It shines from you. You are everything a woman could desire in a —" She dared not say the last word.

But he must have guessed, for his eyes lit and he whispered in a low rumble, "In a husband, Summer? Am I desired as a husband?"

His dear face became blurred with the rush of tears that filled her eyes. "Yes, as a husband. As *my* husband."

"Ah, Summer . . . Always summer has been my favorite season." He pulled her to his chest again, although not in a rush as before. The movements were slow and graceful, as if orchestrated from the beginning of time. He held her there with her cheek pressed to his rough shirt, his heartbeat thrumming beneath her ear. She closed her eyes, drinking in the scent and sound and feel of the man she loved. "How happy you have made me," he murmured against her hair.

"How happy God has made *us*," she whispered in return, and she felt his nod.

They stood together, eyes closed, while the evening sounds and smells of the prairie filled their senses. Summer could have remained in Peter's arms forever — held in just that way — but voices intruded. Nadine and Thomas were returning. Peter released his hold by inches, his hands sliding along her spine and across her waist, catching her hands for a moment, then finally letting go and stepping back just as Thomas bounced onto the porch.

"Look at all the flowers we picked, Summer!" He pointed over his shoulder to Nadine, whose arms overflowed with a variety of wild flowers in yellow, purple, pink, and white.

Summer took a step toward Nadine. "Oh, they're beautiful."

Nadine looked at Summer's face and then at Peter. A knowing smile climbed her cheeks. "Yes, they are. Which will you choose for your bridal bouquet?"

Summer covered her cheeks with her

hands. "Nadine!"

But her mother-in-law merely laughed. "Am I right? Will there be a wedding?"

"A wedding?" Thomas looked from Peter to Summer, his blue eyes wide. "Really, Pa? Summer, you'll be my ma?"

Summer looked at Peter, whose ears glowed nearly as pink as the spiderwort in Nadine's arms. A sheepish grin tugged at his lips, and he shrugged.

"It is all right with me if it is all right with Summer."

Summer burst out laughing. "Peter Ollen-burger, that will not do as a marriage proposal."

He ducked his head and stroked his beard for a moment. When he looked up, the expression in his eyes took Summer's breath away. He moved toward her with deliberate steps. He stopped in front of her and held out his hands. She placed her hands in his work-worn palms and felt his strong fingers close around hers. Their eyes locked, he slowly bent down on one knee.

"Summer Steadman," came his voice of distant thunder, so tender Summer's heart ached with the beauty of the moment, "the God we serve has brought us together. He has opened my heart to loving you with a love that endures. You would do me much honor if you would agree to become my wife."

Warm tears ran down Summer's cheeks. She could not find her voice, but she gave an eager nod and allowed her smile to speak for her.

He rose, lifting her off her feet in a hug. She clung, laughing against his neck.

Thomas's feet pounded against the porch floor as he ran to the edge and leaped onto the ground. "Pa and Summer are getting married!" he sang as he danced across the yard.

From the corner of her eye, Summer saw Nadine slip into the house, but not before her mother-in-law sent a smile filled with approval.

As Peter set her back on her feet, Summer looked out across the yard, across the graves, to the Kansas sunset that streaked the sky with brilliant colors. She sighed, completely content.

The arm at her waist tightened. "You are happy, my Summer?"

She smiled into Peter's dear face and reached up to stroke his beard once. "I am more than happy. My joy overflows."

Peter leaned down until his face was mere inches from hers. "*Ich liebe dich,* Summer Steadman."

She needed no translation. "And I love you." She raised onto tiptoes, closing the distance needed for their lips to meet in a kiss moist with happy tears.

And Thomas crowed, "Woohoo!"

ACKNOWLEDGMENTS

There are many who contributed to the completion of this story. Thank you to each of the following:

Mom and Daddy, Don, Kristian, Kaitlyn, and Kamryn, my wonderful family, whose support is something on which I can always count. You are my biggest blessings. I love you muchly!

Jill, Beverly, Eileen, Margie, Darlene, Staci, Ramona, and Crystal, my fabulous critique partners, who offer advice and encouragement and prayers. You are the best!

Kathy, Ernie, Ginny, Rose, and Carla, the "prayer warriors" who lift my writing ministry before the Father. There is no way to measure the gift of steadfast prayer support. May God bless you as richly as you have blessed me.

Lois Hiebert at the Tabor College Library, who pointed me to the information I needed to bring the setting of Gaeddert to life in my imagination. You are appreciated.

Charlene and the staff at Bethany House — thank you for making this experience so wonderfully pleasant. (I still feel the need to pinch myself occasionally to make sure I'm not dreaming!)

Finally, and most importantly, thanks be to *God,* who planted the seed of desire in a little girl's heart, who watered the seed and brought it to fruit. In your Word you promise that He who began a good work will be faithful to complete it. Thank you for keeping your promises. May any praise or glory be reflected directly back to you.

ABOUT THE AUTHOR

Kim Vogel Sawyer is a wife, mother, grandmother, former elementary school teacher, and child of God. A nearly life-long Kansas resident, she is fond of *C* words like cats, children, and chocolate. She is active in her church, where she teaches adult Sunday school and is a member of both the voice and bell choirs. She relishes time with family and friends, and in her spare time she enjoys quilting, calligraphy, and participating in theater.